GAMES WE PLAY IN THE DARK

Nicole Johnson

Games We Play in the Dark

Copyright © 2024 Nicole Johnson

ISBN-13: 979-8-218-46234-5

"Here in the chaos of life is a complexity so divine it defies all odds, and it is you.
In the terrifying veracity of existence, here you stand.
For all of time you are dead, but for the moments you are alive."

Table of Contents

31) Tightrope _______________________ 316
32) Arrived _________________________ 327
33) Unhinged _______________________ 337
34) Toxins _________________________ 357
35) Eventide _______________________ 362
XLII _____________________________ 371

Before

"Whoa, man, look at that plane." Brad pulled the blunt from his mouth, tapping the end before passing it to his buddy, Ryan.

"Nah." Ryan drew a long inhale, rolling down the car windows to release some of the smoke. "It's a spaceship, my dude."

Ryan, too entirely high to see straight, stumbled out of the car to get a better look up at the star-speckled sky. Between the tall fir and pine, a screaming red and orange tail sliced across the night.

Ryan joined Brad seated on the hood of the car. But as the object shot beyond the trees into the distance, Brad leaned back against the windshield, gazing out down onto Donner Lake from the cliffside overlook.

The impact rumbled through the earth deep beneath them, triggering the car's alarm. Ryan and Brad held tight to the hood as the car shook and the piercing blare rattled from the rusted sedan.

"Holy shit," Ryan drawled. The car listed forward, slowly approaching the edge of the overlook. "That was a rock."

"Ryan?" Brad asked. "You didn't happen to set the emergency brake, did you?"

Ryan let out a long low laugh. "We just saw a space rock." Then the front of the car rolled over the edge and into Donner Lake.

Chapter 1

Tainted

If ten-thousand hours made you a professional, I was overqualified.

As I rounded the corner, the bank's ATM sat as empty as I predicted.

My perfect opportunity.

Which is why I added this particular ATM to my rotation of thirty-seven.

Drawing my hood further to cover my face, I glanced over my shoulder and slinked down the street while my palms, per usual, dewed up at my sides in their angst.

Tonight was... *nearly* the last time I'd make a criminal of myself. I was good— overqualified professional and all. But the thing with committing crime is no one ever *intends* to get caught— so I'd gone in knowing my days were numbered.

But the thrill, it was electric.

And I didn't know if I'd ever truly be able to hit the kill switch.

I glided to the ATM. Swift. Quiet. Unnoticeable.

Placing my hand on the screen, electricity from the ATM danced through my fingertips. I tried to not tilt my head back in the euphoric rush of power seeping into me. I ran through the account names searching for a particular one. Eyecon. Perfect.

Eyecon was a powerhouse. Their accounts would be fine after my measly little withdraws, especially considering their latest quarterly reported earnings. They had so much money on the books my minuscule slices were inconspicuous.

Money spat from the slot. I grabbed the first fist full and jammed it in my bag. Pushing my body closer, I concealed how much money was jutting from the machine.

The only reason I could even steal from a cybersecurity company is that I wasn't stealing from *them*; I was stealing from a bank with access to their accounts— overcoming the ATM's security measures.

I grabbed the last wad of cash and stuffed it in my bag. Here was the most critical part.

I navigated to the security settings as the energy danced between my palm and the screen. Video surveillance? Account records? Time stamps? Deleted.

I was done.

As quick as I'd appeared, I smoothly sailed down the sidewalk onto Virginia street, the main thoroughfare, and melted into the other pedestrians deep in their after-work hustle and bustle eager to ignore anyone who'd delay the escape from their nine to five.

Even after all this time, the thud of my heart, the hitch in my breath, and the deadly calm that came over me when slipping deep into my powers. Nothing could make me feel more alive.

The sidewalk was wet from a recent rain, making the city more aromatic, drawing the sagebrush scent into the concrete jungle. We were deep into monsoon season as the Truckee River flowed higher and swifter than usual. A slight chill brushed my face, reddening my nose in the cold as I passed people. I had to make it home before Ben.

I was a professional and it was all at the touch of my finger. Normal jobs were for normal people.

Plus, I didn't buy into all that capitalistic bullshit.

The saving grace of Reno, Eyecon, was a homegrown cybersecurity enterprise that had won the hearts of the city by boosting Reno's economy and funding climate change projects with their massive amounts of profit— saving the little gem of the Mountain West. But by the looks of Reno, I didn't know if you could claim it had been *saved*.

Besides, between the alcohol and nightclubs, I couldn't hold down a job anyway. I never stole enough to raise suspicion, just a sliver more than I needed to get by. I wasn't an idiot. If my secret, my identity, got out, I was toast. Because let's be honest, if the government found out about me, I'd never even see a judge; they don't put people like me in prison. They put people like me behind plexiglass and in test tubes.

A hand landed on my shoulder, stopping me mid-stride. I tightened the grip on my bag, preparing to make a run for it. There was an alley only near feet away, but as I looked up, the hand belonged to a man in a rather rough condition asking for spare change. The weight of my bag suddenly sat heavy on my shoulder.

I slipped my hand inside, grabbing a few bills, but as I glanced at the condition of the man's teeth, I widened my grasp in the bag.

"Take care of yourself with this," I said, shoving a large wad into his coat pocket. I left before he could comprehend what had happened— before he knew how much money I'd shoved in his pocket.

Gliding down the street, I slinked through a few alleyways, inhaling the summer scent of rain on stone. The city's mountain air was a warm sticky cocoon. Utterly overwhelming. Even through the summer, I nearly always wore jeans so my goddamned thighs wouldn't seal together amongst the sweat.

The only thing this city had left to offer me was a one-way ticket out. And even though it was nestled in majestic purple mountains next to the pristine beauty of Lake Tahoe, there were darker things at play here.

Once home, I closed the apartment door behind me and shed my hoodie and other clothes in routine so I could rattle through my closet and find something more suitable. I settled on a black pencil skirt and a boring blue blouse. Then I drew my hair into a bun, not a perfect one because after a long day of work, no woman had perfect hair.

Right on time, a knock on my door sounded as I dropped a fresh pair of heels in the walkway. As always, after opening the door, Ben planted a kiss on top of my head, and I mumbled something dramatically about 'wishing it was Friday already'.

"Glad that's over. I've done three root canals today, and a crown," Ben said, sliding past me into my apartment. We did dinner together a few nights a week after Ben was done with dental school and I finished up... *work*.

"You sure you want to follow in your dad's footsteps?"

Ben sat his bag on the couch and sprawled out amongst the cushions.

I lobbed over to Ben and took a seat in his lap, tracing my fingers on the side of his face as he unwound. I always found Ben's amber eyes and curly blond hair quite striking.

After a moment, he asked, "What are you thinking about?"

"How much money it would take to convince you to leave Reno."

"I'm taking over my father's practice, Dani," he sighed, "I can't just leave."

We'd, of course, been over this many times. I swallowed bitterly at the realization Ben would never come around to the idea of leaving this city, even if I'd nearly saved enough for both of us to get out and start fresh somewhere else. I couldn't stay here. A whispering of my name was still on the streets. I had exit plans and intentions to execute them. And Ben had no idea.

Ben twisted me in his lap to look at my face again. His expression softened. "We're almost there."

He pressed a hand to my cheek, delicately holding part of my face. The warmth of his palm and gentle touch freely flowing. He reached up, twirling a bit of my loose hair.

Somewhere along the line of hiding who I was, I'd lost who I was. Nearly two years ago, Ben had found me in some pitch-black ecstasy-filled club packed with people looking to let go of their real-world cares. What he saw in me? I didn't know. But he'd somehow saved me from a downward spiral into an ocean of darkness. He was my lighthouse, and he never even knew it.

I was rough around the edges—— ok, maybe more than just the *edges*.

But, *this*. I would be walking away from this...

"You know what next week is?" He lightly challenged me.

I bit my lip. My last ATM hit. But he couldn't have known that.

"Don't tell me you forgot," Ben teased as he held out in anticipation.

Did he somehow know I was leaving? "Are you not going to tell me?"

"It's my graduation."

Oh shit. It had snuck up so quickly. He watched my face shift.

"Ben," I sighed, sliding off his lap.

"You forgot, didn't you?"

Uneasiness settled into my throat. "Ben?"

His eyes scanned over me. They were a beautiful golden hazel brown, painfully searing through my conscience. I didn't deserve his devastatingly gentle gaze.

"I, uh, wanted to tell you something." The words fell out more quietly than the last, followed by a hauntingly long moment. He looked at me, eyes patiently waiting for me to say something in the silence. A tangle rose in my stomach. I didn't know if I could handle watching his face twist under the truth.

"You ok?"

No. I was a freak with electromagnetic powers. A girl who could kill you if she got too upset. And after confessing I was a human anomaly, I was going to blindside him with an invite to give up his father's dental practice, change his name, and move across the border with me. Major miscalculation.

I'd been holding off on this for so long because it felt good to pretend I could have him. Pretend that whatever lay beneath wasn't going to spiral out of control and take me with it. Pretend that once I got out of here, things would be different. But I wasn't only hiding from the government. My life was a ticking time bomb, and one day I'd be eaten alive by whatever those electric powers had in store for me. And Ben had no idea.

"I wanted to maybe look at some apartments with you."

I couldn't do it, watch the sheen in his eyes shift as he learned the truth. Enough. After all, Ben would never leave Reno.

"Yeah? Well, it's about time." A smile as grand as his good looks ripped across his face from ear to ear. "Best graduation gift ever."

I glanced down at my stupid blue blouse. "Mhm." I'd leave before then. To keep him safe, away from me.

A knock sounded at the door and Ben jumped up to grab the food he had ordered us on his way over.

Soon enough we were eating chow mein from to-go boxes. Ben flicked on the newest Blade Runner movie on the TV, then said, "You know, the original title was 'Do Androids Dream of Electric Sheep?"

"They don't," I said. Because *I* was an electric freak, and my dreams were far from peacefully counting sheep. They were haunted by the events that sent my world spiraling.

"If bio-engineered replicants tried to take over the world," Ben said, "I'd protect you."

"With your dental drill?" I teased, shoving another fork full of chow mein into my mouth. Ben smacked the side of my leg and then turned his attention back towards the TV. I stared at his profile, wondering if Ben had any idea about the secret I held... about the person I really was, even outside of the electricity. What kinds of dark things lingered just below the surface.

Eight years ago when I was seventeen, that darkness reared its ugly head in a moment that nearly swallowed me whole. The meager life I'd had with Anna and Darrel, my foster parents had all come crashing down on me in one crowning stroke.

I remembered watching from around the banister, the smell of dirty whiskey filling the room. I remembered Darrel's unbecoming, his red face and balled fists as rain relentlessly pounded the windows. Above all, I remembered the electric charge that had filled the air. As if the storm outside was brewing within the walls. The energy danced around the room as if waiting to release into one giant flash-bang, a sinister and mocking game of duck-duck-goose.

Or how a river of tears flowed down Anna's cheeks. It had only taken him one hand, one hand and Darrel had taken control of everyone in that house. His grip around Anna's throat.

I remembered how the spark of electricity was left on my fingers, evaporating off the ends like boiling water. Anna's scream. The fear in her eyes. *What have you done?*

She chose Darrel. She chose that vile man who I was trying to protect her from.

Because whatever she saw in me, it was far more terrifying.

That night, I lost control of myself somewhere in that mess, and there was no way in hell I would dabble in that tainted darkness again. No way I would show anyone else what I was concealing inside.

That's why Ben couldn't know. If I stuck around and let him slip that ring on my finger, it would be a betrayal. Because he didn't even know the half of me.

And if I let him learn the other half, if I told him everything, well, perhaps his eyes would glaze over like Anna's.

I couldn't do that.

So I kissed Ben goodnight and leaned against the wall as I watched him leave my apartment for the evening. Tomorrow was my final ATM withdrawal.

Chapter 2

Anomaly

My stomach churned. I poured wads of cash into a pile on my bedroom floor, flattening all the crumpled bills and stacking them on each other. One last time and it was over.

According to Google, there was an annual salary that was enough to live a life of *satisfaction*, whatever the hell that meant. So, I erred on the side of caution. I wanted three years to find myself and start over somewhere new. So I tripled Google's *magic* number.

Here I was, at the grand finale withdrawal. I'd saved nearly every dime— well, bill— I'd need, and tonight, I would score my last two grand. It had taken me nearly eight years to get here. Paying for living expenses while saving proved harder than I thought, considering I could only steal small amounts in order to go undetected... and considering all the costly alcohol and molly filled night-clubs. That was behind me though— largely thanks to Ben.

I put the rolls back into their place, being sure not to damage my new fraudulent passport and ID as I slipped the container back into its hiding spot.

Ben would have never set foot in the club that night had he not been attending the bachelor party of his childhood best friend. In my 25 years, he wasn't like any guy I had ever met. And even though I couldn't keep up with Ben's intellect, there was something special in the way he existed.

And for some unbeknownst reason, he was centered on me. A criminal.

I slid into a black hoodie and a dark pair of jeans, lacing my sneakers in tight knots. I grabbed my bag and was out the door.

As I trekked the sidewalks, I thought of Darrel's promise. *You better run girl, 'cause I'll come for you.* It had been eight years, but word on the street was that Darrel and his cronies were still looking, and if he found me, who knows what would happen. Reno was the 'Biggest Little City in the World' after all. If I had to fight him, his buddies— I didn't want to think of that, the things that crept alongside that power.

It was too risky to live in a city where I could run into Darrel or Anna, or someone who knew about me. I needed out. Maybe I stayed in Reno so long because I childishly hoped I would somehow run into my long-dead father— as if he would casually walk down the street. It was a stupid delusion primarily fueled by the nights I danced away in the dark thrum of those clubs. But now I was set to turn a corner.

I wanted a new world, one where I could recreate myself, one where Dani Colburn didn't exist.

The wet night sky kissed my skin as my music blared in my ears, drowning everything out. This was the last ATM hit. I had to get my mind right.

The city was quiet, well, as quiet as Reno really got. A hum of partying drunks just a street over hopping from bar to bar competed with the rustle of homeless people, shuffling in the dark for their next spot to sleep.

When I arrived at the bank, there was only one person in line for the ATM. I leaned against a light post, tucked my earbuds into my bag, and waited.

For all the times I had done this, this would truly be the last.

To scout which ATMs were the best to hit, I'd learned police patrols, guard shifts, street camera locations. I tracked which accounts had an influx of funds and movement patterns so I had the best shot at taking my slice undetected. It was exhausting.

As I watched the woman finish her transaction at the ATM, I got excited over what this last crime meant.

Somewhere on a warm beach was calling my name. I could spend all my off-time bathing in the sun, reading all the books my heart desired, favor some fruity little drink with a pink umbrella hanging out of it.

But, to get from here, to there, severing all connections between my past and future was vital. I would be in a new city where there wasn't a single soul who knew I, or my abilities, existed.

My palms began to sweat as I rehearsed, for what was probably the thousandth time, what my steps were.

The woman stuffed her belongings into her bag and left. Time to wrap this up.

An anxiousness crept down my spine. This was it. I pressed my hand firmly against the ATM's screen, igniting the electricity. The energy swirled inside my head, daring to distract my attention from the task in its intoxicating frenzy. I pushed to maintain focus as I drew through the accounts, finding what I was looking for. Eyecon.

Money began dispensing from the ATM. I stashed the first wad into my bag.

Ok. Come on.

Final stack of cash.

I was so close to being done. Calculating the necessary steps to finish my transaction.

A man appeared behind me in line to use the ATM. He edged up on my heels. The exhale of his hot breath on my shoulder raised goosebumps on my skin. My stomach churned and that anxiety sprang deep within my spine as I realized what was happening, but it was too late. Something sharp protruded into my back. This wasn't part of the plan.

"Don't scream."

I didn't dare make a sound to cause a scene. I slowly held my hands up. To him, he would see this as a sign of submission, but he didn't know better.

"Hand it over." He tugged the strap of my bag.

Hands still raised, I turned to face him. I wanted to give up, let him take the money and run. But I was all charged up, finding it difficult to tame the savage coil of energy bounding through me. And that darkness creeping inside me, it wasn't going to give up and let him go so easily.

I pulled my shoulder back, trying to regain control over my bag, over *my* cash, the money *I* had stolen. He jabbed his knife at me. As I blocked his blow, the blade slid across my forearm, slicing open a section of my skin. Prick.

I wasn't going to play nice anymore. Something inside me, once it took control, wasn't capable of it.

I clenched the wrist of his knife-wielding hand. His eyes darted up at me, wide in surprise. Electricity throttled through my grip pulsing into the mugger. He yelped, dropping to his knees. I restrained him in my electric grasp as he convulsed, metal rang out against the pavement as his weapon fell to the ground.

As soon as I released the tension, his eyes snapped open. The mugger skittered backward on the sidewalk, bracing himself with his elbows.

"Not so tough now?" I stood over him, my palm thrown out in his direction, ready to make a second strike. Ready to show him how wrong his calculation had been. I was going to crush him, squash what little power he thought he had over me. *I* was the one in control now.

Then his face hollowed, and I saw it in his eyes. He had come to understand.

I was a monster. A dark sickness.

So I let him go. I let him pull himself up off the ground and run.

My outstretched palm shook.

I had... I'd almost lost it.

My heart beat wildly out of my chest. I was just *protecting* myself. I mean, he could have stabbed me. I could have been hurt— more than just the slice across my forearm.

Sirens rose in the distance. Damn it.

I pulled my hair back over my face and kept my head down, making my escape in the opposite direction of the mugger's path. Getting caught would ruin everything.

Slipping into the overhang of a closed shop, I ripped a section of fabric from the bottom of my shirt and wrapped my forearm with the crude bandage.

I should have just played the part I was supposed to. He was the mugger; I was the victim. That was how things were supposed to go down. But *nooo*, I'd gotten sidetracked by that pulse of power rippling deep down.

On top of it all, I made a mistake. And not a small one.

Shit. Shit. Shit. In my panic, I forgot to delete the ATM security footage.

I had to go back and get rid of the evidence. This was bad— like an arsonist returning to the crime scene watching his work burn to the ground— bad. But there was no other choice. The longer I let that footage stay in the system, the more likely I was to be caught.

I kept my face down with my hood pulled as far over my head as I could manage. Two police cruisers raced by. Don't look suspicious. The cop cars rounded a corner, heading in the opposite direction of the bank. Maybe no one had caught my quarrel with the mugger after all.

I'd been meticulous in my ATM choices, but life had a way of providing intervening anomalies you couldn't plan for. Stupid mugger.

I approached the ATM once again and pressed my hand against the screen. This time I was sure to double-check over my shoulder before doing so.

Energy blasted through my palms, lighting my hand on fire with an electric buzz that swirled up my arm, but I had to focus, this was purely business. I had to get rid of the evidence. This was the last item on the agenda before I could execute my exit plans. I filtered to the security settings to delete...

"Stop! Police!"

My stomach dropped below my feet. The air left my lungs. Oh shit.

I pulled my hand from the ATM as I took off. My feet smacked the pavement so hard I was surely creating earthquakes as I attempted my escape. No. No. No. The thud of the officer's boots was not far behind me. My heart was racing. This was supposed to be the last time. It should have all been over.

Spotting a dark alley, I made my turn into it. It lined the backside of a row of businesses. As I dashed into the dark my foot caught the corner of a large dumpster bin and I fell to the ground. Just my luck. Grasping my bag tightly, I crawled around to the other side. I tried to squeeze and tuck myself completely behind the mass of the dumpster.

The Officer's feet fell silent. I suspected he was paused at the opening of the alley, speculating if I was hiding in its welcoming dark shadows. I didn't think I was even breathing.

The thud of his shoes began again, and to my terror, they were growing louder. He had chosen to take the alley. I crouched, ready to attack if found. The ball of energy was constructing itself inside of me. The unknown was building, feeding my power. Everything was riding on these next few seconds.

Metallic keys chimed as he stalked through the dark. His radio crackled with voices and static. He was getting so close. I closed my eyes and tried to focus on the sound of his feet, trying to zone in on his proximity. I would risk everything if I used my powers to fend off the Officer. I would be revealing myself and what I could do.

Yet, getting caught and arrested seemed like it would lead to a worse crisis. How would I ever explain how I was stealing money from ATMs? They would have my fingerprints. They would cart me off to some government lab where I would become a guinea pig.

No beach sand or drinks with pink umbrellas.

The Officer sprinted past the dumpster. He didn't see me. I sprang up and jolted around the bin as I made my way to the mouth of the alley.

He turned back in my direction.

The universe hated me.

"Stop!"

Suddenly, two sharp burning sensations were thrusting electricity through my veins, one on the back of my shoulder, the other on my hip. My delayed brain finally clicked. He shot me with a taser.

The prongs burned themselves into my skin. I fell to my knees trying to contain the rapid rush of electricity.

You can't, Dani. Don't do it.

I placed my hands on the ground, trying to hold the biting monster inside me as the overwhelming rush of electricity called to something deeper within. But the taser was charging me up, giving me intoxicating amounts of energy.

The flow of electric shock stopped, and I heard his boots run toward me.

"Stay down!" He snarled.

I tried to get my feet under myself but tripped on my bag, rolling over to see the officer racing in my direction. It was a bad dream. Nothing was working, and I couldn't get away fast enough. I tried to push away the dark circles threatening to tunnel my vision. Just as I jumped up, the officer reached his hands out, grabbing my shoulder.

Then shock.

Utter shock.

Not the electric kind.

His touch pulled the taser's stored energy from my abdomen and up to my right shoulder. Pushing it from my bicep into his palm. I stopped fighting the flowing exchange. Instead, I stood there baffled. The officer looked at me, mouth parted in astonishment. His face turned into a wild expression as his eyebrows lifted.

He felt it too.

We stood there, staring at each other in silence. What the hell was going on?

My breath hitched. I had never felt this happen with any other human before. Never. No words escaped either of us as the moment dragged on. Neither of us made a move as the electric tingle pulsated between our touch.

I stepped back and made a run for the mouth of the alley. As I reached the entrance, I glanced back into the darkness. The officer was unmoved, staring in my direction. What had just happened? Had he seen it? Had he seen me— what lay underneath?

I scrambled back down the sidewalk, racing home, letting my hair hang over my face, looking at no one I passed. I ran and ran and ran. But I couldn't run from the revelation that had just happened.

I laid my hand on the doorknob of my apartment door. Closing my eyes, I moved the metal inner workings of the lock to open it. I slammed it behind me as I rushed inside. With my back against the closed door, I slid down until I sat on the floor, huffing and sucking in air. Had I just been made? Did he know who I was?

On top of it all, I fucked up. There was now video evidence clearly showing me using my powers to *magically—* and illegally— withdraw cash. I couldn't delete the footage from either incident tonight. Shit. Shit. Shit. If he didn't already know who I was, he would soon.

Tears swam onto my face, soaking my shirt. All the unanswered questions. The moment the officer grabbed me. That moment. Nothing like that had ever happened before.

The feeling that oscillated between our skin, the energy that pulsated through me while seeping into him. It wasn't the same as when I zapped the mugger. For the mugger and Darrel, my powers had crumpled them in pain. But the touch with the officer, it felt like, at that moment, we were resonating. We had been on the same exact page. Thinking, feeling, echoing each other— as if we had been on the same energetic frequency. This exchange— this connection with him. I knew he had seen me for what I was, a freak anomaly.

This fuck up tonight... this would end it all. I was done for.

Chapter 3

Hazard

I dumped the rolls of cash into a backpack. Covering the money, I shoved a sweatshirt over it all and zipped the bag closed. It was all happening so fast. I laced up my sneakers and frantically grabbed a few last things I would need to make my disappearance easier on myself, making sure to grab my fictitious passport and ID.

Now. It had to be now.

Ben could help me, take me somewhere. Get me out of here. I dug in my pockets and found my phone, dialing as fast as humanly possible.

"Ben? Ben, I need a favor." I breathlessly poured into the phone. I hesitated, trying to decide whether involving Ben was even a good idea. But I couldn't hang up now.

"Dani? What's going on? Are you ok?" The hairs on the back of my neck raised at the sound of Ben's voice. My call had woken him.

"I need you to pick me up. There's that cafe on the corner not too far from my place," I pleaded, trying to hold the panic back from my tone with a wavering voice. But, even *I* could hear the cracks of frantic utterances splintering my words into pieces.

"I'm on my way. Are you ok? Will you tell me you're ok?" Ben urged.

"I'm ok. I'm ok." Totally not ok.

"I'm leaving now." My hands shook. I hung up the phone and sprinted to the front door. As I made my exit, I studied my apartment, absorbing what might be my last time in my sanctuary. This was not the way I intended to leave things.

The door slammed behind me as I made my escape and ran full speed down the hallway, bursting from the apartment building. The wind broke against my face, tightening my skin in the chill. Rain from an incoming monsoon started to fall as I pulled my hood over my head.

I just had to get to Ben and I would be safe. Safe? It was almost laughable. The cafe's lit sign appeared in the distance, drawing my eyes to the parking lot in search of Ben's car. A red Ford Bronco. It was here. I rushed to the car, pulled the handle, and tumbled into the passenger seat.

"Dani, what's going—"

"Go, just go!" I slung my seatbelt on. The engine revved and screeching noises filled the lot as we peeled out.

"Please, just talk to me. You're really freaking me out." His eyes captured his reeling brain. Reeling maybe even faster than mine. This was the first time I had ever seen such a serious look on Ben's face.

The street lights steadily passed over the car like a strobe light. The warm air flowing from the vents of Ben's Bronco. It was all making me dizzy. I let the silence linger a little too long between us as I fretted about the incident over and over inside my head.

"Are you in some sort of trouble?" He finally spoke.

"Ben, there's something I need to tell you." I almost regretted it the second the phrase left my mouth. But I owed him an explanation.

He glanced at me in intervals, trading me with the view out the windshield every couple of seconds.

"Are you ok?" He repeated, "You have blood on your face." I reached up to grab the sun visor's mirror, noticing the blood on my wrist had seeped out from my sweatshirt. Some of the leaking blood must have gotten on my face at some point. Pulling down my sleeve, I exposed my bloodied arm poorly wrapped in its failing bandage. I didn't know what to say to Ben.

"I was mugged," I blurted, trying to explain the blood.

"You didn't call the police? What happened—"

"No." Panic engulfed me. "I can't call the police, I've done something stupid." Ben wracked his brows together in confusion. "I ran from an officer."

"I don't understand."

"I stole some money, and I was caught."

"I don't understand, Dani. Were you caught by an officer or were you mugged?"

"Yes," I answered. Ok, that didn't help, evidenced by a still clearly confused Ben. "I was mugged *earlier* tonight and *now* I'm running from an officer who caught me stealing money."

Then his face twisted into an unreadable expression. A mixture of doubt, and disappointment, and so many other emotions I couldn't pinpoint. But before I could get anything out of my mouth, Ben's mind was already in overdrive. Maximum rotations per minute.

"You were mugged?" his eyes glazed with anguish. He tapped his fingers against the steering wheel with his rising nerves. "Why are you stealing money?"

"I don't have a job, Ben. A cop— a freaking cop chased me down an alley before I lost him." I drummed my fingers on my knee.

His eyes drained of light, his expression falling with a sort of stiff awkwardness. Maybe he was debating on driving me to the police station himself. The silence persisted with painful restlessness. Maybe that's where I belonged.

"Please say something," I barked. His expression almost appeared torn, then mellowed into something different.

"Dani, I don't know what to say. Are we running from the police right now? Are you a fugitive?" He stopped himself and drew in a deep breath. "What's our plan?"

I uncoiled my fist for the first time.

"Are you helping me—I mean, I can't go home," I said, running my fingers through my hair. "Come with me."

Ben's head cocked a bit to the side. He was quiet. Maybe he thought it was an irrational suggestion I had just come up with, considering he knew nothing about the more than 200k currently sitting in my bag on his floorboard.

"I think I should take you back to my place. The best thing we can do right now is get off the street."

The rusted red Bronco made a speedy U-turn. A few screeches rang out from the large tires.

I gazed at Ben. I had never seen him like this before. There was a certain stillness in his face. A bleak statuesque-like expression painted on him, and it stabbed straight through my heart.

He rolled his lips against each other as he privately calculated, and I was sure he was considering the pros and cons of our relationship. Ben had his life all mapped out, and he thought it was going to be me as his partner. But he didn't know me. And he didn't deserve me. Or rather, I didn't deserve him. I was a hazard.

The wheels jolted us as they nudged the curb. I pulled my bag close to my body and reached for the door handle. Ben was looking out the windshield in front of us, lost in thought, his eyes unseeing.

"Look, I understand the position I put you in. If—"

"No." His voice was soft, a warmth injecting my body.

"Ben, really. I get it."

"Dani, no." Ben's voice was stern, unwavering while I searched for the lie.

I nodded, recognizing the grace and care he had always laced into our relationship all along.

He looked up at me. His face softened ever so slightly. A little bit of my Ben was returning. He raised his hand, swiping a few fingers over my cheek as he cleaned a spot of blood from my face with his thumb. Maybe I hadn't lost him.

A sea of guilt set in. Maybe it would have been better if I had, so he wouldn't be involved in any of this.

There had only really been one dispute Ben ever passionately refuted. Last summer we had spent as much time as possible at the lake. Ben loved to read books, so we'd always packed a picnic and stayed for hours.

"It's philosophic," Ben had laughed, pushing stray hairs from my face. The wind lapped at the shore as we lay spread out on our blanket, soaking up the sunshine of Lake Tahoe's Sand Harbor.

"This is the silliest ending to a book... ever," I complained. "It's idiotic."

"Considering you always end up playing Tetris on your phone, this is probably the only book you have *ever* read."

Well, I couldn't deny that one. "I don't get it. How is the meaning of life, the universe, and everything equal to 42?" I turned over, closed the book and returned it to Ben. "And what the hell does that have to do with hitchhiking the galaxy? No wonder I skipped this in high school, it's stupid."

"It's not stupid." Ben firmed his expression and pulled back slightly to look at me. "We are all just trying to find our 42. Some spend their whole lives and never figure it out."

Ok, whatever the hell that really meant. "It's just some dumb rudimentary number. You know, I bet you he just had writer's block."

"I think you just don't get it," Ben mused, clearly offended. "But I hope you find your 42, Dani."

"Maybe I'll find like a 37 or something," I teased, as if you could even 'find' a number. "Or maybe we can find it together or something."

"Or something," he sullenly echoed. I smirked at him and let it go. He was disappointed, but he hadn't let the argument spoil the rest of our afternoon. He'd still been the soft, warm Ben I'd come to love. But that was books, and this was... this was complicated.

Warmth flowed through my hand. Ben had swooped it up in palms that engulfed mine. His tender warmth pulled back at the emotional coup threatening to supersede me. He led me up a set of stairs, then down a hall to his door, maintaining his hold on me, even while placing his key in the lock.

I made my way over to his couch, sitting somewhat awkwardly. Ben sat next to me, silently placing his hand on my knee. Neither one of us said anything for a long while.

"I'm sorry I've dragged you into this."

"If you needed money, why didn't you just ask me? When you said you were a finance manager, this is not what I thought you meant. Why didn't you call the police after being mugged for god's sake? This isn't adding up."

Ok, those were all very good points.

"I know it's not." A pulsating lull of energy bounded inside me. "I need you to know this isn't the first time I've taken money. It's been... a few times." Really we were at an uncountable impasse, but for the sake of saving myself, I was mitigating circumstances here.

His stiff posture, vacant eyes, and dull face resurfaced. I distinctly heard him gulp. And as if things couldn't get worse, his face washed over with a sullen hollow expression.

"Are you in danger?" He asked, barely a whisper.

"I'd say I've gotten myself in a little too deep." A few long seconds ticked by. He shook his head, he didn't understand. How could he? I kept everything from him. The corner of my heart was beginning to tear, and if he kept looking at me the way he did, soon it would be nothing but a pile of scraps.

"Ben, look, I don't want to put you in any danger."

"I can't help you if I don't know what's going on." He slowly nodded. " But, I'll wait 'til you're ready." I stood, and as I did, he stood too. He swooped me into his arms and carried me down the hall. The last of my wet hair dried as it bounced with Ben's stride. I listened to the rhythmic beat of his heart as his chest warmed the side of my face, his sweat reminded me of the lake's misty mornings as it settles on dry rocks— a smell Ben once called petrichor as we raced to the car in a summer storm.

I didn't deserve it. I didn't deserve him.

Ben set me on the bed and returned to his side, sitting next to me as he scanned my face.

"So the work clothes," he said. A pang of remorse raced through me.

I lifted my eyes just enough to read his face as my admission spilled out. "A lie."

He shook his head in a soft nod, coming to grips with reality.

His eyes traced over the disheveled wrapping of my wound. "Can I clean your arm for you?"

I gulped at the thought of saying yes. How was it fair? But I nodded. I so desperately wanted his comforting touch, his warm fingers across my skin.

Ben unwrapped the pathetic bandage from my arm. His gaze drifted from the cut to meet mine. I knew what he was thinking. The cut was deep and probably needed medical attention. His eyes lifted in curiosity.

"I'm not going to the doctor," I declared. A low chuckle rumbled through his chest as he grimaced and nodded. He was careful to clean my wound with a wet rag.

"I can't believe you hid this from me. For all this time." I bit down on my lip. Nothing. There was nothing I could say to comfort Ben to make the situation any better. And yet, he still didn't even know the whole truth. So I didn't say anything.

Ben rubbed some antibiotic serum onto my wound then wrapped it securely with gauze. "It's late. Do you need a pair of sweats?"

I agreed but decided to wash my face first. I smiled at him, my best attempt at an apology I could manage at the moment. He gave me a crooked smile in return. His signal all was well. For now at least. I excused myself from the bed.

I stripped my clothes then scrubbed the evening off my face.

As I left the bathroom and returned to Ben's room, he playfully whistled, lightening the mood. With a red face, I chuckled. He grinned, his eyes lingering as they traced up and down my body. A fresh pair of sweatpants sat on the corner of his bed. As I took a few steps closer to grab them, Ben slowly extended his arm out and withdrew the pants from my reach. He raised a finger and signaled for me to approach.

My lips curled into a small smile I could barely muster as I advanced toward him. He wrapped his arms around me and pulled me close. The covers fell on top of my shoulders, then his arm returned to its place around me as he let his lips press at the base of my neck, molded into a permanent kiss.

And although I was here in his arms, I didn't know where that left us.

I pleaded with myself to just let it go, to scrub my mind of the sullen image of Ben from today's unveilings. That look on his face, no, that would never leave my mind. But for now, I had his strong embrace, his tender warmth holding me close, folding me into his arms.

Sleep was calling me into its deep abyss, and I couldn't fight it anymore. I finally closed my eyes and drew my brain to a still— so I thought.

The look on Ben's face tonight wasn't the only one to haunt me.

Tonight was the first night in a while I dreamed of him again.

Fog was rolling on the forest floor. Trees swayed back and forth in the wind. I could smell the wet earth under my feet. Smell the crumpled leaves kicking into the air. I was running, but my feet barely budged, and the trees didn't move past as expected, as if I was running on a treadmill. Moving so fast, yet finding myself in the same place. Moonlight sparkled against the forest floor briefly between clouds and dense dreary mist.

"Dani!" He was searching. I tried to make my feet move faster, but they resisted.

"Dani." Sheer panic and torment seethed through his voice. It was so distant. The stationary trees mocked me with their creaks and whistles in the blowing wind. Howls echoed in the distance. Why couldn't I find him?

Falling. I was falling. My stomach was ravaged by that all too familiar feeling. The darkness made it impossible to see what was going on as I endlessly fell in the dark.

With a splash, I found myself in frigid water. The icy cold sucked the breath right out of me. No air. I had no air. I tried to swim to the surface, using the little glimpses of silver moonlight to guide me. I fought so hard, yet I was struggling, still sinking like a brick in the glacial-like water. I needed oxygen. In an instant, his voice rang clear, close.

"Dani, Dani. What are you doing?" His voice circled me in the water. It was so vivid. So clear. "Get out of here, you're not safe." I fought the water frantically, still sinking. Breathe. I needed to breathe. I was drowning, battling to hold tight onto the waning air.

"Dani, go!" and with that, my breath could no longer hold. Waves of water poured in, filling my lungs.

I was overtaken by a sharp terror and a flood of frenzied anxiety. Moonlight dimmed as I fell further into the water, my fear replaced by a slow-coming calmness. Peacefulness. A warmth spread through my body as I sank.

"Dani, get out!" his voice screamed. His eyes floated in front of me as we drifted down into the darkness, emerald eyes filled with anger and rage as we sank further and further into the water. I held my hand out, reaching to place it on where the side of his face should have been.

"GO!" My father yelled.

I sat straight up in bed, gasping for air. I coughed up the water that wasn't in my lungs, trying to grasp reality again. To collect myself, I recounted the events that occurred in the last couple of days, trying to convince myself those woods were a distant past, that those things my brain dreamed of didn't really happen the way I remembered them. But things were falling apart.

Ben still lay asleep next to me as a stampede of panic overtook me. The echo of my father's warning blared like an alarm in my head. I jumped out of bed, grabbed my bag, and snagged a pair of jeans, slipping into them in record time.

Out. I had to get out. I had to go. I finally made my escape to the door, ran through the hall and down the stairs. I broke free of the building and flooded into the street. Would Ben forgive me? Would it matter?

Chapter 4

Entity

My father's eyes lingered in my mind. Deep green emeralds stared at me every time I closed my eyes, and every moment I caught myself staring back, his warning repeated in my mind. I had a hard time resisting the feeling he was trying to tell me something important.

I made a good pace on my departure from Ben's apartment. The wet air brought the floral High Sierra's scent to life. An uneasy feeling settled in my stomach. I was going to buy a bus ticket and never look back. Let Ben pursue a real life.

There was a late-night diner only a couple of streets over from here. It was close to the bus station, and I would be able to tuck into the diner and get a ticket first thing in the morning. After all, I had to get off the street.

Deciding to take shelter at the diner, I cut over a couple of blocks, making my way across midtown. My sweatshirt hood needed constant adjusting as I used it to cover as much of my face as possible. I tried to focus on listening for sirens in the distance. I wanted to be ready, they were surely looking.

I had never imagined this is what my escape from Reno would look like, but I wasn't expecting this.

The city was still sound asleep. The occasional car made itself known by the hum of its engine and the splash of water when it hit a pothole in the street. The sidewalks were empty, just the echo of my shoe soles thudding on the pavement. The street lights made an electrical buzz as I passed under them.

I was going to flee somewhere south of the border. A place where I could be as far as possible from any forest. Far far from here. I was going to get away from this, from Reno, from Darrel who was still out there looking for me, and surely those woods.

I became a ward of the state after my father died. More precisely, three months after my father had died. Because those three months after his death I spent lost in the wretchedly wicked woods. Something wasn't right out there. The way the birds mocked you, the way the trees crept around when you weren't looking. And surely, the way time worked, as if it subscribed to one of Einstein's theories of special relativity. Those woods were a fucking black hole. And once I emerged from them, the things that lingered haunted me, edging to take control.

The diner's half-lit neon sign glinted in the puddles of water. The door gave a light ring as I entered and found a seat at a booth. A long crack in the leather seat exposed the dingy yellow padding within. Menus, on the table in front of me, were encrusted with little pieces of food. No thanks. My only interest? Coffee, to fight off my exhaustion.

Every time I'd been there, a live band played horrible stints of smooth jazz. Tonight, on stage was a single older gentleman who seemed to have been woken by the door ring. He put his saxophone to his lips and started playing.

I glanced around to check my surroundings, making sure I wasn't being followed. A man in rough shape slept in a booth towards the back. He rested with his head back and his hands across the top of his exposed belly. I could make out the shaking of his hands as his rumbling snore gnawed on. I should have picked a better spot to hide out. But it was late, and my options were limited.

The coffee cups already sat on the table. I pushed one to the edge as I made eye contact with the waitress behind the bar. She nodded. The waitress poured my coffee and I consumed it as if my life depended on it. Already, it appeared the saxophone player had fallen back asleep only a few notes into his song. I didn't know what I was going to do.

The caffeine pushed my mind into a vicious cycle of thoughts.

Maybe it was impulsive to leave Ben. It would be for the best if I left without a trace, cut ties, and ran. But I imagined Ben waking to my absence. I could picture the look on his face as his heart raced with worry. Would he know I was gone for good? Would he come looking for me?

And I thought of the empty hurt and sorrow in his voice. The anguish that washed over his face when he had said it. *I can't believe you hid this from me.* He unknowingly loved a monster. Ben did nothing but care about me, and I did nothing but continuously find ways to lie to him, to hurt him. God, I *was* a monster.

I at least owed him a clean break.

If I told Ben I was leaving of my own will, he wouldn't come looking for me. If I hurt him this one last time, it would ensure he was safe. Even if it meant breaking his heart and betraying mine.

I had to get out of here, to do the one thing that would kill me inside. I had to make things right with Ben... or wrong with Ben? I didn't know what the right words were here. But I couldn't leave the threads of our relationship so tattered and unwoven. Ben deserved a better ending. And even if I couldn't give him the right one, the perfect one, Ben deserved better than the dark I had left him in.

Tossing some cash on the table, I stood and left. I exited back onto the sidewalk and pulled my hood on to make my return to Ben's apartment. Maybe I would get hit by a bus on the way back and my worries would be over.

I thought of the lifeless vacant grief that would undoubtedly fill Ben's amber eyes. Or how I wouldn't be able to say goodbye without ugly crying. Or how I would have to pretend to be adamant this was the only way— that ending things was what I wanted. I would have to stand my ground and not cave into Ben's pleading eyes or warm comfort. He would try to convince me I had things all wrong.

Part of me wanted him to be right. Ok, all of me wanted him to be right, that I had massively overthought things in my head. I wanted him to convince me things hadn't gone awry, that there was no threat, no danger— to him or me.

But that was wrong.

I wanted Ben's warm embrace, his palms brushing against my cheeks. I wanted his reassurance. But deep down I knew the truth. I was a monster and there was only one way things would end. I would drag Ben down with me.

Rubber squealed against the pavement, startling me. Wet roads reflected brake lights into my squinting eyes as I stood in front of Ben's apartment. A dark van with its rear doors open came to a screeching stop in the middle of the street. My heart dropped into my stomach. My brain screamed at me, telling me to run. But I just stood there. I held still, stupid and frenzied with paralyzing adrenaline, frozen on the sidewalk.

For a split second, I was convinced I was, yet again, the scared girl standing in front of the limp body of my foster dad. I shook the thought from my mind.

Two men wearing black ski masks hunched in the back of the van. I tightened my position, crouching in response, ready to strike when the opportunity presented itself. Energy simmered in my gut, my predator inclination consuming me. I wasn't going to go down without a fight. Sweat beaded on my palms, my feet were glued to the ground.

One of the men raised his hand when I noticed a third man sitting in between the two masked ones. He sat kneeling on both knees, his hands hidden behind his back, his head obscured by black fabric. A hostage.

With one swoop, he removed the black hood from the hostage.

Brake lights still shined brightly into my squinting eyes. The dim light on his face made it hard to make out his features.

One of the men violently tilted the chin up of the hostage. Blonde curly hair threw off shards of light. Amber gold eyes melted across the way towards me. Ben. No. No. No.

My thoughts were racing. I raised my hands, instinctively throwing my palms out. Sparks sputtered from the ends of my fingers, failing to ignite the way I wanted them to— needed them to. This was the moment. Here it was. Presenting itself. Hesitating. Why was I hesitating?

I had to save Ben. I couldn't do it, I couldn't convince my powers to rush out of my palms the way they had that night with Darrel.

And if that darkness opened up and swallowed me…

No. I had to stop this. But the electricity only stammered, dwindling at my palms.

I ditched the pitiful attempt of using my powers, but just as I pulled my feet from their deep quicksand, tires squealed again.

"Dani, No!" Ben quivered. The hostage-takers pulled the doors closed as they sped off. My feet were failing me.

"Ben!" Oh shit. Oh shit. My mind was racing, sprinting, galloping.

My soles slapped the pavement as I ran dead center down the street. My heart jumped from my chest. It was sitting right behind my ears, pounding faster than my shoes. As I gulped down cold air, salty tears fell on my tongue. The taillights of the van faded into the distance and I lost sight as it jerked around a corner, the city gobbling it up.

Overwhelming hollowness and a nauseating dread clutched me in its grasp.

Ben. I didn't understand. Those men must have wanted me. These criminals broke into Ben's apartment for *me*. I put Ben in danger. I should have never called him to pick me up.

I had been playing with fate far too long.

I struggled to pull the hair tie off my wrist. I had to get my hair out of my face.

"FUCK!" I gave it all my might, bending my body in half to give it all my strength. I had completely fucked up. Worse, was I didn't even have a clue who was responsible for this. This was certainly not the police.

I had always been so meticulous, so careful to not leave a trace. My apartment lease didn't even have my real name on it, as I paid in cash every month.

This couldn't have been a coincidence. My dream was a warning to get out. My father was trying to tell me something, trying to hold this off. I was too selfish to not warn Ben.

The sky started to lighten as dawn readied to break in the distance. Time was passing so quickly, like my opportunity to save Ben was drifting away with the night sky. I pictured the van driving, just driving into the horizon, disappearing. Ben was slipping through my hands as quickly as the time was. The darkness threatened closer like an entity lingering over me.

I needed a plan. Something to go off of. Calling the cops was not an option. Not after our untimely run-in earlier. Not after the security footage from the ATM they surely had.

I was smart— well maybe not, but *I was* a professional. I could figure something out, use my resources.

The idea hit me like a speeding train, perhaps the abductors weren't as cautious as I was while committing a crime. There had to be cameras somewhere. I turned on my heel and made my way back to Ben's apartment where just outside, the whole scene unfolded. A row of businesses lined tightly together across the street from Ben's apartment building. I let my eyes wander up near the roof of each shop. Bingo.

An office across the street had a security camera fixed to their roof, aimed towards the street. The window read *Foreman Law*, right above the listed hours. Nine to five. Well, that narrowed my options. I didn't have time for this. I peeked into the narrow alley next to the building. It was going to be a tight squeeze. I pushed my bag into the small alley as I turned my body awkwardly to make the fit. The space only allowed me to shimmy sideways and I did so as quickly as I could, going so fast I almost tripped over my own feet. The small alley opened into a larger one which backed behind the law firm and other businesses.

My eyes swept the scene behind the building, finding the back door deserted. This was a risk, but it was something I had to do. I needed to get Ben back. And let's be honest, it's not like I had a squeaky-clean record. No point starting now.

My hand fell over the deadbolt as I pushed the magnetic feeling through my fingers. I was imagining the lock as I pushed it from the frame allowing the door to be opened. Before I yanked it free, I drew in a deep breath. Let's keep this quick.

With a creaking groan, the door swung open, allowing a stream of light to illuminate a small slice of the dark office. I pushed inside and waited patiently, trying to slow my breath so I could listen. No beeps. No alarm.

I forced the door mostly closed behind me. Peeking around the corner, I found a small room towards the back of the office. A monitor tucked in the back, separated from the many other computers in the room, was attached to multiple external hard drives. Running over, the screen blared brightly in my face as I woke the computer. I placed my hand on one of the external hard drives, filtering through the files, looking for the security footage application. When I found it, I opened the application. The monitor revealed all the screens from the multiple cameras around the business. Including the shot picturing me in the little room staring at this very computer.

One angle viewed the road in front of the business. I reviewed the footage. As I rewound and replayed the events, a large brick sat in my stomach. There it was. The van. My face pushed close to the screen, straining to see the plate number or any other identifying clue. I attempted to zoom in on the still shot, but the footage was too grainy. A false hope. A dead end.

I picked the computer mouse up and threw it against the wall. Putting my hand over my temples, I rubbed out the rising stress. What a waste of time.

I needed to get out of here. The cold metal of the computer tower sent a frenzy through my hand as my palm pressed against it. I absorbed the electricity through the computer, recharging my nearly empty wells. With a sudden thrust, I pulsed a wave of energy through my hand, effectively frying the hard drive. The air ignited with a smell of burnt plastic as the hard drive fizzled and cracked.

I reached out for the other two external hard drives, sending electricity deep into their circuits. It was necessary to rid them of evidence I was here. I jumped up from the chair in front of the computer and ran towards the back door where I had entered.

Getting Ben back seemed even further out of reach. I didn't know how the hell I was going to pull this off.

Just as I pushed the door open, the morning light gleamed at me. Turning to face the door, I placed my hand back over the lock and focused on feeling the deadbolt move back into place when a voice broke the silence.

"Police! Stop!"

I yelped in surprise, jumping from the loud noise. Great. Exactly what I needed. Turning immediately to locate the source, I tensed my legs as I readied myself to run. A black and white car with its signature blue and red lights on the roof sat behind a man staring at me. My legs were utterly unable to move.

A police officer stood frozen only feet away. He was completely motionless as I crouched into a defensive stance. Why wasn't he doing anything? He was still just standing there, looking over the barrel of his gun.

It was him. It was the cop who had chased me down the alley hours ago. The very man with whom I had shared a remarkable experience— the one who had seen me for what I was.

My defensive stance loosened. The barrel of his gun slowly dropped as he stared at me, his eyes so large I could almost make out the numerous questions racing behind them. Our unusual encounter replayed in my mind.

Sirens blared in the distance, building, getting dangerously close. My window to make a run for it was closing. The officer holstered his weapon.

"We need to go." He turned his back towards me, returning to his patrol car. I looked to make my escape down the alley. "Did you hear me? I need to get you out of here."

I glanced at him over my shoulder, weighing the option of the alley and his offer. My chest tightened. He pulled his door open and revved the engine in warning, waiting for me to quickly get in. I hesitated, swallowing the not-so-little voice screaming in the back of my head. What was I doing?

I pulled the passenger door open and threw myself in just as the car took off.

Chapter 5

Wild

"What are you doing?" My body slid across the seat as the car skidded around a corner. The purr of the engine grew as the car accelerated. City buildings blurred on the sidelines as we sped through intersections. The sirens blared so loudly, I had to focus my attention on the cop to make sure I didn't miss his response.

His dark eyebrows were furrowed together, creasing a line across his forehead as he calculated the necessary movements of the car. He replaced his handheld radio to its spot on the dashboard. "I'm helping you."

"Why?"

"Why did you get in?" He quickly questioned back. My mouth was left open as I began to piece together a response.

"Did you expect me to stay there? I could hear the sirens coming."

"Exactly, I offered you an out, and you took it."

"But, why?"

"You know why." His short responses irritated me. I stared at him, taking in his features. His hair was covered by the ball cap he wore, a few pieces swept out here and there. His dark hair matched his blue eyes as they sat above his wide-angled cheekbones and stiff-set jaw.

"No riddles. Seriously, what's going on? What are you doing?" As I questioned him, the car sped faster down the street. My heart was pounding, and things felt riskier with every passing second. "What are you hiding from me?" My accusatory tone took him by surprise as his face went from stern to apprehensive, but he kept silent.

"Ok, so we both know what happened last night in the alley, right?" I tried to offer a truce. "I am a risk to you if I'm caught by... the police, the other officers. I could expose you too. That's why you let me go. So will you please tell me who you are?" I was firm with my words, deciding I was going to push for answers.

"You're quick." He raised his eyebrows as a smirk crawled across his face.

The car slowed, coming to a normal speed. The officer flicked off the sirens, leaving us in awkward silence. He gazed over at me, likely determining if his decisions were worth the liability. "I need to know who you are, and where you came from." His words were abrupt, warranting a response. His dark blue eyes bored into me.

"Look... officer? I don't know who you are, and the last time I checked, you're a cop. I'm not exactly going to incriminate myself. I'm not an idiot." Ok, maybe I was an idiot. A cop? What was I thinking?

He glanced at me while weaving through traffic, almost annoyed. "I'm the least of your concerns. I don't think you realize the danger that's out there for our kind."

"Our kind?" The idea that there was more than just me, more than just him, out there in the world nearly took the wind out of me.

"I don't know you either. I'm risking just as much as you are, probably more, just by being here, by doing this." His words felt worried. For him being a policeman, detecting fear should have been a difficult task— unless he was just as afraid as I was.

"What's your name?" he asked. I debated for a moment and then gave him his first straight answer.

"Dani. Yours?"

"Jack." He extended his hand toward me. I looked at it, letting it sit there too long, the memory of our last interaction flared in the back of my mind. No way. I was not going to shake his hand. He pulled away, returning his grip to the steering wheel.

"You could at least give me your real name, *Jack*," I scoffed.

A chuckle escaped the tense hold on his jaw as he loosed a breath, finally seeming to relax a little. "When were you taken?"

"Taken? What are you talking about?"

One eyebrow raised as he shook his head in confusion. "How long have you been like this?" He asked.

"I don't know. Quite a long time. How long have you been... like our kind?" The idea was so novel to me the words felt strange leaving my lips.

"It's been about three years since I was changed. Well, Infected."

"What do you mean?"

His face turned even more quizzical— if that was possible. "You're really serious?" His tone was a sort of sour. Jealousy maybe. I didn't know how to respond, because *I was* serious.

When the silence persisted, Jack looked over at me. "What happened to you?"

"No, you first," I said. He paused and I thought for a moment he might decline to share.

"I was just recovering from a bad injury I got on the job. When I got home from the hospital, I realized some strange things happening, but I brushed them off. I did, however, become concerned when a black van pulled up in front of my house one morning while I was bringing my trash cans back in.

Two men with masks piled on to me and threw me into the back." Jack fell silent, his eyes staring into the distance, his jaw clenched as he gazed out the windshield. We turned another corner.

"Then what happened?" I asked, curiosity consuming me, breaking his concentration.

"I was there for weeks. They kept me in a dark room, testing... you just need to know that I was injected with some serum, some virus. When they were done with me, I was thrown on the street. Hence, the change. I didn't even know where I was, or what had really happened to me. This doesn't sound familiar to you?" His face went taught with the remembrance of the events. My chest tightened too. This could be who had Ben.

"Look, my boyfriend's in trouble. There was a van that took him last night."

"Give me a few minutes here." Jack looked down, grabbing the radio attached to his dashboard. He listened for a break in the traffic. "Dispatch, Charles two-four-five"

"Two-four-five, go ahead," a very soft, professional voice flooded the patrol car through the radio.

"Ten-forty-two, goodnight." Jack turned his attention towards me. "Look, I'll help you. I need to park this thing at the station and pick up my car. Wait here a few minutes."

"You're kidding. I just told you my boyfriend was abducted, probably by the very same men who took you, and you're turning in your patrol car? Shouldn't you be radioing other cops? We can't just let them take him. You need to do something—"

"You really think this is a good idea to do this on the clock? To involve others? Let me just radio it up," his stern voice took on a mocking edge as he mimed reaching for the radio. "Hey guys, I picked up this *strange* girl that I found robbing an ATM last night. I let her get away— oh and then this morning when we were responding to the silent alarm for a business break-in, and when I heard you guys arriving at the scene, I helped her escape— *again.* Only to lie to you all over the radio and tell you 'the coast was clear'. Now she cries wolf because her boyfriend was kidnapped. Yeah, it's real time-sensitive. They might change him into an electric freak. You know—"

"—OK. OK. I get it. You're a real asshole."

He cocked his face into a twisted smile. "Like I don't get that all the time."

Jack seemed to have much more knowledge and experience on this subject than I imagined. And not only on the police side of things but on the 'electric freak' side of things. If I was going to find Ben, I was going to have to play nice with Jack. Yuck.

I reached for the door handle, propping myself up to get out of the patrol car. Jack caught me by the elbow. Where our skin touched, a reminiscent flutter raised goosebumps. I glanced back over my shoulder, half stuck in the car. He tilted his head with a crooked sideways smile, apologetically. A charmer. Great.

Shutting the door, I slid across the sidewalk onto the bus stop bench. The morning light pierced my eyes. I pulled my hood up to keep my ears warm, all the while letting the sun soak my face in warmth. The sky was a soft pink with wisps of clouds peeking over the eastern mountains. I could have fallen asleep. I hadn't realized how tired I was, and how little sleep I was running on.

My mind finally had a few minutes to catch up on the overload of details. Jack had been through a lot, that much was obvious, but his story raised more questions than it answered.

Maybe I made the wrong choice and stole funds from the wrong accounts. Questions swirled in my head as I tried to piece together a culpable story, but there were so many holes.

My stomach squirmed under the weight that Ben could be facing the same fate Jack had gone through, *right now.* If I hadn't run away and left him by himself at his apartment, maybe I would already have all the answers to my questions.

A sleek black sports car pulled up in front of the bus stop, the windows tinted so heavily they concealed anyone inside. The delicate morning light reflected off the glass as the passenger window rolled down.

"Let's go," Jack's smooth voice called. His shiny muscle car matched his cocky attitude, and not an ounce of me was surprised. I bounced off the bench and let myself into the car. "Before we do this, Dani, I need to know I can trust you," Jack pressed, the tension suddenly stiff between us. I drew in a deep breath.

"How do I know I can trust *you*, Jack?"

"You don't. However, you do know I had the opportunity to arrest you twice now, and instead, you're sitting in my car. my *personal* car."

Point taken. I had just never told anybody about myself like this before. I had never shared my ugly truths. This stranger knew more about me than I had ever admitted to Ben.

"I was involved in an accident when I was a teenager that left me lost in the woods for a bit. Anyways, I started noticing differences... and voila." I flashed a fake smile, relishing in the awkwardness. I had never told anyone that before, not even this pathetically short explanation, but the facts were all there— short and to the point, but there. I *had* been in a crash. I *had* been lost in the woods. And I *most certainly* had noticed differences.

"Right..." Jack slowly breathed in a brash tone. "What kind of car crash leaves a kid lost in the woods?"

"It wasn't a car," I paused, preparing for impact, "it was a plane." Jack's face ran quizzical. I was unsure if he believed my story. But it was true, my father was a small aircraft pilot. He would occasionally run business routes for his work partner, or take me on fun flights to pique my interest in learning to fly.

"So, no men in masks? No injections?" There was a longing in Jack's voice.

I shook my head. Nothing like Jack's experience had ever happened to me. Silence fell over us. We drove down the street, and I still wasn't sure where we were going. I couldn't help but feel like maybe Jack and I were slightly different breeds. He was man-made, created in a lab, domesticated. I was of lesser quality— Wild. Untamed and uncontrollable.

"What about Ben?"

"Don't get too upset," he countered. His grip tightened around the steering wheel ever so slightly and his jaw seemed to lock into place. "Ben isn't in any trouble. We have him."

Relief washed over me, followed by a thick rage.

"Oh thank God. What do you mean *we have him*?" I wound my fist into a ball, aiming for Jack. He held up a hand, anticipating the hit. "Why the hell would you do that?" I furiously yelled, throwing my fist across the gap toward him.

"You missed out on the fun," Jack said, "when you weren't there, we took him instead."

"We?"

"Well, my guys. *They* took him."

"But why take Ben? Why couldn't you just leave him out of this?" I couldn't believe this. My hands combed through my hair. Half of me was sighing in relief. The other half was outrageously irate. Seething.

Ben was safe.

Jack was a psycho.

The small ball of energy that constantly sat in the dark pit of my stomach rumbled around, waking up with a growl. I adjusted my position, trying to contain myself. Anger threatened to grab a hold of me, shifting my focus to taming the savage coil of energy inside.

"Look, first I needed to find you. And once I did, I then needed you to feel exposed enough to trust me. If you couldn't trust me, I couldn't be sure you were safe to bring in."

"And you thought *this* was the answer? How did you even find me, you fucking asshole?" The words ripped from my lips.

"Well, I had other plans, but you threw those off when we found out you'd slipped away."

I was beyond ready to throw him out of the car. I turned to face the window, ignoring Jack and his stupid bullshit. It took everything I had to restrain the electricity from releasing into a full affliction.

I had to behave long enough to get Ben back. Behaving felt so very hard right now.

Outside the scenery shifted into an industrial area of town. Small green weeds littered the cracks of the sidewalks. Most buildings were unoccupied, as boards with blue and green street art covered broken windows and doors. One board had 'Sparks' craftily spray painted across it.

The car glided down the street, making turns every so often. I wasn't sure if Jack was taking the most direct route to wherever it was we were going.

"You didn't answer my question. How'd you know where to find me?" I repeated, still very irritable. Jack's expression unexpectedly changed as he rolled his lips.

"Car registration," he smoothly said, "I lost you after our run-in at the alley, but I spotted you once you hopped into that Bronco." He had used the car registration to pull Ben's address. It had already been too late. I had made the biggest mistake by calling Ben the moment I returned to my apartment after my untimely meeting with Jack.

"So why take Ben? Why didn't you just pull us over and arrest me?"

"Number one, you wouldn't just sing like a canary," Jack shook his head before continuing. His grip stiffened on the wheel. "Secondly, if you are who I think you are. I was not going to put myself in that situation. Things could have gone bad, quick. I needed my team."

"Look, you got what you want from me. I don't know anything more about our 'kind' than you do. I didn't steal your life and then toss you on the streets. Give Ben back and let me go, you masochist." I let the words tear out of my mouth. The amount of concentration it took to contain my untamed ball of energy, meant I wasn't so cautious in other areas, including my tone. Mean, but safer in the meantime.

"Are you done yet?" Jack let my insults bounce right off of him, his softness gone. I rolled my eyes. This was going to be just lovely dealing with him.

"I told you, I wasn't sure I could trust you," he said.

"Great. That's just dandy, Jack."

"Well, you're clearly in a good mood. At least he's safe." I was glad I irritated him with my childish fit. The feeling was mutual. We were quiet for a few moments. The city scenery continued to grow darker. This neck of the woods gave me the creeps as we rode past more abandoned industrial buildings. Another board covering a window appeared again after some time. 'Sparks'.

"Where are we going? We've already been down this way, just a few minutes ago." I pressed Jack for more information.

"Cool it. I'm making sure we don't have a tail." We turned down a narrow road. A giant metal rolling door stood at the end of the asphalt. Large buildings towered each side of the car, making the way considerably dark. As The metal door rolled up, a black van sat inside the building.

"Dani, I want you to meet the Rebel Collective."

Jack's sports car pulled into the doorway, flooding into a large spacious warehouse. A few men stood by, waiting for us. Ben's unmistakable curls appeared. Relief roiled through me, I had never felt so weightless before. I thought I had lost him.

Jack was the ultimate asshole.

Chapter 6

Replicating

Jack led us deeper into the warehouse after dismissing Ben's captors. We entered a large room furnished with old drab desks, a space not very appealing to the eye.

"What is this?" I asked, traveling down the row of computers and technical equipment. The narrow room was lined with makeshift desks filled with desktop computers picturing multiple angles of camera surveillance. The many electrical components in the room let off an audible buzz, leaving a charge of electricity in the air. Nearly every computer was manned as I pulled Ben behind me, investigating the space. This room was like many other spaces we had passed through in the warehouse, matte white walls, polished concrete floors, an older industrial building with electronics that didn't match the time of the warehouse.

"These are our efforts. We're constantly tracking movements, trying to find Eyecon's next strike." Jack puffed his chest ever so slightly.

I didn't know what Eyecon had to do with any of this ."And what do you know so far?"

"Not nearly enough." Jack moved toward a table, pulling a chair out as he nodded toward me and Ben. I took his offer, momentarily releasing Ben so he could sit.

"Eyecon is responsible for singling out individuals and injecting them with— for lack of a better word— a virus. We're constantly trying to watch for the next attack, but we're always a few steps behind." Jack stared at Ben, watching his facial expressions twist. The world as Ben knew it no longer existed. I wasn't sure how much he had been filled in while we were separated, but his stiff posture gave away his awkward feelings. "We trace their vans on street cams as they leave Eyecon, and we follow the van along its route, but we always lose it. Never fails. We watch the money move through the dark web, then it somehow becomes untraceable. We get a lead on one of the insiders in Eyecon, and they go underground, never to be seen again. We can't tie anyone down to hard evidence. Can't pin anything down."

"How are you any different?" Ben's hand curled into a fist. Jack smirked, his face hardened. Ben had hit the mark, Jack was also guilty of kidnapping.

"Well, while this all sounds delightful, we'll be going now." I stood, my chair screeched as it slid against the concrete floors. I nodded at Ben, giving him the signal to get up. Ben's face reddened, he held his hand in a tightly clenched ball as he stood.

"How could you think we would— *she* would agree to this? After you tried to abduct her? After you took me?" Ben bitterly asked.

"I know, I get it. The kidnapping thing might not have been... tasteful."

"You think," I chided. Jack shot me a look and sharply exhaled. "Look, Jack, what do you want from me?"

"Theoretically, Dani, you are Eyecon's biggest threat. You aren't quite like the rest of us here. That makes you extremely desirable by Eyecon. We can offer you safety." *Safety?* "Well, for the most part." My damn face always betrayed me.

"Safety from what?" I asked, "Eyecon?" Ben placed his hand on my shoulder, nervously rubbing his thumb across my back.

"This company is stealing lives. I'm risking everything to shut it down and keep people safe, keep all hybrids safe. I'm using stolen top-notch security clearance codes to access traffic cameras, digital programs and databases, records, and federal intelligence agencies. I am all in on this thing. But, we need more help, before it hurts more people." I stared at Jack, who held a begging plea in his eyes. I wasn't sold.

"You're telling me that *Eyecon* is behind all this?" I asked. The beloved tech company Reno hailed a savior?

"Yes. They are, beyond a doubt, the industry leader in cybersecurity technology. They know what they're doing, how to cover their tracks."

"Well, aren't you just a hero? No wonder you can't stop them. I'm already a hybrid, I don't think I'm in any danger from Eyecon." I dismissed Jack's proposal. I didn't need his protection.

"Oh boy, well don't you have that wrong," Jack uttered. "Your blood changes everything."

"What are you talking about?"

"I told you, you aren't quite like the rest of us. I need to show you something." Jack stood and we followed him through a door into a larger space. Microscopes, test tubes, and chemical lockers were scattered about in what appeared to be a lab. The lights shined much brighter, giving it quite a desolate feel as the air smelled sterile and stagnant. And the walls were the same matte white. A man sat hunched over a microscope, facing away. Jack continued towards him.

"Samuel, she's here."

Without looking up, Samuel responded. "I knew it was only a matter of time. You're pretty fast, Jack." Samuel adjusted knobs on his microscope, moving a slide into position. Finally, he looked up, snapping blue gloves off the edges of his fingers.

He was a middle-aged black man, with a few too-early gray hairs atop his head. His eyes offered a sense of wisdom as he extended his hand out toward me. I glanced at Jack and returned the handshake with Samuel. A very slight tingle exchanged between our palms, not as strong as I felt with Jack, but noticeable. *Our kind.*

"Hmm, you were right about her." Samuel nodded, still gripping my hand. I needed to stop doing this hand-shaking thing, it was beginning to freak me out. "She's the strongest I've ever felt."

"Told you there was nothing like it. At first, I wasn't sure if it was just due to the taser or if it really was her. But it's her. Certified electric freak," Jack scoffed as a smirk overtook his face, his eyes holding hope I would agree to join their efforts. Ben rested a hand on my hip, pulling me a little closer.

"So Dani, welcome to the Spectrum."

"What spectrum?"

"Samuel's our scientist, of sorts." Jack shrugged, pulling himself onto a lab table, his legs dangling over the edge.

"I am very curious to study you, I suspect your DNA is quite different from ours," Samuel said. Ben winced, his fingers nervously tapped against my waist.

"Different how?" I asked.

Samuel reached down again for my hand. "Do you mind?" I wasn't sure what he meant, but I caught sight of a lancet and took a step back.

Ben closed his arms around me, pushing himself in front of me. "How about we just slow down here."

A giant pompous grin surfaced on Jack's face. "Scared of needles?"

"No, I'm not scared," I bit out, "but why would I be so quick to hand over my blood after you told me it changes everything? I don't know who you are."

"What do you think we're going to do with it?" Jack laughed, "Drink it and turn into Thor?" If Ben's grip wasn't so tight on me, I would have flown across the room to throttle Jack.

"Can someone just tell me what exactly is going on?" I blurted with a level of irritation even Samuel could pick up on.

"Haven't you a clue? Eyecon is creating a silent army. Waiting for the right time to release the real virus on the street. Never get sick, do you, Dani?" Samuel asked. Ben grew stiffer by the moment. Of course, the answer was no. Obviously, Samuel knew this too. "They're creating a super race. We are a kind of human hybrid. After the change, our bodies are less susceptible to normal human things. Don't get me wrong, you're still human. You can still die," Samuel continued.

Well, that was *charming*.

"What does this all mean?" The question came from Ben.

"Dani is quite different from the rest of us hybrids. Stronger, physically and biologically. Her body handles the virus differently. Ben, right? As you know, when you get a virus, Ben, your body sends different types of white blood cells to stave off the attack. That's normal. Your body also sends antibodies that bind to the virus to stop it from replicating, This tags the viruses so those white blood cells know to destroy them.

"Now, when Jack and I had a special virus— the Spectrum virus— introduced to us, our immune systems tried to fight it off. It almost killed us. Instead of choosing to fight the virus off until death, our bodies learned to cope with the infection. It lives inside us, constantly replicating like a cancer, but our bodies aren't able to get rid of it. It's replicating as fast as we can kill it. It just so happens that this virus, so long as you are infected, is designed to give you irregular symptoms. Electromagnetic Spectrum Manipulation. Besides being immune to all human viruses and infectious ailments, we can control, to some degree, electricity and magnetism. Most who are infected don't survive. And those who do, don't usually last long." Samuel shifted on his feet, sifting through little glass slides of blood samples.

"Their bodies can't handle the infection?" I asked. I don't even know if you could seriously say that *I* could handle the infection.

"Other complications," Jack said, turning his attention back to Samuel so he could finish.

"Now, the strange part enters here. I suspect Dani has built up a tolerance to the Spectrum virus. Similar to a vaccine. It was slowly introduced, so her body could stave it off with small doses, using those small doses to become stronger and more resistant to it. However, she has been so massively exposed for such an extended time, I believe the virus has snuck by her immune system by attaching to her antibodies and blinding them. If her antibodies can't detect the virus and tag it for destruction, it can't kill it. Nothing inside her is signaling to attack the virus. She's tolerated it for so long, that her body has accepted it as a part of her being. It's not like a cancer for Dani.

"This is why Jack and I suspect she is much more powerful than the rest of us. We are stuck constantly trying to fight the infection. But, Dani's body has fully accepted it, allowing her to harness its abilities. Theoretically, of course."

Jack was smug, impressed by my biological weirdness. Ben's face turned somewhat green. He swayed ever so slightly as he audibly swallowed.

It was hard to take in the scientific details of it all. Even among the electric freaks, I was the freak of the freaks. Great.

Samuel opened a cabinet of glass shelves where several microscope slides filled with blood samples were meticulously labeled and displayed. Vials of blood accompanied each slide.

"How many people are these samples from?" Ben asked.

"So far I've collected seventy-one," Samuel said. I swallowed. Seventy-one? Considering most who are injected with the virus don't survive, how many people had Eyecon victimized?

"How many have joined the Rebels?" Ben questioned.

"All we've spoken to have joined. They don't wish this life on anyone. We've lost a few along the way. Others were killed by Eyecon, recaptured and tortured, never to be heard from again." Samuel spoke bluntly. Jack's eyes fell to the floor. "But I need a sample of *your* blood. It's the strongest sample we know of."

"How would this virus have been introduced to me and nobody else besides Eyecon's victims?" I asked.

"Well, if you were never at Eyecon, were you ever alone for a long time? Somewhere no one else has gone?" I winced at the deep pang that ruffled through my stomach. Jack saw it, but Ben felt it. He tightened his grip, turning me to face him.

I knew where to look for the source of my infection, but this was dangerous information. I didn't know Jack or Samuel, or any of the Rebels. I had no reason to trust them. And their track record with me wasn't exactly squeaky clean— you know, kidnapping and such.

"What would be the point of finding the source of the virus?" I asked, looking from Jack to Samuel. Jack tapped his fingers on the table, Samuel turned his attention from the display case of blood samples.

"If I can find the source, get a raw sample of the virus before it binds to antibodies in the blood, I might be able to find a cure. It won't stop Eyecon, but it could save lives." Samuel made it clear. A cure could save those who had already been infected. It could save *me*.

My heart sputtered in excitement.

"What about me?" If there was a cure out there, I would beg to take it. I could be free of the impulsive rage that took me over. Or the worry that a split-second reaction could make me lash out and hurt someone, hurt Ben. I could shed this monstrous thing inside me, this darkness always chomping at the bit to gain control of me. I could be free.

Samuel nervously glanced at Jack.

"Potentially," Jack said softly. "We just don't know enough about you yet." *Freak.*

I rolled my lips together as I calculated the risks. Ben's eyes softened, filled with worry. "Are you seriously considering this?"

"Ben, a cure could fix me, give me a fresh start." But Ben didn't know the extent of things, because I had fucked up. I'd never told him about anything. I'd never even told him of my plans to run and start over.

There was a price to pay for a normal life. And the price? Returning to ground zero of my trauma. A cost I didn't know if I was ready to pay.

Even if Samuel did figure out a cure, it was a shot in the dark it would work for me. But if there was even a chance I could escape the iron gridlock of my power— a minuscule possibility I could start fresh— I couldn't pass on the opportunity. I could be *free.*

But I didn't know them. I didn't know Jack, or Samuel, or any of the Rebels. I'd merely stumbled into this world hours ago. Yet, the potential for a cure?

A massive amount of concern plastered Ben's face. He dropped his arms back around my waist to pull me closer. "I don't like it. We don't know him, Dani." The words fell from Ben's lip as a whisper.

But Ben didn't know me either. The desperation of running away from this, from myself. I had to get rid of this darkness inside that was tainting me.

I nodded to Jack, giving him my approval. Jack smiled, jumping down from the table as he exchanged excited words with Samuel.

"Well, first things first. Where're we headed?"

"I think I know where to start."

My thoughts turned to the trees as they closed around me again. Wind whistling through my hair, echoing like a river through the treetops. Cool air swirled around me, and bone-chilling anxiety flooded through my veins. I stood at the edge of the water, staring at the moonlight glimmering off gentle waves. I looked deeper and deeper, searching for my father's eyes again. I was seeking another warning, looking for an answer.

Ben's warm hand landed on my shoulder. His touch pulled me back to reality. "You ok?"

"Yeah, I think I'm just tired now." I might have gone delusional due to sleep deprivation.

"We have you covered." Jack slid by to lead the way.

He walked down a long hallway with many doors. Stopping at the first one, Jack let us into a room with concrete floors like the rest of the warehouse, walls bare and white. A bed pushed up in the corner of the room was the only furniture, across from a narrow door leading into a very small bathroom.

"Sheets are clean, what's ours is yours. Towels under the sink," Jack informed, pulling the bedroom door shut.

Ben rubbed my shoulders as the door softly closed behind us. After a few long seconds, he turned me around to face him. "How long have you been hiding this from me?" My stomach sank.

Ben had done nothing but love me, and I had done nothing but hide myself from him. He had never known me, not truly, but like always, I didn't know what to say, so instead, I said, "Ben, it's... it's just complicated."

Ben nodded his head. His eyes grew vacant and his face betrayed his disappointment. Once again, I kept choosing the wrong words to say. *Gold star, Dani.*

Ben blew a frustrated swath of air from his mouth as he shook his head.

"I'm sorry," I whispered. But that wouldn't be enough to fill the gaping tear in our relationship. As Ben pressed his lips against my forehead, I could tell he wanted more, *needed* more from me, but he let it go.

My thoughts spun, but I was so tired. I too let it go in defeat, disappointed in myself. I was a monster in more ways than one.

My heavy feet trudged forward to the bed. My body sighed in relief as it hit the mattress, but my mind was awake, wandering into the dark abyss of my past.

I could remember the booming noise like it was yesterday. An alarm, deafeningly loud, screeched from the dashboard of controls. Dense black Smoke filled the cabin, infiltrating my lungs in what felt like a dry drowning. And there was the familiar free-falling feeling in my stomach engulfing me. My brain was panicking, neurons on fire. Hot adrenaline raced through my blood threatening to take over. I sucked down air, but I wasn't able to get enough oxygen.

"Dani is your seatbelt on! Dani!" my father yelled in the same frightened tone. I couldn't respond. I was frozen like a deer just before its monstrous death. You know the look. It's the frozen pause and stare before a car plows it off the road. Except I wasn't going to be hit by a car. We were crashing into the earth. Everything was spinning in an intense web of panic, keeping me paralyzed as my dad yelled the same question over and over again. Loud sounds of ripping metal roared as we hit the treetops. Our eyes met as I pleaded to make it stop.

And then it did.

Everything was black. I don't know how long I was there, or maybe I just blocked out whatever happened. Maybe I should have been more grateful there was a gap in my memory for whatever reason. It would have been worse to have known.

"Dad!" I stumbled over tree roots, frantically calling for my father. Cuts, dings, and scrapes covered my body. It was dark out, but the plane crash had awakened the forest as an eerie silence set in. Pieces of the plane sat scattered every hundred yards or so, as if it had glided across the thick treetops while falling apart, dropping pieces of itself here and there over the forest floor. My chest tightened. Trees circled and enclosed tighter and tighter around me. Creeks and clacks echoed in the distance as the pines swayed and uprooted themselves to creep closer in. I became intensely aware of the awful event that had occurred, altering my life forever. Devastating, dark, desolate, loneliness. The trees squished me into each other as they overcame me, forcing me into the pitch-black darkness.

I sat straight up in bed, gasping, hyperventilating. Blood rushed to my head. There was no oxygen in this room. My chest knotted, excessively heavy and tight as I kept sucking up air, but nothing was changing. Breathless and gasping. Where was the air?

"It's ok," Ben said, sitting up, wrapping his arm around my shoulder. "It was just a dream." He attempted to soothe me back into reality. I drew in a long cool breath of air. *Just* a dream?

Chapter 7

Martian

I woke before Ben and stroked my fingers along his bicep as he slept. His face was soft, peaceful while he snored and his curly blond hair sat snarled by the pillows.

This. This could be mine if I wanted it. Endless mornings of this perfection, to wake up in bed together, to make our perfect little life together. These things that had happened to me, who I was, all the little broken bits underneath, I could just pretend they didn't exist. *Pretend.*

But Ben never realized how long I'd been pretending. He had saved me from a downward spiral, deeper into my own darkness. I was a sinking ship, my walls constantly springing leaks. I was going down, drowning in clubs full of ecstasy and alcohol. Except Ben stepped in, standing in the engine room. And when a new rupture broke through, I had him, to unknowingly patch it up, help me hold it all together. With Ben, I was no longer sinking. I could keep my head above water, just enough to keep from going under.

But now that Ben could see more of myself than I'd ever shared, I wasn't sure he would be willing to help me swim through my ocean of darkness. I wasn't sure I could *pretend* as

I once had. Things weren't anywhere close to what they had been when we first met.

The first time Ben kissed me, it had been in the most 'Ben' way possible. One of my dearest memories. It had nearly been a week since we first met— after he had captivated me with all his bookish words, his intricate conversations— even if I didn't know what they meant. What he saw in me, I wasn't sure.

He had taken me out to dinner, whereafter we had wandered up to a swing set on a hill overlooking the main drag of downtown. He moved from behind me, to watch my smile as I enjoyed the cool August night, mindlessly swinging free. He reached out, grabbing the chains of the swing, stopping me right in front of him. Slowly, he pulled the swing, pulled me, straight toward him. He smiled and my heart stopped. Complete flatline.

"Can I kiss you?" He asked.

I was too speechless, caught in Ben's gaze, unable to respond. I'd never had a man ask me for permission, instead, they thought I was always theirs for the taking.

He leaned in, placing his hot breath on my ear, and asked again. "Can I kiss you, Ms. Colburn?" to which I had finally given a breathless nod. Our lips met, flooding my body with a rushing warmth.

But, I didn't understand. I didn't understand how he could have fallen for someone so broken and empty. Maybe he couldn't see how vast the damage was, how many thousand little shards made up the mirrors. Or more simply, maybe he had never seen me at all or the way I used him as my silent crutch. Because I only ever showed him what I wanted him to see.

I loved Ben. And I hoped he would forgive me, that when I showed him all of me, he wouldn't turn away in disgust. I didn't know if I could do that.

Ben had no idea supernatural freaks existed a few days ago, much less his partner was the biggest freak of them all. Even if Ben was upset. Even if my secrets had hurt him. All things considered, he was handling things exceptionally well. Far better than I would've handled them if the situation was reversed. Especially if a group of masked men had kidnapped me. I couldn't have forgiven Ben had I been abducted like that and I sure as hell couldn't have forgiven Jack. He used Ben as a lure in his game. Asshole.

Jack spoke so effortlessly about trying to help others, about stopping Eyecon. Had Jack known about me? Or had stumbling into each other merely been fate?

Perhaps it was luck, and I only agreed to this mess out of greed. Because who really believed in fate and destiny? It was mere folklore to console us humans when life played its cards. For better or for worse.

Ben tossed gently in his sleep, slowly exhaling a large breath while he tried to get comfortable again— my cue to stop tracing patterns on his arm.

The bed creaked as I rolled out. I slid into the jeans I kicked off during the night, making my way to the bathroom. Splashing cool sink water on my face, I attempted to fix myself up for the day. But when I looked up from the sink basin, my reflection in the mirror caught me for a long moment. I stared at my eerily bright blue eyes.

A cure. I just had to get Samuel the raw source of the virus.

Before leaving the room, I took the sight of Ben sleeping soundly. Maybe things would turn out alright. Maybe I was going to make it through this awful return to the woods— to hell. And maybe, whatever it really was, we could find our 42 together.

I grabbed the door and let myself into the hall. Peering back and forth, I wasn't sure which way to go, so I ventured deeper into the opposite direction we had come from the previous night, walking at a fast pace. If you walk with purpose, people hesitate to stop you.

The hall led into a large opening of the warehouse. Light flooded in from windows mounted high on the walls, preventing anyone from seeing in or out. A few tables stood scattered close to one side of the large room, contrasting with the polished cement flooring. Groups of people sat around, talking or eating. It all felt natural. I paused, debating if I should return to my room.

"Dani, right?" a voice called from behind. The source was a blonde in her mid-twenties who was approaching me. I nodded, too caught off guard to say anything. "Shauna." She extended her hand. Her blond hair fell over her shoulder in a wave with the movement.

I hesitated for a second but placed my hand in hers for a quick shake. "Hmm, well ok," she chuckled.

Stop. Shaking. Hands. Dani. Stop.

"I'll introduce you to everyone." Her hips were wide, yet she was pretty thin. Her fast stride gave me the impression she was the just-cut-to-the-chase kind of girl. I followed behind as we made our way across the large room. There must have been thirty people strewn about the tables, eating from cafeteria-style trays. As we walked, voices began to quiet. Eyes followed me. *Freak. The* certified electric freak of freaks. Lovely.

"Guys meet Dani, Dani meet guys." Everyone seemed kind. Smiling. I awkwardly lifted my hand, blatantly out of place.

"Ben still here?" One man sitting in the back asked. His question prompted the memory of the first time I saw Ben after his abduction. This was the same group who had carried out the act.

"Yeah, still sleeping."

The man broke out in laughter. "Hah, Gus, he probably had so much adrenaline in him, he'll have to sleep for a long while to recover from that van ride." My eyes flared toward the man who spoke to Gus. "I'm Aaron," the man said. He had dark skin and striking olive eyes with flecks of amber. I gave him a fake smile. *Nice, Aaron. Real nice...*

"Nate," the man sitting next to Gus introduced himself. Short black hair, dark eyes, and alabaster skin. Shauna smiled at Nate, and he gave one in return, clearly greater than friends.

Shauna glanced at me, then back at the group. "Alright, not that you are going to remember these idiots now, but this is the crew. We'll save the chitchat for later." Shauna nodded toward me, signaling to follow as she guided us over to a kitchen window.

A few moments later, a man appeared, holding a plate of hash browns and sausage. I was so thankful for the food. I hadn't realized how long it had been since I last ate.

Shauna thanked the man and passed the food to me, followed by a fork.

We returned to the table to the rest of the group. I was positioned in between Shauna and Nate. The food seemed to be going into a bottomless pit, and I, apparently, wasn't the only one to notice.

"Ok, ok. We see you, Dani. Next time, I'll bring you a bucket and a shovel," Aaron laughed.

I don't think we are going to get along, Aaron. I lifted my fork, pointing it in his direction. My face flushed with heat, giving rise to a fit of anger in my gut. Just as I aimed my fork at Aaron and got ready to say unkind words, I was interrupted.

"Don't pick on the new girl." The voice echoed from across the room. Suave. And not to mention, right on cue. "Clear out, we've got a trip ahead of us. Gus, work with Samuel to pack up some of the things from the lab," Jack ordered.

Gus glanced at Aaron, then gave me an apologetic look as he adjusted his glasses, trying to clear the air from Aaron's snide remarks.

"Welcome, Dani," Nate said as he and Shauna left.

The group cleared out as Jack strode over to stand across from me at the head of the table. The rest of the cafeteria thinned as well.

"Get enough beauty sleep?" Jack questioned. Glaring at him, I rolled my eyes enough to make sure he saw it. I looked far from rested. "You doing ok? Ben still sleeping?"

"Fine, thanks. When are we heading out?"

"Well, we have some planning to do first. I need some more information before I can send my crew out into the field," Jack countered.

"Well, what do you need from *me* then, Jack?"

"Where's the site of the crash?"

"I don't know." The words spilled out with a wince. This was the unrelenting moment that changed my whole life, the Big Bang if you will.

"Well, where were you in the forest?"

I responded more firmly, "I don't know."

"How can you expect us to go out there and find anything, Dani?" Jack's eyebrows wracked together as his jaw jutted out with a decent amount of frustration, his voice ringing firm.

"Look, Jack, in case you didn't realize, I was *lost*. If I knew where the hell I was, well, I wouldn't have been lost." *Captain Obvious*, I silently added.

Jack circled over to my side of the table, taking a seat next to me. He straddled the bench, biting his lip, looking away from me, his muscular chest highlighted by his white cotton T-shirt. His casual outfit was nothing like his bulky police uniform and bulletproof vest that had kept him covered during our last encounters. The uniform had hidden the black ink lapping at his neck. His chin and jaw were well defined, making it easy to spot when he tensed it up in uncomfortable situations, like right now. With a sigh, Jack's head rolled back towards me. My fork scratched across my plate as I anxiously pushed the last of my hashbrowns around.

"Can you tell me what you know?" His voice was softer as he let go of the frustration.

"It's somewhere in the Plumas National Forest, north of Lake Davis. I don't know the exact spot, but I think I could recognize the area," I offered.

"Can you recognize it on a map?"

"Look, I was never keen on going back, but it's, unfortunately, a place I can never forget. I'll recognize it once we find it." Maybe.

Jack's eyes lingered on me, reading the pain on my twisted face I was trying so hard to cover up. He placed his hand on my shoulder. His touch buzzed with electricity, and the energy danced in my stomach, floating up through my body, engulfing and comforting, like some sort of nexus. I looked up at him, trying to understand the feeling.

"We'll find it." Jack's eyes lingered on me as silence fell over us for a moment. "Have Samuel clean your wound up for you." When I glanced down, the bandage wore enough red peeking through the white gauze to raise concern. Then Jack left.

After replacing my gauze with Samuel in the lab, I returned to my room. Ben turned over in the bed to look at me as I made my way in. With squinting eyes, he held up the covers and made room for me to crawl in. I took up his offer, snuggling into him as he wrapped his arm around me.

"Want to talk about it?" Ben asked. I didn't. So I didn't say anything. Instead, I pressed my body closer to his and pulled the sheets over my head. This was going to suck.

We laid there for a while and I let my mind wander off into all the different scenarios that could play out in the woods. My heart started racing as I recalled the awful place that stole my life.

It reminded me about how Jack's life had been stolen from him too. He had been thrown out on the streets. His creators had kept him in the dark about his new self, much like what the woods had done to me. Mocked my humanity. Took advantage of my vulnerability. Chewed me up and spit me out as its own creation. A monster left in the dark with nothing but a twisted mind and unthinkable disparities. 'Electric freak' Jack would call it. An atrocity, I would say. Jack and I, connected and brought together by nothing but our oddities.

A pit grew in my stomach. I was much different than other humans, but now that I was even stranger than other hybrids and Jack, I felt like a mutant— A martian making contact with the people of this land for the very first time.

"Your friends are asking about you," I mumbled into Ben's chest.

Rumbles of a low laugh quietly shook through his body. "Gus and... Aaron?"

I nodded, pressing my nose awkwardly into Ben. "Why is that funny?" I peeled my face from under the covers and pulled back to look at Ben's eyes.

"I'm guessing you didn't take well to Aaron?" He continued to chuckle. "As you can imagine, I didn't like them initially, but they really aren't bad guys. They were under Jack's orders."

"You have got to be kidding." Ben *liked* them. Gross.

A knock at the door prevented the situation from turning into a heated debate. I jumped up to answer the door as Ben flattened his curls, trying to look presentable. Shauna stood in the doorway, peering over my shoulder to see the whole room.

"Grab your stuff, we're heading out," Shauna notified us. "Morning, Ben," She said before turning away and disappearing down the hall. *Morning, Ben?*

I turned toward Ben, rolling my eyes with a smirk. Gag me. "Well, you just went and made friends with everybody, huh Ben?"

A subtle grin rolled across Ben's face. He was good with people, something I was not capable of.

"They're nice, I like them," he shrugged. As if he had forgiven everyone for his abduction... with the exception of Jack, of course. I don't think I could forgive Jack for his sins either.

Chapter 8

Omen

Ben and I met Jack and the others at the rolling garage door of the warehouse. As we approached, Shauna tossed a large duffel bag at me. I clutched it trying to lessen the impact.

"What's this?" I pulled my eyes from the bag to look at Shauna.

"You're about my size, I threw together some things for you." She reached down, picking up another duffel to toss at Ben. He caught his bag more gracefully than I had. Of course. "Gus and Aaron donated some clothes to your cause," she said over her shoulder, walking towards a van. Two black vehicles idled as everyone stood around, waiting for the game plan to come out.

"We don't have much gear, but it'll be enough to get us in and out all in one piece. Dani, I want you in the first van with me," Jack ordered as he placed the rest of his gear in the back of one of the vans. "Shauna, you and Nate ride with us. Gus and Aaron are going together. Ben, do you mind riding with them?" Jack swirled questions and directives around as everyone started to pick up and organize gear.

"Wooo, yes. Ben's coming with us," Aaron exclaimed with a little too much immaturity. Gus's eyes shifted from Ben to me as he adjusted his glasses, catching my hesitation.

"Ben is coming with us," I told Jack, trying to command it to be true.

"Too dangerous. The guys are going to run surveillance. There's a high chance Eyecon has eyes on our movements, which means they may be in the area. We want to send in a small team, and let the others keep a tight watch on the outside. We need to be careful not to tip them off. Eyecon's been getting closer," Jack explained.

"Nate can't stay back?" I needed Ben there. The holes in my ship were sure to multiply. I would sink without him on this journey. Ben rested his hand on my shoulder, giving a tender squeeze.

"Nate's too good to be eyes only, he's Jack's second in command," Shauna muttered. Jack shot her a look of condemnation. She clearly had overstepped her bounds.

"Ben's with the eyes," Jack said again, sterner this time, foregoing a kind request.

"Yeah, yeah, not an issue," Ben chimed in, using his grip on my shoulder to turn me towards him. "Dani, what's the problem? I thought this is what you wanted," Ben whispered to me.

"I just got you back, Ben."

"It's ok. I'll be just fine," Ben non-convincingly whispered. "You signed us up for this. You have a job to do here. In and out as quickly as possible. Then we're done." His hushed tone wasn't quite low enough for only us to hear. "I'm not going anywhere," Ben reassured me.

I swallowed a deep breath, still not ok with the dynamics of our teams.

"Let's go," Jack ordered. Ben's hold on my shoulder pulled me in. He wrapped his arms around me, letting them fall to the small of my back. Ben was nothing but genuine grace, seeping into me where we touched. I clenched my arms around him, resting the side of my face upon his chest. He set his lips on the top of my head in an extended kiss.

I didn't want to leave this moment. Ben's words had always soothed me, but the moments like this, his touch washed away any adverse feelings that lingered. At least in the moment. Because all too soon, it was just Ben and me left standing in the garage. Ben disembarked from our embrace as he let his arms fall from me, only to grab one of my hands. My eyes locked with his.

"I'll see you soon," he said, backing away to his assigned van, "I love you." A faint smile appeared on my face. I was positive my pulse shot up for a brief second.

His hand released mine as I watched him disappear into the van. The loud horn of the car closest to me blared in my ear. *I'm coming, Geez.*

Shauna had leaned over from the passenger seat to press the horn. As I opened the door to the back seat, Jack sat with a map spread across his lap.

No one said anything for quite some time. As Nate drove, Jack studied the map. He crinkled it and made marks with his pen every once in a while.

"I think I've established a perimeter or at least a decent area to start with. We can hike in cross-sections until you recognize the area. Still think you can, right?"

"Jack, I don't know. I'll give you what I can."

"I don't mean to push you too far. I just don't want to expose the team to any more risk than they have to. They've been through enough." He was almost apologizing for separating me and Ben. But, he wasn't.

Push me? "You don't even know me," I hissed through my teeth. Guilt automatically bit at me because he was trying to be nice. Jack's jaw tensed. "But, thanks." I tried to patch up my rough words. Jack returned his eyes to his map and concentrated again.

Already asleep in the passenger seat, Shauna rested her head against the glass. I was sure Nate couldn't hear us over the hum of the air conditioner and the radio.

"Can I ask you something?" I softly spoke again.

He didn't look up. "Sure."

"You knew where to find me, that night at the ATM."

"That's not a question," Jack responded, maintaining his focus on the map, seeming irritated. I had probably pissed him off. I let the thought wander off, deciding not to bother him. After all, did he owe me an explanation? I thought so, but I wasn't sure of anything anymore.

Mimicking Shauna, I rested my head against my window. Butterflies fluttered in my stomach. I attempted to ward off all the different simmering feelings and scenarios trying to play out in my mind.

Had it not been for the nightmares, those eyes adrift deeper and deeper into the water, my father's eyes, I didn't know if I could have said yes to this. I was desperate for a cure. Desperate. But there was something about the mind that wanted answers, wanted closure. And the woods were bound to give me something more than I bargained for.

The window pressed too cold against my cheek, pushing me to turn my head to escape it. In doing so, I could now see Jack, obsessively studying the area on the map.

"I'm not sure how much that's going to help," I spoke up. Jack took his eyes off his work to look at me, folding the map softly in his hands.

"Why's that?" He asked.

"Everything gets messed up in there."

"What do you mean? In the forest?"

"You think you're doing one thing, going one way, then suddenly you're back at square one." I closed my eyes, trying to shake the oncoming memories of my captivity. "There's something wrong with this place. We need to mark our path in, so we can find our way out." Jack didn't respond at first. Instead, he rolled his lips as he touched his chin, planning, I assumed.

"This place really screwed you up, huh?" Jack finally asked.

I gulped in a breath of fresh air. Yes, it certainly did. The static curling in my stomach threatened to wake the electricity in my veins. "More than you could imagine. If you can't trust your own mind, how do you learn to trust anybody else's?" A truce, for my abrasiveness from earlier. The closest he would get of an apology from me.

"Looking forward to the challenge." I couldn't tell if it was sarcasm or not. Maybe he was genuinely looking forward to battling the twisted games of the woods. I was surely on edge to go back. But there was a bigger purpose here. Find the source of the virus. It was my ticket for a cure.

"I'm sorry for what this is going to do to you. Being back here and all." Jack's face twisted in an uncomfortable smirk. Apologetic, surely, but there was also some determination there. This was something that had to be done. We had to get the samples for Samuel.

"What about the others?" I asked.

"The other hybrids? What about them?"

"What does the virus do to them? I mean, what can they do?"

"Nothing close to what I'm betting you can." He tapped his pen on the map as he looked at the road in front of us. I stared at Jack, hoping the silence would convince him to talk. It didn't.

"You didn't answer my question."

"Surprised?" One corner of his mouth peeled up into a crooked smile. Snide little prick.

"What kind of powers do most hybrids have?" If every hybrid I met always commented on how 'strong' my electric force was, they certainly had some sort of power.

"It's not like you," Jack said, highlighting once again the reason why I would never anchor down and call the Rebel Collective home. "It's mostly just a spectrum of human tasers, biologically elite in the sense that hybrids never get sick or have ailments." He crossed out a section on the map with his pen. "Oh, and the unrelenting battle of energy addiction withdrawals, that's probably the biggest flaw."

I wanted to ask more. I wanted answers, but Jack was being short with me as he scanned the map on his lap. We didn't speak any more in the van after this, of how we were unalike.

I knew I was different. Although, my powers were easy to handle in small doses, like controlling small electronics or moving bits of magnetic metals, or lighting my fingertips up to see in the darkness. There were parts of me I dared to tell no one. Parts that were beyond what I was willing to comprehend. Parts I tried to pretend weren't there, lurking for me. The night I had confronted Darrel, I opened a gateway into a black hole. And ever since then, I had been desperately pleading with myself to not acknowledge what lay underneath those unfathomable electric abilities.

Because summoning something bigger also summoned something darker. And every time I dared to get close to that kind of power, something gnashed its teeth so close and so deep... I knew there would come a day it would sink its claws in. That I would be able to do nothing more than stand by as the darkness engulfed me.

"We're almost there, maybe a ten-minute drive on this dirt road to the parking spot," Nate said over his shoulder, waking Shauna. She combed her fingers through her hair and pulled the wavy mop of blonde into a ponytail. We pulled off the highway and onto a narrow dirt road as the other van continued on.

"Where's the other team going?"

"A small town nearby. They're setting up base and making rounds to keep an eye out."

For a brief moment, fear struck me. What if I couldn't trust Jack? What if he was an associate of Eyecon and it was just easier for them to take me in on my own will, to convince me of his scheme and coax me in? This whole Rebel thing could very well just be a hoax— separating me from Ben so they could carry out their plans. I tried to let the thought pass as quickly as it came.

Jack was too authentic, too caught up in it all for it to be fake. He would certainly be putting on a good show if it wasn't real. He was genuine. An ass. But a genuine ass.

The van jostled us around like rag dolls on the dirt road. Nate's white knuckles gripped the wheel as he drove, trying to miss large rocks and dips. Thankfully, we stopped. Nate pulled the van off the trail, tucking the vehicle out of sight.

We all made our way to the back to collect our gear. I grabbed the duffel bag Shauna gave me and noticed Nate looking at me while stretching from the ride. I didn't know what to make of the smirk on his face. Possibly sizing me up.

Nate combed his fingers through his short black hair, grooming it off of his forehead. His skin was flawless and smooth, not what I expected as Jack's second-in-command. I thought scars and tattoos would have been more fitting.

"Here's your pack, put your clothes in this. Nate packed all your food, Aaron and Gus packed your gear." Jack handed me a large backpack that easily towered over my head. I did as I was told and shoved the clothes deep into the bag. Shauna passed me a pair of boots which I thanked her graciously for.

Jack convened with Nate, giving him the new details he had thought of during the van ride. But there was no way Jack knew, no way he could warn Nate of what we were about to encounter. The woods beheld a wicked sickness, a staggering eerie entity that seeped into your mind. What the forest had to offer, it was something you couldn't put your finger on, a muddied reality that came and went without reason. And if it did have a purpose, I was unaware of what its intentions were.

By the time I finished lacing my boots up, everyone was staring at me.

We started our trip into the forest without the help of a marked trail, merely meandering through. The bubbling and twisting in my stomach grew stronger with each step. My mind was clouded, but I fought to keep my focus on moving my feet, attempting to make sure I didn't miss anything. It was my job to notify Jack when I recognized anything. Every fifty yards or so, Shauna lagged behind to tie trail markers onto trees as we passed, marking our escape plan.

The forest grew thicker, darker, and more intimidating. As harmless as this place may have seemed with all the proper gear, it would catch you off guard. The birds above mocked us, screeching loudly as if trying to spook us. A twisted warning to get out. A dark omen of what lay ahead.

"Here ok?" Nate asked. He pointed to a small opening between some trees.

I struggled to catch on to what he was saying. "Huh?"

"For the night. Do you think this spot is ok?" For the night? Already? I looked around. It was nearly dark out. The sun was due to set in the distance, giving off a faint and final glow even dimmer through the trees. We had just started hiking, it couldn't have been longer than an hour, maybe two at the most. We should have had all day. We must have had all day. Panic crept into my mind. How could I have missed the whole day? Been so checked out of reality? I was supposed to be focusing. The wave engulfed me in its grasp, threatening to overtake me and send me into the undertow.

"You should go wash up, I'm going to make us some food," Shauna said, recognizing the emotional attack written all over my face. She led me a short distance to a stream then returned to camp. Gratefully, I knelt to the water and took a few handfuls to splash on my face. *Wake up, you need to wake up. What the hell is wrong with you? Why are you always so fucking lost?*

I tried to scrub off the confusion with the cold stream water as I let it soothe the hot anxious panic inside. Tomorrow, I'd need to be more focused.

I returned to camp where Nate and Shauna tended to a fire. Shauna already had laid out bowls on the ground, filled with some unidentifiable mush. I sat next to Shauna on a fallen tree, eating silently. I was too busy trying to make a conscious note of every detail going on, afraid that if I let my brain wander off, time would slip away again. I even tried to pay attention to how many times I raised my spoon to my mouth. Maybe if I just focused hard enough, paid attention to every detail so closely my mind wouldn't be able to slither away from me.

Shauna leaned in and asked, "You ok?" What was I supposed to say to that?

"Yeah, yeah, I'm fine. Just a bit creeped out by being back here."

"Can't blame you for that." Shauna stared at me in a silent moment that lasted a fraction too long then peeled herself off the log we shared. Nate excused himself, walking over to his tent, Shauna following close behind.

"Goodnight," Shauna called over her shoulder. They were sharing a tent, confirming my suspicion they were a couple. I peered around our camp. There was Nate and Shauna's tent, then another, maybe thirty feet from theirs. Two tents? I studied the area, comprehending there were no more than... *two tents.* I glanced at Jack as he caught my moment of realization.

"It's not middle school summer camp," Jack laughed. Prick. First-class prick. "Plus, it's safer sleeping in pairs."

I sighed. It was going to be a long night. Or maybe not if my brain was so checked out, so mysteriously adrift. Maybe I could use that to my advantage and just drift quickly away to sleep. Yet, I didn't see how I was going to be comfortable enough to sleep next to Jack. Don't get me wrong, there was a reason Ben and I had met the way we did. I wasn't *little miss purity.* I had gone to clubs in an attempt to drown myself in molly and alcohol, to find a cute man who could fill my needs. I had slept with plenty of men before, but not like this. Not in such a platonic manner. And not like Jack.

We rolled out our sleeping bags inside our tent. I eagerly got into my bag and tried to make myself as comfortable as possible. Jack seemed just as uneasy, laying stiff as a board.

We laid there side by side in silence as I prayed sleep would find me. It was strange to be laying so close to someone so unknown. Very strange to have such a rapid encounter with someone that had led to sleeping mere inches away from them in only a matter of days. I just needed to focus on getting my mind right for tomorrow. How could I be so careless as to let everything slip by me today?

"Me too," Jack suddenly spoke. I sat straight up, my sleeping bag awkwardly wrapped around me.

"What?"

"Me too," Jack tiredly spat out again.

"I didn't say anything," I confessed. He rolled over to look at me.

"You said something about being careless with the time, letting things slip by you today."

"I didn't... say that out loud." This had finally caught Jack's attention.

Chapter 9

Whisper

Jack stared at me, just as speechless. I was being consumed by the idea Jack quite possibly heard my thoughts. I surely wasn't making this up. It had to just be a coincidence. He couldn't hear my thoughts, could he? I was supposed to be safe, inside my mind, my black box. Perhaps it never happened, and it was just the woods messing with me.

Jack now sat up in his sleeping bag. "I swear, it was just as if you said it. Sounded just like your voice. You had to say it aloud without realizing. I heard it." He seemed unable to come to grips with the same idea. "You did say it aloud, didn't you?"

I was tempted to go along with it. To let it all be put to bed. The stark reality was, if it happened once, it could happen again. I shook my head.

"I would've never told you that." There was no possibility of me letting Jack in— I had never even let Ben in.

Jack gripped his forehead, rubbing out his temples.

"And what did you mean, by 'me too'?" I quietly asked.

"I thought we had just started hiking, and before I knew it, we were here. Like incredibly fast. Did you feel that way?" Jack conceded, all cockiness absent in his tone. "Like everything was cloudy. As if I was watching things happening before me, but I was standing back, in a different part of my brain. It was all from my perspective. But I wasn't there."

A knot formed in my chest. I had known this place was crooked, that these woods messed with your mind. I had gone mad under the grasp of the forest. And now I had led others here to become its newest victims.

"Do you think Nate and Shauna are having the same problem?" I asked.

"It didn't appear that way. I mean, Nate and Shauna didn't look... well, not like you anyway." A smirk spread across his face.

"Like me? What's that supposed to mean?" I retorted sharply.

"Dani, let's stop pretending that you aren't an open book. Shauna and Nate knew something was up."

I swallowed the ball of anger forming in my throat as I tried to pretend I wasn't bitter. Jack flashed a smug smile— he saw right through it. I glared back at him. But he was right, Shauna even asked if I was ok.

"Is that the first time?"

"—I've noticed you being an open book?" Jack scoffed.

"No," I snapped, "That, you know, you've heard my thoughts." Jack fell silent, failing to make eye contact with me.

"So it's not." I exhaled in frustration, my pulse rising behind my ears.

He still didn't look up. "Not exactly. It's just been a feeling, a closeness."

I felt something similar when Jack had touched my arm at breakfast but never had I thought it would turn into something like this.

"Why now?" I didn't understand. It had to be this place. What if it was amplifying our abilities? Or scrambling them?

Jack was caught up in his thoughts. Tense jaw, staring blankly.

We sat like that for a while, until Jack finally asked, "Can we try something?"

"What are you talking about?" I sharply raised an eyebrow.

Jack held out his hand, an open palm, face up. He looked at me, an invitation in his eyes to place my hand in his. I hesitated, recalling our past run-ins. When Jack had chased me down the alleyway, tasing me as he tried to grab hold of me, only to reveal we had a strange connection. Then again, at breakfast, when he had placed his hand on my shoulder. I had felt the sensation, the exchange of electricity. The connectedness.

My right hand floated above his. If we built this connection, would I be able to sever it? I'd be letting him in. Opening Pandora's box. Never had anyone known about my abilities, but maybe Jack was just as much of an electric freak as I.

I gave in, letting my hand fall into his.

Bounds of energy poured through my palm and into his. His electricity seeped into my skin, mixing with my own, but differentiating between the two was easy. The way we shared our power was seamless, natural.

Energy rushed around my body and a humming filled my ears. That same electric hum from high-powered machinery, like lights in a football stadium. It was almost euphoric, recharging as his power caressed my body. I removed my hand from his and shook my head. I didn't understand.

Nothing like this ever happened when I shook hands with Shauna. Or anyone for that matter. Why had this been so much stronger than any other interaction I had with Jack before? When Jack had placed his hand on my shoulder at breakfast? When we had met in the alley?

A smug look laced Jack's face, as if he'd just proven his hypothesis. And then his lashes fell over his eyes as he glanced down. A softness washed over him. For the first time, he too had taken down a wall. Jack, the all-knowing, fearless leader, with his guard down. "Why are you so different, Dani?"

This was new for him as well.

"Can we try again?" He was eager to repeat the phenomenon. I didn't extend my hand. "It's ok, I just want to try something." Jack lightly picked my hand up and cupped it in his own. The sensation returned. The charge jarred around my body as a hum rang in my ears.

"Focus, close your eyes, and focus." I watched his lips as he said this, only to be sure he said it aloud. Conforming to his wishes, I shut my eyes, letting the current take over. The connection returned.

Can you feel it?

I pulled my hand back, spooked by the sound of Jack's thought.

"You can, can't you?" He searched my eyes for confirmation. Somehow, this electric freak thing was on a spectrum, and Jack was suddenly closer to me than anyone else ever had been. He was tuning his frequency closer and closer to my exact number. The edges of my little lonely world seemed to stretch just a bit thinner. I'd been comfortable with those edges, but now, I caught myself imagining what lay on the other side of them. Uncharted seas were dangerous.

Jack's teeth gleamed through his smile, he was thrilled. I wasn't as elated.

How could I have such a bizarre connection with Jack? It was supposed to be Ben. It had always been Ben. It was always supposed to be Ben. He was my person. My lighthouse who called me safely to shore, showing me the way.

But, I couldn't simply ignore the fact Jack and I were connected somehow.

"I won't say anything to him." He let his eyes fall from mine. "I understand this could threaten your relationship." Jack shifted awkwardly in his bag. I didn't know how to respond. Jack was always so quick.

I shot him a small smile out of gratitude. But ultimately, I tried to give him some sort of hint to let the conversation go. I laid back down and stared at the tent ceiling. I couldn't have been more hopeful for sleep to wash over me. Or for bigfoot to eat me. Or for aliens to abduct me. How was I going to explain this to Ben?

In the morning, we ate quickly and broke down camp. I was eager to try and regain my focus today. "I want to be in the front," I told Jack. Nate overheard and looked at Jack for his response. Jack nodded towards me, I had the go-ahead. Not that I needed permission from Jack, but it would keep Nate from overtaking my position. Shauna made a show of rolling her eyes.

We began hiking again, making our way further north towards the area Jack had singled out. Nate took over the map. I assumed Jack gave him this duty after feeling so cloudy yesterday because there was no way Jack would have given that map up by the looks of how hard he studied it before embarking on this trip.

"Dani, wait up," Shauna yelled. I shook my head out of my stupor as I turned to locate her voice.

I didn't see her. I didn't see anyone. "Shauna?"

"We're coming, stay there." I looked around, not being able to remember how I got so far ahead of everyone. I waited for Jack, Shauna, and Nate to reach me. We drank some water and had a few snacks for some energy. This was my warning, I was failing to 'be present' so far on our hike. I had to do better. I was determined to keep my focus, to keep track of what was happening.

Once we were ready, I started the group, heading northwest. Quickly, I was interrupted by Nate.

"We should go this way."

I paused and turned to face him and the rest of the group. Nate held the map and compass in his hands, as Jack stood in the back peering around Shauna to see.

"I think it's this way." I held out my hand, pointing to the northwest. I knew it, I could feel it. Something, *something,* was pulling me in that direction. A gentle whisper. A vibration. A mellow attraction. It was the woods coaxing me into its deep trap.

Nate looked back at Jack to get a read on how to proceed. He likely speculated something was peculiar with both Jack and me. Jack didn't seem the kind of man to let go of the reins so easily. And I knew Shauna and Nate both were picking up on the fact I was checked out lately.

"Follow Dani," Jack suddenly commanded. Nate glanced at Shauna, having a silent debate on the idea as they exchanged subtle facial expressions.

"Let's just go," Shauna said, nodding towards me.

The word begrudgingly left his lips, "Ok."

I let the forest pull me in deeper as my mind wandered into the abyss, the strange darkness that took me so long to escape from. The trees seemed to be larger, the canopy thicker with its growth. Less light made its way to the forest floor. I'd spent nearly three months out here, surviving how? I didn't have a clue.

"That's it, Dani, no more tonight," Nate demanded. It was dark out, dark inside my mind too. I had missed so much again, yet this time I was more sure I was doing part of my job. I didn't feel helpless— although I didn't know where the time was going, I was sure we were getting closer. Worrying about focusing on what things looked like, or finding some physical sign wasn't the cue I should have ever been looking for. This place had been waiting to cajole me back into its belly. A beast trying to sink its teeth back into its prey. If I wanted to find the source, I would need to let it pull me deep into its trap, and pray

I would still have my mind intact if I could ever make it out of here.

We made camp, ate, and crawled into our appropriate tents.

With Jack laying so close, I was concerned he would hear my thoughts. I didn't know how to protect myself. The Trojan Horse was at my gate threatening to crumble my cracking walls. But if I let him in, he was free to infiltrate deeper and deeper. I wrapped my bag a little tighter around myself as I begged for sleep to find me. I closed my eyes, trying to get comfortable, trying to drift off. Finally, letting sleep come to grasp me.

The forest rested, calm and dark. Trees swept in, growing larger as they threatened to encircle and crush me. I had to keep moving. To get away from their death trap. Howls in the distance grew closer as birds stirred above. They squawked loudly, uneasy. I picked up my pace and ran until my legs felt like rubber. Trees blurred past me. Something wretched was on the precipice.

There was nowhere to run anymore. I had deadended into the face of a large rock cliff of granite jutting straight out of the ground, the top so high I couldn't make out quite where it ended in the darkness. Then I heard the growling. I turned, semi-crouching, ready for whatever was next. Eight floating blue orbs danced in pairs. The ravenous growls continued.

I realized the orbs happened to be in pairs because they were eyes. Four large wolves staring at me. Their silver fur stood tall in the darkness as it reflected what little light there was. The wolves bared the position, ready to strike, to take me out. I kept crouched as well, I wasn't going to back down. Backing down surely meant death.

These wolves were not like any other. Their blue eyes struck me as quite strange until I placed what they signaled. Their eyes were like mine. Only changing into a uniquely bright blue color after being massively exposed to the Spectrum virus. Suddenly, one let out a long whimper.

A light appeared several feet behind them in the distance. A fire. The source was a man who held a lit torch. He was calling them off as he ran towards us with his fire. The wolves fled as he closed in.

The man was about twenty feet away from me, his face blocked by the brightness of the flame. The orange glow concealed his identity. He turned, quickly running alongside the face of the cliff. Running away. Wait. Where was he going? He had just saved me.

"Wait!" I ran after him, failing to keep as close as I wanted to. Then he was nowhere. And I was at the edge of a lake. A dark, glass-smooth lake reflected the full moon across the water. Without the canopy cover from above, the night sky flooded the lake in silver moonlight making it hard to see around its perimeter.

"Hey!" I yelled across the water as I tried to get his attention wherever he may have gone.

Silence. Complete utter silence. No echo. No cawing birds, no howling wolves. I dropped to my knees, cupping water into my hands to splash onto my face. As I opened my eyes, they were met with a returned stare. Two deep emerald green eyes peered back at me from under the water's surface. I began to make out his face. My father. My father had saved me. His face sank deeper into the lake. He needed help. He needed to get out. He was drowning. Slowly fading into the depths of the dark water.

I dove in, breaking the surface of the glass as it shot shards of moonlight over the wavy water. I pushed myself, deeper, deeper into the cold depths. I had no more air. He drifted down, down and away from me. I needed air. He was slipping out of my reach. I had no oxygen. He was disappearing from me. No oxygen.

I sat straight up and gasped for air, my head in a whirlwind as I awoke from the nightmare. Jack's hands held my shoulders.

I couldn't stop coughing up the water that wasn't in my lungs. I needed air. I was hyperventilating as I attempted to suck in all the oxygen in the tent.

"Where was that? Where were you?" Jack bewilderedly asked, his grip slightly too hard on my shoulders, his eyes just as frantic as mine.

Chapter 10

Unflawed

"How did you see that?" I screeched at Jack in horror, knowing he had likely impeded on my dream.

He shifted on an elbow. "You were restless, having a nightmare. Yelling 'wait'. When I grabbed your shoulder to wake you…"

"Well, it doesn't matter," I spat. Jack's face twisted, taken aback. Bitterness crept up my throat as an inkling of guilt trickled into my conscience. "It always ends the same way."

"You drowning?" Jack chided. He laid back down, resting on his pillow.

"No," I gritted through my teeth, "well, yes, but I meant his eyes, in the water."

He quickly sat up again before asking, "Ends the same way? You've had this dream before?" Great. The last thing I needed was Jack inside my head.

"Look, I don't want to get into it." I laid back down on my pillow, rolling over so I didn't have to see Jack. My sleeping bag was tucked tightly around me in an attempt to keep him from seeing my face, pretending the Great Wall of China existed inside the tent with us.

Jack had seen my dream— I'd never even told Ben about those dreams. There had been so many nights where I woke in a sweat, screaming, choking, coughing, and Ben was there, holding me together. He had never asked me to explain myself. He must have wondered at some point what could have possibly caused me to have all these nightmares. Yet, he had always been so respectful, always so careful to never step on my toes.

I remembered the way Ben's eyes had looked as they traced over my face, scanning my cheekbones. Jewels of amber.

"It's ok. It's all ok." I remember soaking his words in, inhaling them like my drug. Ben had known, somewhere inside him, there were a lot of fragile parts to me.

The only control I seemed to have was deciding who to let in and how far.

Maybe that's why I resented Jack so much. I hated how everyone looked up to him. How he held the reins in his hands to their little Rebel circle. He was the Trojan Horse, holding such a commanding presence to him. His words were spoken with such conviction, the path he walked so clear. He drew in all the other Rebels because he was a leader, a natural.

A leader, not an outsider like me.

I forced myself to push the thoughts away and tucked them into the folds of my mind.

I'm sorry. It was Jack. Trying to chip away at my wall, battering with his Trojan Horse. My shields suddenly didn't feel tall enough nor strong enough.

The back of his hand lightly touched the nape of my neck. He withdrew and returned his arms to the inside of his bag. So I laid there, pondering if my resentment for him was just that, or if it was jealousy. Jealous I couldn't hold myself quite the way he did, with such a presence.

Even when I tried, I couldn't stop the pieces from falling apart, because my demons were like weeds. They grew through the cracks even in the driest of droughts.

"Jack?" I whispered, half hoping he was asleep.

"Yeah?"

"Why are things so clear at night?"

"My best guess?" he offered.

"Ok. Let's hear it."

"Things are cloudy during the day. As if you're just a bystander in your own brain. You've lost all control of your thoughts, perceptions, mental processing. But at nighttime, it's like you have all the time in the world to think. I didn't even catch a wink of sleep the first night. I was wide awake. So what's different about day and night?" Jack rambled as if he'd been anticipating, waiting to see if I'd felt the same.

"The light?" I offered, not making the connection on how this could be responsible.

"Yes, obviously that too," Jack quickly bit out after my faulty guess, "The forest is clearly protecting itself from anyone lurking too close. But why would the veil fall at night?"

There was a quickness to his voice now. A smidge of excitement building.

The feeling of inadequacy racked through me, squeezing my chest as I realized how idiotic my answer must have sounded. The light? He probably thought I was a special kind of stupid. "I don't know, Jack."

"Whatever this virus is, whatever these woods hold, I think it feels at home in the darkness."

An intense howl rented the night. Close to our camp. *Too* close. Jack jumped up, yanking open the zipper of the tent. Trying to slide boots on my feet, I failed to get them on quickly enough to keep up with Jack, who was out of the tent long before me. Making my way out, I looked around to locate Jack and saw Nate had unzipped his tent too, only revealing his head and an expression of concern.

"Jack?" I called, hoping he was close by. The darkness kept everything hidden, only small patches of moonlight scattered along the forest floor through the thick canopy above. Jack was suddenly behind me. His hand fell on my shoulder.

There, over there, look. I searched the distance, following his outstretched finger. I could feel Jack's body position change into a defensive stance. Tensed. Ready to fight. And right on cue, I saw it, two floating, electric blue eyes. They were mounted on the largest wolf I had ever seen. The wolf watched as it crept around a large tree trunk. There was only one— that we knew of.

It watched with a scowl, stalking us. My palms were on fire as the wolf snarled into a glowering crouch. My adrenaline was lighting me up with its energetic charge. I was losing control of the ball of energy as it threatened to burst at the seams, swimming through me.

Get a grip, Dani, Jack thought, sensing I was on a very dangerous edge.

The wolf was ready to pounce as it pushed its body closer to the ground to gain a larger strike. I pushed myself down into a position matching Jack's as I prepared for the fight too.

The wolf bounded up. It was running, except it was running in the opposite direction. And without warning, I was running too, bounding full force as I tried to catch up to it. I had to chase it. How could I not? There were bound to be answers to all the questions my dreams had caused.

The wolf slowed, almost as if it knew I wouldn't be able to keep up. It flashed its eyes over its broad shoulders to check my progress. But its feet picked up the pace and it shot into the distance, out of sight. The wolf was gone.

Then the forest opened up to a lake, still as glass, moonlight reflecting perfectly against its surface. An all too familiar lake. The lake from my dream.

Feet thudded through the woods behind me.

"Dani!" Jack was calling.

I stood paralyzed at the edge of the water as I stared across the lake, not daring to look into its deep abyss. I knew how this all ended. My throat tensed as the fear engulfed me. This had to be another dream. Please be a dream.

"Dani!" Jack's voice was sharp and frantic. But it was as if I was caught in sleep paralysis. I couldn't move, couldn't speak. An atrocious tragedy unraveling before my eyes. I didn't want to look into the water, but I couldn't leave its side. It wasn't just a dream. It was real.

"Dani," a whisper now from right behind me. Jack was silenced by surprise, just as much as I was. "How is this possible?"

My mind was losing itself in its internal circles. Jack caught me by the elbow and turned me around to face him as he placed his arms around me. I gave in, letting my head rest on his shoulder.

The link we shared pulsed alive with the meeting of our touch. All the familiar sensations flooded me with their electric buzz. The familiarity gave way to a feeling of warmth and refuge, of connectedness. A caress far deeper than our touch. I couldn't pull away. I didn't want to.

His mind was racing. *Why here? This place has to be significant somehow. She has to have been here before.* Jack was utterly Jack. Trying to use his logic to piece it all together. Trying to solve the puzzle I longed to forget.

I'm sorry, you don't have to look if you don't want to, he thought, realizing we were connected, picking up on my wordless commotion. I tried to keep my thoughts, or at least any coherent words, to myself. The truth was, I had been here before. I knew I had been here many times, but I couldn't exactly recall anything. The connection with Jack tingled at the edge of my skin.

"Have your eyes always been blue like that?"

"No," I admitted, "I didn't know they had changed until after I was found."

"The wolves... their eyes are like yours." I lowered my lashes. I was a different breed. Wild. "I think they led us here for a reason. You're somehow connected. What does it all mean?" Jack contemplated.

I traced over Jack's thoughts. They led us here, that was true. We had to be connected, I could feel it. We had the same eyes. How would they know to lead us here? What would the lake, the wolves, and I have in common?

"The water." I backed from Jack's embrace. "It's in the water. The wolves' eyes, my eyes, my father's eyes, it's in the water." Jack joined me next to the edge. I kneeled at the shoreline and made myself brave enough to glance in. This time nothing stared back at me but my reflection, my father's emeralds long gone. Half of me wished his eyes were there. That I could have the chance to rescue him, to plunge my hand in and pull him out. Or at least have some sort of goodbye. My childish imagination hoped my father was just lost out here, that we had been somehow missing each other during those long few months, that we had been walking in circles in the grasp of the forest. But, I knew he was gone.

Hate. I hated this place, despised it with all my being. I placed my hands in the lake, but as my fingers broke the surface, it tinted with a bright bluish-green. As if there were tiny neon krill swimming around wherever my hand traced. Fluorescent bioluminescence, triggered by touch. "Do you feel that?"

Jack leaned down, dragging his fingertips across the surface. "I do. This water, it looks... it feels... I've never seen anything like this before."

I dragged my fingers over the top of the smooth surface, making little ripples of the blue-green fluorescent light. It started to click into place. Everything was beginning to make sense. I could see it. The connection. The wolves' eyes were electric blue. My eyes were electric blue. We were drinking from the same water source. The lake was the source of the virus, it had to be.

"We need to get the test tubes to take samples for Samuel," I claimed. We both stood. I caught a glimpse of Jack's weary eyes. "What?" I asked, anticipating something wrong with my assumption the lake was the source.

"We left Nate and Shauna." Jack tucked his face downward.

We started back in the direction we had come from. It was vital we got the samples for Samuel. In a way, I was getting answers for myself, as if it was some crazy DNA test. Something to tell me what I was. To signify maybe I wasn't all that different from the others...or maybe I was. This cure Samuel was making, I was so hopeful it was capable of curing me and getting rid of that slow-coming darkness that would one day swallow me whole if I dared to get too close.

We had been walking for over a half-hour when Jack's hand flew out across my chest, stopping me in my tracks. "Something isn't right."

"What?"

His hand dropped. Jack headed off the side into a thicket of trees. I stood motionless behind him, curious as to what he was trying to get a better look at. Were we being stalked by another wolf? Perhaps it would eat us and my problems would be over.

"No..." Jack whispered in confusion. He cocked his head back towards me, signaling to join him. When I did, I came to the grim realization of what Jack had figured out. Just a few yards away, the moonlight glinted off the surface of a smooth lake. This couldn't be. This couldn't be the same lake.

Chapter 11

Ember

"That can't be the same lake," I coughed up to Jack, still shocked with disbelief.

"We must have almost looped around the whole thing by now. Look, there's the beach we were at." Jack pointed across the water.

"It won't let us go. It's pulling us in. Even when we think we're walking away, it's drawing us back to it. What a sick joke." I threw myself on the ground, resting my back against a large tree. "I told you this place screws with you. Just plays tricks on your mind. Dark, twisted little forest," I more or less muttered to myself.

Jack was deep in thought, trying to figure out how any of this was possible. Trying to put his good logic to use.

"You think Nate and Shauna are going to wander into the lake too?"

"Eventually, I don't think they have as strong of a connection," I said. I understood why this place had such a strong pull on me, but I didn't understand Jack. Why did this place have such a strong connection to Jack? Why not Nate or Shauna? Would Nate and Shauna even be able to find their way here? Then what? We waltz on out? Mission accomplished? How the fuck were we actually going to get out of here?

"We're going back to the beach." Jack walked away. I didn't want to move, but when I realized Jack leaving meant I would be alone out here, I peeled myself from the tree and jogged to meet up with him.

"Maybe if Shauna and Nate aren't as connected, they will be better at navigating us out."

"Such an optimist," Jack sarcastically muttered.

"You think Shauna's still tying those trail markers to trees?"

"Not sure. I haven't been the most observant as of late." Snide. So snide. We walked in silence after that. Once we returned to the beach, Jack lay on the sand.

"What are you doing?"

"Laying down." As if I couldn't tell. Smug little prick. This was going to be a long night.

I walked over to Jack and sat in the sand next to him. "Maybe they're waiting for us to return to camp. You think they're going to come for us?"

"They'll probably wait through the night. Hopefully, they'll come find us tomorrow. I'm sure they won't hike in the dark, especially after seeing that wolf."

"*You* ran through the woods after seeing that wolf."

"Yeah, that was stupid. We have bigger things to worry about. You're just lucky it worked out. Both Nate and Shauna are reasonable enough to recognize the mission as their priority. Nate was a soldier."

"Your priority wasn't the mission? Just a mistake?" Part of me didn't want the answer, the other part intrigued at the driving force behind Jack's actions.

Jack's eyes broke from mine as he tilted his head back to gaze at the stars. A tight-lipped smile he was trying to conceal very subtly peeled across his face, flashing a small portion of his teeth.

"At that moment, whatever happened to you was more important to me." Guilt panged through my gut. Guilt, because I liked his answer. Guilt, because it was wrong. Guilt, because of Ben. I didn't ask any more questions.

Instead, I leaned back, laying in the sand, watching the stars with squinted eyes against the abundance of moonlight.

After a few minutes, Jack got up. He walked to the water's edge and peered across the lake. His arms rose and he pulled off his t-shirt, exposing the breadth of his shoulders. Black ink shadowed up in misty swirls, leaving his chest, lapping up to the edge of his neck. I had seen the edges of the ink before, barely visible at the crest of his shirt collar, but now shirtless, half of his back revealed a snarling wolf. He began kicking off his boots and stripping down to his briefs.

"What are you doing?" I asked, barely loud enough for him to hear. The words were so quiet, almost not escaping my lips in shock.

He placed his feet in the water, slowly wading out into the lake, a trail of the bioluminescent blue light activating in the ripples which trailed behind him.

"Jack, what are you doing?" I stood in the sand, then made my way to the edge of the water. "Jack."

He waded deeper into the lake. Hesitantly, I peered into the water, just a few feet out. I convinced myself this wouldn't be the same as all my dreams, pretending the depths of the water didn't end in the dark suffocating abyss I knew all too well.

I slipped my feet out of my boots and set them aside. Was I going to do this? Shit.

I peeled my shirt from my sweaty skin, placing it on top of my boots, doing the same with my shorts. Standing on the edge of this all too familiar lake, I was only in my bra and underwear. A bubble rumbled in the pit of my stomach, a nauseous churning that soured my bravery. It was entirely quiet. My ears picked up on the very unique sound of nothing. Not even a breeze blew the branches of the high treetops. Only the dull sound of white noise, the echo of my blood rushing through my ears.

My toe found the edge of the water. With a flash of blue reflecting at me from the ripple, I felt the charge. It called to me, to slip deeper and deeper into it. As I walked through the shallows, the energy built, swirling in my brain. Goosebumps on my skin gave rise to a tingling sensation just behind my ears. The water rose to my belly button, warm like bathwater, making the coaxing of the lake easier to agree with, easier to obey.

The electric charges were astounding, flowing through my veins with the pump of my heart, zipping to my toes. Each beat pulsed my electric drug. An energetic numbness that complemented the serene silence of the lake. Euphoria. Pure euphoria.

I waded out close to Jack, following his blue and green trail. When I reached him, he turned towards me. *This is so amazing.*

I noted we weren't touching, but could still hear each other's thoughts. The lake provided the connection between us, the bridge which attached us.

I splashed some water towards him, a wave of bright green and silver moonlight. He chuckled, lost in his electric splurge. He drifted closer to me, his eyes brighter. Through my squinting vision, I tried to decipher if it was the reflection of the moonlight off the water, or if Jack's eyes were dancing with electricity. *Your eyes,* I told him.

Yours too. You should see how beautiful they are. His eyes flashed, glowing with the energy we were absorbing from the water. *Look at the moon.* I glanced up. *Such a sorry lonely rock, spinning its circles through the night sky,* he thought.

And he was right, it was kind of sad to think about. *Do you think it knows its beauty?*

I laid back and kicked my feet to the surface of the water to float calmly on the surface, watching the moonlight glisten over everything it touched. The water still surged with power, overdosing me in its depths, pulling me into a deeper trance, allowing me to ignore the ever-chaotic reality of this world. Granting a peaceful harmony. My eyes were closing as I tuned into the whisper of the lake. I would stay here forever if I could.

Like a violent reminder, under my eyelids, I saw my father's eyes. Those dark greens pulsed me out of my float. My head almost went underwater in panic as I fought to break to the surface.

Jack, we have to go. I was swimming back to the beach. No response from Jack. As I looked back over my shoulder, he was still floating in the water, wading further out. *We have to get out.* Jack didn't move. He was just drifting. It didn't appear he had any intention of returning. *Jack, listen to me.* Again, nothing. *Jack, it's not going to let you go. You have to fight it or you will die here.*

Then I made a terrible mistake. I turned around and swam towards Jack. The water became cooler as it deepened with every stroke. The electric drug was overdosing and I struggled to keep my strokes steady, thrashing through the water. I was almost to him now, but blackness was settling in on my vision, encircling it like peering down a tunnel. My breathing became labored.

I wrapped my arm around Jack and pulled his body to mine, towing him back towards the shore. But his weight was pushing me under the surface as I struggled to keep my head above water. He was limp. That's when I noticed I couldn't hear anything from him. His brain was completely blank. The feeling that usually washed through me when we touched was absent.

Was he already dead? The dark tunnels grew longer, and my breath shallowed evermore.

I closed my eyes and tried to draw in air in tempered rhythms, nodding in and out of consciousness. The thought of my familiar dreams returned, encroaching on my mind. A dark reminder of the consequences of losing. So I let the memory of my dreams pour into me, using the fear like a primitive form of adrenalin. I was drawing on it, counting on it. Complete fight-or-flight mode.

Jack's weight made the trek back to the beach excruciating and nearly impossible. I was going to die.

I couldn't die. I had to do this. One arm after the other. Fear fed me, beckoning me to keep going. But its flame was turning from a bright fire to a small ember. And I wasn't sure if it was going to keep the way lit. The tunnel was becoming very dark and I didn't think I would be able to swim out of it, to escape it. Was Jack dead?

My thoughts reverberated around inside me as the euphoric drug hijacked my body. I was losing the battle for control, slipping further back down the tunnel, farther from its exit. I wasn't going to make it. Was Jack dead? Should I leave him? Keep swimming. Come on.

On my next paddle, my finger swept sand. The shallows. I was in the shallows. A burst of adrenaline kicked my feet under me as I helplessly and pathetically dragged Jack from the water onto the beach. He was so muscular and so much taller than me, an impossible task. I pulled his arms over his head and tugged as hard as I could to get the rest of him out of the lake. With a final huff, which I thought would tear his arms off, he was finally out of the water.

And I collapsed. Exhausted. Afraid. High. Spent. I lay in the darkness on the beach too weak to avoid the crash, so I gave in to it.

Chapter 12

Rookie

When I came to, Jack was still lying in the sand. Almost too afraid to look, I drew in a couple of uneven breaths. I watched his chest, trying to see if it was rising, but my body quivered so intensely, I was unable to tell if he was breathing. I crawled closer to him and focused on steadying myself. Movement, I could see movement. He was alive. My body fell back into the sand like a boulder, absolutely exhausted. My muscles convulsed and my fingers trembled restlessly. A soft sting ran over my skin and my breath swelled in a shallow pant. My mind was still spinning, clouding my thoughts.

I recounted the events which had occurred. Lead in my gut plagued me as I considered what would have happened if we didn't make it out of the water. We were counting on Shauna and Nate to find us, hopefully by morning.

Jack just had to hold on. Then we could get out of here and I could get back to Ben. I would convince Ben we needed to get the hell out of dodge, immediately. Convince him to run with me to the warm sands south of the border, far far from these wretched woods.

Ben flipped through my mind. I pictured him here right now in the sand next to me, combing his hand through my hair, lulling the nerves away. I could already hear him trying to soothe me with his easy words.

"Here, try this," Ben had said, pressing a cold rag filled with ice into my palm. I had clumsily burnt my hand on the stove and was biting back the threatening tears. Yeah, it had hurt, but I had been fighting to keep something much stronger at bay. The shock of the burn had almost triggered an electric reaction from me. That had been why I had almost cried, I could have lost control and hurt Ben. I could have killed him. But, Ben hadn't known that. He had simply thought I burnt myself and rushed to get me some ice. Ben had sat me down on the couch with a kiss and permission to do nothing else but watch for the remainder of the time it took him to finish preparing dinner.

I let the thought of Ben lying next to me, rubbing his hands across my cheekbones, run warmth through my body.

Eventually, I stopped shaking. I sat up and rested my head on top of my knees as I attempted to get my bearings. I shook the sand from my clothes and pulled them back on.

As I peered across the deceiving water, I revived the thought that shook me into action. The thing that saved me from this place. My father's dark emerald eyes. In some unknown way, I knew he had saved me. This was another one of his warnings that had appeared right before things went south.

Jack groaned as he turned over onto his side and pulled his legs in. I crawled over to meet him where he lay in the sand. He placed his hands on his stomach, holding it.

"Jack, you awake?" I tried to hide the cracked voice of my crying. He swallowed and smacked together his dry lips. I stared at him, trying to decipher his condition. My fear and concern were fading, now being replaced by a new emotion.

"You almost got us killed," I spat at him in a rapid rush of anger, "How could you be so stupid?" It rang out, and I didn't attempt to hold it in. The familiar ball of energy boiled just under my skin. I was supercharged and finding it hard to maintain any sense of calm. "You were just going to let us die out there? Too busy getting... getting high?" Jack rolled over to his back, legs still pulled close. He shot an arm across his body and pushed me. From kneeling, I fell onto my butt in the sand. Rude. But, I sat for a second. How come I didn't feel anything when he touched me? No familiar sensation was present, nor did I hear anything. I blew it off, too angry to let it stop my tirade.

Jack turned over, crawling toward the water.

"What are you doing?" I pulled myself from the sand and ran closer. Reaching out, I grabbed his shoulder, trying to rip him from his course as he crawled toward the lake's edge. But as we made contact, I flinched. Nothing was there. The connection was gone. I tugged as hard as I could, but I was failing to stop him. I simply wasn't strong enough.

"Get off," Jack grunted with slurred speech. I pulled harder, trying to keep him from gaining any distance to the water.

"I said, get off!" Jack growled loudly as he threw out the arm I had a hold of. With the sudden release of tension, I fell backward onto the beach sand again. In a moment, Jack was on top of me. My arms pinned down above my head. His massive size made me feel like another pebble strewn about the beach. My wrists burned under the pressure of Jack's weight pushing into them.

"Stop getting in my way," he spat. His eyes showed the slew of emptiness behind them. The person I knew, or at least thought I knew, wasn't there.

What are you doing, Jack? But he couldn't hear me, and I wasn't receiving any kind of signal from him either. The electric pulse, the drawing sensation that linked us, was absent. Complete loss of contact.

Jack's eyes were filled with electric energy, still high from the overdose of lake water. Panic was charging me up. A boiling ball of energy danced around inside, waiting to pop. It circled like a hungry pack of coyotes singling out their prey for the strike. I had to get Jack off of me. Things were bound to end ugly.

I could feel the intensity of the current building, threatening to race through my arms and exit where Jack and I touched. But as the fear raced through me, I couldn't hold it back any longer.

A burst of electric blue power released from me, pulsing into Jack where we touched. It was an attempt to get him off of me, sending bright blue light glowing over our faces. But Jack didn't crumple in pain like the mugger or Darrel.

His eyes closed and he inhaled with a grin.

Shit. I was making him stronger. No. No. No.

In a moment of frantic panic, the power withdrew, stopping the current.

Jack's eyes threw open, threatening me to continue.

I resisted.

Jack's jaw tensed, he drew in a deep breath. His hands moved from my pinned-down wrists, sliding to my neck.

My stomach was a nervous pit of electricity threatening to burst, but it would only make him stronger. His grin stretched with a growing greed.

His hands tightened around the soft skin, choking me. Trying to force me to pulse my energy into him again. My fingers wrapped around his forearms, pathetically trying to pry him from me. I was gasping, barely getting bits and pieces of air. I was going to die. I was going to die at the hands of Jack, overtaken by this perverse forest. Darkness shaded my peripherals, closing in on my vision.

I was trying so hard to force my throat, my airway open. I had to get him off of me. But the power only sputtered, shooting sparks from my fingertips. Please. Please. Loud ringing of white noise boisterously racked my ears as static took over my body. He was killing me.

His fingers pressed harder into the softness of my neck, closing off the last of the air I could narrowly gasp down. I couldn't get the electricity to obey. The ringing in my ears sealed off any noise but the outrageous thud of my heartbeat as I lay helplessly under his weight. Jack was going to kill me.

Then a familiar warmth rushed through my veins, something inside me clawing to the surface. It was wrestling to take charge. It wanted to watch Jack shatter under its control. *I* wanted to watch Jack shatter under *my* control.

The energy siphoned, drawing down into my palms. I would show Jack how it felt to be a pebble on the beach. Tiny and helpless. I'd watch him beg. Beg *me* to make it stop—

"Jack!" a threatening growl rang out. And before the electricity broke from my palms, I turned, trying to use my waning peripheral vision. Nate was running through the trees, Shauna on his tail. Nate dropped his bag and gained speed on his sprint. Jack's head cocked to the side as he interpreted what was happening. With no intention of slowing, Nate bounded across the beach and tackled the boulder off of me, effectively freeing me from him. My lungs lit with fire as they expanded in a desperate breath. I skittered across the sand, pushing myself away from Jack. Oh my god. Oh my god.

Shauna ran to meet me, helping me up off the sand. Before I could look up to see what was happening between Nate and Jack, Shauna pulled me away.

"Let's go," Shauna whispered sternly as she picked up her bag. Anxiousness swept her voice. She pulled me behind her with no plan on stopping. When I tried to pull my sore wrist from Shauna's grasp, she met me with more resistance. She wasn't going to let me stay and watch. What was going on?

"Shauna, Nate has to get a sample of the water... for Samuel. He's going to need the viles." I hoped she would cave and let us return to the beach. I wanted to see what was happening. Shauna kept her eyes up, looking for the tags she had been tying on the trees. She had kept up with it all this time, after all. Shauna handed me the boots she had collected from the shoreline before fleeing. I slipped my bare feet into them.

"I'll give Nate the vials when he catches up to us. He can return to collect the sample. We need to go." Abrupt. Matter of fact. She wasn't asking any questions. I was glad for that part. I didn't want to explain what had happened. I'm sure from Shauna's perspective it was all the more confusing. The last she had seen me, I was chasing after a very large blue-eyed wolf, only to later find me washed up and pinned down on the beach by a half-naked Jack. I shivered, thinking about what could have— *would have* happened if Nate hadn't interrupted our quarrel in time.

Shauna didn't appear to be shaken up by the situation at all. Yet, I didn't know her well enough to determine if this was just her personality or if she was accustomed to Jack behaving this way. She was so anxious to get out of there, for me not to see. She was protecting him.

"Has this happened before?"

"Jack?" She barely threw her head over her shoulder so I could hardly hear her response. She wasn't trying to encourage conversation.

"So this *has* happened before," I said.

"Not Jack, only the rookies after they've gotten their first taste of power."

I wanted more. I deserved an answer. "What do you mean?"

"After the change... it's an addiction. When you're coming off of it, essentially, you're going through withdrawals. Except, the withdrawals are worse than any drug humans use. You will do anything to get it. I mean it. Anything."

"That's happened to you?"

Shauna stopped so abruptly I almost ran into her. She spun to face me. "Yes, it's happened to us all... except you, I guess," she bitterly snapped.

Heat rose inside me, but before I could say anything she peeked her head over my shoulder at the sound of rustling leaves and breaking branches. We turned in anticipation. Perhaps Jack had slipped free and was after us. Instead, a rather breathless Nate appeared.

"I'll get the samples and meet you guys back at camp," Nate exhaled through winded breaths. Shauna reached in her bag and tossed Nate the containers for the samples. He caught the vials and then turned out of sight again. With that, Shauna and I silently followed the flags she had tied to the trees back to camp.

"Here, hold this." Shauna handed me Jack's sleeping bag from inside my tent. She replaced Jack's bag with hers. "Let's get some rest. We'll only have a couple of hours before sunrise, and we're going to need it."

I crawled into my bag and blankly stared at the ceiling of the tent. It would go on like this until it got lighter out. I wasn't able to sleep. Not after a night like the one I had just experienced.

I remembered the lifelessness that had been in Jack's eyes as I pushed the electricity into him as if he were a zombie. As if there was zero cognitive functioning taking place in his brain. Just actions that had pushed him closer to the energy he needed. My pleas had ricocheted in the empty cavern of his skull.

It felt as if I understood nothing about hybrids. I had never experienced craving electricity.

Whatever was deep inside of me wanted power, but not the electric kind that had enraptured Jack or the others. What lay inside didn't want to consume, it wanted to crush, to make others feel tiny and helpless. It made me disgusted with myself.

My powers were restlessly yearning to jump in the driver's seat. And I couldn't control it, the way it overtook me, the way it felt so good to crush the power my foster dad thought he had. Or to take control of the mugger who had tried to exude his will over me. I did everything to restrain myself, to keep that darkness locked up, because if I gave into it, I don't think I would come back. I wouldn't deserve to.

So, in a way, I did understand. Because for me too, every day had been a fight to not lose myself.

But even among my own 'kind', I had endless reminders I was not like anyone else. A completely separate breed. Shauna was already fed up with it. How long until others couldn't stand me?

"How long have you been a hybrid?" I asked as we laid in our sleeping bags.

"Almost two years. I came about just after Nate, he and Jack really helped me get on my feet, out from under the cycle of withdrawals."

"I'm sorry."

"I had been a competitive gymnast before this. I was in the last competition year at my university. Probably could've gone to the Olympics." My heart sank with Shauna's admission. Was this why she was so hell-bent on finding a cure? Even so, how do you return to your former life after something like this has happened to you? How would you ever explain your absence? It's not like people didn't notice she had suddenly gone missing from elite gymnastics, from the world stage. And it's not like she could waltz back in.

"But that's gone. It was stolen from me," Shauna said sharply. I didn't know what to say. So instead, I said nothing. Maybe that's why Shauna disliked me so much. I didn't have to walk through the compound as everyone stared with pity in their eyes. It had hardened her.

In the morning, Jack remained in the tent as Nate helped pack up camp and kissed Shauna goodbye. We hiked in silence, my thoughts remaining absent, a relief to be so checked out during the daytime. Before I knew it, nightfall was upon us.

"We're almost back to the van, we're hiking out tonight," Shauna commanded. "I'll drop you with the other group and come back for Nate." A flutter struck my stomach, to know I was going to be returning to Ben. Not only a stable human being but one I trusted. Someone I knew, through and through. I was ready for that.

Shauna had never mentioned Jack's name again since revealing he had slipped up like a rookie. Maybe she was disappointed. As was I. How could I ever have thought I was so profoundly connected to someone I knew nothing about. It was sickening to think I let Jack chip away at my wall, almost let him in. Come to find out, his wall was a lot higher than mine. I hated him for that. It was like he had been putting up this facade, bluffing as if he had nothing to hide. Wearing this sense of bravado, yet he was still hiding in a tower of his own. He was the Trojan Horse. And pathetically, part of me still wanted to let him in.

Chapter 13

Tumbleweed

Ben's arms were a warm bed on a bitter winter morning, nearly impossible to convince myself to leave his comforting hold. Sheltering me from the brutal storm threatening to take hold and remind me of the merciless agony these last few days had stirred up. I was safe at this moment.

Aaron, Gus, and Ben had been waiting with the other van Nate had parked off the trail a bit. We began packing up at Shauna's orders as Gus took my bag and tossed it in the back. Ben walked over to offer me some water and another embrace.

"You've got some dirt on your face." Ben extended a finger to wipe my cheekbone. Out of embarrassment, I turned, pulling my face away as he tried to clean it.

"Dani, What happened?" Ben's words were frantic, suddenly very serious. Gus and Aaron rushed over to us as my stomach dropped. I raised my hands to hold my still-sore neck. Ben's eyes flooded with worry. I caught the shyness on Gus's face before he looked to the ground.

"Is that a hickey—" Gus elbowed Aaron, but not before he could finish his idiotic assumption. Ben remained unmoved, his eyes begging for an answer. My stomach weighed heavier than a cinder block. Before I could get any words out, Shauna's voice cut me off.

"They're not hickeys. Why do you think we didn't come back as a group?" Shauna said, tossing an empty water bottle into the back of one of the vans. Aaron made a loud swallow and glanced back at her. Ben's eyes never left me.

How was I supposed to say what happened? How were the words supposed to come out?

"Nate?" Aaron asked solemnly, wondering who the culprit was. Shauna shook her head.

"Jack? What did he do to you?" Ben pulled me closer to him, grasping my wrist a bit too tight. "I swear, I'm going to hurt him. He put his hands on you?" I had never seen Ben so worked up and irrational before. I'm not sure his response was all that inappropriate. What it came down to was I'd never seen Ben angry before.

"Dani, will you tell me what happened?" Ben quietly whispered, seeming to have returned to a more Ben-like manner as he collected himself. Shauna had already disappeared back into the woods to find Nate and Jack. Gus and Aaron ducked out of sight to give us some privacy.

I couldn't. I couldn't say it.

"I'm fine. I don't want to talk about it. It wasn't Jack. Well, not really." A minimal offering. But I hadn't yet dealt with the emotional trauma of the event. Nor the whole trauma of even venturing back into the forest. My world was still spinning and now that I had been saved from the woods and returned to reality, the clarity in my thoughts was returning, too. I was trying to rapidly process everything that had happened over the last few days. As if all the events had just unraveled and dumped in my brain only minutes ago, like jolting awake to reality. Some of the details were emerging from the fog, and I didn't know what to say to Ben.

"He hurt you, Dani. What happened?"

"No. It was just a misunderstanding."

"Misunderstanding? Misunderstandings aren't allowed to end that way. I thought the enemy here was Eyecon, this virus. Jack wasn't supposed to be the one we needed to worry about." I felt that in my gut.

"Ben, I said I'm fine!" Overwhelmed. My brain was overwhelmed. "Stop talking about it."

"I don't even know what *it* is!" Ben's sudden anger took me off guard. This was the first time Ben had attempted to pursue an argument, to try and push me, to force an answer out. I was stunned, frozen in place. For a moment, I questioned if I knew Ben— really knew Ben. What if Ben was just as good at hiding things as me... or Jack?

"Dani, we aren't just talking about your feelings or your past, we are talking about something that physically happened to you. Something right now. Someone who hurt you. You were attacked for God's sake." Ben tried to dial back his tone a little bit.

"Sometimes, Ben, what hurts the most are the things that can't touch you." I turned my shoulder to loosen his grip, trying to play down the seriousness of the event, but I didn't think I was successful in convincing Ben. "This is nothing. Let it go."

I put the rest of my belongings in the van and sat on the edge of the bumper while I untied my boots. Ben hadn't moved from the spot where we last spoke. He stared at the ground, deep in thought, upset.

I was pushing him away. The only thing I knew how to do? Keep others out.

I tossed my boots into the back and exchanged them for my sneakers which I had left before our venture.

"We found it, you know." It came out as a whisper, almost falling off my lips. I wasn't sure if the words had reached Ben. I waited a few seconds. Ben finally pulled his eyes up to meet mine. He joined me on the edge of the van.

"The source?"

"It's the water of a lake."

"Did you get the samples?"

"Nate has them."

Ben blankly nodded. "You know Dani, I'm sure this was hard for you. But, please don't pretend like I haven't been left behind worried sick about you. And rightly so." He was calm, even though his words were fierce and bitter for me to swallow.

"Thank You." I didn't have anything else to say. I didn't know how to respond.

"Let's go," Aaron yelled out. A door thudded closed as Gus walked behind the van by us to get to the other side. Ben gave him a soft smile and got up to walk with him. Ben and Gus exchanged words, but I couldn't quite make them out. The only thing I caught was Gus saying, "I'm sorry, Ben, I know you care about her, but that wasn't really Jack. I'm just sorry." As if Gus was trying to make amends on Jack's behalf.

I shuffled around some belongings, pretending I wasn't eavesdropping. Loudly closing the trunk door, I made my way to the opposing side of the van and crawled into the backseat. No one spoke as we made the drive back in the direction of the Rebel's warehouse. I'm sure Aaron planned on getting the details from Nate or Shauna. Even as forward as Aaron was, he had some recognition of boundaries. Barely.

I spent the time running through the few memories I had, like a marathon on repeat. The hardest part was most of what I could remember was Jack. How we had connected in the tent and in the lake's water. How I could hear him, and he could hear me. I reveled in how strange all of it was. Having such a connection with Jack was exciting and beautiful, but terrifying, sickeningly terrifying. My wall was under attack. Well, perhaps not anymore. I shivered, remembering the lifeless feeling, the absent electric connection the last time I had touched Jack. Or rather the last time *he* had touched me, with his hands around my neck. He was nothing but a blank space, a black hole sucking all the energy into its gravity.

Honestly, I wasn't sure how to feel about Jack. I didn't know what I was going to do when I had to face him. Attempting to put up a front of everything-was-ok to Ben, meant playing it off while in front of the both of them. But like Ben, I was angry. At least parts of me were, the other parts of me found comfort in knowing Jack was just as lost as I was. His strong persona had hints of weakness, matching me in a way. I found a bit of solace in that. To know Jack's fearless leader facade was just that. A facade. And now that the connection was no longer there, maybe I would return to having the safe space of my mind.

Ben would barely look at me in the van as we drove back to the warehouse. The heaviness of remorse weighed on me for not telling him the details of everything. He had no idea the connection that sparked between Jack and me when we merely touched. That we were able to have conversations without speaking. I was counting on Jack sticking to his word. He had told me he wasn't going to say anything to Ben. I wasn't sure when, or even if I could, tell Ben, especially now.

This was all going to be over though. I wouldn't have to face it for much longer. Nate got the virus samples for Samuel. I may not even have to see Jack before Ben and I could skip town and start over, just pretend none of this ever existed. A cure was on the horizon. Maybe Samuel could just FedEx a life-saving dose to me. Ben and I could escape, find our meaning, our purpose in life, our 42. Whatever the hell it really was or meant.

Although, I still needed to break the news to Ben. He had no idea I planned to leave. And I had no idea if he would ever come with me... Especially now.

Aaron pulled the van into a gas station, stopping at a pump. Aaron and Gus hopped out as Ben's eyes wandered to me, pursing his lips together. He didn't know what to say. And seeing him this way killed me because Ben always knew what to say. He always had the right words. A lot of them. No. Nope, I cannot do this.

"I've gotta use the restroom." I excused myself from the car—from any confrontation that would have arisen. Gus pumped gas as Aaron disappeared inside the store. Before pulling open the convenience store door, I saw Ben join Gus at the pump. Was he trying to get more details from Gus? Answers? Could I blame him? I surely hadn't filled in any gaps.

I marched to the bathroom throwing open the door in frustration. As I approached the sink, I saw what Ben had gotten riled over. Dark bruises laced either side of my neck in an ugly mixture of purple and yellow. A hollow feeling overtook me as a shiver raced across my skin. Was it just the electric high? Or had Jack wanted me dead? Was I, and my powers, a threat to him? The ugliness on my neck didn't show Jack's intentions, but they were an indicator of what the outcome of the situation would have been if Nate hadn't shown up.

My face looked rough, covered in dirt. I splashed the cold water across my forehead, trying to scrub the incident from my mind. But the bruises were still there, staring back at me. I pulled my hair out of its ponytail and draped it to cover the crime scene on my neck. Regardless of Jack's intentions, it stung knowing how close to the end I had come.

I left the bathroom and paid for a bottle of water with the cashier before returning to the van. Ben and Gus still stood at the pump chatting. Upon joining them, Gus's eyes flitted to my neck, which was now mostly covered by my long dark hair.

Ben placed one hand on my waist and the other on the small of my back as he leaned in. He kissed my forehead then drew back enough to meet my gaze.

"I'm sorry." But I didn't know what he was sorry for. Sorry for his behavior? He shouldn't be. Sorry Jack attacked me? It was out of Ben's control. Sorry I ever had to go into the woods?

It was my choice. Before I could open my mouth to tell Ben, Aaron's voice overtook everything.

"Gus, get in the van, let's go!" Panic filled Aaron's commands. As I looked to find Aaron, he was sprinting toward us. An unknown man stumbled out of the gas station's door, looking dazed. The man's hand raised to his head, rubbing out his temples. He locked his stare onto Aaron as his stance firmed. Then with striking clarity, he began running in our direction.

He was coming after us.

Gus ripped the pump handle out of the van, letting it fall to the pavement as he dashed to the driver's side. Ben and I tumbled into the car just as Aaron pulled his door shut. The van's engine revved as squealing tires filled the lot. Gus peeled out of the gas station and onto the highway.

"Who was that?" Ben said, just as panicked as Aaron.

"He recognized me," Aaron breathlessly admitted. Adrenaline pumped below my skin, making my heart race.

"Aaron, who was that?" Ben asked again. Gus was pale as a ghost.

"Eyecon?" I questioned. Aaron gave a nod as he tried to catch his breath.

"What did he want?" Gus glanced over at Aaron as he maneuvered the van. We were speeding down the highway, and I would have much preferred Gus to maintain his focus on the road.

Aaron exhaled a large swath of air. "The wild one." A grumble raced across my stomach waking the electric monster. My leg tapped in nervous anxiety. Me. The man was looking for me. Eyecon was looking for *me*. How had they known?

"Oh shit. Get your seatbelts on." Gus's eyes were glued to the mirrors, watching behind us as he drove. I pulled my seatbelt on and twisted my head over my shoulder to look out the rear windows. Ben's hand found mine as he squeezed it.

A black sedan weaved through traffic, catching up to us. My palms were on fire and I forced myself to let go of Ben's hand. If my powers took over, who knew what would come of it. I could hurt Ben. I could hurt everyone in the van. But I had to keep my emotions tamed, before everything spiraled out of control.

I tried to replay the scene inside the gas station shop over in my head. There were a few patrons inside, but none seemed suspicious, none appeared to have taken interest in me. Had the Eyecon man seen me? Had I been made? Or had he not realized we were there until he recognized Aaron? Did Aaron give me up? Tell him my name?

The black sedan raced right behind us now. Sweat dripped down Gus's face. Flutters of electricity were flooding through me. My hands were nothing but pins and needles as they attempted to contain the energy.

The sedan was smaller and faster than the van. It swerved into the adjacent lane, cutting in front of another driver who then lost control of their car. Crushing metal and squealing brakes rang out as the crash took place behind us. The innocent driver's car smashed into the cement median divider, rolling and tumbling as other cars avoided being squashed.

The black sedan raced right next to us in the left lane. His position edged closer and closer, attempting to get in front of us. As I peered out the window I saw the muzzle of a handgun. The Eyecon man was aiming right for Gus as our vehicles raced neck and neck. Ben pushed me down across the backseat just as the van made a sudden jerk. A barrage of noise broke out. The van was spinning. Everything was spinning.

Just as the Van stopped circling, I saw the black car rolling across the highway like a tumbleweed in the wind. The Eyecon agent crashed into a berm of trees. Gus floored the gas and the van fishtailed into action.

"Holy fuck," Aaron yelled in relief.

"Is everyone ok?" Gus asked. Ben's hand touched my chin as he pulled my face up to look at me. His eyes filled with concern, checking to see if I was alright. I nodded, but my hands were shaking and shock was setting in. The monster inside was lightning hot, and I was struggling to convince it to return to calmness.

"They were after me." They were after *me*. I needed to breathe, to focus. To be grateful for how things had ended.

"No shit," Aaron chimed. My stomach was going to engulf me. I was falling prey to the ensuing panic. A shaky breath left my chest. Eyecon knew of my existence. Shit.

I swallowed the wave of emotion threatening to take control. I had to hold it together. I couldn't afford to hurt anyone. I exhaled deeply, pushing the monster aside, focusing on containing it until the ball of electricity sat undisturbed.

We made it back to the Rebel's warehouse without further incident. Gus pulled the van to a stop behind the rolling doors and shut the ignition off. We all sat in silence for minutes. No one said a word. No one moved a muscle.

"That could have been bad," Aaron finally said.

"That could have been a lot worse than it had turned out," Ben admitted, "Thank you, Gus, for your good driving skills." Gus didn't say anything. He nodded as his gaze was stuck staring straight ahead, not fixated on anything. Shock. We were all in shock.

"Jack's gonna be pissed," Aaron said before pulling his door open and leaving the van. Ben's attention turned toward me.

"Are you ok?" Ben's eyes glued themselves to me. I didn't know what the real answer to that question was. I was ok *physically*.

Ben swiped his fingers across my cheek as he slid his hand behind my head, pulling me in for a hug. My chest tightened and tears threatened to overtake me, but I held them in. It was my existence that threatened the lives of every individual in the van. It wouldn't be fair for any one of them— Gus, Aaron, or Ben— to have to console me. So I pushed the tears back down, choking back my words. Because if I said anything, a flood of water would appear from my eyes. My existence was a threat to everyone I surrounded myself with.

Chapter 14

Pawn

"Why did you ever stop?" Jack snapped. I couldn't help but stare at him, to inspect him, to see if he looked any different. This was the first time I had seen him since Nate had tackled him off me at the lake.

"I had to take a piss," Aaron bit back, "what, I'm not allowed to pee?" We were gathered near the vans inside the warehouse. Nate, Jack, and Shauna had shown up minutes after us.

"Did they see her?" Jack's face filled with a red hollowness. Lifeless anger.

"No," Aaron quickly said, "Well I don't think so."

"Neither do I," I intervened, interrupting Aaron and Jack's banter. "I went into the gas station to clean up, but I don't remember seeing that man." At least, I didn't think he saw me, and if he did, would he have known who I was— or rather what I was?

"Yeah, that's because he was busy pissing next to me. And when he recognized me, he flew across the bathroom like a fucking ninja."

Jack's face was stone, a carving of a roman warrior, his jaw so tight I was convinced it would crack. "What did he say?"

"Something about knowing we have her. He was trying to find her. Luckily I was able to sock him in his stupid face." Well, that explained the dazed look and staggered steps the Eyecon man had barely taken when he exited the gas station. "He called her the wild one." My stomach churned once again at that phrase.

"Yeah, that's 'cause they didn't create her." I was convinced Shauna took every opportunity to remind me of how different I was. How I didn't fit with the rest of the hybrids.

Jack pushed his hand through his hair. "Everything's a fucking mess."

Was he talking about the wreck? They would have passed through the same strip of highway on their return. I imagined Nate would have floored it to return to the Rebel's compound, to make sure we had made it out alive. Or was he referring to my near-death experience at his hands? Or our lost connection? Or so many other nuanced things that had felt awry?

None of these situations were ones Jack, or anyone had anticipated. Jack's hand fell from his head as he turned to leave the space.

"Where are you going? You just gonna walk away? We almost fucking died," I bit out.

Jack stopped. The hand at his side balled into a fist. "You think I would walk away? From this?" He gestured to the dent in the van. "Let's go, there's something I need to show you." Jack tossed the words over his shoulder as he turned down a hallway.

Ben's grasp found my arm, briefly holding me back. Not now, Ben.

But I knew what this was about. Ben was weary of Jack, of his capabilities, of what he had done. I nodded for Ben to come with me, not because I was scared. I wasn't. But it would console Ben's worry of me being alone with Jack. And part of me selfishly didn't want to let Ben out of my sight, especially after the crash.

Jack led us to the surveillance room, lined with computers and a number of Rebels scattered about, tapping and clicking away. Their screens were filled with articles, city surveillance, databases, windows of coding, and other records. Someone gathered papers and stood, readying to approach Jack, but he motioned them away before they could even leave their desk.

"We're running all the specs, trying to get ahead of Eyecon before they make the next strike. Missing persons cases are up, and you'd think there was a rhyme or reason, or even just some kind of pattern to follow, but Eyecon leaves no trace. We are failing to make predictions, failing to prevent any more abductions. Eyecon has gone so far underground, they're nearly impossible to detect." I followed Jack as he led us through the surveillance room. Ben kept his hand on my elbow as he traced my steps.

"Preventing the next abduction is great and all, but that isn't stopping Eyecon."

"Any suggestions?" Jack snidely remarked.

"Go after them, stop playing defense." If Jack ended Eyecon, I could slip away with Ben. I wouldn't have to look over my shoulder in constant worry.

"Who are you going to go after, Dani? You just going to waltz in and start blasting people?" Jack snapped back defensively.

Me? I wasn't involved in this, in stopping Eyecon. A few wandering eyes left computer screens to stare at our quarrel. Ben stepped up close behind me. Jack's harshness reminded me of the scenario at the beach as I lay pinned beneath him.

I bit my lip. Ben didn't know I could project my energy, Jack didn't know the extent of it either. Maybe he was just referring to guns. Or maybe he wasn't. Bitterness filled my mouth. Jack had never seen it the way it had happened the night I 'blasted' my foster dad, Darrel. He had never seen the horror on my foster mom's face, or stared at those accompanying viciously cold and scared eyes Anna donned that night.

Jack's shoulders tensed. "It's a bit more complicated than that. First of all, Eyecon is a very large corporation, and not everyone in the company is associated with the Spectrum trials. You can't just walk in and hold court."

"Ok, but obviously, you have been failing to solve the issue at hand. Eyecon just tried to wipe out members of your team. They almost killed us, killed me."

"You think I don't know that?" Jack growled, blowing through a door and into the next room. Before I could follow, Ben placed his hand on my shoulder, holding me back— it set me off.

"Ben, I can handle myself," I spat in his direction as I stormed off after Jack. Ben didn't follow. Immediate guilt. He was wound tight due to the incident from the woods. Could I blame him? I could only imagine the scenarios rising in his head since I had failed to fill in the blanks for him.

And if Jack was going to piss me off, I didn't want Ben near. If my powers decided to consume me, if I couldn't hold them off, I could hurt Ben. He wasn't a hybrid like me or Jack, Ben would crumble under the electricity.

Murmurs between Rebels buzzed, talking under their breath as they stared while I took off after Jack. Great.

And maybe that made me stupid to be alone with Jack, but he said he needed to show me something. And I wanted answers.

I recognized the room as the same one Jack had sat me and Ben down in to tell us about the underground doings of Eyecon. It was Jack's planning room, his office of sorts. Jack faced a wall away from me, his hands tugging on his hair atop his head.

"We almost died, and by the looks of it, you're going to do what you have been, a whole lot of nothing." Bitterness flooded my words. Jack had to stop them, keep hybrids safe.

"What do you want me to do, Dani? I suppose you are finally going to agree to help us, you know, since you've got it all figured out," Jack snapped.

Figured out? "I don't have shit figured out."

"Then don't talk to me about *doing nothing*," he snarled. "There's nothing we can do until we catch a break." Jack exhaled, rubbing out the rising stress at his temples. "Let me be blunt with you."

I waited as Jack finally dropped his hands from his face. "Look, you are the strongest of our kind, probably ever. Stronger than me. What you did on the beach, your powers," Jack exhaled, pausing his words so he could turn to face me, "No one has those capabilities. Not only can your touch discharge an incredible voltage, I saw you withdraw the money from the ATM that night."

"So when I tell you I need your help, I'm saying we can't do this without you. You're a vital component in stopping this. I need you on board." How could he be so sure of that? I had never even been to Eyecon. I was just Dani. I had no control over this, over myself. If I let those powers run rampant... I couldn't do that.

"What about the cure? If Samuel can make some sort of cure and I'm no longer a hybrid, this all goes away right?" I wasn't going to commit to Jack's mission. It was too much. Too dangerous. Ben was getting mixed up in all this, the crash was too close of a call. The only thing I committed to was helping get the samples for Samuel. I just wanted a cure. Then Eyecon would no longer have interest in me. Free. I could be free. That is, if the cure would be effective on me.

"There is no time for that! Did you not see what happened? Eyecon is clearly coming after you. And Samuel could take years to develop a cure or even a vaccine." Jack walked over to the table, placing both hands flat across the surface as he leaned over.

"And if I say no? If I just walk away?" I could start my life over fresh. Even without a cure, I could slip away and cut all ties with this place. Wash my hands and be done. Jack's face fell. He bit his lip, jaw stiff as granite.

"And just where are you going to go? You aren't safe, Dani. As soon as they've got the formula right, who do you think the first target of their army will be? They're going to eliminate any threats." I swallowed hard at Jack's words. "I don't know how much time we have left."

I drew my eyes to Jack, trying to think through the rising anger. "They don't even know who I am, I'm not one of their little lab experiments. If I walked out of here right now, who's to say Eyecon would ever be able to find me? To track me down? If Ben and I go now, we could get out of this," I said sourly as I nodded toward him.

Nothing could happen to Ben, not because of me. Walking away now would give Ben the best opportunity to get out of this unscathed, to run, and run now before things got worse.

"Is that so?" Jack questioned lightning fast as he pulled himself back from the table. He moved to stand in front of me. My nerves fluttered under my skin. "They *know* you exist. And they know we either have you or we know where you are. If you think you can just flee to some beach in Tahiti and forget your life here, I think you're mistaken." Jack threw his hands in the air as he turned and marched a few steps back. Well, Tahiti was a bit further than I was planning. But I'd take it. Anywhere with sunshine and a fruity little drink with a pink umbrella.

"If Eyecon knows about you, that a wild hybrid exists. They will go to the ends of the earth to figure out how. They will stop at nothing until they have you in their grasp. You can only run for so long. Because they will find you. They're just trying to keep us at bay long enough until they get their opportunity to wipe us out and take you. It's all just a game of fucking cat and mouse until then." Jack stepped so close to me I felt his body heat radiating from his chest. My stomach churned in a knot.

"If we don't stop Eyecon first, they are going to end us. All of us. They'll take down every soul you ever knew just to get to you." Every soul. That included the Rebels. Jack paused, pulling in a cool breath of air. "Dani, they'll hang Ben in front of you like a carrot."

And there it was. I was risking Ben's life by associating with him. Just by existing. I inhaled a long deep breath, trying to hold off a wave of anger. How could Jack have so soon forgotten? "You hung Ben as a carrot in front of me. Remember that?"

Jack glanced down over his sharp cheekbones, looking away.

"That wasn't the same," he said, trying to put enough emphasis on his words to justify them. The vein on Jack's neck pulsed. His face was bright red.

Seconds ticked by as Jack took a moment to flex his jaw and exhale.

"That incident on the highway was the first of many more to come. Eyecon's going to change the world if they have their way, and it won't be for the better. Society as you know it will be over. There will be nowhere to run off to, nowhere to hide, Dani. It's going to be ugly."

Ok, so maybe I wasn't being realistic with myself. It was clear Eyecon was after me. And It was even more clear they were willing to do whatever it took to get me. The Eyecon agent had caused an accident of an innocent driver. He was going to shoot at us. Kill. He *had* killed. And he was going to kill again. *They* were going to kill again.

What would the Eyecon agent have done had we wrecked? Had he gotten his hands on me? On Ben? I would have traded my soul for Ben's release, even if it meant giving myself over to Eyecon. That man would have killed anyone to get me, Jack was right about that. The crushed car of the innocent driver had demonstrated as much. Jack was also right that they wouldn't stop until they had me, confirming what I already knew after narrowly escaping the wreck. My existence threatened the life of everyone.

"Look, the longer we wait, the more people die. I know that, I carry that on my shoulders every damn day. But, how many more do they have to infect or kill before you decide it's enough? And once Eyecon perfects the virus, they'll be turning out hybrids en masse. Do you know how many people will die in that process, inside that hell hole?" Jack pursed his lips, inhaling a deep breath. "The ones who do survive will be turned into Eyecon's good little soldiers. And the ones who get tossed out on the street, they won't last but a day or two. Eyecon will tear humanity apart to get what they want."

I was quiet for a long while. It should be easy to be like Jack, effortless to choose what was right, to be so committed to justice.

"Do you know what's going to happen once they get their hands on *you*?" Jack asked, echoing my thoughts.

"I can only imagine the lab rat I would become."

"It's worse than you think. But that's not all," Jack's eyes flitted away from my face as he turned his wrists over in examination. "The idea is to perfect the virus. Modify it to give hybrids more power, remove the cravings and withdrawals. To make *you*," Jack admitted, "You could be the most dangerous weapon. Imagine taking elite soldiers and giving them your powers." I gave a hard swallow. "And the key to their success lies within your blood."

Jack's eyes locked onto mine as he took a step closer to me.

"You have no idea what Eyecon is going to do to you to get what they want, and if you live, you won't come back the same as you went in." It was a dark warning that sent chills down my spine.

Jack slowly approached me, stopping only mere inches in front of me. He held out his palm, an invitation. I was reluctant to comply. The last time we touched, there was a void, an empty space. Like our connection had been lost while Jack floated out to sea, the line to the life preserver snipped.

"Dani, please." Jack's voice sank softer, pleading. Desperation in his face, in his words.

I gave in, letting my hand fall in his, warmed by his touch. The indistinguishable sensation breathed to life, burning through my palm, running up my arm, dancing around my body. We hadn't lost it.

Our exchange was not only in words but images.

A room appeared, as if I was standing in it. As if I was Jack. It was the room they had kept him in during his apprehension at Eyecon, a space of empty hollow darkness, bleeding into his mind. It had only taken mere... Days? Hours? Minutes? He didn't know. Everything slipped away from him as insanity crept in through a darkness beyond fire and brimstone. His mind had only been filled with a single burning desire, the need for electricity. He had been consumed by nothing more as that burning, unyielding flame endlessly singed every nerve in his body. Agony. Uncompromising agony. A stream of unrelenting thoughts of killing himself decaying his mind— to end it all, for there was no hope of it getting better, of getting out. There had been no ounce of light— in the room, nor left in Jack. Nothing but a bottomless pit of emptiness, a free fall into a void that existed somewhere between here and death.

Anger. So much anger inside. A clasp around his neck kept him chained to a medical gurney. Notches of raw skin were made absent from his wrists as he ceaselessly fought to free himself from the wickedly cruel bondage. A caged animal, brutally neglected. He couldn't end it. Even when he had wanted to. Suspended infinitely in an escapeless unforgiving nothingness.

I so foolishly thought it was *me* who was misunderstood. *Me,* who had it so hard, haunted by the bits and pieces of the patchworked memories. All the while, Jack bore the most vivid never-ending memories from every minute of what he endured, engrained, burned, perpetually stained into his mind. To relive, over and over as a lucid dream. A vivid ghost to haunt him wherever he persisted. And instead of running from his demons as I did, they edged in the crypt of his mind, fueling his need for vengeance— to end Eyecon.

When I opened my eyes, I was met with the face of a broken man, as broken as I was. An ache in my heart rose a throbbing hole in my chest. Words. I was devoid of words.

Jack's experience had shown the visceral truth of Eyecon. No one else. No one could go through this.

Believe me, if that forest—that lake, was a living person, I would have killed them, a long long time ago, without a second thought. But the moratorium of Eyecon's kill list? Eyecon's impending martial law if they succeeded? Ben?

Eyecon's willing to shatter everything to take control. They'd infect others with whatever this tainted virus was.

No. No more. Eyecon had moved the first pawn in the game. And it was our turn.

"I'm in."

Chapter 15

Bulldozer

Ben sat quietly for a moment. I didn't know if that was a good or bad thing. I didn't want to talk about it, but I owed it to him. When Jack had gotten irritated and raised his voice, Ben had pulled me away and tried to insert himself between us. A commendable quality, but Ben didn't know Jack the way I did. Ben had no idea what it was like to have an electric monster pulsing through you, making your emotions so much more unstable, threatening to overtake you at your most vulnerable moments. He didn't know what it was like having to cope with such a virus.

But did Jack really know? We were different breeds. All I really knew about the other hybrids was their insatiable affinity for electricity, but was there that deep dark something else that craved power, the non-electric kind? Did he really know what it was like to have that same darkness lingering below the surface? Or was he perhaps the first person to look my way who I thought could understand. Maybe I was naive for not being afraid of Jack. Because, at the end of the day, I didn't really know him.

"I understand. But I just can't let it happen again. And now considering we'll be here longer... Look, I don't want you to get hurt. You can't push it with Jack," Ben said. I smiled a little crooked, trying to hide the expression. I'm sure I would push the limits with Jack. "It's like you're drifting away. I'm not sure I know who you are anymore."

Who I am? I tried not to let the rising anger snarl from me in the way it had rushed over me. I was angry, and yet, I was sad. Ben never even knew who I was.

Because who I wasn't was the perfect little housewife Ben's mom was hoping I'd be. Who I wasn't was the girl who had a prized career. Who I wasn't was the one who held it all together. I... I was a sinking ship, leaching onto Ben's lighthouse to stay afloat. And he didn't even know it.

"Ben, you just have to back off a bit. Trust I can handle myself."

"And if Nate wasn't there?"

"It only happened because of the water, It's not like I alone had done that to Jack."

"Again, and if Nate wasn't there? —I'm just saying that now you know what happens when he's pushed too far. He's unstable. I don't know what I'd do if anything ever happened to you," Ben sighed, shaking his head. "So just... be careful. Ok?" Ben pleaded to end the conversation right there. Unstable? Ben had no idea *I* was unstable.

"I can do that," I lied. I wasn't afraid of Jack, even after the incident on the beach. Even if Jack was much taller and stronger than me. But I had to agree I would try to be on my best behavior. Ben had done nothing but care about me and I owed it to him to try to care about myself too. *Try.*

Ben had told me to be careful one time before, but it wasn't in the same sense. It had been with his lips pressed against my ear, a pretentious warning.

We had just brought an armful of groceries from the car as we ran to Ben's apartment door in the summer storm of the year. Upon entering, I had slipped on pooled water in the entryway and brought Ben down with me. We had been soaking wet as the fall sprawled us over the mess of grocery items. Ben fell on top of me as he held his weight above my body, trying not to crush me. Frozen. I was struck by the sheer laws of attraction. The way Ben's delicate eyes had melted over my face. Or how his lips bore the most beautiful color, somewhere between plum and the pink wisps of a sunrise. I lost my breath as I stared at him. Partially embarrassed, partially telling myself I needed to plan these kinds of happy accidents more often. Ben lowered his body, tight and muscled, drawing his lips across my chin and up to my ear, causing my back to arch.

"I'm going to need you to be more careful," he whispered. My heart sputtered in my chest. Ben drew back one of his hands supporting his weight as he shifted his attention. His arm flexed with strength I was begging him to use on me. He lightly swept his fingers over my exposed midriff, drawing them up to the center of my chest as his lips traced down the side of my neck before finding their way to mine. He wasn't just late to dental school, he had missed class entirely.

But that felt like ages ago. And things felt... Well, things felt so complicated now.

A knock on the door withdrew my attention from Ben. Shauna appeared as I opened it.

"We're meeting, Gus has an idea."

We followed Shauna to the meeting room, the same one where I agreed to help the Rebels. Gus sat at the table nervously tapping his thumbs, looking lost in thought. Aaron and Nate made small talk while Shaunna took her seat beside Nate. Jack steepled his fingers as he leaned back in his chair, his lip tucked between his teeth. Jack's uneasy taps flooded my nerves. He'd already been privy to Gus's idea. Why did this not look good?

"Alright Gus, lay it out," Jack started. Ben and I sat across from Jack at the table.

"So, Aaron and I have been looking into how Eyecon stores their data. Essentially everything is stored on computers that are shared between their servers and since it has an internet connection, we have access to all that, given that we can beat the firewall and get in undetected, we can look but we can't touch." Gus paused, "the issue is we can't locate any data about the Spectrum program." Gus glanced at Aaron for confirmation as he spoke.

"If this is the place." Gus's eyes fluttered to Jack. "They are very careful to keep information inaccessible. It would have to be stored on computers without connections to their servers or the internet. It's a closed-circuit system. There's no trail of crumbs to follow."

Shauna's brow furrowed as she waited for the plan. Jack tapped his steepled fingers together.

"So, if we really want to figure out what is going on and who exactly is involved, we have to figure out where they are storing their data— that's the only way to come up with a plan to shut Eyecon down. And to do that, we need to have ears on the inside. We have to plant a bug. Once the bug is planted and we determine where the data is, we can formulate a plan to collect it or destroy it. We'll be able to figure out who to target and how to stop them." It went quiet for a moment. Everyone knew what that meant. One of us was going to breach Eyecon. Hence, Jack's uneasiness. Shit.

"And who's going to do that?" Nate looked from Shauna to Gus as he asked. Jack's fingers stopped fiddling and his jaw tightened. Aaron's eyes were trained on the table as he sat across from me.

"Ben," Aaron confessed. Fire hot rage.

"Are you kidding me?" I choked out, throwing my hands onto the table. "No, absolutely not."

Ben placed his hand on my knee. Jack leaned forward, Gus wouldn't look at me, and Aaron sat back in his seat, rolling his eyes. The posture of every single person in the room ran stiff, save for Aaron. Cocky prick.

"Once we have the data, we can figure out who exactly is involved. We can begin to build targets and take them down, figure out how to end Eyecon," Gus shyly offered.

"Ben is the best option. They don't know who he is. We're going to send him in on a job interview so that he can plant the bug. Then it's over. In and out," Aaron tried to summarize it as if it was no big deal. As if we weren't sending Ben into enemy territory as a spy.

"And if they *do* know who he is? They just let him waltz out? I don't think so! We both know what happens if he's caught. It's too risky." My eyes were on Ben, curious as to if he was in on this plan. How else could Gus have offered up his name so effortlessly? Had Aaron, Gus, and Ben thought this up while the rest of us were looking for Samuel's sample in the woods? While Aaron and Gus filled Ben in on the details of Eyecon?

And Jack had to know. That's why his eyes were glued on me as Aaron announced Ben's name. Why his nerves were so heightened with his stupid steepled fingers. How could Jack have not come to me first?

"Every scenario requires us to infiltrate Eyecon somehow, think about it. It will always come back to us needing to send someone that isn't on their radar," Aaron continued, justifying Ben as the best choice.

"And why Ben? This isn't something we can hire an actor for? Bribe an associate who already works there?" I asked in rage.

"Dani, it's ok," Ben whispered to me. Trying to calm my nerves. But this was nothing to be calm about.

I stared Ben in the eye as I announced it to the team. "Ben isn't going." Final and unquestionable.

"So then it's you," Shauna said, standing up. "You've never been in their facilities, they didn't create you. They haven't seen your face yet. They can't change you, you're already infected. The only thing Eyecon could do would be kill you, and why would they do that? You're too valuable to their cause." There was a sharpness to her words that sliced right through me. Ben's grip tightened on my knee. I rocked back in the chair, biting my lip as I internally debated.

"That's a risk," Jack intervened, "Dani can't go. If they've already identified her, it's game over. And, the last thing we need is for Eyecon to use her as a lab rat to further their progress. Dani's out of the question." Rock-hard eyes.

"Well, then it has to be Ben. We can't involve anyone from outside the collective, it's too risky. It could expose hybrids," Aaron said. Gus wouldn't stop looking at me with apologetic eyes as everyone spoke. I couldn't stand that right now, him pitying my situation.

"Jack, I swear to God. Ben isn't doing it. If you want a player in the game, I will do it." I wouldn't risk Ben's life. Not more than I already had.

"Everyone out," Jack ordered. Shauna rolled her eyes, but everyone started leaving the room. Ben stood next to me, reluctant to move. "Ben, you too," Jack said in a low grumble. Ben hesitated. I knew what this was about.

"I won't push it," I mumbled to him in a bold lie. Ben nodded and left me in the room alone with Jack.

"What is wrong with you?" Jack questioned through the slits in his teeth.

I was taken aback by his harshness. "Excuse me?"

"You come on board with the team, and then the first thing you want to do is head a suicide mission? I don't understand."

"So it's a suicide mission if *I* go, but it's ok if they take Ben? Are you serious right now?"

"Are *you* serious? You know we can't lose you. Dani, if they get their hands on you...," Jack paused, drawing in a breath. "Ben agreed. He volunteered." Volunteered?

"If you try to send Ben... it's not up for discussion. I'm your only option, Jack. Did you really think I was going to be ok with letting Ben go?" I asked, amazed at how Jack ever thought sending Ben would be plausible. "And as Shauna mentioned, I'm *too valuable to kill.* So we better bet on them not knowing my face yet."

Jack's jaw set in such a hard line I thought it was going to crack. He lifted his fist and slammed it down on the table. I tried not to flinch as the rumble reverberated through me.

"Do what you will, but you're on your own in there. It's a fucking suicide mission. They are going to torture you in absolute hell," Jack paused again, straining to send the rest of his words through gritted teeth, "And I'm not sending a rescue team, Dani. I won't subject any of my team to that. Not again." He stormed out of the room. I stood there, trying to process everything that had just happened. What had I gotten myself into?

The door slowly opened, Gus shyly peered in. "Jack said it would be you." I knew he wasn't looking for a response. "We have some details to work out."

Ben hurried in after Gus, his balled fist gave away how furious he was, but I didn't need to see Ben to know he was mad at me over the situation.

"Dani, are you kidding me?" His voice was so stern I wasn't expecting it. "We just talked about you not putting yourself in stupid situations. You not pushing the limits. You remember that? And then you come up with this?" This was not the Ben I knew. Ben had never been confrontational. He never had the need.

"You aren't going," I reiterated.

I hated fighting with Ben. It was new and awkward. Anger steamed from his face which was redder than I'd ever seen. The whites of his knuckles thinned.

"I never would've thought up the plan if I knew you were going to take my place."

This was Ben's idea?

Before I could say anything he burst from the room, brushing shoulders with Aaron as he left. A brick of lead pitted itself in the bottom of my stomach.

"You sure know how to clear a room," Aaron offered up. *Well, aren't you just charming?* I bit my tongue. Igniting Aaron's ego was not something I was going to feed into.

Aaron sat some papers down on the table. Gus and I joined him. Aaron and Gus were discussing all the details of the plan, but I couldn't focus on it. I kept tabs on the conversation, like a B roll, soaking the information in so I could replay it in my head later. The only thing at the forefront of my mind was how both Jack and Ben were angry with me, over the exact same thing. Was I making an irrational decision? There was one sure thing. I would not put Ben at risk. If anything went south, he needed to be able to cut all ties and flee with his best odds. If Eyecon knew who he was, Ben leaving wasn't a plausible option. Maybe Jack couldn't see that. Or at least Jack couldn't see why keeping Ben safe was so important to me. Or maybe he could and he didn't care. Prick. Giant prick.

Ben was going to have to accept this. If he had the power to, he would have done the same for me. And he wanted to. He wanted to go in place of me. He had planned for himself to infiltrate Eyecon. He had helped think up this plan during his time with Gus and Aaron as they ran surveillance while the rest of us were looking for the source of the virus in the woods. Aaron would have had no problem filling Ben in on all the questions Ben ever had. I didn't want Ben involved.

I narrowed my eyes at Aaron. His light green hazel eyes gave a challenging raise in response as Gus spewed details at me. Just another reason to keep Aaron on my list. We were not going to get along.

We finished discussing the details of the planned interview over dinner in the dining commons. Wandering eyes and stares of the other Rebels made clear that the news had spread about me. A nauseating wave curled inside my gut. It only took one Rebel to cough up information about me and my whereabouts to ruin everything. One leak in the Collective and Eyecon could come to scoop me up. If that happened, my bets were on Aaron being the leak.

But he did make us sit away from the other Rebels, wanting to keep the whole operation quiet until it had gone successfully. An order from Jack. No sense in spreading unneeded panic or fear among the other Rebels who were already on edge about the incident at the gas station. I looked around searching for Ben or Jack, but I came up empty. I didn't find either of them here in the cafeteria.

Gus was going on and on about how I needed to ask for a tour if one wasn't offered during the interview. Aaron attempted to give me pointers on tactics that could sweet talk the interviewer into showing me around. He was sly as a mountain cat, knowing how to push people in the ways that favored him. And the more he spoke, the more evident it became. He had been purposely trying to get under my skin this whole time.

The goal was to get the bug placed in the most sensitive area. Somewhere they could get the most valuable information. I knew this was all important, but it was so very hard to digest right now. I attempted to keep my brain on track, asking questions as they occurred to me during our conversation.

"What about handshakes? I can't risk shaking hands with a hybrid."

"Sneeze into your hand or something, it's not like you're going to accept the job if they even offer it to you. You just need to lie enough to make it not look so suspicious. Gus has given you the rundown on the cybersecurity consulting you need to scrape by. The goal is to get in, plant the bug, then out as slyly as possible. You can't get caught," Aaron scoffed, "Nowhere did we say you had to actually land the job."

You better believe that earned the eyeroll of the century from me.

When I returned to our room, Ben was lying in bed, his gaze fixed on the ceiling. He didn't bother glancing at me as I walked in. The tension was so thick, I was swimming through it to get to the bed. Slipping off my pants, I crawled under the covers.

Knowing it was the right and the only choice, I stood by my decision. But it didn't stop the guilt. Not only was Jack upset with me, but Ben. I opened my mouth to try and say something, to reconcile all the harsh encounters Ben and I recently had, to attempt to return to normal. And as I tried to push the words out, Ben turned over, facing away from me.

I had ruined this relationship— hit it with a wrecking ball and driven over it with a bulldozer, crushing whatever we had built together. This may have been the final time Ben allowed me to run over our relationship. Maybe he's had enough.

"Why?" I asked, the words drifting towards Ben's back.

"You said you wanted to be free."

I sighed. *Free.* I couldn't be free if Eyecon existed. *We* couldn't be free if Eyecon existed. Not anymore.

"Ben..."

"Don't."

For the first time, Ben didn't want to talk. I had nothing to say to fix anything anyways. He knew the reasons for my decisions. I had no solace to offer him, other than I cared for him so deeply. If losing my relationship with him meant keeping him safe, I was more than willing to give it up. A cold chill ran through my body. Leaving things so crumbled like this with Ben... things were in ruins.

I emptied the thoughts from my brain of Jack and Ben and succumbed to the dark sleep welcoming me into its depths. Shutting everything out, at least for the moment.

Chapter 16

Crash

When I woke, Ben was missing from the bed. In the dining commons, I found him sitting alone at a table, staring intently into his cereal. Gus watched from the other side of the room, a concerned look on his face as I placed my tray of food down across from Ben.

"You didn't wake me," I said, trying to coax Ben's eyes from his food. He didn't say anything. His thumb gently tapped on the table. "Ben, I'm not going to apologize, but I am going to say that it would be nice to talk before going into Eyecon."

Ben's thumb stopped tapping, he enclosed it with the rest of his hand into a tight grip. His eyes finally swept across my face, reading my expression. My throat bobbed with a swallow. I was scared. Scared I was losing Ben, scared I wouldn't be coming back to him, scared my lighthouse was out of commission and my ship would crash among the harsh waves and rocks.

"Aaron has orders to restrain me if I get in the way. You've made your choice, Dani." Ben got up from the table, leaving his food untouched. He disappeared from the cafeteria. My chest gave a giant ache. I was a gold medalist in destruction.

I returned an awkward look with Gus who tried to look away in embarrassment, pushing his glasses up on his nose. He stood as if he was going to come over to join me in my misery. But his expression changed as he looked past me. Gus sat back down, shifting his focus to Nate who was across from him. Oh no.

A warm shiver tickled through my shoulder. *Hello Jack. What do you want?* I hostilely pushed through to him. I didn't bother picking my face up to turn around and look at him.

Come on, I want to show you something.

I let out a hard sigh. Things just really couldn't get more irritating. I followed Jack from the dining commons and into a van. The rolling door went up and we pulled out of the warehouse.

We let the silence awkwardly sit upon us, Jack as quiet as I. We'd been creating a streak of bad interactions lately. And I assumed this pow-wow would be another tally in the books if we were keeping score.

The van sailed through the streets. We were edging closer to the limits of the city when I noticed Jack making a lot of turns.

"Are we being followed?"

"Just precautions." Jack pulled off the paved road and onto a dirt path with no room for oncoming traffic. The incline made it difficult to see where we were going. There were no buildings, just sagebrush and iron-rich dirt.

Maybe Jack was going to leave me here so he could send Ben to Eyecon instead. Desert and abandon me so I couldn't make it back to the city in time to interfere with his plans.

Or maybe Ben was right, I had been pushing Jack's limits. Maybe he had enough and he was going to kill me here. If he killed me, that would mean one less source of the virus for Eyecon to target. If I was out of the picture, the only thing left to target would be the lake— And Eyecon didn't know about the lake.

I swallowed, this was the first time I had been alone with Jack since the incident at the beach. I mean seriously alone. No one else in earshot a room away. No Nate to come to my rescue. Whatever Jack wanted to do, there would be no one here to stop him.

The van came to a halt. Jack got out and continued walking straight up the hill, following a foot trail carved into the steep mountainside. My hand hovered over the seat belt release in a deadlock.

Run. Turn back and run, Dani. The voice itching in the back of my head made my skin crawl. I could duck into the bushes and run back to town. Though I'd never make it before Jack found me of course.

I released my seatbelt and started up the hill quite a ways behind Jack. He never stopped to wait for me.

I made my way to Jack as he stood at the top of the hill. He stared out over the distance in front of him. Behind us was all of Reno, partially lit by the rising sun, the other illuminated by building lights that had yet to turn off in their morning transition. He was surely going to throw me off to my death. I imagined my fouled-up body lying shattered on the canyon floor, only to be discovered after washing out in a monsoon-incited flash flood.

Jack sat with his feet dangling over the cliffside. I stopped myself from getting any closer, standing behind him for a long moment. I should push him off. I should push him off before he has the opportunity to kill me. I edged up close behind him, readying myself to strike. Power simmered under my anxious palms, my insides twisting in intricate knots. Jack finally looked back over his shoulder.

"What are you doing?" He chuckled, with a puzzled look. I was not sure what my face was doing, but I guarantee I was not smiling at Jack. Caught in a panic, I joined him on the cliff edge, putting distance between us. He raised his eyebrows at me. Maybe he knew I was onto his plan.

He studied my face. "Why are you acting so weird?"

"Why are we sitting on the edge of a cliff?"

Jack broke into hysterical laughter. He held a hand over his stomach as a grand smile ripped across his face. His laughter rebounded from the canyon below, echoing obnoxiously in my ears. Heat flushed my face. After more than a minute of unrelenting laughter, he closed the large gap between us. Sitting together as friends would. We were not friends. We were... We were... I don't know what we were.

"You thought I was going to kill you?" Jack snickered.

"You still could." I glanced at the cliff bottom.

"I'm not going to throw you off." The words bounced off his lips as if he was trying to hold in another case of laughter. "Not today at least." How charming.

"Then why did you bring me here? What else was I supposed to think?" My face was stone. I could not be blamed for my assumption Jack was going to kill me. It wouldn't be the first time. Jack's light expression stiffened, his cheeks flattened. Silence stretched between us just long enough to make it awkward.

"You see that building?" I traced Jack's outstretched finger and focused my eyes on the building below us in the canyon. It was a small building etched into the side of the canyon, a large number of power lines leading in and out of it. "It's a hub for the energy company before the powerlines stretch up the canyon and over the mountains."

"So?"

"So this is where I come when I don't think it's worth it," Jack admitted.

"What do you mean?"

"When I think I don't want to be a Rebel anymore. That it's pointless in fighting Eyecon and their stupid plans."

I raised my eyebrows. "You threaten yourself with suicide?"
He let out a chuckle, softer this time.

"Something like that." He brushed it off, clearly seeing this conversation was not going the way he planned. Jack thumbed the scars on his wrist. The wind whistled as it blew through the canyon, brushing the hair from my face, blowing it out behind me, the only noise between us.

"Ok, so why?" I asked Jack. He rolled his head from looking down, up to meet my gaze, exposing the edges of his ink just under his collar. His eyes held mine, dawning a beautiful deep blue color. His gaze held me for a little too long. Also not long enough. A flutter ruffled through my stomach. I tensed my gut, trying to quell the feeling. Finally, Jack rocked back onto his palms.

"I came up here on a call once. A body was found by the power company near their facility here. I didn't know it at the time, it was before I had been changed, but now I look back and know exactly what happened." Jack drew a deep unsteady breath, keeping the line on his jaw stiff.

"After Eyecon threw me out on the streets there was only one thing I could think about: Getting my next high. The problem was I had built up such a tolerance that I couldn't find anything strong enough to get the job done. Until I remembered this place." He paused for a moment, his lips parted.

"I scaled that building, climbed all the way to the top to reach the power lines, and just as I went to wrap my hands around the wires, it clicked. That man had died because he was a hybrid, on the hunt for the same thing I was trying to get my hands on." I shifted stiffly as Jack spoke.

"I think he died so I didn't have to. It was here I decided to take my stand against Eyecon. Decided I would find the others who had been a victim. On patrol, I would listen to every call that came out, trying to head off any of the officers who were assigned to calls that felt out of the ordinary. Nate was the first, a trespassing call for the city bus parking facility. I found him clinging onto an electric bus charger, barely alive." Jack looked down, his bottom lip tucked between his teeth. "He was supposed to be a soldier, he'd already done a couple of tours in Afghanistan, only for Eyecon to shred what he had made of himself."

"When I wasn't working, I spent my time frequenting different spots trying to find more hybrids. Trying to help them resist the temptation. And you know what, Dani? You can't save them all. As hard as you try, you just can't. When a hybrid wants to kill themselves, sometimes you have to let them. I just hope your death ends up being for a good cause." I flinched. His words were a knife, gouging straight into my chest. Jack's hand coiled into a fist. His eyes lined with silver, but there wasn't enough to roll down his cheek.

"You really think it's a suicide mission tomorrow, huh?" I mumbled out.

"I think you're dead in the water. You'll be a sitting duck in there."

"Like you said, hope it's for a good cause," I reiterated, a little sharper, hoping to poke the word knife back into Jack. The tears rolled down, but they were on my cheeks, not Jack's.

Energy simmered below my skin and Jack moved to rest his hand on my knee, gently gripping each side. *I brought you out here so you could ask yourself if it's worth it.*

I was ready to give up my life if it meant saving the others and ultimately, saving Ben. If there was no way out, this wouldn't be the worst cause to die for.

So this is goodbye, Dani. And before I could move, Jack's lips were pressed against mine, parted. A wave of hot anger and fire-red fury rose over me, but quickly faded, replaced by a feeling of bliss. A complex tangle of electricity danced back and forth between the edges of our mouths. The noise of the wind was drowned out by the pounding of my heart, racking my ribcage. My pulse was raging behind my ears. I felt every thought inside of Jack's head. I could almost touch them, taste them. The colors of his emotions brightly bounded back and forth inside him, suspending us in complete ecstasy.

Connected. As if I knew him my entire life. As if I had known him for lifetimes— I mean if you believed in that kind of thing. The feelings were indescribable as they raced through me, as if the other half of my brain was suddenly awake, suddenly alive. Filled with a color I'd never seen before, one that didn't exist in this world.

His fingers wrapped through my hair, caressing my head, his lips softly pressed against mine in a desperate ache. Something inside fired to life, a bond that solidified something between us, braided us together somehow. And in an impossible motion, I pulled away. Jack's hand still rested on my knee, the other cupped around my face. My eyes locked with his in an unwavering hold. Jack was still trying to process everything. His thoughts were wordless. I was wordless too.

In an instant everything was gray. Everything I knew about myself, everything I stood for, everything I was searching for. It was all lost. I had crashed on the wretched rock and all my pieces were falling to the bottom of the ocean. To the dark abyss.

I no longer knew who I was.

Chapter 17

Game

Ben wasn't in our room when I returned to the warehouse. Part of me was grateful, the other half was scared he may never come back. How I could face him after having the moment I did with Jack in the canyon? I didn't know. I couldn't come to terms with the fact I had just experienced the most incredibly beautiful thing. Because it was with the wrong person. If there was ever going to be a moment like the one I had, it should have been him. It should have been Ben. But, Ben wasn't a hybrid. He could never understand, not truly.

The incident with Jack wasn't the only thing on my mind. The crawling beasts in my stomach were beginning to swallow me. The interview was approaching. All of this worrying would be for nothing if I couldn't plant the bug in the right place. Forcing myself to push anything and everything that wasn't about preparing myself for tomorrow out of my head, I decided best to wash it all away. After showering, I crawled in bed. I was in store for quite a lonely night as Ben had still not returned.

I tried to close my eyes and let the void that he left take over, let the blank space sway me to sleep in its wrath of white noise.

But the thoughts replayed over and over in my mind. All of them.

Every interaction I had with Ben over the past few days rehashed inside my head. Recounting how he had always been so gentle with me through our entire relationship. He had always been so understanding, but now? The disapproval of going into the woods, pushing me to tell him what had happened while I was there... and now this? Going into Eyecon— this changed everything. Ben would do anything for me, I knew that. And I hadn't told him the truth. Pathetic.

And even more so, I hadn't told him anything about Jack, not really. Especially now that I had pushed Ben so dangerously close to the edge. If I told him, and told him everything, I might push him over. It would all be too much for him to accept. It wasn't right to expect him to either. Perhaps he would choose to not come back, to leave me in my downward spiral deeper into my darkness. Maybe I had hurt him one too many times. Maybe it would give him enough reason to leave. Maybe it would be enough to keep him safely away from all of this, from the things that could hurt him, from me.

The kiss from Jack still lingered on my skin, a constant reminder of my betrayal of Ben. Further proof Ben would leave if he knew the truth. Why did I find it so hard to return love to Ben in the easy and seamless way he would give it to me? It was so effortless, so natural for Ben.

It was the way he had said I love you over the edge of his book on a late Tuesday afternoon. It had carried over a breeze to me as I let the Sierra sun kiss my skin. The way he held my head in his lap while he had tucked his face into the pages. He could so easily wrap me in his words, but that day he'd absent-mindedly let his light touch play with my hair as he read.

"Eventide," Ben whispered, peeking down at me.

"Huh?" I didn't understand. Of course. Ben was an intellectual, and I was, well I was just me.

"The second most beautiful time of day," he said.

"And the first?"

Ben's lips snapped into a soft smile. "Being with you." And I had been at the center of the universe. No one else had existed as we laid on the blanket spread across the sand for hours. The breeze carried wafts of lake water lightly through the air as the tide ebbed, creating small waves washing up along the banks of Sand Harbor.

Second to Ben, there was nothing I loved more than Lake Tahoe. How it swaddled you in warmth. How its colors made you feel alive in the waning light of the day as if all was well.

Eventide. It was now my favorite part of the day, again, second to Ben.

I replayed the memory, over and over in my mind, trying to pretend things were ok between Ben and me. But they weren't, that much was evident by the empty space next to me in bed.

I spent my whole night with my eyes trained on the same spot of the ceiling until a knock on the door came in the morning.

When I opened it, Shauna stood outside with a bag and an outfit on a couple of hangers.

"Well don't I have my job cut out for me? So much for beauty sleep." Shauna smirked to herself. I let out a huff of air and opened the door wider, reluctantly allowing her into the room. "Here, change." She forced clothes hangers into my hand and pushed me towards the bathroom. They were very nice quality business clothes. Black slacks with a nice collared shirt and matching suit coat. Gross.

"Do we really have to do the makeup thing?" I scowled at her.

"You look like shit. You're applying for a cybersecurity consulting position at a successful corporation after all. You have to pretend like you're interested in the job. Don't be suspicious, remember?" Maybe the makeup was a good choice. I couldn't go to an interview looking like roadkill.

A lead brick sat in my gut to think of the prospect of actually working at Eyecon. How many people working there didn't know what was going on? How many people did? What if I did land the job? Ok, that last one was a fat chance I shouldn't have wasted any brain energy on.

After Shauna completed my hair and makeup she paused to look at me, proud of her work.

"Reminds me of gymnastics competitions," she sighed, remembering a past long gone. I could imagine all the athletes preparing for their performances. What a feat it was to pull off the kind of work they did, all the training and painful wear on their bodies.

"Do you miss it?"

"Sometimes. I mean, it was a high-stakes game anyway. Always just one injury away from retirement. You could go out of the game at any time, any of us could have." Shauna looked down, breaking her eye contact. And these were the things we humans said to ourselves, to justify how our lives had happened. Especially when what had happened had been out of our control.

Shauna walked me out to the vans, revealing a town car with a chauffeur holding an open door. The Rebels who knew about the plan were there: Nate, Shauna, Gus, Aaron, Jack. Only one person was missing. I couldn't believe he wasn't here. A hole in my chest throbbed. Maybe he had come to his senses and realized how dangerous being with me was. Maybe he had already made his choice to get the hell away from me.

"Remember the script. You don't have to say too much, but you can't be too vague. It will give you away if you can't follow up your lies." Gus adjusted his glasses.

"Good luck." Aaron's voice was so sincere I almost couldn't believe it.

Shauna wrapped me in a hug before returning to Nate. That would have been unusual outside of these circumstances. Nate didn't say anything aloud, but his face sat sullen. He wrapped his arm around Shauna, pulling her closer to him and they both turned and left, followed by Gus and Aaron.

I looked at Jack, the only one remaining.

"You know the plan?"

I nodded. I had spent the last few days incessantly reviewing every detail, especially last night as I stared at the ceiling, begging for sleep to find me. Jack passed a small bag to me. A purse containing the bug and a few other things.

"I hope this isn't goodbye," Jack said.

"Me too." Ben's voice echoed across the pavement.

My heart lifted.

He had shown up.

He was here. Ben walked over, his eyes red and swollen. I wrapped my arms around him, burying my face into his chest. Listening for his heartbeat.

"I thought you hated me," I admitted.

"I hate what you are doing, but I would do the same. I want to do the same," Ben whispered as he pressed his hands firmly over my shoulder blades, almost pleading with me. "I wanted to stop them. To keep you safe." Ben's eyes welled, but he bit his lip in a fight to hold back tears. "Please, Dani, please be careful."

I inhaled deeply, trying to take in the scent of him. Trying to memorize it. Morning mist. My lighthouse.

Then I remembered what had happened between Jack and me. My lungs seized, nearly choking my supply of oxygen. Anxious flutters rose alive, overtaking my body.

This wasn't the time, I had to pull it together. I couldn't let the guilt overtake my emotions, threatening to rock the focus of my mission.

"I'll come back," I promised. I had to, because I had to make things right with us. I had to figure things out. I had to find my 42, my purpose, my meaning in life. I had to find *our* 42.

Ben squeezed me into his chest again. After a long moment, he released me. And when I stepped back, Jack was missing from the room.

"We'll be late," the chauffeur said. I caught the look on Ben's face. My spirits fell further.

Ben wiped a tear from under my cheek. "Don't do that, you'll mess up your makeup."

The driver cleared his throat as Ben walked me to the car, taking the place of the chauffeur at the door.

"I'm sorry I wasn't around for you the last few days." Ben barely let the cracking words escape his lips as he choked up. I knew what this was. This might have been our last goodbye. The door closed, but I didn't take my eyes off of Ben.

The car pulled away, and I watched as he got smaller and smaller, until we turned a corner and he was out of sight.

I was a mess on the inside. Throwing my head back onto the seat rest, I knew I had to pull myself together. But I was so on the verge of having an ugly cry.

"Jack's a good guy," the chauffeur said, "I told him I was only doing this for him because I owed him." I gave the chauffeur a small soft smile, I couldn't chit-chat. Not only was I incapable of such social niceties, there were other things on my mind. A lot of other things.

When the car stopped, the chauffeur opened my door. I paused, grasped by uneasiness.

For Ben, you have to do this for Ben. For him. For us.

I pushed my body out of the car and up the concrete stairs toward the skyscraper. The building was as the rest of them in the area: Modern, sleek, and expensive-looking. However, Eyecon was the decadent centerpiece outshining the surrounding competition in the business district.

Act like you've been here before. Like you belong. Whatever 'belong' really meant. I coached myself using Aaron and Gus's instructions. I peeled open a large glass door and walked with a purpose to the receptionist, trying to keep my head down the best I could. I didn't want to be noticed more than I had to. The minimum amount of exposure was key.

The lobby was a huge atrium reaching to the top of the building, letting sunlight flood in across the white marble flooring.

"How can I help you?" the receptionist quietly asked.

"Yes, I have a ten o'clock appointment with Derek Rodgers."

"Oh yes, Ms. Davis, please follow me. Is there anything I can get you?"

"No, thank you."

She stood and led us across the open floor to the elevators. Inside was a panel of numbers with the top three floors sectioned off to the side, access clearly restricted. The receptionist inserted a key before pressing the button for the top floor. Thirty.

I focused on maintaining my composure, keeping my face poised. The elevator ascended slowly, but to me, it felt like a descent... into hell. The floor indicator dinged and the receptionist shuffled me towards an assistant waiting nearby.

"Ms. Jennifer Davis," the assistant announced, "Right this way, please." I followed her down a hallway and into a large conference room made of glass with a large oak conference table. This all seemed very grand for an interview but felt like a decent place for the bug. Should I place it here? Maybe I should use the mountain cat's advice to sweet talk the interviewer, Derek, into a tour for better options. Was it worth the risk to wait for a better spot?

"Please have a seat Ms. Davis, Mr. Crowe will be right with you." Crowe? No. No. No. Something was wrong.

"Excuse me," I intervened before she could shut the door, "I believe I am supposed to be meeting with Derek Rodgers." The assistant smiled and nodded her head before closing the door. The pit in my stomach was overwhelming, opening its large mouth and eating me bit by bit. But before I could come up with an ejection plan, the door opened.

"Ms. Davis," A sleek man in a very expensive suit said as he entered the room, crossing the vast space. I smiled and stood, extending my hand. My heart geared to leave my chest with its furious pounding. Shit. Shit. Shit. His jet-black hair was combed back, exposing the lines across his forehead. I tried to stay calm, but my mind was screaming at me. This was not Derek Rodgers, this was Victor Crowe, the CEO of Eyecon and suspected leader of the Spectrum program. Enemy number one.

"Mr. Crowe, It's a pleasure to meet you." He stood tall with sleek hair and dark eyes set wide and deep into his face. He wore summer-kissed skin and the kind of suit I expected from a CEO.

Mr. Crowe stretched his arm out. As I reached to shake his hand, I let my watch slip off my wrist and onto the floor. Not only did I become accustomed to hating handshakes, but I also couldn't risk shaking anyone's hand, especially his. I wanted to wind my arm back and punch him in the face, use all the boundless energy to blast him from his feet. 'Hold court' as Jack had called it.

Mr. Crowe kneeled and picked the watch from the floor.

"Oh, thank you, I've been meaning to get that clasp fixed," I feigned embarrassment, beginning to pick the watch out of his hand, careful to not touch his skin. Before I could retrieve it, his hand closed around the watch, sealing it from my reach. Victor extended both hands, placing one on top of mine as he pushed the watch into my palm. A volt of electricity stunned me as our skin touched. A sick grin spread on Victor's face.

"The wild one," Victor sighed in relief. The pit in my stomach grew teeth.

I had fucked up.

This had been the major miscalculation Jack and Ben had warned me about.

"Please, call me Victor." A curt smile struck his face. "Let's not pretend we both don't know what the other is." A hybrid. Victor was a hybrid. I tightened my jaw. The jig was up, but I didn't know what to say. Jack was right. Dead in the water.

"I've waited a long time for you. And I am so pleased Jack has made the right choice." My stomach dropped so far I thought I was going to be sick. He saw my expression as I broke my composure. I couldn't believe what he was saying. Jack? Right choice?

"Well, I must say, you were quite the trade," Victor surmised. "Jack has gotten the story wrong. Although I can't blame him, the electricity can turn your head into a dark place." His voice was calm, and his face soft. Victor sat on the sofa as he encouraged me to join him. What was I to do? Send a surge of electricity through him, so I could supercharge him the way I had Jack on the beach? I hated the position this put me in. He was a hybrid, and the electricity, my only shoddy weapon, wasn't going to free me of him. I placed myself next to Victor, as far from him as the sofa would allow.

"You see, Jack is convinced what we are doing here is malignant." Victor touched his chin, pausing. Electricity raced inside me. The rage of knowing Jack had far bigger plans than I was aware of threatened to consume me, but I couldn't trust what Victor was saying. Run? I should run. But there was nowhere to go.

"It is, I know what you do here," I rebutted, trying to push back on his words. his lies.

"I guess it would be hard to see the light if you only knew darkness," he inhaled, bringing his eyes up to meet mine. "This is going to sound a bit harsh at first, I know, but bear with me." Vomit rose in my throat as I prepared myself for what was to come next.

"I want you to think of the virus as a gift." I was right, the vomit was very hard to hold back. "I'm sure you are now aware of the benefits of infection. Because you never get sick, do you?" I knew that much to be true, not only because I never came down with colds, or the flu, but because Samuel had also confirmed hybrids don't get sick.

"You see, the virus protects against more than just the common cold. The virus protects against the coming radiation poisoning."

"What are you talking about?" I was so lost. No one had ever mentioned anything about radiation. Victor smiled warmly, placing his hand on my knee, the electricity fluttered under his touch. It had caught me off guard, and I almost released a wave of energy right then. I pulled my knee back, but it didn't seem to bother him. Maybe he wasn't aware of just how 'strong' everyone claimed my powers were— or maybe he was. He could not see what I was capable of, under no circumstances.

"In the next ten years, the climate will be a major threat to the human race. The destruction we have caused on this planet is due to come for us. Simulations show Mother Nature is striking back, trying to rid herself of the disease we are. We're her worst plague.

"Things are worse than you may have been led to believe. Natural disasters will be nothing compared to the rising thermal and solar radiation levels. We can attempt to protect ourselves all we want from these disasters, but we have to change ourselves in order to even think of surviving the radiation. Evolution simply doesn't have enough time."

"That's not why you are doing this," I blurted out, "You want control, you want power."

"Oh, Jack has really gotten into your head. Why do you think Jack wanted you? Why he found you?"

"His team is making a cure." I left out the part about the source of the virus, I wasn't going to hand that information over to Victor. He chuckled lightly.

"Jack thinks what we are trying to do here at Eyecon is to create an army of hybrids, that we are somehow power-hungry." And I almost lost it at that. How could this man possibly have it all wrong? How could he not have come to terms with the fact he and his corporation was the very definition of twisted and evil— partaking in killing innocent people in a ploy for power. "I need to be honest with you. I too have darkness on my hands. It's my fault Jack has been consumed with such an idea. You see, I used him in such a way one shouldn't be used," Victor admitted. An admission? Ok, I didn't expect that. I let my brain go quiet so I could carefully listen to every word leaving Victor's mouth.

"We picked him from the very beginning and it worked out better than I could have ever imagined. You piqued our interest when we kept finding money missing from our accounts. We have the best security and accounting, how could this be? Lo and behold, a hybrid using unheard-of powers. A hybrid, one we weren't aware of. One we never created. How can that be true?"

They knew about me all along.

"You created Jack to find me?" Jack was more than just a product? He was Victor's vision?

"Jack was the best soldier we had ever seen. He was designed that way. You were his mission. We picked *him* for *you*. We had been following Jack for a while, checked his files, and his personality met all the right criteria. We know what choices he is going to make before he even makes them. Add the virus to that formula, and it makes everything more clear. Then I got greedy, hoping if we found you sooner we could have more time to perfect the radiation vaccine."

"What are you talking about?"

"I pushed Jack too far," he exhaled, "I broke him."

"He worked for you?" My heart sat heavy, thumping so hard I almost couldn't hear Victor.

"Yes, that is, until he went rogue and came up with this power trope idea on his own. He has targeted all of our researchers, our doctors, driving us underground," Victor said. "Look, I don't want to hurt Jack, he provides shelter for the released hybrids, he trains them how to conquer the electricity addiction. Jack, unbeknownst to him, is still a vital piece in helping Eyecon."

"You are stealing lives, kidnapping people—"

"I never said I was a saving grace. But the reality here is everyone is going to die. The coming radiation poisoning is a ticking time bomb. You think we enjoy doing what we do? I have watched the ill side effects of the virus consume hybrids, making them kill themselves. And that's only the hybrids who survive the injection." Victor lowered his head, his lashes falling over his eyes. "This isn't some far-out prophecy. This is science. This is a cold hard fact. And we are racing towards the end of society as we know it. There is no time to juggle the ethics of what a life is worth when life itself is at stake." When Victor raised his head again, his eyes looked like wells, ready to burst. This certainly was not what I expected.

"How could nobody else know about this?"

"Do you see how easy it was for Jack to turn on us? This kind of information could create an uprising. Our government isn't going to incite chaos. You can't simply tell the people they are doomed and offer no hope, no plan. People will not hold hands and go quietly into the night. Rightfully so, we need fighters if we are going to survive the radiation. If we are going to make it past the mark, we don't need people fighting each other, we need to preserve as many lives as possible. This has given cause to the need to be incredibly careful with the information we share." Victor ran his fingers over the edge of his sleeve cuff.

"And I'm sure it may come as a surprise to you that I value human life." Lies. Down-right lies. They had to be. How could I have not known any of this? Jack would have told me.

I shifted awkwardly on the sofa, leaning away from Victor. "Why are you telling me all of this?"

"Because I have been looking for you for a very long time." The edge of Victor's lip twitched, threatening a smile. "You have the strongest powers, which means you have the strongest strain of the virus. You should be invincible to radiation." Victor was going to take what I had and infect others? Force them to endure the torment which lingered just beneath the surface. Condemn them to a world where the monster inside threatened to take the driver's seat at any moment.

"You can't do this to people, you can't give them the beast that comes with the infection. They will destroy themselves. You will destroy humanity."

"I agree, that's what our doctors are working on. We need to perfect the virus to stop the radiation poisoning and then edit out the electromagnetic side effects." Victor took a long pause. The silence sat over us for a moment while my brain struggled to place all the pieces together. Did he actually say 'edit out the electromagnetic side effects?' as in no more powers? He had to be lying.

"I know what you are going through, constantly fighting the feeling of becoming unhinged." Victor stopped himself. "Trust me, I don't wish this on anyone." Yet, here he was, subjecting people to the unhinged monster. How could he possibly understand?

"I would have done anything to find you, to save society, to save our people. Even if I had to take out the Rebels. And I know it's not right, but can you see how important this is? How limited our time is? I can't afford to play cat and mouse with Jack." And the way the words 'cat and mouse' escaped Victor reminded me of how Jack had said those very same words. It was moments before I had agreed to help the Rebels in their fight against Eyecon.

"He traded me for the freedom and safety of his team," I exhaled.

Victor bit his lip and nodded. This couldn't be true. Jack would never have handed me over like that. We were connected.

"He knew how things would end if he didn't give you up. I'm sorry, I know it's not right." I shifted rigidly, pulling my hair out of my face, trying to breathe evenly. "Jack thinks we are trying to strengthen the electric side effects. He thinks that's why we wanted to find you. But like I said, you already have the key to the radiation poisoning, we just need to figure out how to stop the electromagnetic abilities."

"That's what Jack wants."

"Yes, but think about it. Jack knew of your powers. Why do you think he has been collecting hybrids? Who do you think is making an army? He wants to bring us down, he wants his revenge. He is consumed by it. You think his one-man-band scientist, Samuel, can really create a cure? There was never a prospect of a cure. Jack doesn't stand a chance against us, and he knew it."

"I... I can't believe I didn't see it." I couldn't trust Victor's words. This had to be a card in his deck, because I could see what he was doing here. He was trying to wrap me around his finger to get what he wanted. And two could play at this game.

"I'm sorry," Victor said, "I'm sorry he lied to you, that he didn't respect you enough to at least tell you the truth. I'm sorry he used you." Victor sat silent, scanning my face. "You don't have to believe it, not yet. I'm sure it will come with time."

I forced the vomit back down, refusing to believe Victor. Understanding this trade meant accepting it was all a farce. That Jack had pretended our connection was special. I couldn't believe that. Because if I did, everything would hurt like hell. It couldn't be true, it just couldn't.

"Will you help us?" Victor asked, "Well, you don't have to decide that quite yet either. I want you to meet our team first. I think you will find them quite welcoming."

Panic ensued at Victor's proposal because I knew what this meant. He was trying to entice me further into his trap. I didn't know what to do, so instead, I gave him a warm smile. I still had the bug in my possession. And now I had to play the game better than Victor himself.

Chapter 18

Bond

I had asked to relieve myself, to go find a private restroom as shelter and pull the overwhelming thoughts together.

I bent over, ill, trying to pull air in through my nostrils, trying to calm myself to think clearly. The room was cold and empty, and I was alone. My brain was racing to dive off a cliff into the abyss I feared. A place where I would never be able to retrieve it.

Victor was really trying to suggest Jack had betrayed me. Disgust. Absolute disgust. Jack's work for the last few years had been about nothing else than destroying Victor. I was part of Jack's team now, and Victor insinuating Jack had traded me for the safety of the Rebels was insulting. *I* was a Rebel.

Regardless of how righteous Victor thought his reasons were, nothing he could say would convince me of his cause. Even if the world was going to be ravaged by rocketing radiation levels, how could Victor justify murder as the means to saving humanity? How could he believe Jack was still his little toy soldier? And how could he actually think I would be interested in helping him?

No, Victor was smarter than that. Whether I believed his story that Jack had traded me or not, he knew where my loyalties lay. Victor was expecting a fight from me, using his words to crawl under my skin, trying to poke an angry bear. He wanted to pull my strings to see what kind of dances I could perform, what kind of powers I possessed. But I was playing the long game and I had to maintain my focus. I had to learn what made Victor tick, find out what would take down Eyecon's entire operation.

All the questions swirled in my head, threatening to consume me in rage. And I had no time to think. No time to give them the answers they deserved, because Victor was waiting just outside the door. And I had to play nice if I was going to make it out of Eyecon alive. So I swallowed the red-hot rage threatening to overtake me. Because my life depended on holding myself together right now.

As Victor led me across the marble lobby, employees nodded and waved as they passed. Did any of them truly know Victor? We came to another set of elevators, confirming my suspicion this trip across the lobby ended with us going to the lab. This was my last chance to escape. I only had a split second. I could make a break for it. But, of course, it would end in disaster. The front doors were clear in the opposite direction and any shot at pretending I believed Victor's lies, pretending like I was playing on Victor's team would be gone as soon as they caught me. Game over. If the Rebels were going to take down Eyecon, planting the bug in the lab— learning how things operated— would be vital. And if this is what it took, giving my life so the Rebels could stop Eyecon's plans to destroy the world as we knew it, this was a sacrifice I was willing to make. A sacrifice that would keep Ben safe.

Victor swiped his hand— not a keycard— over an access pad as it flashed green. Once inside, the elevator revealed two basement levels to choose from, as it only serviced the basement-level floors. Victor selected B1.

"Before I introduce you to the team," Victor said as the doors closed and we began our descent, "there are a couple of touchy subjects I would advise you avoid."

I raised an eyebrow at Victor as we descended. "What would that be?"

"Jack is the reason we have had to go underground, hide our work and our identities. These researchers are paying a hefty price. But it's a sheer sign of their commitment." Victor's voice was smooth, free-flowing, and I could swear there was almost a hint of care contained in it. But my senses had to have been tricking me. Care? How could he care for the researchers when he kidnapped and killed people the way he did?

"They have taken a leave of absence from their families in order to continue their work. I mean, we pay them a great compensation for their devotion, but it's taken a toll on the doctors. They have been waiting a very long time to figure out the right formula so they can return home."

"It's a sensitive topic. Noted." I wanted to believe Victor, his words appeared sincere. But how could I believe anyone after Victor proposed Jack had betrayed me? Victor was a con artist.

I tapped my toes, easing my rising nerves. As the elevator doors slid open, we exited into a pristine white hallway. And just like that, I knew I was sealed into my enclosure, the lower levels of the building.

A wall of glass separated the laboratory from us. The lab was filled with researchers donning white coats, about twenty or so, who were all working in different aspects, some in groups staring at diagrams projected onto the wall, others independently with microscopes and other equipment.

Victor turned towards me, stopping in front of the lab entrance.

"I want you to stay," he offered, "I mean, at least for a few days." I whipped my head in Victor's direction, unsure of what to make of his offer or how to respond to it. "We will house and feed you for as long as you like. I just want you to ponder the idea." I was trying to not let my jaw hit the floor, but I knew my face was likely betraying me. If I was going to beat him at this game of false motives, I had to get better at controlling what emotions crawled across my face.

"Thank you." Bile almost moved up my throat, the words likely coming out more robotic than intended.

"One last thing. No phones are permitted on this level. We work on a closed-circuit system. For obvious reasons, we keep our work very secure." Victor held out his hand towards me, catching the hesitation scowling across my face. "I assure you can have it back once you leave the lower levels of the facility. It's just a precaution. Should you choose to leave, the receptionist in the lobby will return your device to you." I begrudgingly gave Victor my phone. Yeah, that puppy was long gone.

He smiled and swiped his hand over the lab access panel. As the doors slid open, our presence garnered several stares.

A small scientist with hair red as fire came to greet us. Her curls laid over her shoulders as her blue eyes gazed at us from her pale freckled face. She extended her hand towards me, and I curiously accepted it. She wasn't a hybrid, just a regular ol' human.

Victor leaned in with his hands clasped behind his back, a large toothy grin on his face. "This is the wonderful Ms. Burns."

"Emily, Head Microbiologist," she corrected, raising a brow toward me.

"Dani," I returned.

Emily glanced at Victor curiously. "Another researcher for the team?" she asked, noting a title didn't follow my name.

"Quite the contrary." Victor's face lit with enjoyment. "Dani is the wild one."

Emily's eyes went wide and her mouth parted in surprise. I hated being called that. *The wild one.* It sounded as if I had no manners. Clearly, I did. Because I was refraining from burning the entire place down.

"I suspect you will be giving our new guest a tour," Victor suggested, "Make it a good one, we want her to stay awhile."

Emily nodded, one side of her lip curled into a grin as Victor turned to leave.

"I hope Victor was warm to you," Emily said. "Sometimes the stress from our work can get to him and he can be short."

The words scalded my throat as they left my mouth. "He was kind." Victor Crowe was nothing but a middle-aged man with a crooked moral compass.

"This is the main brain of the lab, we all get together and collaborate here." Emily nodded towards the tables in the center of the room covered with papers, microscopes, and digital tablets. The entire table's surface was an electronic touch screen. A few of the guys in lab coats quieted, their eyes trained on Emily and me. I blankly nodded my head every time Emily opened her mouth to say something, looking for the perfect spot to plant the bug. I had to turn it on and cue the Rebels in on what was happening.

Emily showed me to a massive storage room where file cabinet upon file cabinet sat. My eyes wandered over the rows of cabinets, imagining how many documents they must store. How long had these scientists been working on the radiation vaccine?

"Why so old school?" I asked.

"This is all on our closed network, but out of security, we ensure there are hard copies of everything. Just in case something were to happen to our electronics. I know it seems dated, but we've spent way too much time working to lose our progress to a couple of failed hard drives." And that explained why Gus couldn't access the information about the Spectrum trials, it wasn't a part of any accessible network.

"How long have you been working on this project?"

"Over a decade, I've seen a few researchers come and go." It made me wonder how long ago she left her family. Did she have children? A partner? But I heeded Victor's warning to not ask about the doctors' families. She had given everything to devote herself to this project, and I didn't want to tread on touchy territory. I wanted to stay on Emily's good side to suck as much information out of her as possible. I was playing a game I couldn't afford to lose. Because it would likely cost lives.

We left the storage room and made our way into another large room filled with bookshelves that housed hundreds of books with scientific names above my understanding. The colors of the books clashed with the pristine white of the lab and the glossy sheen of the glass.

"I don't think you understand how much you're going to help our research," Emily admitted. "You will catapult us into a new era. Kiss these books goodbye because they will rewrite them all after what comes from you. You are the news of tomorrow."

"This isn't what I asked for," I bluntly stated, instantly regretting the words. Emily was Victor's toy and I needed to play the same facade I was giving Victor. Her face flushed red.

"I can understand that," Emily almost whispered, "Sorry, I didn't mean to make you feel like the shiny new toy. I think all of us are just really looking forward to solving this problem and returning to our families." Emily shyly rolled her lips. I didn't say anything else as she finished her tour.

She returned us to the main part of the lab where we had met. This would probably be the best place to plant the bug, it appeared this was where most of the researchers conglomerated. I had to find my opportunity.

Emily turned her gaze toward me as we settled into some stools at a table. "I'm sure you have questions." And I did, I had a ton of questions. I placed my hand in my bag, simultaneously grabbing my chapstick and the bug, keeping it hidden in my palm as I applied the chapstick.

Then I took a calculated risk.

"You know, I'm not sold on what Victor told me," I admitted, rolling my lips back and forth. I let my hands fall from my face to my lap.

"I'm sure it all can feel overwhelming." Emily tucked some of her bright red hair behind her ear. "I can help you work through some of that." She had fallen right into what I was asking of her. I wanted more information and she was the prime target to give it to me.

"What do you mean?"

"Victor mentioned to me before that you had met Jack." Emily's eyebrow raised. "A charmer, huh?"

My spine tightened and my muscles grew stiff. I was taken off guard by the anger filling my veins. With my hand out of Emily's sight below the table, I hesitated to switch the bug on. That was one of the first thoughts I had ever had about Jack. It was just after he had picked me up in his patrol car. You know, when he was pretending to help me find Ben— the very same Ben he had kidnapped. Even if Emily had gotten to know Jack, it was no indication he had actually betrayed me.

"He used me." This was the card Victor played upstairs, and I had to follow the same narrative.

Emily leaned forward in her stool. "I don't doubt it for a second. He's smart, and a sly little manipulator."

I wanted to ask more about Jack, but the tangle of electricity in my stomach was growing. I wanted to know what they had done to him here, what Victor had subjected him to. I wanted to hear how Emily's hand played in this mess, to learn if she was just as guilty as Victor. I hesitated to turn on the bug. Emily was Victor's pet.

I wanted Emily to give me more information, but if Jack was innocent, I wasn't going to let Emily's lies sow doubt among the Rebels, let her spread misconceptions.

But I wanted—needed to know more. I slipped the bug back into my purse for the moment as I put my chapstick away. I was going to pry more information from Emily about Jack before planting the bug. But before I could ask, Emily turned her attention to a set of microscope slides resting on the table.

"Ok, I want to show you what we have all been so excited for. Here, look." Emily slid a microscope across the table toward me. I peered down the tube but wasn't sure what I was looking at.

"This is what normal blood looks like under the scope. Now, here, look at this." Emily pulled up a digital file on the touchscreen table the microscope sat on top of. A video. "Here is what our current samples of hybrid blood look like." The video showed red cells dancing across a slide, but they were more active than the sample of human blood Emily had shown me. They were vibrating in place. It was something out of this world.

"Can you see the difference?"

I nodded in almost disbelief. "It's like they're charged with energy."

"Well, you're in luck today." Emily slid off her stool, gesturing for me to follow. We walked towards a larger group of scientists who were gathered in front of a window.

"Today's test day," Emily said.

A scientist behind the window stood dressed in protective gear. He even had an oxygen supply running from a hose connected to the ceiling. A clean room, designed to keep contaminants out and also protect the researcher.

Next to the window was a viewing screen. It showed whatever the suited-up researcher had under his microscope. I recognized the red smear as the blood cells vibrated across the slide. Hybrid blood.

"Lincoln's injecting the sample with a radioactive isotope to measure its response," Emily whispered. Some of the researchers bantered with each other, taking bets on what the outcome would be. Eyes wandered over to me, but no one approached. I was grateful for that.

As Lincoln released the radioactive isotope onto the sample, little flashes of blue began lighting up like sparks. Some of the red cells from the sample turned dark, but only a few remained healthy-looking.

"Well, it was better than last week," Lincoln surmised in an English accent.

I leaned in toward Emily. "So no test subjects? I thought the only way to test the virus was on humans?"

"We only have live test subjects when absolutely necessary. It's a very serious event to use a live subject. And we don't take it lightly."

I bit back the rising bile. Somehow I doubted what Emily said could be true. Lies. Such blatant lies. How could there be so many hybrids? So many Rebels? "How is Victor a hybrid?"

Emily looked cautiously over her shoulder. She pushed me further from the group of researchers arguing over their failed bets.

"Look, I'm not too sure Victor would approve of me discussing this with you, but I think it's only fair." Emily pulled me along as she walked through the lab, finding a relatively secluded space.

"Victor was one of the originals to work on the virus. There's a reason why Lincoln is suited up in a clean room, and it's not just the radiation." Emily's eyes swept our surroundings, ensuring we were still alone. "Victor became infected with one of the earliest forms of the virus. It was an accident that nearly killed him. He almost lost his mind to the electric side effects. He had gone mad, and now the only form of the virus we have has been derived from his blood." Her voice was leery and discreet.

"That's what's been taking so long." It made sense. Maybe it was Victor who had caused the hold-up to creating the radiation cure.

"In his rage, he ruined everything. He killed his lab partner and used all the samples in the lab trying to intensify the outcome of whatever electric high the addiction creates."

My brain was trying to click all the pieces together. Victor alleged he knew what it was like to battle the energy and withdrawals other hybrids had gone through. He claimed he was so desperate to edit out the electromagnetic side effects of the radiation vaccine. But, Victor was lying.

And in the same breath, maybe I was luckier than the others. Maybe my blood, my infection was one step closer to the truth Victor declared he was searching for. Because I had never been drawn to electricity. I mean, electricity and the energy from the lake dazzled me when it wrapped me in its euphoric grasp. But never had I lost control of myself afterward, never had the power taken me over, spiraled me into withdrawal. Not like Jack. Or how Victor had been consumed by the need to fill his craving. Did Victor care enough to not want to pass on the electric traits? Or did Victor begin to crave a different kind of power?

Because there was one obvious truth. There was something other than the cravings the Spectrum virus brought on. Something dark lurked in the back of my head wherever I went. A void that crept so closely it almost drew me in like the gravity of a black hole, final and unforgiving. Its weight made me question what was make-believe and what was reality. A parting gift from the woods.

"Can I ask you something?"

"As long as you promise to keep that information from Victor. He would be devastated you knew the truth." I nodded in agreement, internally rolling my eyes.

"If there's a way to create the radiation vaccine without the electric side effects," I paused, watching Emily's face. "Could there be a way to somehow edit the virus that already exists in a live subject?" Maybe Samuel could actually pull it off.

"You mean a cure?" Her face fell into a soft expression as her hand raised to her mouth in contemplation.

"Dani, I, I don't know," Emily softly let out. Maybe I shouldn't have been so disappointed. Maybe the prospect of a cure was a long-lost hope. One I had already been warned of— by both Jack and Victor.

The researcher who ran the radioactive isotope test approached Emily and me, automatically extending his hand out.

"I'm Lincoln," he said, glancing down at his palm. He had a thick English accent and tan olive skin. I grasped his hand in a firm shake. Human.

"When did you discover manners?" Emily snorted at Lincoln.

"Don't be silly," Lincoln chided, "*I* am a prince." Simultaneously, Emily and Lincoln let out a loud bellowing laugh.

"Ahh, I see what this is. You find her attractive." Emily leaned in towards me, lightly squeezing my arm, her eyes lit with amusement.

"Being down here, I have been deprived of beautiful women," Lincoln joked.

"Mmm, I think those manners have suddenly died." Lincoln's face flushed and he opened his mouth to awkwardly correct himself.

"Not saying that I'm desperate, or that you aren't attractive. I just— sorry, it seems I don't know how to behave." Lincoln stopped short of embarrassing himself further. Emily gave another loud snort at his attempt to patch up his words.

"Dani's not the shiny new toy," Emily suggested, echoing her words from earlier as she pulled me away from the interaction. Lincoln followed as Emily guided us over to the table, what appeared to be her workstation. She cleared the surface, then began pulling out a tray and filling it with tools she plucked from different drawers and cabinets.

"Hope you aren't afraid of needles," Lincoln mumbled. My gaze shot to Emily, she hadn't told me what was going on. But I knew what they were after.

"Lincoln," Emily reprimanded, "I haven't asked her yet."

"I just can't seem to not mess these things up." Lincoln pressed his palm into his face, covering his embarrassment. "I am so sorry."

"If it's ok with you, Dani, we would like to take a blood sample." Emily's voice was soft and apologetic as she gritted her teeth at Lincoln. My heart raced. If I refused, I couldn't just walk out of Eyecon. Victor would not give me up, especially after he admitted how he was prepared to find me. He would kill for my blood. Even though Emily was being kind about the blood draw, ultimately, it wasn't a choice.

Samuel had said it was important to study the virus before it binded to any of my antibodies. This led me to believe, along with the fact Eyecon's research had stagnated with the limited resource of Victor's blood, whatever the virus was, it was more desirable in the form of the raw source. My blood was created from that very source and it frightened me what kind of information I would be handing over to Eyecon.

I didn't know what kind of clues would be in my blood, or how much it could help Victor's cause. But there were two very clear things that could not happen. I could not hand my blood over and I surely couldn't let Victor find out about the lake. I didn't want Emily or Victor to even suspect there was a raw source of the virus that existed out in the world.

"Is she mute?" Lincoln whispered to Emily. She shot Lincoln a silencing expression.

"No, I'm not mute. And I'm not afraid of needles either," I bit out toward Lincoln.

A smile lit his face. "She talks."

"You're ok with the sample?" Emily asked.

I pushed to my feet in refusal. "No, we aren't doing this."

Emily pulled off her blue latex gloves, setting them on her workspace, her reaction far gentler than I anticipated.

"Can I ask you something?" Emily's eyes were kind as she lowered the vial to the tray containing the tools for the blood draw. "Did you by chance give a sample to Jack?" My chest thudded. What was I to say? My omission was a clear indication. Lincoln glanced at Emily and then back towards my gaze.

"It's ok, love," Lincoln whispered, "we understand." No, they did not understand. Because Jack couldn't be this monster they were all making him out to be.

"It's not your fault, Dani. There was no way you could've known his intentions. As I said, Jack's quite the cunning manipulator." Emily thought Jack had duped me into giving him my blood. I wanted to scream at her. I wanted to yell about Victor's lies. I wanted Emily to know the truth. Jack wasn't the bad guy here. Jack hadn't traded me. I would have known. Because there was no way Jack would have given me up, not after the things we experienced together. I saved him from the lake, he owed me his life.

"Does she know?" Lincoln asked Emily, but before Emily could respond, words had finally found me.

"Do I know what? That Jack traded me like an object for peace with Victor?" It stung to let the words leave my lips, to pretend I had been enlightened by Victor.

"He was created to find you, Dani. But he went off the rails a bit," Lincoln said.

"Victor already told me."

"I'm sure he didn't tell you the full extent of the situation," Emily softly whispered, "and I know you have questions."

"You're going to do it, aren't you?" Lincoln rolled his eyes at Emily, sucking in a heavy breath of air.

"How could I not? Wouldn't you want to know if someone sent a soldier after you? Created one to find you?"

"Perhaps I wouldn't want that kind of weight on my shoulders," Lincoln said, raising an eyebrow, offering me an out.

But I wanted to know. I wanted to know who I'd left Ben with. I was the reason Jack was created. He was the consequence of me. Jack could have easily submitted to Victor. I could have hopped in Jack's patrol car, and our ride could have ended a lot differently. Because the reality was, Jack had done what he was designed for. Jack found me. And if his intentions were to obey Victor, Eyecon would have had what they were after a long time ago.

Most importantly, I wanted to know about our connection. Because that was the single most important thing confirming why I knew Jack hadn't given me to Victor. Our connection was the unique bond Victor could never have anticipated. Our bond was the reason I didn't fall into Victor's trap, the reason I knew his lies were false words. I wanted to know what made Jack different. Because I knew Jack had not betrayed me. He couldn't have traded me.

"Do what, Emily?" My eyes locked on hers. Emily inhaled slowly and turned to leave the table.

"Dear lord, she really is going to do it," Lincoln exhaled, "she'll be back."

As I watched Emily duck into the room with numerous filing cabinets, Lincoln's eyes traced over my face. "You ever been to London?"

"Why? You going to ask me for a hand in marriage?" I prodded at his earlier behavior.

"I could certainly warm your bed, but no, I was not inviting you home."

"No, I've never been to London. Why?"

"You just look a bit familiar I suppose." Lincoln let it go. Emily returned with a stack of papers wrapped in a manilla-colored folder. Lincoln looked at her, studying her expression. Emily paused, momentarily doubting if she wanted to do whatever it was she had planned. A rumble of acid wracked through my stomach.

Finally, Emily sat the file on the table and pushed it across to me. His name was printed across the label: Jack Ryker.

Chapter 19

Commission

"What is this?" I asked Emily.

"You ask, and you shall receive," Lincoln slid in before Emily could respond.

"It's Jack's file. I know you have questions, and I think it will help put some of the pieces together for you," Emily said.

Grabbing the file, I slid it closer to me, properly orienting it.

"Look, I know you have no reason to believe him, and I don't blame you, but it sounds like Victor told you the truth." The truth? Laughable. But, here it was, Jack's story, all typed up and ready for me to read. This file would finally shed light on how Victor exploited Jack, on how our connection came to life. Perhaps Emily thought this would reveal the final pieces of information compelling me to join Victor's cause. But it wouldn't. Nothing could convince me Eyecon's malevolence wasn't what I knew it to be. Eyecon was the echo chamber of Victor's creations, he would make damn sure nothing repudiated his rule.

"Do you mind if I read this in private?"

"I'll show you to your room," Emily offered, trying to change the subject. "You are going to stay, aren't you?" I almost fell off my stool at Emily's words. How could she form it in a question? Was she unaware my presence was in fact not a choice? There was no way Victor would actually allow me to leave.

"Of course." I smiled softly. What the hell was I doing? But I had yet to plant the bug.

"Don't let Victor see that if you run into him. He isn't proud of that project," Lincoln whispered before I turned to leave after Emily. Rightly so, Victor should be ashamed of what he has done to Jack, of all the things he has done with the Spectrum trials.

Emily led me out of the sliding glass lab doors and down a hall. She swiped her badge over an access panel that illuminated green. When the doors swung open I was expecting a dark room flooded with medical devices. Instead, I was met by small quarters with an attached bathroom. I sighed in relief. It was nothing like what Jack had shown me.

"We'll get you a badge tomorrow," Emily said, "and it'll be official."

"What will?"

"You'll be a member of our team." Words evaded me, too disgusted to think I would be helping Victor to move his plans along. Too ashamed I would be expected to surrender a blood sample to his team. I had squeezed out of the request today, but I knew better. Victor was going to get antsy, and shortly it wouldn't be my choice. The demand would come down the line soon enough.

"There's a robe in the closet. I'll see that some fresh clothes are delivered to your door before morning." I thanked Emily, expecting her to turn and leave me in the doorway. Instead, she looked down and exhaled.

"Everything alright?" I asked.

"I'm just relieved," she sighed, "I never thought I would actually get to work with someone like you. I'm excited to see what kind of insights you bring to the team." I didn't know what insights she could be referring to. And if I did, I wasn't sure if I wanted to share them.

Emily finally left me to myself in the room. I closed the door behind her and took inventory of what was laid about. There wasn't much furniture, but the furniture present was sleek and modern. The room was filled with warm woods and contrasting shades of black and gray.

I placed Jack's file on the bed and began pulling open doors, running my fingers over shelves, inspecting everything. But, nothing. There was nothing suspicious about any of the artwork or any other object in the room. I couldn't find any evidence a piece of furniture or decor was concealing a camera or microphone. I mean, Victor could be very good at hiding such a small piece of technology, and it's not like I knew what I was looking for. As far as I was concerned I had to assume I was under surveillance one-hundred percent of the time. They surely couldn't trust me. Victor had taken my phone after all—little did he know about the bug concealed in my bag.

Placing my ear against the cold hard surface of the door, I couldn't hear anything. This was the first time I was left alone and unmonitored at Eyecon.

I pulled the door open and was surprised to find it unlocked. Could I really just leave? I pushed past the door, lodging a small trash can in between the frame so it wouldn't lock behind me. I didn't have a key or a badge to get back in if it closed.

Walking down the hallway, I expected to hear alarms blaring at any moment, or to see guards running my way, but neither of those things happened. A laugh broke the silence as I rounded a corner. Two researchers were chatting as they walked through the hall. One gave me a curt nod and waved as they passed. I continued to the lab, of course without a badge I couldn't get in, but through the glass, I could see a few researchers still working, everyone else had melted off.

"Taking evening strolls, I see." The voice came from behind. I knew who it was before I had turned to see his face. Victor held a stack of fresh clothing in his arms.

"I heard you require some items." Victor pushed the clothing towards me.

"I don't understand."

"You don't understand clothes?" He raised an eyebrow.

"I can really leave?"

"Of course," he responded, "I mean, I wish I would have known before I hunted down the clothes you needed." But it was quite convenient Victor had shown up before I decided to test my boundaries.

"I'm not," I paused, "I'm not going anywhere. I just thought..." Coy. I had to play coy. Dumbfounded. Victor needed to think I was really buying into his crafted story that he wasn't the villain I knew him to be.

"Us hybrids have been held captive by ourselves for too long. The last thing you need is another cage." Victor's eyes were light, honest. The moment held us while we let the silence linger. Maybe he truly believed it, but I didn't care. The very place I wanted Victor was in a cage, a physical one, where he belonged.

"Are you opposed to a blood sample?" He asked, breaking the train of thoughts rushing through my head. Here it was. I knew what Victor was going to do next. I couldn't bring myself to respond to his words. "It's ok, Dani, I can understand your hesitation but we both know what is going to come of this." A threat.

"And what is that?"

"This was the trade. You can provide a sample with grace or we can take one by force." Punch him. Clock him in his face. Oh, the anger boiled just beneath my palms. I had to pull it together. Victor's words were clear. I was caught in a panic. I wanted to refuse. I wanted to kill Victor, but I was powerless against him.

"I don't want to do this, you know that." And for a moment, his words felt too kind, too sincere for the vile atrocity I knew him as.

A test. He was attempting to confirm if I bought into his story, his lies. Stiffness took hold of my jaw and I was unable to respond. My mind was begging me to run, but there was no escape.

A very careful trap. We were playing a delicate dance of wits.

The words stung as they left my mouth. "The thing is, I'm just a bit queasy around blood." Bold-faced lie. One I hoped would make him falsely understand why I hesitated to agree to the blood draw. I was entirely disappointed in myself, but what other choice did I have? Refusing would put others in danger, and Victor would get what he wanted from me eventually. He wouldn't let me go. This was the only option to keep me in the game, keep me in his grace to wander about the lab. To stay close and work my way in, to figure out how to annihilate him and all of his work. At least that's what I consoled myself with.

He chuckled softly, "Ah, I can help with that." A smile crept across his face as he turned. He closed the distance to the lab door, swiping his hand over the access panel. "Come."

I begrudgingly obeyed Victor's gentle command, following him into the lab. He set the folded clothes he carried onto Emily's desk, gesturing me to sit. I found a stool and kept my eyes trained on him as he pulled the tray of tools Emily had prepared earlier in the day. The taste of blood leaked into my mouth as I bit the inside of my cheek. Victor selected a latex band from the tray.

"May I?" he asked, gently plucking my arm up to rest openly on the table. An electric sensation raised goosebumps under his touch. I didn't say a word, because if I opened my mouth nothing that obliged Victor would come out. He tied the band around my arm then glanced up at me.

"Not so bad so far?" Again, I gritted my teeth, clenching my words from escaping. I was trying to keep my composure as Victor swept his thumb over the crook of my elbow, smiling in delight. My stomach twisted. He wanted a rise out of me. Teasing me with his touch to demonstrate the power he had over me, how he could hold me under his thumb. I couldn't believe I was even doing this, giving in. I was going to be sick.

"It will be over before you know it," Victor said. And I hoped truer words had never been spoken, because I couldn't wait for this disgraceful exchange to end.

Then Victor glanced up at me with a snide little smile. My chest sputtered in panic as he leaned in, drawing so close that if I pushed any further back, I'd fall from my stool. He slipped his mouth up to my ear, heat radiating from his chest, leaking the wet movements of his fowl trap. "Or we could let this game go on for a while longer."

Words evaded me. I swallowed rising bile in my throat. Was he talking about our game? The clash of wits we were ensued in? How he would play his next move if I had refused? About killing the Rebels? He would enjoy nothing more than to maliciously pick them off one by one. Or more simply, was he talking about my life? Because I only remained alive by the grace of Victor, and if I didn't comply, he could order me killed or locked up in an instant.

Victor leaned back, sliding the needle from my arm. And like that, the draw was over.

"The trick is surprise," he admitted, "to draw your attention away from the act."

Victor placed the filled vile on the tray as he glanced up to catch my gaze. "You look a little ill." A smile of bluster filled Victor's face as a sparkle caught his eye.

He had seen me.

I wasn't ill from the sight of blood, I was sick over the exchange, and Victor knew he had won the quarrel. He was satisfied with himself. I felt nothing but disgust.

"Shall I escort you back to your quarters?" Victor asked.

"I know the way." The words snarled from my lips as I stood to excuse myself. Victor grinned and placed the clothing in my arms, nodding to see me off for the evening.

I had never been so disappointed and repulsed by myself. Victor had taken more from me than my blood, he'd stripped me of my dignity and relished in it. I would find a way to vindicate his transgression.

I returned to my room, removing the trashcan and closing the door as I entered. Pulling on a robe left in the closet, I retired myself to the bed. Jack's file sat near me where I'd left it. Victor had done atrocious things to more than just me.

I pulled the file into my lap running my finger over the label. *Jack Ryker*. Did I dare read the words in his file? Did I truly want to know? What if his file confirmed my fears? What if everything that had happened between us was all a ploy? A detailed decoy designed by Victor? But there was no way. My interactions with Jack couldn't have been fabricated. I knew it in my soul. I could feel it in my bones.

And had Victor been sharp enough to intentionally create a hybrid so profoundly connected to me, he wouldn't have needed Jack to find me. He could have gone after me himself. Victor was failing to perfect the virus as it was, he certainly hadn't been the mastermind behind the connection Jack and I had.

The first page of Jack's file was an intake report, reviewing his background and current mental standing. But instead of a detailed report, it was vague, suggesting Jack was healthy and fit for testing. Near the end of the form, there was a profile written by hand: Defiant, Oppositional, High-risk.

I swallowed, remembering how Victor targeted Jack for his traits.

Listed was a daily log of Jack's status. It contained notes about the subtle change of color in his eyes. Bandages were replaced daily on his bound wrists which showed no sign of healing. There were constant injections and IV drips for sedation, antipsychotics. And at the bottom of one page, a haunting number. Patient: 00184. Release: 00012.

Was Jack the 184th patient who had been injected? Were only 12 released at the time? The reminder that Eyecon was responsible for so many crimes sent rage through me. If they had taken live subjects to be such a serious manner as Emily claimed, how could they have stolen so many lives from people? The injection was nearly a death sentence.

There was nothing that would have answered my questions about why exactly Jack was chosen or what sort of mental state he was in during his stay. I guess that kind of information wasn't necessary for Emily's team to determine how the vaccine was responding in his body. A psychological decision would have been out of the scientists' hands. Victor was the only one who must have held an answer to that. But whatever state of mind Jack was in, it wasn't a good one judging by the numerous recordings of necessary sedatives and antipsychotics.

On the very last page of Jack's file was a red stamp which read 'Selected for Commission'. Vomit rose in my throat as I recounted how Victor talked about Jack, about his 'perfect little soldier'. The one I was supposed to be reporting to.

Pulling the bug out of my bag, I stared at it for a long time. I could imagine the Rebels eagerly awaiting an update. Maybe they already thought I was dead or being tortured. I had to check in and say something, let them know I was alive.

Would they come for me? Even if Jack said he wasn't sending a 'rescue team'. My stomach flipped. My major miscalculation of Eyecon being able to identify me had ended in disaster. Jack warned me, but I was too naive to believe it, and now I was condemned to whatever Victor had in store for me. I couldn't blame Jack for his decision. I wouldn't want to subject the Rebels to the horrors they had been through, not again. Protecting the Rebels was the very reason I gave my blood up to Victor. But, I couldn't admit that to them, I couldn't tell the Rebels I willingly let Victor take a sample from me, that I didn't put up the fight our world deserved. I was too soft to be the brave hero the world needed.

I turned the bug on as it sat in my palm. I had to at least let the Rebels know I was alive. I couldn't put Ben through that—thinking I was dead. It was too late to keep my mind stuck on my loss to Victor. Now was the time to plan the next play. I had to inform the Rebels I was looking for a place to strategically plant the bug.

Relocating myself to the bathroom, I simultaneously turned on the shower and sink faucet to mask my words in case Victor was monitoring me. I held the bug in hand, pretending to adjust and remove the earrings Shauna made me wear as I spoke.

"I want to let you know I'm alive, and that I'm working to get as much information as possible. It was too risky to plant the bug today, so this is my update. I'll try again tomorrow. I'm fine, and I think I have currently convinced Victor Crowe, the CEO, I'm interested enough in being complicit." I paused, rolling the bug across my palm with the earrings.

"I know this isn't what any of us were expecting— Ok, maybe some of us. But maybe this is how we figure out how to take Eyecon down, from the inside out." And that was a commitment I had already made to myself. Find what matters most, then crush it, take away whatever progress Victor would make from obtaining my blood.

"And Gus, you were right," I admitted, "they keep all their research on a closed network disconnected from the internet and the rest of their building." That's all I wanted to say before I got too choked up.

I turned the bug off, praying my transmission was received. I hoped the news would be shared with Ben, who was probably worried sick right about now I had yet to return to the Rebel compound.

As I lay in bed, an itch in my brain kept flaring. I couldn't help but chew over the words Victor had repeated to me. *Cat and mouse.* Jack had said those very same words to me, they were part of the reason I had decided to go in on the plan with the Rebels. Because I knew Eyecon had wanted me in their grasp, and it was clear they were going to do what they needed to accomplish that goal. It was only a matter of time until they nabbed me.

Who would Victor have killed to find me? And housing me was a giant risk to the Rebels. Maybe Jack really had traded me for the safety of his team. He would do anything to keep the others safe. *I won't subject any of my team to that, not again.* I shut the thoughts down as soon as they crossed my mind. They were the sprouts from the seeds Victor had planted, and I wasn't going to let the doubt grow. Jack hadn't given me to Victor, he hadn't betrayed me.

Tomorrow I would plant the bug.

Chapter 20

Crow

Emily arrived at my room the next morning. She gifted me a badge granting me access to the lab and my quarters. Just as we entered the lab, Lincoln looked up from a sheet of legal paper covered in scribbled notes and diagrams.

"Find anything you didn't want to know?" Lincoln asked, glancing up from his writing. I took a seat across from Lincoln and Emily as I slid the file across the table.

"How many people survive the injection?"

"The earlier forms of the virus had a ninety-percent kill rate after the first administration. For those who survived the first round, about half died after the second." Then, cautious of the other researchers, Emily whispered, "Only one person has made it to the third round."

"Jack?"

Emily didn't say anything, she only nodded. Victor had told me he had gotten greedy, that he had broken Jack. Was this what he meant? Had he subjected Jack to three rounds of the virus? Was this why Jack wanted his revenge? Jack had shown me his terrifying experience at the hands of Eyecon.

Victor chose to subject Jack to three rounds of the virus, could this be why we felt so connected? Samuel said Jack and I had the closest level of infection. Was this the explanation I was looking for? Victor mentioned he had broken Jack, that he became greedy in order to find me sooner. Victor put Jack through unspeakable pain unknowingly creating the connection between us. The very thing that prevented me from buying into Victor's deceitful stories.

"Look, I know it must be hard to wade through all the lies and figure out what the truth is, but one thing I can guarantee you," Emily paused, looking at Lincoln, "There's no way Jack told you the truth."

And maybe some of Emily's words made sense. There certainly were things Jack kept from me. He never mentioned Victor had singled him out with purpose, created him to pursue me. Nor had Jack ever admitted he knew I existed or that he had been looking for me, as if running into me was merely a coincidence. Why would he keep that from me?

"I'm sorry, Love," Lincoln whispered. For a split second, I almost lost control of myself, of my tongue. Because everyone kept apologizing to me, Victor, Emily, and now Lincoln. I felt their pity. They thought I was naive for buying into Jack's grand lies. But they were failing to consider, to question if Jack had gotten things right, that he had seen Victor for what he was.

But maybe I was a little more reactive to Lincoln's apology because I was irritated Jack had kept pieces of the truth from me. I was so enraptured by him and our linkage, how could I not know I was the reason, the cause of Jack's creation? Weight stacked heavily on my chest.

We sat in silence as Emily and Lincoln recorded more of their work. Occasionally, another researcher would come over to exchange items and words. But I couldn't pay attention to any of that. There was so much on my mind. A pinwheel spinning wild in the wind.

Lunch was pushed in on carts. The entire lab ceased their work to grab their trays of food. I followed suit, returning to our table where Emily cleared some additional space for our meal.

"In other news, you are simply spectacular," Lincoln energetically said, trying to make conversation over our meal.

"You better record the date, because I have never said this before— Lincoln's right, your blood is fascinating," Emily smiled. I nodded, pushing some of the food around on my plate with my fork. "It just seems like your infection is quite old, it looks pretty mature in your blood— quite the unique set of antibodies."

"Hmm, the same thought crossed my mind. I noticed that too," Lincoln confirmed. "How long have you been a hybrid, Dani?"

"Nearly a decade. I was fifteen."

"Do you know how you happened to be contaminated with the virus?" Emily asked. I hated how she phrased it. *Contaminated*. I hated it because it was true. Dead on bullseye. It wasn't the 'gift' Victor had spoken of, it was a contaminant. Something that destroyed what was natural.

But this was the mistake I was trying to avoid making again. I was not going to give away the location of the raw source of the virus, the lake had to be more valuable than my blood. My exchange of blood would still take Eyecon plenty of time to solve their little puzzle. Look how long it had taken Eyecon to get to this point with only using Victor's blood. But the lake? The lake had to be kept a secret at all costs.

"No, I'm not sure what the point of infection was." I didn't want to elaborate, it would make it harder to sell the lie.

Her voice was sincere, curious. "Were your parents infected?"

"Not that I know of. My mom wasn't in the picture, and my father passed away quite some years ago."

"I'm sorry to hear that," Emily gently said.

Lincoln nodded in agreement. "Well, I've got to go get some work done, I'll catch up with you two loves later." Lincoln excused himself from the table, leaving Emily and me to ourselves.

"I can't help but feel responsible that you all are stuck in this lab," I admitted.

"Why do you say that?" Emily pushed her tray away, leaning on her crossed arms.

"Without me, Jack wouldn't have been created."

"Well, I can't deny that part. Try not to dwell on it, it's not your fault. None of this is." She paused and looked down at her food. "But it looks like you will have the opportunity to stop it."

"What do you mean?"

"I mean, you've held it together long enough to get to today. To not fall victim to what the virus demands, what it takes from you. And because of your strength, we will save the human race from succumbing to the nearing radiation poisoning."

I didn't want to correct what Emily said. Because I hadn't been holding it together, I had been relying on Ben as a crutch. All I ever did was become another victim of the virus, praying it didn't take too much of me along with it. Praying I didn't lose myself. I didn't have any strength, I was merely a leaf in the wind, pretending I would somehow land somewhere safe. Pretending a new start wasn't a far-off hoax. And look what all this pretending got me, nothing but a trip deeper down the rabbit hole. Alice in fucking wonderland.

Perhaps Emily thought it was somehow fate that brought me to Eyecon. If my blood was truly the key to saving humanity, it would be just one great big stroke of luck. The humans once again remain living by the grace of the universe. But it wasn't true, because Victor's plans reached further than a cure for radiation poisoning— and it surely wasn't saving humanity.

"I used to think we would be condemned to this lab for eternity. That there was the possibility you didn't exist. That *any* wild hybrid didn't exist. And we would never solve the radiation vaccine." Emily leaned back on her stool. I tapped my thumb on the table nervously. She thought I was the key to the radiation vaccine, but she had no idea there was a body of water out there which contained the virus.

"Between us?" Emily raised an eyebrow. "Part of me guiltily thought Victor had lost it, that he didn't know what he was talking about."

"You still think he's telling the truth?" I was curious as to her thoughts.

"We solve the vaccine, we get to go home. We get to save our families, save our neighbors, save the world. Eyecon's promised all of us enough money to disappear with our families after the vaccine formula is perfected. This vaccine is our one shot at having a normal life."

And I couldn't hold back the words that found me.

"I would like that too," I said, "a shot at a normal life. Is that even on Victor's radar? If he hates himself so much for what the virus has done to him, why would he not want to rid himself of it?"

Emily didn't say anything. Instead, she pursed her lips. A softness fell over her face.

"We'll figure something out," she said, "you deserve more than what life handed to you."

A salty wave of dark bitterness crashed over me. And I almost broke down right there, letting the hurt bleed out onto my face. But I held firm. I didn't want her to think I pitied myself, I didn't. But what I did want was for an ending, for a brighter future. And every corner I turned seemed to just bring darkness and brick walls. I was fed up with it all.

I wanted to end Eyecon, end Victor for the things he had done, for the things he planned to do. But more than that, I wanted to be with Ben. I wanted to escape it all. My stomach churned. I may never see Ben again. I may never even see past the walls of Eyecon again— an animal sentenced to its enclosure.

"I don't even know what kind of life I am going to return to," Emily admitted, "I have a daughter, Adeline. She's eleven now." Victor had warned me this was touchy territory, so I decided to tread lightly.

"I'm sorry."

"I thought I was doing well, balancing my work life with my home life. But the judge didn't see it that way. My ex used my work against me, granting him full custody of Adeline. And I guess the judge was right. Because where have I been for the past decade?" Emily's tone was bitter, her words dropping with a sharpness, a certain heartache.

"I'm terrified she'll also lose her father. Life is strange. All it can take is being in the wrong place at the wrong time, a bad accident." The weight of her words fell on top of me. Life had placed my father and me in the wrong place at the wrong time. Life wasn't strange, life was cruel.

"My father died in a plane crash," I whispered. I left out the part about my involvement in the same crash. No need to give rise to suspicion, to plant ideas about where my possible exposure was. Emily was quiet for a few moments. I knew my admission wasn't consoling to her, but if she cared about her daughter, she should have never let her go the way she did.

"Although I know little about you, I'm in awe of what it sounds like you've been through. The virus, Jack, two missing parents. And at that, one taken at the hands of a tragic plane crash." Emily shook her head. "Did he go down before or after your infection?"

"Before."

"So you were all alone in this?" Her lower lip wedged between her teeth as she struggled not to let the tears roll down her cheek. I nodded. "I'm so sorry," her gentle voice barely carried the words over to me.

"I'll give you some space," Emily softly said, reading my crumbled face, "I have to deliver some of our progression notes to Victor." Emily collected a folder and stood. "Victor's going to be pleased with you, you know." A short smile flashed across Emily's face. "I already am."

But it wasn't me she was pleased with, nor Victor. Deep down I knew what she was truly pleased with. It was what I was, what my blood contained, and what I could do for them. That much I knew. Because life had taught me better than to trust anyone.

"Lincoln should be back shortly." I nodded, not knowing what to say or how to act. I was just trying to avoid the pain and hurt, the incessant mind spinning its circles, its web. I wanted to sink into myself, to feel tiny and helpless. Because the world just seemed as if it was passing me by, using me in the way it needed, but neglecting that I too had needs. Isn't that the saying? Life sucks and then you die?

"Speak of the devil," Emily blurted just as she turned to leave.

"Hello Love." Lincoln sat at the other end of the table. I pursed my lips and gave a soft smile. If I opened my mouth to say anything, only tears would come. So instead I kept it shut.

"Just want the company?" I nodded in confirmation.

I spent the afternoon observing Lincoln and the rest of the team work. A buzz filled the air. Excitement about my blood had infected all the researchers, just to again remind me of how I was the awkward puzzle piece that sat in the wrong box, the wrong world. So out of place, I would perpetually never fit into whatever landscape I came across. More so, their excited chatter was the reminder of how I had given into Victor. Anguish and sourness filled me.

The stares from the researchers had dwindled since they had first seen me. I no longer garnished the curiosity that had consumed them when I first arrived. Thank god. They were much too busy toying with their new blood sample, drawing Lincoln off to work with some of his colleagues.

Pulling the bug from my pocket, I rolled it across my palm. Victor's office was likely the best place for the bug, considering the most vital information came at his directive. But, I would never be able to surreptitiously plant it in his quarters, because I would always be in Victor's company during our visits. And if I slipped up in front of him, it was game over.

I turned the bug on and placed it on the underside of Emily's desk. This was as good as it was going to get.

When dinner was rolled in, Lincoln brought me a tray, letting me stay where I was. As with my other meals, I barely picked at my food. I couldn't focus on eating when everything felt so wrong.

Lincoln walked me from the lab to my room. I wasn't sure if he was chaperoning me, or if it was just an attempt to be kind after recognizing how upset I was.

Upon entering my room, I found my bed, making the mistake of letting my mind take over. As I laid in bed, I tossed and turned trying to find a comfortable position, but my brain was pondering the mess I had found myself in. I was in over my head. A devastating landslide.

A barrage of noise overtook my senses, pushing me to my feet. But the floor was soft, leaf-soiled dirt. When I looked up again, a flock of crows circled overhead, diving down onto me, picking at my skin and hair. Stop. I flailed my arms, trying to rid myself of them, but they mercilessly dove at me. Stop. My heart raced as the electricity turned up another notch just under my skin. Stop. I reached out, catching the next bird that dove towards me. As soon as it was in my grasp, the other crows stopped their diving. Instead, they returned to circling overhead, cawing in warning as they darted through the dark treetops.

The crow in my hand stared at me with its beady little eye, trying to bite at my fingers which trapped it. The electricity now boiled, I was ready to pulse a wave into the bird, make it feel weak and small like it had done to me. But it stopped and looked straight into my eyes. And instead of doing anything to the bird, I just held it, encapsulated by the grip of my hand. The crow's heart beat like a train. Afraid. It was afraid of *me*.

I opened my hand, throwing the bird back towards the sky, showing it mercy, to prove I wasn't the threat, the monster it thought I was. Just as the bird joined its crew, the entire flock pushed down on me in one uniform dive. I fell backward. My body gave out a splash as the water surrounded me, wrapping me in its grip.

Engulfed in a familiar feeling, I was in the lake again, my arms thrashing as I fought to get free, to swim for the beach. Pulling my body onto the moonlit sand, I breathlessly heaved the water from my lungs. Over my coughing came his voice.

"Dani," he frantically shouted. But I already knew where to look for him as I turned my attention back towards the water, peering in.

"Dani," he yelled again. I wanted to plunge my hand in, to pull him out. I wanted him to wrap his arms around me. But none of that happened.

"Save yourself," he screamed in his panic. My heart beat so alarmingly, like a bass drum racking my chest.

"I can't," I cried out, "I can't."

"Save yourself, Dani." And his emerald eyes were slipping deeper into the darkness. "No one is coming." I sank my hand into the water, sloshing waves in search of him. My body plummeted into the lake, sinking down. Adrift into the darkness.

My eyes flew open as I tried to make sense of where I was. The room was filled with modern furniture and I all too soon remembered my room at Eyecon as I lay in my bed. It was a dream

My father had returned once again to warn me. The last time he had told me to run was the night Jack had come for me. Had Jack gone after me because Victor asked him to? How else would Jack have known about me? I had seen Jack's treacherous experience at Eyecon. Perhaps he was desperate for freedom, to escape the fear of returning to Eyecon's lab. I had seen the pain on Jack's face as he ran his fingers over the scars on his wrists. I had felt the grief and hopeless despair during his imprisonment at Eyecon.

And most importantly, I had felt the empty darkness inside Jack when he held me pinned against the beach, caught in the electric madness that had overtaken him. Fear can cause people to do unimaginable things. Could Jack have done the unspeakable? I couldn't believe it. I didn't want to think Jack had it in him to betray me. But just maybe I had been condemned to this fate when I failed to listen the first time to my father's warning. *No one is coming.*

Chapter 21

Destroyed

When I entered the lab the next morning, I hoped to pry as much info from Lincoln and Emily as possible. The bug had been planted and it was past time to start feeding the Rebels important information.

"Good morning, Love," Lincoln greeted me. He had walked me to my room last night and knew I was in the thick of it.

Emily sat a mug full of coffee down on her workspace as steam rose from the cup, giving me a warm smile as she slid into her stool. Part of me wished Ben could meet Emily and Lincoln had they not been tainted by Victor. He would have taken a particular liking to Lincoln. They would all be able to talk about the kinds of things you found in books. Intellectual things.

I gestured to Emily's coffee with my eyes. "I'll take some of that."

"How unfortunate, I had you pegged as more of an Earl Grey kind of girl," Lincoln said, his accent laying thick.

"A what?"

"Oh, good gods, you Americans and that damn tea party in Boston," he drawled.

"It'll have to wait." Emily's gaze settled on something behind me. "Looks like Victor wants to talk." When I turned, a guard was approaching. He motioned for me to join, and I excused myself from Emily and Lincoln. What did Victor want now?

I followed the guard as we exited the lab and entered the elevator which serviced the basement levels. He didn't say a word to me as we crossed the lobby and rode the alternate set of elevators to the top. Once the doors slid open, the guard escorted me down the hall to what I assumed was Victor's office.

Maybe Victor had got what he wanted and was setting me free. Fat chance.

After a single knock, the large black door peeled open, and Victor motioned me in. The guard stood back, taking a posted position outside in the hall.

The entry gave way to a large sprawling room. The walls were made of windows running from floor to ceiling, spotlighting the view of downtown Reno and the surrounding snow-capped mountains.

"I just wanted to check in, see how you were doing," Victor said. "Sorry for the formality, I would've run down to the lab, but it's a little more private up here." Victor's hand swept out, inviting me to sit in twin black leather armchairs, separated by a small end table. "Would you like a drink?"

I opened my mouth to ask for coffee, but cut myself short when I realized Victor was reaching for a crystal decanter of liquor. Instead, an awkward mumble left my lips.

"No worries, just promise not to judge. I'm not often a day drinker, but every once in a while there's good occasion." A light easy chuckle escaped him.

"I am delighted about the strides we'll make due to your kind donation of blood." Victor smiled, tipping the glass against his lips. He strode from the bar cart to the chairs, taking a seat.

I didn't donate it, I was robbed, a stick-up.

"Was it really a choice?" My father's warning bit at the back of my mind. *Save yourself.* I had to cut the attitude and play nice. *No one is coming.*

"I suppose you are correct in your assumption," Victor inhaled. "Perhaps that was the only thing you didn't have a choice over. However, are you finding the rest of your accommodations up to your standards?"

"I have, thank you for your hospitality." Gag me.

"I know I have put you in quite the position. I do want to say thank you." Victor tilted his head down, breaking his eye contact with me. I crossed my ankles, trying to soothe my nerves, my electrical circuits. "And I want to apologize. Had I never done what I had, I never would have put you, or any of the researchers, in this position."

"What did you do?" As if I didn't already know. Emily had already filled me in.

"I made a grave mistake that started this whole thing. I was accidentally infected with one of the original strains of the virus while working with my lab partner. And, well, as you probably can guess, the power consumed me. The cravings were unbearable. I was lost in some... black hole, and when I had escaped, so much time had passed me by. In the process, I destroyed everything in our lab." Victor's dark eyes were two large inky wells, threatening to drip. "Had I been stronger, I wouldn't have given into the rage. I wouldn't have destroyed everything in my path."

"It's not your fault." Gross. Did I just say that? But it was true. Victor gave a dry doubtful chuckle in response. I knew about the violence and cravings that could ensue had Victor accidentally infected himself. I thought about Jack on the beach, glazed-eyed as he pinned me down. My hand slid up to my neck, remembering the bruises that had remained. A reminder I could have died. And when I tried to connect with Jack, it was like reaching a busy tone. He wasn't there. His mind was just… gone, deep in the black hole Victor had mentioned.

"I spent more than a decade learning how to control it. Trying to overcome what had been made of me." Victor's expression was stiff, drawing in a deep steadied breath. "But alas, I have made peace with myself." Perhaps Victor had made peace with the fact the cure was an elusive dream. Maybe I would be forced to make the same acceptance.

"Here is what I need help understanding." Victor swallowed the last of his liquor. "Our researchers have been studying my blood for a very long time now. And it appears you have a mature infection, similar to mine." Shit. Emily and Lincoln had already mentioned this to me. I knew what Victor was going to try and get at. "As I said, I am so grateful for your donation. But what you don't understand is all the lives that have been lost on the way to this point. And still, there is a multitude of testing to be done before we can release the vaccine. That means live subjects are going to be put at stake while we iron out the details of your variant."

"You know I don't want any more tests on humans. No more deaths. But, there is nothing more I can give you, Victor"

"I truly mean to not push you. But it's just I, too, don't want to see any more people get hurt. And I want to end the need for Jack to hate us so much." Victor wanted more from me. I had been a hybrid for a long time, and he was coming to that realization. He wanted me to confess how I had become infected.

Like I'd told Victor, I didn't want Eyecon to steal more lives by testing on humans. By using my blood as an excuse to murder. The blood of innocents would be on my hands.

"I don't know how I was infected." I protected the secret of the lake. I'd been made a fool once, and I wasn't eager to repeat history.

"You know, you're a very hard person to find details about," Victor said.

I stiffened as Victor fiddled with his sleeve cuff. "What do you mean?"

"What's your last name, Dani?" Victor pulled his attention from his clothing to look at my face. "I tried to have my team look into your past, but it's like you are a ghost."

"That's by design," I admitted. "As soon as I was on my own, I never left a trace of myself. I've never used my legal name, worked a job, opened a bank account."

"Very smart and careful." Apparently, it wasn't enough. Victor cleared a stray strand of black hair from his forehead. "Had the government found you first, we would have been in a very different position. Perhaps fate has brought you back to us then?" His hand fell to his knee, dusting off his slacks.

What? What did he just say? "Brought me back?"

"It's just I can't help but wonder if you are who I think you are." Silence sat over us for a moment, stretching on forever. Victor rubbed his chin.

"You don't think I'm a wild hybrid?" I asked, trying to put together Victor's hintings.

"You aren't still working for Jack, are you?" He dodged my question.

"Jack lied to me and then betrayed me." Not much of a confession at this point, because those words were from Victor's lies.

"Good, I don't want you to get hurt, because I don't want Jack knowing what comes next." Victor sat back, resting his elbows along the arms of his chair. "If Jack finds out who you truly are, he'll want you dead too."

"Why's that? Because I helped you with my blood?"

"I suppose that would give him something to seethe over, but that was the trade. The deal. He's already aware we have your blood, knew it would happen the moment he gave you up to us."

"Then why?"

"How were you infected?" Victor repeated his question. A trade? He wanted me to tell him about the source, and I wanted him to tell me what he was holding out on. On why Jack would want to kill me.

"I told you, I don't know." But Victor's wager was tempting. Because I wanted whatever information I could get my hands on. I wanted the pieces to the puzzle. I wanted to fully understand the landscape I had been competing in. I needed as much information as possible to strategically plot my plans.

"See, here's the thing." Victor placed his glass on the side table, clasping his hands together, and rested his elbows on his knees. "You're lying to me."

I gave a hard swallow. I *was* lying.

"You've come home, Ms. Ophelia Colburn." The air escaped my lungs. The oxygen was absent so long inside me I was convinced I had forgotten how to breathe as static overtook my body.

Finally, I took in a deep painful breath.

"How do you know that name?" I snarled. My palms itched with fire. I pressed them into my legs, trying to contain myself. Trying to prevent my fury from taking over.

"You aren't the only one with secrets." Victor's lips curved up into a thin smile. "Look, I'm not trying to scare you. I want to help you."

"I doubt your intentions on this."

"If Jack figures out who you are, then it's game over for you. You will never be able to start over," Victor admitted, "He will come after you, and he will find you. He already has once. After all, it's what he was designed to do."

"How do you know my name?" Filthy, rotten scum.

"Because, my lab partner was your father, James." Eyes, in my mind. My father's emerald green eyes. What? No. No. No. I was so shocked, so baffled I couldn't respond.

"You gave yourself up to Emily, your only misstep, the only indication of your identity. You see, your mature infection perfectly lined up with the death of your father, coupled with the absence of your mother. There was only one explanation for your existence. You are James' daughter." And I tried not to let the gasp escape me, but it had.

Victor pushed himself to his feet as he paced in front of me. "How could I have missed this? You do look quite like him. But then I remembered, it's in the eyes. You had James's eyes when you were younger. It had thrown me off." And again, Victor was right. My eyes had changed from my father's emeralds to an electric blue color after I had made it out of the woods. He was telling the truth. If he hadn't known me or my father when I was younger, there was no way he would have known that information.

"So, no, you aren't a wild hybrid. You are an *original* hybrid, like me. James must have turned you." I... I couldn't believe it.

"But there simply has to be more, Ophelia," Victor paused. His eyes jutted up from the floor to meet mine. "How could your sample be as strong as it is? How could your eyes change color? There is more to your story than the tragedy of your father." Victor was smart, putting together threads of information quicker than I could keep up, weaving together the fabric of my story, my past.

"I don't know how I was infected," I repeated. I would not lead Victor to the lake.

Victor stopped in front of me, kneeling. "Please don't make me do this." He swooped up my palm into his. A wave of electricity danced between our touch. A tornado of emotions whirled through me, settling on a sickness. It was too reminiscent of Jack, and all I wanted to do was pull my hand away. To run from Victor's office and find a private place where I could crack open and unleash everything I had been carrying inside. Every corner I turned, I had been met with the unveiling of another lie. I was constantly playing the naive game of 'catch up'. And I hated myself for not seeing it, not seeing any of it sooner. Not being able to put the pieces together as quickly as Victor did. "Please, Ophelia, I am begging you to choose what is right here."

"Make you do what?" I asked.

"I don't want to put you in another cage," Victor's voice cracked as a tear rolled down his cheek. "If you walk out of this building, Jack will pounce on you like a circling predator." Victor was going to do it. He was going to justify why he couldn't let me leave, why he was going to hold me against my will. "I can't let you kill yourself. I need to keep you safe until you come to your senses. Until you can tell me how your hybrid powers came to be."

He was going to twist my arm until he got what he wanted from me. But the thing was, even if I gave up my secrets, Victor was never going to release me.

"Victor," I exhaled, "you don't have to do this."

"We are talking about saving the human race, Ophelia." Victor raised from his kneeling position, straightening out his suit coat. "I owe it to James to see to your safety. And I cannot risk the future of humanity on your ignorant sense of integrity." *Save yourself.* Was I supposed to give it up? Let go of the secret of the lake? I couldn't. I couldn't betray innocent lives, our city, our world. I wasn't worth it.

I stood, my eyes almost level with Victor as I pushed a finger into him. The electric hot anger lingered dangerously close to pulsing through my fingertip into his chest. Before I could get any words out of my mouth, Victor let out a whistle. Two guards breached the room with me in their sights.

Their hands grasped my shoulders. One guard got a hold of my wrist and I could feel they were hybrids. Even if I could, blasting them with electricity would be senseless. It would charge them up like it had done to Jack on the beach. Instead, I complied as the guards pushed me out of Victor's office.

"I'm sorry Ophelia," Victor said, barely audible over the shoulders of the guards. "I'm so sorry." I was forced back into the elevator where we began our descent to the lab. I was seething, and the pent-up energy made it hard for my brain to think clearly. My pulse boisterously thumped behind my ears. My chest hummed with the weight of my anger.

It was *her*. Emily had given me up. She had taken my words, my confessions, and turned them straight over to Victor.

The guards escorted me back to the lab. Once the doors slid shut behind me, Victor's soldiers returned to the elevator we had come from.

Emily and Lincoln immediately ran to me.

"Don't you dare do that," I bit out at Emily. She pulled her hand back from the touch on my shoulder.

"Dani, what's going on?"

"Don't you dare pretend you care what happens to me," I snarled. Emily's poor apology yesterday ate at my mind. *I'm so sorry*. She was only sorry because she was going to turn around and betray me to Victor. And everyone was 'sorry' it seemed. So full of fake pity and insincere emotion. They saw me as nothing but a tool in their quest.

Lincoln's gaze moved from my face to Emily's. "What have you done, Emily?"

Emily's face started as an expression of denial, but quickly faded into one of acceptance. And I then knew Victor's words to be true, I had given myself up to Emily. She betrayed me to Victor so he could pull the puppet strings and try to manipulate the needed information out of me.

"What had to be done," she admitted. Eyes from all over the lab began to wander to the situation. Our words were not subtle and quiet, but instead sharp and intense.

"She told Victor I was James's daughter." Lincoln's face shook with surprise. He took a step back, finding a stool to brace himself with.

"No wonder you looked so familiar," Lincoln whispered in astonishment. All the pent-up rage consumed me. I still hadn't had enough time to piece all the bits together, and it was so hard to think clearly with the pulsing anger running through me.

"Why didn't you tell me?" I took a step closer to her as she took one back.

"James is the real reason we're all stuck down here, Dani. How long do you think we've been here? Since Jack turned on Victor?" A dry giggle escaped her. "Oh, it's been much longer than that. When James fled, Victor ensured no one else would leave too."

Words evaded me as the anger rose.

"I had to do what's best for society, and you have been lying to us. All of us. You're too selfish to realize the future of the world depends on our success." That's what Victor had mentioned upstairs, I had an *ignorant sense of integrity*.

"Do they know you're stealing the lives of innocent people to do it? As in murder?" I yelled. Lincoln rose from his stool, the screech drew even more attention as it slid across the floor.

Emily's face turned solid stone, her finger pointed in my direction. "You don't know what you're talking about."

"What do you think is going to happen Emily? Do you think you're going to find a cure? Some little vaccination that will stop the radiation? At what cost? Do you think Victor is going to let you return to your family after you've solved it?" My voice rose with every word leaving my mouth. The electricity was building, threatening to take control. My palms simmered with a charge dancing just beneath my skin. How could Emily not see what

Victor was doing here? He wasn't planning on editing out the electromagnetic side effects, he was planning to take advantage of them. Emily was refusing to look up at me.

"And by you doctors contributing to this formula, don't think there isn't blood on your hands. Don't think that for one second it wasn't your fault you aren't passing the life-gifting torch to Victor yourselves. And for what? For all you know, your family is already dead. Once you perfect the virus, *if* you perfect the virus, you all know too much. If you decide to defect your loyalty, he will kill you too. Victor's never going to let you go. Things are never going to go back to normal." The words flowed so freely from my mouth like the electric river pulsing through my veins just below my hot skin.

"I don't know they are dead. If we don't develop this radiation vaccine, we will all die." Emily countered as if none of my information seeped into her thick skull.

"What if that was your daughter? What if it was Adeline?"

"One day it will be if we don't get it right now." That triggered something deep within me. Emily was a threat as great as Victor. How could she seriously believe her work was worthy of the harm it inflicted?

"Victor wouldn't allow it," I bit out, "He will hold her indefinitely over your head. Even if she dies, you won't live long enough to find the answer to what happened to Adeline. Victor will ensure he writes the ending to your story."

Emily stood red in the face, a look of realization upon her. She had never wondered if it was a hoax? That Victor was never going to let her go? I wasn't sure what to make of her expression. But then she opened her mouth.

"And what? I just stop so he can kill my family now instead of later?" She spat.

"What's so important about your family over the people you are infecting? "

"It's not a death sentence. They can survive if they fight hard enough, and the vaccine has the best survival rate than it ever has." Had this been how Emily justified her work to herself?

"You can't play God!" I screamed at her.

"They are saving us all. One at a time we learn a little more. Their contribution is saving my family. It's saving the world."

"What does a cybersecurity company have anything to do with radiation poisoning anyway?" I angrily asked, "Think about it."

"The virus produces the electromagnetic spectrum. Electric means programmable."

My jaw parted in utter disbelief. Oh my god. Victor intended not only to create, but to program an army of hybrids.

"You knew this was his plan?"

Emily bit her tongue in refusal to answer.

"Once the general population is vaccinated, they will need updates. We will need to make changes as radiation levels rise. It's the only way to keep the human race alive, Dani," Emily said.

"Oh, isn't that just so fucking convenient?" I shouted. "That's what Victor wants you to believe. You said it yourself. The virus, if perfected, will make hybrids programmable. What do you suspect Victor will do with that? Why is Eyecon not collaborating with anyone? Why isn't the government involved? Do you think it's just good faith Eyecon will provide the cure you are creating to the public? Do you think that's why they have locked you down here and kept everything so secretive? The reality, Emily, is this isn't going to go down the way you think it is. It's not going to happen the way Victor has explained it to you. Victor wants to create an army of hybrids—That's why he wants the virus to be programmable. Yeah, the world is changing, but Victor is going to be damn sure that it is him who is on top. Him who is holding the reins. He wants to seize power before there's ever a power struggle to question.

Think about it. It's not about radiation poisoning, it hasn't been for a long time. Are you ok with Victor playing God? Because it's all led up to this. The radiation vaccine is his justification for power." Lincoln stood between Emily and me, encouraging me to back off as his hands pressed against my upper arms.

The red-hot electricity inside my body rose, warning that my skin was going to melt. The power was overtaking any last control I had over myself. One of the scientists fled towards a phone fixed to a wall, calling for help.

My only opportunity to get rid of Emily, to subtract a truly evil person from the Eyecon team, from the world, was dwindling. This was my only chance to take down one of their head scientists. She was incapable of being convinced to see the truth.

There was something inching inside, begging to let it take me over in its dark consumption.

I pushed Lincoln off to the side with a pulse of electricity as he stumbled to regain his balance. I focused on my stance, stretching my arms out in front of me. Pulling the energy from my core, drawing it out of my legs and up through my body. Reminiscing in the high feeling as I concentrated it through my arms and pushed it ever so closely to my palms. Building it up for one large strike that would desecrate her, to end her where she stood. To kill her and give those who she had murdered at the hands of Eyecon justice. The energy was simmering, fleeting, and I didn't know how to control it. But there was something deeper inside, resting over the edge, lurking with an eager grin. It egged me closer to it, pleading to let me give it sway.

Just as I let the dark corners of my brain take over, pushing the electricity into a bundle for use at my hands, the doors of the lab slid open.

"My, my," Victor waltzed into the lab, giving a slow clap. "Ophelia, you don't cease to amaze me. Go on, let's see what you are capable of." He let his hand slide out in front of his body as if displaying a scene, waiting in anticipation. The energy fogged my brain, grasping for total control, mere seconds away. But I couldn't do it. I couldn't live with myself if I took her life. She was a product of her environment, of Eyecon, of Victor's lies.

I turned towards Victor instead. I could take out the biggest enemy on my list. I wanted to release the roar of energy inside me, to eradicate Victor where he stood. That not so little voice inside was bartering to let the flood gates open.

"Please, it would be my pleasure. I haven't indulged myself in such an amount of energy in quite a long time. I would love to see what you are capable of." He smiled, fixing the cuffs on his sleeves, preparing his stance to support himself for the blow. "Those eyes didn't change color for nothing."

I wrangled the energy rummaging around me fighting to escape. I couldn't do it. It was helpless. I was helpless.

I had to Swallow it. Stop it. Learn to control it. Every muscle in my body burned, ached in torture as I attempted to quell the crude electricity pumping through me, as I tried to force that darkness back into its ugly little box.

I painfully forced my hands down, containing the ball of energy as it dispersed back through my body. Victor wanted to see what cards I held in my hand. And although I had a shit poker face, I wasn't going to give him the satisfaction of playing them. The energy boiled just below my skin, threatening to blow the lid off.

"Hmm, cat got your tongue now, Ms. Colburn?" It took everything in me to stop myself from giving Victor what he wanted.

"How unfortunate, I really thought you were going to be an asset to this team," Victor sighed as he turned on his heel to leave. "You can take her now," he ordered the guards, tossing a lazy hand up. All traces of the soft and kind persona gone.

A syringe pressed at my neck. Part of me hoped whatever liquid it contained would put me out of my misery for good. It would be better than facing the darkness of my mind all alone in my prison cell for the rest of eternity. The metal of the gun which held the triggered syringe dug firmly into my neck. The guard had one hand on my hair, pulling my head backward so my chin tilted upwards. The muscles of the guard tightened as he readied to pull the trigger of the syringe, to jolt that needle into my neck.

"It's my fault, Mr. Crowe." A small voice sliced through the thick tension in the room. Victor stopped in his tracks, still facing away from us. Every single set of eyes in the lab were glued to the situation.

"I'm sorry, did you say something?" He questioned aloud, turning on his heel. What was she doing?

"I pushed her a little too far, I know she is James's daughter, I guess it was out of spite." I didn't know what to make of her words, what to believe.

"You have risked the lives of all these valuable doctors, Ms. Burns. Did you not think of the consequences of your actions?" Victor spoke down to Emily as if she was small and weak, as if she was a child.

"I did not. I'm sorry, Mr. Crowe." Emily fell in line, she knew how to play her cards, because she was far from the superficial giggle she had given me in her play of bravado.

"Her too." Victor nodded towards another guard, signaling him to take ahold of Emily. "Oh, and I almost forgot." A smile grew on Victor's face. He slid his hand into the pocket of his suit coat, removing a small black transmitter. Shit. It was the bug. "I'm not going to tolerate your games, Ophelia."

The transmitter fell from Victor's hand to the floor, and before my brain could calculate what he was doing, the bug sat crushed under the sole of his shoe. Destroyed. "I really thought you were going to choose better. My mistake."

The guard pulled the trigger of the syringe. Everything fell black.

Chapter 22

Foolproof

When I woke, I was inside a small pitch-black room, but I had seen it before. I already knew where I was. It was familiar to me from Jack's memories he had shared. This room had been his personal hell, consuming him with an inescapable craving for electricity, an unbearable dark fire, and a death wish which would never come. I would soon know Jack's experiences firsthand.

I bent over ill, attempting to pull air in through my nostrils. Trying to calm myself to think clearly. I couldn't see my hands in the darkness when I waved them in front of my face, as if I were bodiless, floating in a sensory deprivation tank, in the abyss I feared. As if I was nothing but a flicker of light that had burnt out and now I belonged to nothingness. Condemned to eternity in a void I couldn't escape.

What was going on? My Father— how was my father connected to Eyecon? I had always thought he was a pilot. I had to rethink everything I thought I remembered about my dad. The day he pulled me from my friend as we worked on a school project had replayed in my mind. One of the few memories that had made it through the forest. He had been speeding down the street, his car coming to a screeching halt in front of our house. My dad jumped out and ran inside of our home. When I followed him in, he was madly grabbing papers and shoving them into a briefcase.

"We need to go, get in the car," he frantically spat at me, pushing me out the door before I could ask any questions. His hand so firm on my shoulder it frightened me. He didn't even lock the front door. We had just disappeared down the street like a ghost in the night. Our lifelines cut, leaving all the frayed edges unwoven and tattered.

The only person who had seen anything out of the ordinary was Beatrice, a friend who was over at the house. We had been working on a school project together. And if she was even half as scared as I was, I guarantee you she had never spoken a word about it to anyone.

We had fled for the plane which my dad kept parked at a small airport. He used to take me on flights, pointing out all the little landmarks as we flew. I loved flying so much I used to want to become a pilot. The feeling had changed after the crash. *Everything* had changed after the crash. Why were we on that plane? Where were we going? And why?

I couldn't trust Victor, I couldn't trust anyone. Had things gone wrong? Had James become power-hungry and ran off to placate his cravings? Had he been trying to fly us to the lake? Had the forest happened to just swallow us, aching to fill its hunger? The only thing I knew from Victor's story was my dad had disappeared. But when we had fled, we weren't chasing someone— or something. We had been running. Had James been running from Victor? Had my father seen the inkling of Victor's demons, of the monster he would turn into?

I punched the wall. The tang of blood filled the air. I needed to be careful, I didn't know what kind of surveillance I was under. All of my attention and brainpower needed to go to creating a plan while my mind was still sharp. I needed to gather all the details before I would go mentally insane inside this dark cell. Jack showed me what would happen here. Victor, yet again, had the uptick in our game.

Yet, I didn't know if I could really trust Jack. He was hiding secrets from me. Had Jack already known who my father was? Had he given me over to Victor? Could it be true I was a trade for the safety of the Rebels?

Biting my lip to contain the anger, blood seeped into my mouth. If I did manage to get out, to escape, avoiding Jack would be a whole new ballgame. James had a hand in the Spectrum virus, and I was his daughter. Victor warned me Jack would want me dead if he realized who I was, if he found out my father was responsible for creating the virus with Victor—creating me.

My stomach ran rife with sourness. I was an original product of Eyecon, produced at the hands of a lab and perfected by the lake. And the unique process in which I was created, formulated, was the key to Victor's pursuit. But it was information I refused to give up, no matter how long he kept me caged.

I drifted between incessantly planning and sleeping with my back in the corner of the room, too afraid to sit in the chair which resembled a dentist's recliner. Jack's memories had been a little too real for me to lay in that same chair.

Light flooded into the room as the door opened. A long stretch had passed. I wasn't sure how much time had gone by because the minutes felt excruciatingly long. It could have been weeks, or days, or even just hours.

My eyes adjusted to reveal a guard standing in the opening of the threshold.

"Let's go," he announced. I didn't want to follow him, but I knew it was better than staying in this hole. Anything was better than being locked in the darkness.

As I walked behind him, I thought about where we were surely going. He was likely taking me to Victor so I could beg for absolution. Perhaps Victor would lash me in atonement. There was no number of whippings I wouldn't take to keep hold of my secrets. They were all that was left of me. If I let them out, I would be surrendering everything. The secrets of the lake— of the virus. And Victor would find some way to twist my words, to make me question reality once again. I would not concede to Victor.

But we didn't make the rise in the elevator to the lobby. I was puzzled to see the guard stop at the glossy sliding doors of the lab. I didn't expect to be allowed back in the lab. The guard shuffled me inside and the glass doors softly closed behind the departing guard.

The team of doctors sat around one table, all conversing with each other in whispers. There was no way I wanted to approach them, not after yesterday. Not after I threatened Emily. One thing I was positive of, I was now their enemy. Upon recognizing my subtle entrance, they quieted.

Not sure what to do, I stared at the group— a herd of bison, circled together. A few doctors shuffled from my line of sight revealing Emily, one arm in a makeshift sling and a purple face. Battered so badly, her right eye was swollen closed. My stomach dropped. Was this all because she stood up for me?

"Let's talk," her dry voice croaked. I was hesitant to step any closer. What were their motives? Maybe they were going to circle me, take revenge for what happened to Emily.

Within the awkward silence, I realized they were waiting for me to join them at the table. Reluctantly, I took a seat.

Emily's eye stared at me, dialing in on my face. "We're in."

"In?"

"Destroy the research and get out." The words were barely discernible as they left her cracked throat. I looked around the room. Weren't they watching? listening to us? This had to be another sort of test. Lincoln noticed my uneasy body language. "Cameras mean they'd have to relay the footage on their network to monitor us. Nothing about this project is on their network."

"Why now?"

"Do you see what she looks like?" Lincoln pointed to Emily. She raised her hand to quiet the rumble through the group.

"I never quite realized the tenacity Victor had towards this project. There are no lengths he won't go. I'm not willing to participate in this atrocity anymore. I believe I was holding on to hope that my family would be ok and things would eventually return to normal. I was being too human. Recently, I have been enlightened by an individual with a differing perspective." Emily uttered the words in a husky voice, referring to me.

My gut twisted. I was wary of her proclamation. Emily was Victor's favorite pet.

"Is that so?" I questioned.

"Look, you have no reason to trust me, especially after what I did to you. But we are all trapped in the same position right now. We want the same things." Emily's voice gave multiple cracks. Did we? Her single eye scanned my face, reading my reluctance. She was right about one thing at least. I had no reason to trust her. She had betrayed me once already. But, even if this was a ploy against me, I had no other options. I didn't know what to do. My mind teetered back and forth on the possibilities.

One clear truth settled over me. I had been playing the game alone against Victor, and I was losing. There were no alternative options to consider. After all, what did I have to lose at this point? I was better off having her and a team of people helping to destroy all their work and figure out an escape plan than I was on my own sitting in my cell to rot. The risk meant I was better off at actually getting out of here, of returning to Ben.

"Where do we start?"

"Lincoln," Emily hoarsely whispered, "go ahead." Lincoln rose dramatically as if giving a military briefing to a platoon.

"Before we can even think about doing anything to current data, we have to redact and correct the old archived information. This is probably the most important part. It means no matter what happens, they can't use old files to pick up where we left off.

"Larry, your division will work on reviewing stored hard copies of the earliest set of trials. The documents will need to be scrubbed of any useful information and then recreated to tell a new narrative.

"Jennifer, your team will have to work with Larry's to first figure out what that narrative is. Your team will be responsible for any data that came before the X trials. So whatever you and Larry decide will have to coincide with each other. Remember, this has to sound logical. If they bring in a new team, it needs to be able to pass for credible research that is plausible. This way it will lead them down a rabbit hole and they can't use our work to pick up where we left off.

"Emily's team— my team— we will help oversee the narrative and fix any supporting electronic documents on the drive from Trial X to Trial Y. Once we have completed scrubbing any pertinent info, we will create more misleading documentation for our current trials and research." If Lincoln was second in command, I could only imagine how Emily would sound in this situation if she hadn't had the shit beat out of her. Lincoln's banter reminded me of how Jack would direct the team of Rebels. How a leader speaks to his unit— solid directives which leave no room for questions. It begged me to reason with myself, was this quite possibly why I never questioned Jack's motives?

"Thank you," Emily said. It was unclear if the plan had belonged to Emily or Lincoln, or even between a few of the members.

"Are there any live subjects here now... for the trials?" The words scalded my throat as they left. Lincoln and Emily exchanged an expression of glum.

"There are four, one's already undergone the initial testing phase," Lincoln said. Four? Four innocent lives. Four potential Rebels... if they even survived.

"What does that mean?"

"They've been infected with the newest Spectrum variant." As the words left Lincoln's mouth, I thought I was going to be sick as a wave of sourness hit my stomach. Was this my blood, my doing? I closed my eyes for a brief moment, trying to pull in air through my nostrils. Trying to stave off the nausea. I wasn't going to ask.

"And the others?"

"They're in an induced coma, kept that way until the newest strain is finalized."

"We have to get them out with us," I said, gazing at Emily's only available eye.

"We'll figure something out," she whispered.

"It's not an option." For me, it wasn't. I couldn't leave here knowing we left them behind. "And what about actually getting out of here?" I asked the group. Emily's face turned solid.

"We were hoping you had some ideas," she offered. Murmurs and questions erupted between the group in a sea of chaos, a rapid round of pinball. *What about the access panels? Isn't there a fire alarm somewhere? I don't think they would evacuate us even if there was a fire, they'd just cut their losses.*

"Break up into your groups. We need to get the data out of Victor's hands first," Emily yelled, barely audible as it escaped her scratchy throat. But the group quickly split up and fled to the filing room. "Lincoln, you're with me, have someone else oversee our group for now."

Lincoln returned a few minutes later, waiting to hear what Emily had to say.

"We need to come up with something. Even if it's small or at its early stage. This will make the group more confident in what they're doing." Emily had a very valid point. Having even a meek plan made me feel better about the ordeal— a little seedling of hope.

"We can't lie to them, we have to be transparent while we're doing this, if not, you're going to break their trust. It only takes one to sell us out," I admitted. The thought of Jack crept into the back of my mind.

As the doctors worked, Emily acted as a judge. Researchers referred to her with questions about how to proceed. She presided over each issue, listening to all the information before drawing up her decision. It demonstrated how good she was at withholding information and playing it in her favor. How she was able to pretend she was on my side just to turn on me the second it suited her. Her commitment to this operation, to me, was questionable, but it was the only hope I had of formulating some sort of plan to escape. And I had to get back to Ben.

I spent the next few hours following Lincoln around, watching him help others sabotage information and create new faulty formulas for the trials. Lincoln spent the rest of the day showing me around the lab.

He described all the horrible events the team had partaken in. Explaining Eyecon would incinerate the bodies of those who didn't survive the trials. Those who did survive were usually released, to be recaptured for additional testing at a later point. Survivors were followed and studied to see how they would react in the real world. Most of them overdosed on electricity, killing themselves in the process. Some hybrids fell off of Eyecon's radar, making me wonder if Victor already knew where the Rebel's compound was. Jack and the others had always been so cautious, but if Victor was following released hybrids, he easily could have found the compound by now.

"Why?" I stopped Lincoln, "Why let the survivors go? What kind of information do you get if most of them kill themselves?"

Lincoln looked down, slow to respond. "It closes a decent number of some of the missing persons cases, quelling suspicion for the abnormal number of cases we have in this city. They get written off as drug overdoses. From what I know, Eyecon has paid off the city's coroner to fabricate toxicology reports in place of hybrid electricity overdoses— pretending this city has a heroin problem, not a Spectrum problem.

"Those hybrids who don't kill themselves will never talk. They'll be exploited by their government, recaptured and studied. The single thing they are most afraid of is returning to a lab. Eyecon tries to keep tabs on the hybrids that are still alive. From what I understand, it's a difficult task.

"I can only imagine if I was a released hybrid, my life's mission would be to stay the hell off of anyone's radar. Victor is oh so eager to see how these hybrids will bubble up again in the future. I think he's waiting to see how a perfect hybrid would be able to take on one of the older models." Lincoln was babbling, never stopping to check if I was still following. Although, I was.

"How do we know what a perfect hybrid is?" Did I want to know the answer?

"Guess it depends on survival rates to radiation and other such threats. That's supposed to be the real goal anyway. Victor is obsessed with this idea extraordinary special powers will also present once the virus is perfected. That he will be able to program these powers. I'm not all that convinced, but we've yet to have good survival rates for even a single round of the strain. Very few make it past the first round, even less after the second."

How much did Victor know about the powers the Spectrum virus could offer, outside of biological protections? How did Victor know what goal to shoot for? What was possible? How did he know any of it? Was there someone out there besides me that had the same powers? Was I not the wild hybrid Victor had been looking for? Or more simply, was Victor just as strong as I was? Had consuming whatever samples his lab had on hand made him just like me? And usually, the parsimonious answer was the correct one. Victor had lethal powers.

Lincoln talked about how a small number of other survivors had gone on to be some of Victor's guards. If they had the mental tenacity after infection, Victor liked to keep them around and train them up. That way he could also subject them to further testing if needed.

Everyone simultaneously began shuffling papers and closing drawers at Lincoln's order to clean up for dinner. I joined Emily at the central computer tables.

"I hope you know the team is betting on a plan," she hoarsely whispered.

"We'll come up with something, I just need some time," I reassured her, completely clueless on which direction that plan would come from or go. The rest of the researchers took seats at the tables around us. Lincoln joined Emily and me at our table.

"Any ideas, ladies?" Lincoln asked. I exhaled loudly, attempting to convey the irritation washing over me. Figuring out this plan felt like it solely rested on me. While bothersome, what was truly irritating was I kept coming up blank. Empty. I had nothing. I wish they would just stop asking me until I had it figured out. Usually, it was someone else coming up with the plan. I was just along for the ride. But look where that had got me.

Lincoln exchanged a look with Emily, displeased as she raised an eyebrow.

"I just need to get out of here. There are people I need to get back to," I huffed.

"I'm sure we can't understand," Emily snapped. Lincoln lowered his gaze to the table. This conversation was not helping his psyche or that of the other scientists whose eyes and ears had wandered over to our table.

"Do you think the Rebels would help?" I asked.

Emily coughed, surprised at my question. "Jack? You think *they* would help *us*?" Jack was supposedly their enemy... Jack was supposedly *my* enemy.

"If they haven't gotten you out so far, then what's the point?" Lincoln questioned. "Say we do get a message to the Rebels, and then what?" Lincoln shook his head. "Dani, Jack will kill you if he finds out you are James's daughter— if he doesn't already know." Victor had given me the same warning.

The doors of the lab slid open before Lincoln could finish his thoughts. Guards pushed in carts of dinner trays. We, along with the rest of the team, grabbed our food from the carts and returned to our seats. The guards left the empty carts in the lab before exiting. I kept my eye contact with Emily limited, I didn't want to give away the fact I was nervous about my proposal.

"We aren't doing this, involving them," Emily commanded, "The risk is too large. Even if we could find a way to send a message, we would be relying on outside people with limited information to devise a rescue mission. We would be inviting the devil in." She used her fork to stab a potato on her plate as she spoke, "No way. We don't have any control or say, and we don't even have any two-way communication. And not to mention... *Jack?* We can't trust him. He wants to take Eyecon down, not save those who are responsible for turning him into a hybrid. Not happening."

I pushed my food away from me, resting my head on the tabletop. The electricity of the table tingled where it met my skin.

"What now?" I asked.

"You come up with a new plan," Emily said. I groaned.

She was right. I was so desperate to get out of here and get back to Ben I wasn't thinking clearly. If Jack wanted me dead the way everyone explained it to me, he wasn't going to break me and the rest of the scientists out of jail, nor would he allow the Rebels. We needed a foolproof plan.

Chapter 23

Warm

"You know, I didn't expect them to let you out," Emily admitted.

"I think Victor's trying to convince me he isn't the monster I know he is. He wants something more from me so he's trying to play nice," I proposed to Emily.

Lincoln was busy overseeing the doctors destroying their research. Emily still wasn't back to one hundred percent, so instead, she hung back at her workplace and answered questions that occasionally arose. She jotted down notes on some official-looking documents as we spoke.

"Where did the original samples of the virus come from?" I knew the likely answer, but what I wanted to know was how.

"We don't know," she admitted. It seemed like no one knew anything. As if everything went downhill after my father had left. Or maybe he had jumped ship just in time to escape. I guess the irony is he never did escape.

"Emily, you worked with my father, what happened?"

"James was the first to discover the virus sometime after his wife left him." Emily's eyes steadied on my face as she spoke her words. "We never knew where it came from. I think James had an inkling of what Victor's plans would turn into. When James left, Victor became irate, paranoid, and locked us down. We all kind of assumed Victor had killed James for his defection from the company." There was silence between us. Emily shifted awkwardly on her feet. I trained my eyes on the floor, focusing on my dry swallow. Trying to not let the emotions overtake me.

"He was a good man, Dani," Emily said. "I never met your mother."

The doors to the lab slid open, allowing in a guard. Lincoln made quick to look busy. Emily and I remained at her workspace, waiting for the guard to approach.

"Mr. Crowe is ready for your progression notes," the guard said. Emily winced. Victor still wanted progress after he had just ordered the crap beat out of her.

"Ms. Colburn will be taking them today," Emily hoarsely said. Me? I didn't know anything about this. I stared at Emily in shock.

The guard gave her a long look, questioning her motives. He scanned her battered face, looking into the only eye of Emily's available. "Scared?"

"You want progress? I'm in no condition to deliver the progression notes, and my team has been without its lead. We can manage without Ms. Colburn for the next while," Emily said in an irritated manner, awkwardly adjusting her arm in the makeshift sling.

Oh, she was a good card player. What better way to appear to be batting on Victor's team than to deliver the updates to Victor himself? And if I didn't know anything about the research, I wouldn't have to answer any questions about the progress— or lack thereof. Emily wouldn't risk having to lie to Victor's face. Not after the experience she endured at his orders. She was sending me to apologize to Victor for my bad behavior. My stomach churned thinking of his vile words as he would try to twist something out of me.

Emily extended her good arm to me, handing me a folder, "Thank you, Ms. Colburn," she barely muttered, selling her facade to the guard ever so more.

"Let's go." The guard pushed my shoulder towards the door. I wasn't sure what I was going to do or say. I was escorted into the elevator which was locked by an access pad. He swiped his hand over it and the doors opened.

I focused on the details of our journey. Trying to learn how things were laid out, looking for weak points. I pretended to open the folder, fraudulently skimming the information in front of me, attempting to give no clue I was consuming details about my surroundings, looking for potential escape plans. Now that I was being held captive, my opportunities to get a good look at the upper levels which led to freedom were limited. I had to be as observant and inconspicuous as possible to devise a plan.

The elevator only had three buttons for floors, G, B1, B2. I thought this must have been for the ground floor and two basement levels. What was on the other lower level? The one besides our sleeping quarters and the lab. The guard pressed the button for the ground floor and the elevator rose. So did the vomit in my stomach as we started our journey, getting closer to Victor again.

When the doors opened, we were in the lobby with the large atrium overhead. The guard gestured for me to exit the elevator. I complied. Following the guard across the large open marble floor. We were headed to another set of elevators, the ones I had taken twice before to meet with Victor.

Anxiety flooded my system, the electric pulse growing into a monster inside my stomach, one beat at a time.

People bustled around the lobby, crossing the large floor and disappearing down different hallways. I wondered what their jobs were, questioning if they knew about the Spectrum project— if they knew how many people were locked away right beneath their feet. I could scream out loud right here. Spill Victor's secrets as quickly as I could. Sound the alarm on my captivity. Alert them all to the atrocities of Eyecon.

But I didn't do any of that. Who knows what the outcome would be. Would I incite chaos? Anger? Fear? Or maybe they would just look at me indifferently as if I were a madwoman talking about the voices in my head.

We approached the elevators which reached the upper levels. As we rode, my nerves started to dance. We were going to the very top floor, to Victor's office. We exited the elevator into a hallway ending in a very large door. The guard knocked twice, waiting for a response. The door opened, beholding Victor in its frame.

"Ms. Colburn, what a pleasant surprise. Please do have a seat," Victor said with an eager grin, turning to allow me to pass. The bile rose from my stomach and into my throat. Play the part, Dani. This was supposed to be an apology for my behavior. I obeyed Victor and crossed the room.

Victor closed the door behind us, leaving us alone in his office. I held the progression notes on my lap as I crossed my ankles in a black leather lounge chair. Victor took a seat in the chair next to me. I had never been more grateful for a side table that separated us an extra foot or so.

Victor leaned back, placing his ankle over his knee. He swooped up a tumbler from the side table which contained an amber liquid, tipping his glass to me in invitation.

"No, thank you," I softly declined. "Another good occasion?"

Victor chuckled, reminiscing over our last conversation here in his office, the one where he decided to cage me.

"Your father enjoyed whiskey. Thought you would have taken a liking to it." Victor smacked his tongue against his teeth, making a clicking sound. I swallowed as the bile in my throat burned.

"I am not my father."

"Indeed you are not," he laughed, a little too relaxed.

I extended my arm to pass Victor the folder. "Here are the notes." He raised his hand and shooed them away.

"I'm not naive. I know you think I am some kind of monster," Victor confessed, "But I'm not all that different from you." Victor looked up just in time to catch the expression I let slip out onto my face.

"We are not the same."

Victor let out another easy laugh, swirling his whiskey in his palm. He let the words set among us for a moment.

"There will come a day when your power will eat you alive. And I'm not talking about the cravings." I didn't want to acknowledge what Victor was getting at. But I did know one thing for sure, we were not— and never would be— the same.

"You ever wonder what your mind is so hell-bent on running from?" He asked. My jaw went stiff. I tried to not move, to not let Victor in on the fact his statement was correct, how it had hit home. Victor gazed at me, using the silence to coax me into talking.

"Hard to keep all those emotions at bay," he said, "The tickle in the back of your mind, the one that tells you trouble is on the horizon, it's not telling you about the dangers of others. It's warning you about the danger of *you*. Perhaps that's why you so foolishly thought running was going to save you."

I rubbed my hand across the back of my neck, trying to stifle the anger, to not let Victor win my words.

"One day, you will realize that the monster you feel inside... is *you*. And it has been, this whole time. It's been growing, and it's power-hungry, and it will consume you."

"I will never be like you," I slid through gridlocked teeth. Victor tossed the rest of his whiskey down.

"Listen," he exhaled, "The world is going to change, and you can either ride the wave or get caught in the undertow." The rush of anger pushed me to my feet. "I'm offering you a hand here," he said, "you are James's daughter."

The words snarled from my lips. "I don't want your pity."

"Oh, here come those untamed emotions," Victor chuckled as he rose to his feet to match me.

"I'm capable of handling myself," I spat.

"We both know that's not true." So much of me hated that Victor was calling me out, telling my facts, but he was also trying to get in my head, and I couldn't let him play me like this.

"Life has presented you with a gift. We can save the world, save humanity before they even have to suffer. Climate change will cost more than just our environment, it will cost us everything. You think these natural disasters have politicized us thus far? Wait until the solar flares and thermal radiation wipe us clean. Humans, not just humanity."

Victor spoke as if he was doing the world a favor. As if he was saving people from the ensuing harm. As if he wasn't subjecting innocent people to suffering— Creating hybrids, locking up researchers, destroying lives. "You ever hear of the Fermi Paradox?" I shook my head. No, because that required being an intellectual. "It begs to reason why we are alone in this universe. And you know what the answer is?"

Again, I shook my head, not knowing where he was going with this. "It is the nature for intelligent life to destroy itself. You see, we caused the climate change disasters, created the coming rise in solar and thermal radiation. But, there are simply too many of us to take control of the unstable conditions we have caused, and we are rapidly spiraling into chaos. If we waste this precious time, letting the collective dally in their decisions, their bureaucracies, we will fail in an inevitable self-annihilation of humanity.

"But Ophelia, imagine what we can conquer if we can just confront our own flimsy limitations, if we can transcend into a world where we don't operate under the burden of fear, if we can give in and harness the power we can unlock within us."

Victor swept his curled fingers down the side of my face, smoothing a stray hair. Blood seeped into my mouth as I bit the inside of my cheek. "Ride the wave, Ophelia," he almost whispered, "Things are going to start changing very rapidly. And let me tell you what happens in the undertow. You drown."

"You're asking me to join you?"

"I'm telling you that you'll look back at this opportunity and be disappointed you declined. This is where you belong. When that darkness consumes you, I can teach you to be great, Ophelia. But I need the source of the virus." Victor softly exhaled, then whispered, "*You* could save the world."

"I will never become like you. I will never give you the source of the virus. And I surely will never take up a position in your army." Victor snatched my wrist, pulling me close to him as my body tensed. I pushed my face away, trying not to look at his two black lifeless pits mounted on his face, the darkness in his eyes.

"Let me tell you something, you ungrateful bitch," Victor's breath was hot, the smell of whiskey rolled off his tongue. "You are only alive because of my grace."

"Looks like *you've* really learned how to tame those emotions," I said. I didn't care what the consequences of my words would be. He was a vile man, and he deserved every cut I could carve with my word knife.

"You laugh now, but the darkness will spread inside like a disease. You will never be able to fill its hunger and you will never be able to stop it." I tried pulling my wrist free of Victor's grasp, but his fingers were wound too tight. "You will never have to hide in shame from me. So keep telling yourself you aren't like me, but I can see it on your face you know exactly what I am talking about." Victor leaned in, spewing his hot breath next to my ear. "Once you fall, it's a long way down, and you'll drag every soul you know down with you."

I tugged my wrist again as Victor suddenly released it, causing me to fall backward onto the ground. My chest stuttered. I was scared. But I wasn't scared of Victor, or whatever retaliation he had in store for my disobedience. I was afraid because he was *right*. Because I *did* know what he was talking about. I spent every waking— and sometimes sleeping— moment fighting the darkness that lurked inside.

"You're not ready anyway. You don't know yourself as well as I thought. Just playing a little game of hide-and-seek with yourself. You're just a few tragedies away from slipping over. And let me tell you, there's a blurry little line between a hero and a villain, and it's incredibly thin." It angered me. It angered me so much Victor could think he knew me better than myself. Maybe he could see me more clearly than I thought.

Victor sat back down in his black leather chair as I pulled myself from the floor. He already held another round of whiskey in his glass. I wanted so badly to kill him, to rid the earth of this pathetic scum. But what was I to do? Even if I could manage to summon a desperate blow of electricity, he was a hybrid, and my electricity would just give him power, the power he was looking for. I was weak and defenseless.

"You were right about one thing," I said, "I do think you're a monster." Even though it was a lie— Victor had gotten more than one thing right, I wanted to jab him with my words. His ego was fragile, and I hoped to crack it. Because as much as Victor saw on the open pages of my book, he had let me see him too.

"Out," he yelled in a spat of anger, "Get out."

Before turning to leave, I had to get the last words of our game. I bowed, nodding my head down toward Victor. I opened my mouth and the words cunningly fell out. "Your Grace."

Victor's whiskey glass shattered against the wall after making flight past my head. A guard rushed in, pulling me out of the room by my shoulders. Good. I hoped I pissed Victor off.

The guard aggressively pushed me back into the elevator. We descended the many floors, returning to the lobby. I was seething, trying to contain the energy bouncing like a fireball inside me, because Victor had pinpointed it, he had called me out.

He warned me about the darkness, but somewhere in me always knew there was something darker lurking within. I had always been fighting to push it back down. I was not like him. I refused to *become* like him. But perhaps it was inevitable.

Something hard smacked into my shoulder, and multiple thuds sounded as boxes hit the floor. A man in a delivery uniform had run into me. He knelt, gathering the fallen packages off the lobby floor. I kneeled to help him. The guard stood only a few feet away, waiting for me to finish, an annoyed look had overtaken his face.

"Sorry Miss," the man said. His eyes never left the floor as he gathered the packages, but his voice was all too familiar. I instantly recognized it. A bit of blond hair was sticking out from under his hat.

Ben.

"Don't worry about it," I replied, trying to keep calm. My insides bubbled, anxiety was taking over. What was he doing here? This was the last place I wanted Ben to be.

"Thank You." It felt so good to hear his voice. I had to warn him, I had to tell him about Jack. I had to tell him to get out of here and never to come back.

In the hardest thing I ever had to do, I turned away from Ben and rejoined the guard. We approached the elevators which reached the lower levels. I had to come up with something before the guard pressed the button, before I would be sealed back into the lower levels.

"I'm sorry, I have to use the restroom," I interjected before he extended his arm to hit the call button. I tried to say it just loud enough so Ben would have a chance to hear.

"There's a restroom downstairs." He leaned in closer to the button panel near the elevators, impatiently pressing the button again.

"It's an emergency, I've started my period." The guard immediately dropped his hand and turned on his heel, steering us toward the closest restroom. He walked me across the lobby, all the way to the bathroom door.

"I'll wait out here," The guard said, turning his back to the door as he waited. Without hesitation, I made a beeline for the men's door, hoping Ben was watching from somewhere, hoping no one else was inside to blow the whistle.

Once inside, I checked every stall making sure I was alone. I paced back and forth trying to soothe my churning stomach. *Come on, Ben, come on.*

The bathroom door opened. In walked Ben dressed in a delivery uniform. There was so much relief at that moment, accompanied by so much more angst. The threat to Ben's safety was all the more real at this moment. He was very much out of his bounds.

"Ben." I wrapped my arms around him. "You have to listen to me. They were expecting me at my interview. Jack isn't who he seems, he wants me dead. Get out of here and don't go back to the Rebels. You need to run." My words were falling so fast out of my mouth. We didn't have enough time.

"It's not Jack, Dani, they're trying to get in your head." Ben's hands fell tightly on my shoulders as he peered at my face. "What happened to you?" I knew he was looking at my pale skin and the dark bags under my eyes. He dragged a thumb across my cheekbone. I wasn't doing well when I left the Rebels, and it had all gone downhill after that. "We need to get you out of here."

"Ben, I want you to run. And I never want you to come back to Eyecon."

The bathroom door swung open. Shit. Shit. Shit. Four guards rushed in, grabbing Ben and me. A faint electric current tingled between our skin as they squeezed my arms, practically lifting me off my feet. Even if I could control it, blowing them with electricity was going to be useless, it was going to make them more powerful like it did Jack on the beach. I had to hold it off, I had to wrangle it.

"No, stop!" I screamed, knowing full well it wasn't going to make a difference. Ben yelled my name, his feet slopped out from under him as they dragged him across the lobby floor to the elevator. We were rushed down to the basement level, waiting just beyond the elevator door. The next time the door opened, I knew who would be standing behind it.

"Give him what he wants, Ben. Please. Tell him everything you know. Jack isn't who you think he is." I pleaded with Ben as one of the guards tried to cover my mouth. I thrashed, trying to free myself from their tight grip. All too soon, the elevator doors reopened, and standing behind them was none other than the devil himself, Victor Crowe.

I instantly regretted everything I had done moments ago upstairs.

"Ms. Colburn, you've really outdone yourself," Victor smiled, "I thought I made myself clear, I won't tolerate your little games."

"Aren't you a work of art?" I spat out through the hands still attempting to keep me quiet while I writhed about. I couldn't play nice, I wasn't capable of it while so much anger raged just under my skin. Victor plucked the folder of progression notes from a guard's hand, finally taking interest in them. His eyes fell over the pages inside, sweeping back and forth. Ben concentrated on me, waiting as if I had some sort of cue to give him. As if I had a plan. I didn't.

"Leave her alone." The words slid out of Ben's gritted teeth while the guards forced Ben to his knees. Victor gracefully smiled and approached Ben, looking down at him.

"Hm, so noble," Victor grimaced, holding Ben by his chin, rotating his face as he inspected him. "A prince, but not a hybrid."

"Let him go," I grunted over the guard's hand covering my mouth.

"Oh, one of Jack's little soldiers? Have you taken a liking to this one?" Victor pointed at Ben, electricity dancing in arcs at the end of his fingers.

No.

Victor could project his power too. How had he come to have that kind of power? It surely couldn't have been from Emily's team. They weren't able to produce hybrids of such caliber.

"I'll give you what you want if you let her go," Ben offered. I couldn't imagine what he was trying to trade for my safekeeping. Was it Jack? The lake? Or was it just a bold-faced lie?

"There's nothing you have to offer me," Victor chided, "I mean, I suppose there are a few things you could be useful for." Victor let the electricity from his hand dance closer to Ben, lapping up toward Ben's face.

"Victor, don't," I growled, "I'll kill you myself." Victor's eyes widened, then he sent his electricity deep into Ben's chest. Ben's body shook with electric convulsions as his head rolled across his shoulders. A long painful groan parted from his lips. I screamed under the guard's hand, trying to thrash free. Victor got a rise out of watching the horror in my eyes.

When Victor finally withdrew the current, Ben's head slumped even further.

"Looks like the team has made great progress with the new study of your blood," he devilishly grinned, "How's about we test the allegiance of our doctors on your friend here?"

I screamed, biting the hand over my mouth.

No. No. No.

"No!" Tears welled up in my eyes. They couldn't inject Ben. Please. No. It was surely a death sentence. And who knew what form of the virus he would be injected with now that Emily's team was working to destroy it.

"No?" Victor questioned as he rolled up the sleeves of his shirt. He wound his arm back and punched Ben's face. Again and again. Blood seeped from Ben's lip, carving a trail on his flawless skin. Victor withdrew his hands and stepped back. At Victor's orders, the guards released Ben and he slumped to the floor. Ben's amber eyes opened. He looked like a fish out of water, just lying on the concrete breathless with parted lips.

"It's ok. I love you." But I couldn't hear it over my frantic thoughts. I'm not sure if he even had the strength to say the words aloud.

Victor's heinous smile graced the world yet again as he pushed his palms out in front of him. The electricity pulsed into a stream, scooping Ben up in its grasp. A bright pulse of power thrusted Ben across the room, his body making the most awful noise as he thudded against the concrete wall, bones splintering under the force of the hit. Electricity danced across Victor's palms as he prepared to lift Ben in his electric grasp once more.

"NO!" My voice was cracking, shaking. My screams became hoarser as I begged. Begged. I couldn't hold it together, I couldn't contain the energy coiling inside of me. With a kick and a tug, I forced myself from the hands of one guard, freeing an arm. I pushed it out in front of me, engaging a full force of electric blue power pulsing from my palm and across the gap into Victor. The stream of electricity pinned him against a wall.

But Victor outstretched his arms, taking it in, welcoming the energy as a familiar expression overtook his face. The same look that had appeared on Jack's at the beach. Victor was thriving in the electricity. I knew this would happen, but at least it took the attention off of Ben, at least if Victor was focused on me, he wouldn't be hurting Ben.

And as quickly as I summoned the current, it withdrew. The stoppage made Victor open his eyes, they glistened with strands of bright blue tentacles slicing across his two black colorless pits. He was all charged up. Ben's barely conscious face filled with shock, almost terror as he witnessed the exchange.

"Wow." Victor clapped his hands. "I knew you would be quite spectacular, Ophelia. But I had no idea just how strong your powers really are." His voice was soft, flowing. I had shown Victor almost all my cards.

"Prep him for injection," Victor smiled, never taking his eyes from me, testing to see just how far I would go to save Ben. Victor wanted to see all my cards, and then he wanted me to fold them.

"Please," I begged, "I'll do anything."

"You'll do everything I ask of you," he announced. "Your little friend will be at my mercy." Victor wound back his arm as his fist danced with electric blue tendrils, punching Ben in the gut. A spray of blood met the pristine white floors. Ben's head slung forward as he gasped for air.

"Stop," I breathlessly yelled, "I'll show you the raw source!"

Victor held his hand up, signaling the guards to stop their march to the lab.

"Now, that's more like it," Victor beamed. "I think you finally understand your place in this enigma."

And just like that, I had folded my last card.

Victor paused, just before turning to leave. A vicious smile grew on his face. "Your Grace," he taunted.

The guards dragged Ben towards the lab, his legs limp. I watched, helpless as Victor followed. Thrashing about, I tried to break the grip of the guards. This wasn't happening. This wasn't happening. The walls of the hallway spun as I was dragged through them. Writhing. Screaming.

As we passed the glass walls of the lab, I could see the faces of the scientists, struck with fear. Ben was held by a guard while the other bashed and pounded him with endless punches. Emily turned her eye away from the scene, from Ben's battering. She watched me as I screeched in horror. I ceaselessly fought to break free from the guards as they dragged me to my cell. I twisted my arms, kicked my feet, tried everything to break free of their grasp. They pushed me down into the medical chair. One guard placed my arms into restraints attached to the chair.

I pulled and pulled, but I wasn't strong enough to break his grip as he latched the strap around me, imprisoning me. A fist made contact with my face, creating stars in my vision. Before my other arm was locked into the strap, the cold sharp metal of the syringe was on my neck. I tried to kick the guard who held the syringe. I thought I had hit him, but I was out, everything black again.

I didn't know how much time had passed when I woke. The only light in the room flooded in from the open cell door, proving it hard to make out his face. Victor sat on a stool near the end of my chair.

"Where's Ben?" I demanded, the words slurred from my mouth.

"We made a deal, remember?" Victor grinned, all too eager to remind me of his reward, a certain sparkle in his eye.

"I won't give you anything if you don't let him go," I spat.

His smile widened. "I need a bit more information." Victor furrowed his eyebrows together, eager to hear my words. "You want to keep Ben safe, don't you?"

"It's a lake," I snarled, "the water contains the virus."

"Where?" Victor questioned in fury.

"I need confirmation of Ben's release. Alive."

"Let me be clear. If you're lying, I won't hesitate to kill him." Victor stood. "And I think I like keeping him alive for that purpose." A carrot. Jack warned me of this.

"I won't show you the source if you don't let him go. He can't stay here."

"We've already released him," Victor begrudgingly admitted, "so he can warn your little friends to back off and not get any ideas."

A screen on the wall blared so bright I could barely make out the picture through my squinting eyes. It was a video of an alleyway, black and white security footage. A door suddenly opened and a limp body was tossed out onto the alley pavement.

Ben.

He was laying there on the ground, not moving. Just lying there. Come on, Ben. Come on. And then his hand moved, and his leg twitched ever so slightly. He pulled his arms under himself, slowly pushing his body off the ground, then quickly falling back down onto his face. Finally, Ben staggered to his feet and hobbled out of sight.

It was a relief to see him alive and hopefully uninfected. But at this point, alive was all I could ask for.

Victor leaned in toward me. He pressed a thumb to my busted lip, swiping the extra blood. Victor pressed the bloodied finger to his mouth, inhaling as he lapped his tongue over his lips. A dark crooked smile overtook his face. Then he winked.

My body convulsed, I stirred trying to break free. I wanted to hurt him. But the bindings confined me to my chair. Victor chuckled in response.

"Prep the team. Get the on-call pilot here, now," Victor ordered the guards. The door to my cell slid shut, and this time, I didn't want it to ever open again.

Attempting to pull my arms towards me, I fought the straps, but they wouldn't give. I had to get out of this thing. It was like the memories Jack showed me, except I didn't have to witness it from his eyes. I finally got to experience it on my own— a caged animal.

I hoped Ben took my warning wholeheartedly. I hoped he was halfway around the world by now, hiding. I hoped he was somewhere, anywhere but here. Hell, I hoped he was even under the protection of Jack and the Rebels. Ben seemed to still be captivated by Jack, saying Jack was upset Eyecon had captured me. But it had to be an act, a great deceit, because Ben didn't know I was the reason for Jack's creation. Ben couldn't have guessed it was because of me Jack had been through the horrors of Eyecon.

Maybe Jack was so desperate to get out from under Victor, it was simply a deal he couldn't refuse. Ben hadn't been in the room when Jack said he wouldn't send a rescue team, as Jack had already planned to desert me. It was a game of *cat and mouse* and Jack had knowingly released me to Victor to secure his freedom, a trade to ensure he would never have to return to a lab, a guarantee Victor wouldn't put him back into this very same room. He made a deal for the autonomy of the other Rebels so no one would have to endure the wrath of Victor again. No one but me— a small sacrifice. One Jack was willing to pay, because I was James's daughter— I was the reason for his creation.

And perhaps I was too naive to believe Jack had figured out my puzzle long ago. All the bits and pieces he kept hidden from me, never admitted to. Maybe that's why he had ultimately agreed to hand me over to Victor. Because once Jack knew who I was, that I was created— and who I was created by— he knew I wasn't the original source of the virus, I wasn't the answer Victor was looking for. The answer to Victor's endeavors lay within the lake, and Jack knew it. How could I have been so stupid?

Jack's mind had been twisted under Victor's rule. He could see how Victor's blood kept producing blank answers in Eyecon's pursuit. Once Jack saw the lake, he knew my blood wasn't holding the secrets Victor thought I did. I wasn't wild. I was created, the same as Victor. And Jack saw that. Damn it.

Jack was *selected for commission* by Victor, and perhaps Victor had pegged Jack more accurately than I could have imagined, his dark capabilities. Victor had told him about me, and Jack had snatched me up. I thought I could trust him. I was a fool. Jack hid the truth from me, made me think I was special. I had let my guard down, let Jack chip away at my stone-cold walls. He had given me that guilty kiss, and I let him. And the worst part was, I liked it. I had felt like his other half. Like I'd known him for lifetimes. What a lie. And I had never even told Ben. Maybe Ben wouldn't have come to Eyecon had he known.

Jack had given me to Eyecon in just the way Victor had claimed. I could see it now. Jack hated Eyecon. Hated. I was a part of that messy creation, connected to it. Jack wanted me dead, and he wanted to keep the lake's secrets out of Victor's hands. He wanted to appease Victor in a way that would keep himself, and the raw source of the virus, out of Eyecon. It was nothing but a win-win.

I was a fool for believing Jack had ever cared about me. A fool for thinking there was hope for a cure for me. I was an idiot to think I could just run off, slip away and pretend to start over as if my past would never catch up to me. As if Victor wasn't bound to find me. It was a lie. *Everything* was a lie. And I was stupid enough to believe it. Victor was going to get his way. He was going to figure out how to make his stupid perfect hybrids programmable. There was little hope I would ever be leaving Eyecon.

Victor expected me to take him to the lake. And once he had his hands on the pure virus, things would get ugly. He would crack down on Emily's team, forcing them to work harder.

Maybe once they perfected the virus, he would have no reason to keep them. Leading Victor to the source was a death sentence for Emily's team, for humanity, and for me. Victor would destroy everything if he got his hands on it.

All Victor wanted was power and control, and I wasn't going to give that to him. He was using Ben to dangle over my head like bait. He would hold me captive forever with the threat of Ben's life. And I surely wasn't going to join Victor.

The only way to ensure he wouldn't go after Ben was to take *me* out of the equation. It was the only way to keep Ben safe. Alive.

If there was no Dani, then there was no point in going after Ben.

I could protect him in this way. If I could just hold Victor off from obtaining the pure strain of the virus, he couldn't create his army quite yet. It would give Emily's team time to come up with an escape plan, to get away from Victor. And maybe the Rebels would have enough time to figure out how to take down Eyecon.

Noises filled the hallway, people were bustling outside my cell. I imagined the guards gathering their gear. Victor was probably over the moon learning there was a true source for the virus, and expecting me to lead him right to it. His team was shuffling in a frenzy to get ready for the trip. Stop. Stop. Stop. I had to end this.

I let the rage boil under my skin, remembering Ben's face being repeatedly bashed in by Victor. Replaying the scene of Ben's body striking the wall, wrapped up in Victor's electricity, then falling to the ground limp. Or the way Ben pathetically peeled off the ground after he was thrown on the street. The energy was bouncing around my body, threatening to rip through my skin to escape. If I could just harness it...

In an ugly quarrel for control, I edged the flow to my wrist, concentrating a swath of the energy in one spot. It was getting hot, so hot, it was burning. The smell of leather singed my nose. I pulled my wrist, tugging on the strap. It was loosening. With a final ragged push, I sent the electricity blaring as hot as I could. The strap faltered. My wrist was free.

I quickly freed myself from the rest of the straps and turned my attention to the medical machine attached to the chair. I lit the ends of my fingers up with light to see what exactly I was working with. It appeared to be a heart monitoring device and a defibrillator. This surely had enough power to get the job done. Ripping the front panel off, I exposed the electrical components. Two central wires led to the defibrillator pads. I ripped the pads from their housing, exposing the loose cords. The electricity fidgeted at the end of the exposed wires. Without hesitation, I wrapped my hands around them, letting it in. The flow rushed through my arms into me, swirling around my head, as if my feet were floating off the floor. Instantly suspended in pure bliss.

The noise from the hallway was drifting away as I sailed down a dark tunnel. As if I was back at the lake floating in its grasp. Loud popping noises were bringing me back to my cell, ringing in my ears, taking me away from my high. It sounded like gunshots, reverberating around and echoing in my tunnel of darkness as I traveled. The noise continued, but I was too busy taking my journey back to the lake water.

I let the electricity dance through me. I was fluttering away. My thoughts were flickering in my mind like a candle on the verge of being blown out. The water was so warm as the energy glimmered across my skin, forming pins and needles. The night grew darker. And Jack was there too. We were connected again in that familiar sensation. He was pulling some of my high away. Stealing some of the staggering power flowing through me. *Dani, stop.* He begged. *Stop.* But I had been through this before. Jack's voice was a warning like my father's eyes. This time I wasn't going back to reality, I refused to turn away from the warm waters. I wasn't running from my fears anymore. I wasn't going to give in to Victor's plan.

My high was peeking. I was topping out at the height of my euphoric stage. But, there was more than Jack's voice— a wave of frantic panic. Jack's thoughts were rushing through me, but I gave no input, there was nothing left for me to give. I let his thoughts, his begging pleas, linger in the last bit of consciousness I had. Letting go of the world as I knew it. Finally welcoming the dark abyss I had been desperately avoiding for so long.

Jack screamed at me, like a wave crashing down on top of me, thrusting me around in the dark water. I could feel him. I could feel everything, hear everything. I was very acutely aware Jack was somehow there. And Nate too. Nate yelled at Jack as if he were standing on the beach sand of the lake. I was experiencing it through Jack. Everything was so distant so far off. It was easier to let go this way.

And I did.

I shut off the final inkling of life, giving way to the void, the long gangly dark arms of nothingness, grasping me tighter than iron, snapping my ribs in its clutch. Slow pitiful breaths, dribbling off. I sank into its depths.

I didn't expect death to feel so warm.

Chapter 24

Hollow

She's blank. Still blank. At this rate, she may never wake up. It's my fault things ever went down like this. The thoughts were a stream of consciousness flowing through my brain for the first time, a river that flooded every crease, every fold of my brain. It was like I had only shut my eyes for a minute. As if the darkness preserved my last moments, like they were mere seconds ago.

A high-pitched ring blared between my ears. The light was so bright I couldn't open my eyes. Did I drink last night? What was this hangover? It was far more excruciating than any hangover I'd ever had before. My heart was pounding. Racing. *She's awake.*

My eyes bounced open. I squinted, avoiding the light in high doses. I was alone in my room at the Rebel compound. What was going on? *I'm on my way.* My clothes were on the floor and I was dressed in a large T-shirt with a pair of cloth shorts. My old shirt on the floor sat dirty and singed like it had been lit on fire in places. *I'm almost there.* I tried to make sense of what had happened, but my mind refused to work properly. The door to the room swung open and Jack rushed in.

Jack paused in the doorway as I stared. *What's going on?*

His face was older, the bags under his eyes made him look like shit. My brain was failing to comprehend what had happened. This certainly didn't appear to be any kind of afterlife.

I can't believe you're awake... that your brain wasn't fried. We have to keep you away from electricity. I was perplexed, looking at Jack. His expression was similar to mine, but he didn't appear to be as surprised. *I was starting to think you would never wake up.*

I stared at him, observing the distance between us. I backed away, ruffling the sheets as my back stiffened.

You're not touching me, I noted. His face watched mine, thoughtless as I pieced things together on my own. *I can hear everything in your head, almost like it's my own.* The feeling was unparalleled. Dreamlike. *I can see everything from your perspective too. I can see myself. What is going on? I don't understand how I'm here. Am I here? Am I a figment of your imagination?*

Jack stood in the doorway, staring. His mouth slightly parted as he appeared to be speechless. Thoughtless too. And before I could sort anything else out, my mind flitted to the last moments I had been through.

Where's Ben?

Jack's face went stoic, hard. His Jaw had a familiar clench to it. *There's something I have to tell you.* And before Jack could finish his thoughts, images of Ben laying in a bed with an IV drip were plastered among Jack's mind. He couldn't hide it from me. Ben looked awful, pale, pulverized. Recognizing the room Ben was in, I jumped out of bed and ran towards the door. *Dani, Samuel's revived him twice. He isn't awake.*

I have to see him. I pushed past Jack, getting into the hallway and sprinted toward Ben's room. I didn't know what was going on, nor could I piece together what had happened.

Samuel sat near him, looking at a clipboard. Ben's face was purple, almost unrecognizable. His eyes were swollen. One cheek was raised much higher than the other, matching his lopsided lips. Samuel jumped out of his seat at the sight of me, almost blocking my view of Ben as he urged me to sit.

I ignored him, kneeling next to Ben's bed as I placed my hands on his chest, sobbing. This was exactly what I wanted to avoid. Oh god, Ben's pulse. It was so weak. His soul, his essence had been sucked out of him. He was clinging to life by a thread I was so desperately hoping would pull him through. I combed my hand through his hair. He didn't look peaceful like he usually did when he slept. He was nearly unrecognizable, a lifeless body at a wake. A river of tears streamed down my face.

"Is he going to be ok?" I asked Samuel in a tone probably too harsh.

"I'm not sure. He's crashed twice already. A broken rib has punctured his lung. He's got several broken bones and I don't know he can handle it if he crashes again." Samuel wouldn't look at me. My heart shattered. I did this to Ben. It was my fault he was in this position. If I had just let him walk away after our run-in on the lobby floor, he would be fine right now. Or had I never called him to come get me the night I was caught stealing money by Jack at the ATM. Had I used some fucking common sense, I would have fled right then and there. But I was selfish, and I used him. Ben was my crutch. If I loved him the way I claimed, I should have left and never looked back. I was so selfish.

Where's Emily? Lincoln? Get them in here, they can help.

"Who's Emily?" Jack asked.

"The doctors at Eyecon, where are they?" I stood, desperately looking at Jack's puzzled face.

Dani...

"You didn't save them?"

"We didn't know," Jack admitted

"I can't even trust you! We have to get Ben to a hospital, a real doctor."

"And say what?" Jack bit back. "Samuel found something in his blood, it doesn't quite act like the Spectrum virus." I fell back to my knees next to Ben. A hollowness filled a hole right where my heart had been. The sting so vivid, it tugged at the edges of my limbs. The floor was falling out from underneath me. Who knows what Victor had infected Ben with.

"Does it matter what we say? So long as he lives, who cares what lies we have to tell?" I sobbed.

"You know we can't do that. The hospital can't do much else," Jack said, a solemn tone in his voice.

"What can we do?" I asked Samuel, trying to go around Jack, hoping Samuel would agree to a hospital.

"There isn't much to do but make sure he has everything he needs, it's up to Ben's body. The only thing we can do is try to pull him back from the edge when he's about to go over. Like I said, we've done that twice," Samuel solemnly admitted. Jack was right.

Placing my hand on Ben's chest I felt his heartbeat. It was weak, so very weak.

"What if we introduce the actual Spectrum virus?" I couldn't believe I was even considering this. But if it could help, it was worth a shot. Hybrid was better than dead. And if he was a hybrid, maybe I could give him energy.

Jack's face twisted, full of sorrow. "He isn't healthy enough to fight it, It would kill him, Dani." Awful images filled his head. We both knew the first dose only had a ten percent survival rate. We didn't know what this strain was, but of course, it wasn't the Spectrum virus as we knew it, because Emily's team had likely destroyed it. Ben was infected with a false mutation, for better or for worse. And I hoped so badly it was for the better.

I pushed the smallest dose of electricity into Ben as I monitored the screen. Maybe I could help him. Maybe I could control it.

Ben's heart sputtered wildly.

"What are you doing?" Samuel's eyes glossed over with concern.

Dani, stop... Jack begged. Ben's pulse didn't respond how a hybrid's would have. The electricity didn't give him strength, it didn't improve his heartbeat.

"Dani," Jack whispered, gently pulling me up and away from Ben.

I was embarrassed to think I even considered infecting Ben with the actual Spectrum virus. Samuel's expression filled with sorrow. There was nothing more I desperately wanted than for Ben to be ok. Ben had yet to find his 42— his meaning to life, his purpose. Whatever 42 even was, this surely couldn't be it. We were supposed to figure it out, find it together I thought.

I was weakening, crumbling. This would have all been for nothing if Ben didn't pull through.

I jumped to my feet, making my way to the exit of the room. I punched the wall with all my might as I pushed past the door, leaving a large hole that matched the feelings inside. I was a thousand shattered pieces.

All of Jack's thoughts were there, racing through his head, racing through *my* head. I just wanted it all to stop. Wanted the walls to stop spinning.

Dani, wait. He followed me down the hallway. And I couldn't help but feel I had just traded cages, back into Jack's grasp.

Get out of my head, Jack.

"Wait," he said, a sting pulsing through him.

"You traded me to Victor. You gave me away like an object." This was the first time I was able to confront Jack, to tell him I knew about the game he was playing. To call him out on how he was sitting at both sides of the table, lying to all the Rebels. "And then you gave Victor Ben."

"You think I'm working with him? Do you even know me?" Jack was taken aback.

"No, obviously I don't. But, *he* knew you. Victor also knew I was coming, Jack. The moment I stepped foot in that building, they all knew who I was. I pushed my angry finger into Jack's chest.

"And you think that's because of me? I warned you of this." His anger rose at the accusation.

"Were you just following orders? Or did you betray me?" My words ripped from my mouth in an ugly snarl. Jack's wide eyes stared at me in disbelief. "You are a hybrid because of me. *You* were his plan, Jack. *You* were *selected* for commission."

"Don't waste your time telling me things I already know," Jack snapped, taking an angry step back.

"After you got what you needed from me, you couldn't wait to pass me off to Victor. Did you get tired of playing the martyr? Do they know? Do the Rebels know you willingly gave me up? You intentionally hunted me down, and then used me just like Victor." Yes, Jack. I knew. Victor had told me all the details and I had learned enough to fill in the rest of what I needed to know. My fists wound tight as the words left my mouth. The anger was giving rise to the electricity sitting in an ugly tangled ball in my stomach.

"Were you following orders?" I repeated.

"I don't report to Eyecon," Jack said, ignoring most of my questions.

"So you knew," I chided, "it was a trade." I bit my lip, pulling my fingers back through my hair. The anger bubbled in the pit of my stomach, overthrowing the hole in my chest.

"I wasn't working with them," he admitted, "I never did. But my instincts told me to play along If I didn't want to end up dead."

"Maybe that would have been better for all of us." I stabbed him with my words. I felt it, his internal flinch, the pang of hurt which flooded through him.

"Look, when I found out about you, I knew I had to find you first. If Eyecon got ahold of you, it would have ruined everything. Are you kidding right now? They tried to get me to work for them and when I refused, I was subjected to another round of the virus. I was only released because Victor wanted to see if I would comply with their wishes out of fear. So I pretended. I pretended like I was doing what they wanted, Dani. But the reasons for doing the things I did weren't theirs. I never worked for Victor. "

"Then why did you ever let me go into Eyecon?"

"I told you not to go."

"You also told me you wouldn't come for me when things went south. You knew exactly what would happen," I said. The frustration in Jack's thoughts was building. His anger beginning to match mine. "And when Victor wasn't getting what he wanted from me, you gave him Ben to hold over me."

"You volunteered. We needed more information so we could make a real plan. *You* volunteered for that. I didn't want you to go, Dani, you know what that did to me? When you were gone? I thought you were dead. And If you weren't, I thought you were in fucking hell. And so did Ben."

"And you let Ben go? Let Victor get a hold of him? Do you know what that's going to do to *me*? Why would you do that? Why would you send *him* into Eyecon? And I thought *I* was selfish." I ripped the words out of my mouth, making them as sharp as I could.

"Did you want to be left there? At Eyecon? Looks like you were doing real well when we walked in. *Real well.* Or did you forget?" Jack sliced back. Turning the argument towards me.

"How did you even get in?" I quickly channeled the anger from Jack's reminder of me trying to end myself back onto him.

"Not without blood on my hands." I watched as he replayed the event in his mind. Watched as Nate shot a guard in the back. The guard crumpled to the ground.

Only small bits and pieces were coming through, like a film strip riddled with holes. Images in the wrong order. He was trying to withhold it from me.

Show me it all, you owe me, I told Jack as he tried to hold back.

"Like saving your life wasn't enough?" he bitterly said.

"I wanted to die, Jack. I was protecting Ben. And I was stopping Victor from getting the real virus. I was accomplishing *your* mission."

"Why don't you see it, Dani? Ben was already infected with who knows what. And he already had the living daylights beat out of him, whether you killed yourself or not! Victor only let Ben go so he could use him against you later. And, even if you killed yourself, Victor would never let Ben live. Ben's associated with the Rebels now and he knows what's happening at Eyecon. Even without the source, it's a matter of time until Victor gets it all figured out. He'll come for all of us to settle his game."

"Show me, Jack," I demanded.

Like I'd be able to hide it from you forever anyways. Gus found a flaw in their system, I guess their sub-ground floor isn't as secure as the rest of their building.

Jack showed me how he and Nate had killed four guards as they made entry into the service door which Ben had been thrown out of only hours earlier. Jack's heartbeat raced in my ears. I could taste the dense amount of fear that had laced through Jack's mind. The tension in Jack's body increased every time he interrogated people with the barrel of his gun. Every pounding step he had taken reverberated through his memory as they rushed the lab, shooting through the glass doors to enter. Emily's face was horrified because she recognized him. She had known instantly of Jack and didn't know what to make of his traits: Defiant, Oppositional, High-risk.

Emily pleaded with Jack, trying to explain as quickly as she could that her team was being held hostage by Victor. It was evident Jack hadn't believed it. He hadn't cared. As far as Jack was concerned, these were the people who had administered his death serum. His finger rested over the trigger of the gun as he held Emily in his sights.

Emily didn't want to give up my position, but then Jack turned his weapon on her team and she was forced to. And for a moment, he debated on mowing them all down with the clicks of his gun. A lurid piece of Jack I had not wanted to see. A part of Jack that confirmed he was more than capable of working for Victor, of turning dark if it suited him. He too was holding off the monster in his head.

As Jack turned to leave, Emily commanded her team to take shelter in the archive room. Two more guards raced down the hall. Jack took a shot, successfully downing one, holding his weapon high as he approached the second.

"Put it down and you'll live," he said. The guard obeyed. Terror was written across the guard's face as he scanned the lifeless body of his colleague lying on the floor. "Take me to cell four," Jack commanded. The guard complied and led the way down a dark row of holding cells as Jack pressed the barrel of the gun deeper into his back.

"Open it." The guard waved his hand over the access pad, and as the door slid open, Jack shot him. In a violent jolt, the guard thudded to the floor, blood gurgling from his mouth as he took his last breaths.

In the back of that dark cell, laying on the ground had been me, convulsing in pain with my hands wrapped around the wires of the heart monitoring machine. Jack's emotions ripped wildly through him as he dropped his gun, gaping a large empty hole in his chest. A pit in his stomach, an empty static had taken over his body. He lurked towards me, wanting to rip me out of the clutches of the electricity. His mind teetered between scenarios. My skin was pale, translucent as a plastic bag as I lay limp and lifeless, only stiffening through electric convulsions.

"No!" Nate yelled. Jack had known touching me would capture him in the electric deadlock as well, but there was part of Jack that knew I had been so close to sinking to the bottom of that lake and never resurfacing. He had thought if he could divert enough energy, to save my brain from frying, maybe he could save me, maybe he could buy enough time before it was all too late. So he reached out and grabbed me, pulling me into his lap, wrapping his arms around me, and clutching me to his chest.

I flinched, making the realization that Jack was in my death dream because he was there in the flesh. He wasn't some figment of my imagination. He wasn't a pretentious warning. He was real.

"How'd you stop it?" I asked.

"Turns out there's an emergency power switch, probably for similar hybrid situations," Jack said, "Nate found the switch in the hallway just in time. So I guess it's him you should thank anyway."

"And now what?" I asked, ignoring his snide remark about being thankful.

"What do you mean?"

"I mean, I have to live with you being inside my head like this?" I said.

"You know, I hear every thought you have, feel every emotion that runs through you, Dani," Jack said, "When you were blacked out, I could feel all your emptiness, listen to your hollow heartbeat, feel the black hole you're trying so desperately to cover up. It's not like I asked for that either."

I jammed my teeth down on my lip, so hard I nearly drew blood as I tried to not show Jack how deep the blow had hit.

"As soon as he wakes, we're out of here. I should have never gotten involved." I turned on my heel and stalked back to Ben. I was certainly going to sink without my lighthouse. I re-entered the room, sitting on the edge of Ben's bed with a hand resting on him. I waited patiently until I calmed down enough to feel the dull pulse barely beating beneath his skin. This was all too much to handle right now. He needed to be alright. I needed to know Ben was going to come out the other side of this.

Sorry, I know I hurt you, Jack said. *I wasn't following orders and I didn't betray you, Dani.*

I put my head down. Jack didn't say anything more.

I was forced to accept the biggest indicator screaming Jack hadn't betrayed me. He had infiltrated Eyecon and saved me.

He had saved *me.*

And he had taken Ben in, trying to help him. Ben had invaded Eyecon to look for me, to confirm I was alive, I knew Jack was a part of that plan. If Jack had given me up to Victor, why would he have let Ben go after me? Jack wouldn't have come to my rescue, and surely not Ben's if he was working in conjunction with Victor.

The only reason Jack let me go, was because we were out of options, and we were betting on Victor not knowing who I was yet. And we had bet wrong.

I welcomed the silence, yet Jack still sat somewhere in my mind, waiting for me to respond. Waiting for a signal things would be ok between us. I gave in. Juggling all these issues made me believe holding over on Jack wasn't going to change or help any part of our situation. We were even after all. Both of us had saved each other from an overdose. This was a fight I was begrudgingly going to have to put to rest.

Thank You, for getting me out, I thought. My version of a half-assed apology.

I'm sorry, a shudder ran through Jack, *I'm sorry for not getting you out sooner.*

Had Jack gotten me out sooner, had he never allowed Ben to go into Eyecon after me, maybe things would have turned out differently. But Jack wasn't the only one who kept making decisions that hurt people. I too was guilty of the consequences of my actions.

A shiver ran down my spine as I swiped my hand across Ben's cheek. It pained me to think about losing him. I would be losing my lighthouse, I would sink and drown without him.

I imagined somewhere warm. Somewhere far from the forest, far from the landscape which held me captive and changed me into this monster. Somewhere where the people were nice and didn't ask too many questions. Some little pocket of the wild west desert or warm sands of a beach in Mexico where I could recreate myself. I prayed this could still be a possibility. That Ben would get better and he could be with me. That we could start fresh. It was so selfish because the option to run and hide had been made for him. I had done this to him. I had sucked him down into this world. I was at the center of Ben's world and I didn't deserve it. I had never deserved it.

That had become especially apparent while we had been out walking to dinner one evening. I had expected his eyes to linger on her far longer than they did. But Ben's gaze returned to me so quickly and in a way I knew he hadn't even noticed her, truly noticed her. Ben's features were stunning, and he never failed to capture the attention of every woman that ever looked his way. But somehow, he only had eyes for me.

She had 'accidentally' tripped and fell into Ben as she passed us by. Ben reached his arm out and gracefully caught her from falling. He asked her if she was ok, to which she quickly nodded yes, pretending to be more bashful than she was.

Then, as if nothing happened, Ben returned to our conversation right where he left off while we picked up walking again, leaving the woman standing in confusion. She was beautiful, and clearly, she had been expecting more interaction than what she received.

"That was weird," I said.

"Hm?"

"That woman,"

"It's like this city purposefully neglects their uneven sidewalks. Happens more than you think," Ben confessed.

I had simply just smiled and slid my hand into his as I peeked back to see the woman saddened her maneuver hadn't garnered the attention she had been looking for.

That's why I didn't deserve Ben, because, for some unbeknownst reason, he was centered on me. And If I cared for him so deeply, I would have never involved him. Ben would have been better off had I made it out of town before he ever noticed I was gone. Because just as Ben had never seen her, he had never seen me.

Ben deserved a girl who could fill a conversation the way he could. A girl who could engage with him the way he deserved, to help him grow. Instead, he was too busy holding me together. Fixing me. If I would have just let him go...

If I loved him, I would have let him go.

Chapter 25

Suits

I never left Ben's side except to get my meals from the cafeteria. Even eating was rare. It had been days without a proper shower. My body ached from the worry I put it through every day, and I slept like shit. There was no sign of Ben getting worse, yet, he didn't seem to be getting better. Every time his fever would spike, Samuel let me hold a cold rag on his head and chest— pretty much the only thing we could do at this point. Samuel made sure to keep Ben hooked up to an IV bag with plenty of fluids. I was dying for his eyes to crack open. Dying to get him back. Would he be the same? Would he be a hybrid? Would he even survive this?

There were so many questions that remained. How could Jack not have saved Emily's team? Did Emily think I had betrayed her? That I had come up with a plan and left her team out of it? Had I never succumbed to Victor's lies, had he never crushed the bug, would things have gone differently?

What else did Emily know about my father? So many questions were swirling, and there were zero ways to find answers to them. Fretting over them was senseless. At least I told myself that so I didn't have to feel guilty about confronting the tsunami of anger and helplessness.

I had daydreamed about Ben. About him waking up. About the things I would say to him, the questions I would ask him.

"Dani," Ben croaked with a sigh of relief. I kept my eyes on the floor, too nervous to look. How could I look at him? This was my fault. I smiled, slowly looking up to see his face. I missed him so much. When my eyes met Ben, his lips parted in disbelief. The moment stretched on before Ben said my name again, "Dani," but it was in that pitiful kind of way. I hated that. "Are you ok?"

"Are *you* ok?"

Ben barely nodded as I sat on the edge of his bed, the exhaustion plastered on his face. His cheekbones had fallen flat and pale with dark bags under his eyes. He looked thinner, part of his collarbone protruding more than usual. Not in a way anyone else would notice, because they didn't know Ben like I did.

"A lot has happened, Ben," I tearfully said, "I wish I'd never put you into this situation."

"I volunteered, Dani," he admitted, "if it meant seeing you one last time, it was worth it. I couldn't let you go knowing I did nothing." There was another long pause as the guilt made its home atop my chest, bearing down, threatening to let the tears loose. "It's only up from here then, huh?" Ben barely croaked out with a soft smile.

Gently, I squeezed his hand. His pulse was the strongest since the incident, but nowhere near normal. He was still so weak. He was awake, but he still wasn't out of the woods.

I traced my fingers over his protruding collarbone. "I had planned to run."

"From me?" Ben questioned. He reached up, wrapping his hand around mine.

"Yeah, before you got all tangled up in this," I admitted, "I knew it was only a matter of time, and I wanted to protect you." Ben watched me.

"It wasn't supposed to end this way," I finally choked out. Ben's eyes traced over all my parts, looking at my hair, my worn face, my pale skin.

"I never want you to leave," he whispered, "so where shall we go?"

Pain clutched my heart.

Because it wasn't real.

It was all in my head.

My brain wanted answers, so it started wishfully creating them. I needed to stop the daydreaming because it meant I wasn't preparing myself for both possibilities. Ben would either wake up, or he wouldn't. And that was that. I was only hurting myself more if he didn't pull through.

During my time with Ben, I spent the day listening to everything Jack. Not that I could help it, everything was there in my head whether I liked it or not. It took more energy to focus on tuning him out than it did to just let Jack's mind play in the back of my head. It was like a loudspeaker, buzzing all its announcements, every trivial thought, feeling, emotion, observation. Had I had a mind of my own at the moment, I wouldn't be able to put up with it. But I wasn't competing for my own attention. Nothing of any value was taking place in my empty head.

I learned Jack and the team had been failing to come up with a plausible plan. One that wouldn't get his whole team killed. Eyecon was an industry leader in cybersecurity. Even if we could get in, it wouldn't be undetected. Jack and Nate had already exploited the hole in the system Gus had found. Jack had played his only card by saving me. A stupid mistake. Ben should have never been at Eyecon. Jack should have counted his losses and stuck to his words. No rescue mission. End of story.

Let's go, you need to get out of here for a while, Jack thought. *Meet me at the vans.*

Where are we going?

Don't worry about it.

The canyon? I asked, *are you actually going to kill me this time?* I could feel Jack smile and hear a slight chuckle under his breath even though I was at Ben's bedside and Jack was in the computer monitoring room. A Rebel gave Jack a sideways glance after hearing him giggle at seemingly nothing. And then I felt the bout of embarrassment ping quickly through Jack.

Ben had been somewhat stable for a couple of days now. And Jack was right. I needed to get out of the compound for a bit.

"Samuel, please call, if anything happens at all. I'll be with Jack. Seriously, if anything changes even by a micron, I want to know," I ordered.

Samuel nodded in agreement. I took a long look at Ben. Trying to fathom how he was even still here for the moment, his face still so puffy and swollen. The bruising had turned from a deep purple to an ugly mixture of yellow and green, making Ben look dead. Like a monster or a zombie or something. But it was progress.

The car ride was annoyingly intense. I tried to keep my mind calm to hide everything I could from Jack. This meant I could hear all of Jack's driving decisions. Drop in on all his wandering thoughts. As if I were trapped somewhere with an old lady who never stopped talking. It was overwhelmingly bothersome. When I tried to tune him out in an attempt to rid myself of the irritation, my fear of Ben not pulling through barged in. Maybe listening to Jack's banter was easier to keep distracted, and quell my intrusive thoughts.

"Have you always been like this?" Jack asked.

"What?"

"So much going on inside your head all the time. No wonder you're a mess." He pointed out.

"Can you just try to not pry through my brain? You should see what yours looks like, you old hag. Why are we going up to this canyon anyways?"

"You need a break, need to get out of the compound for a while. You've got cabin fever. Probably going to snap someone's neck pretty soon if you keep losing touch with reality like you have been" Jack bit his lip as he gazed over the steering wheel.

"Seriously?" I scoffed at him, "Maybe I'll just snap *your* neck while we're out here."

"See what I mean?" He was proud of his teasing. I rolled my eyes.

"Oh, I'm not planning on killing you this time," Jack snidely remarked. "We're not going to the canyon."

"This time? I knew you couldn't be trusted."

A grin peeled across Jack's face in amusement.

I began to recognize bits and pieces of the scenery. Buildings grew more familiar the further we drove. But I was still unsure of Jack's intended destination as his mind was focused on directions.

"Where are we going?" Part of me wished it was just a car ride. Then we could turn around and go back. Spending time with Jack felt like a betrayal to Ben. I was much more comfortable being by Ben's side not having to look at Jack's face as a constant reminder of the situation that had come about. Jack's team was no closer to stopping Eyecon, and everything... everything was in shambles.

Unfortunately, being inside of Jack's head meant I could hear all his conversations, with everyone, all of the time. Including those which occurred between the Rebels in the inner group. Jack knew I was aware of how doubt was starting to inflict his team like a fast-spreading disease. Their faith in him and the big picture was dwindling.

After I bailed on the Rebels in continuing to take down Eyecon everybody wanted things to go in different directions. The whole crew was just spinning in circles with no win in sight. And what hurt Jack the most, was his closest ally, Nate, had even mentioned he was unclear about the future of their mission. Jack was at a complete and abrupt halt.

What was Jack's real motive for leaving the Rebel's compound? He pretended it was for me, but he needed to take the edge off just as much as I did. You always had to be prepared for the worst. Even though what I wanted most was for Ben to wake up, I knew better. Life always presented the bait before the switch. Every time I wanted something, cold hard reality was there to remind me to never get my hopes up.

Jack parked the van in the lot of what appeared to be a rundown strip mall.

"How charming," I snidely remarked.

"Take it or leave it."

The bar inside offered a bit more privacy than usual. We sat at a booth instead of at the bar top.

Jack raised his drink with one hand while passing mine across the table toward me.

"My other vice." Jack nodded toward his old fashion. "Nothing says congrats on not dying like a drink. At least we don't have to pour one out for you."

"Not this time," I said. He winced and took a long draw of his drink.

"You really think that's how this is going to end?" His thumb fell across his wrist, drawing languid circles over one of his scars.

"How could it not, we glued a bullseye to my back."

"I'm not going to let that happen," he sternly said.

"Again," I corrected him. He inhaled and looked away, pulling his sleeve cuff over the edges of his scars.

He nodded at the drink in my hand. "This was supposed to be an apology."

"Forgiven," I said bluntly. He and I had yet to make eye contact as I fiddled with the straw protruding from my drink. "Did you come after me because Victor tipped you off about the ATM footage?"

"What ATM footage?" This caught his attention.

"The night you found me," I paused, exploring his inquisitive expression, "I hit that ATM twice in a row because I'd made a mistake. I had forgotten to delete the ATM footage." Jack's mind was racing with this information, as was mine. "Damn it. That's how Victor knew who I was." And Victor had just wound me up in his vindictive lies after that.

"Why didn't you tell me this before the interview?" Jack's anger rose. His mind was reeling, calculating just how stupid it was to send me into Eyecon given the new information he had.

"I didn't know the footage would get into Eyecon's hands."

"You don't understand how far-reaching Victor is, Dani. He even has the damn city medical examiner wrapped around his finger." I hung my head, feeling stupid for not thinking to tell Jack earlier. Feeling like an idiot for falling right into Victor's play. Feeling like a fool for wasting my time warning Ben to escape from the Rebels when we had run into each other at Eyecon. Had I just let him walk away.

Jack's mind was spinning too at the realization. He never would have allowed me to go into Eyecon had he known of the footage. He would never have had to break in, to kill those guards, to see me wrecked with electricity dying in his arms. I winced as the thought crossed his mind.

"How did you find me? And don't give me that 'I don't know' bullshit"

"Luck, Fate. Whatever the hell you want to call it."

"Seriously, Jack." He bit his lip, looking for an out. Debating if he wanted to answer my question. I could feel the turmoil bubbling up inside him. He tossed back the rest of his drink.

"Victor had told me about you. That you existed, what you were doing with ATMs. But they could never pin you down or figure out who you were, or when you would strike. So every second I wasn't out responding to another call, I was watching. I staked out a couple of ATMs and figured you'd hit them at some point. And if I was lucky enough I would run into you."

"How did you know it was me?"

Jack chuckled to himself, taking a long moment to look up. "How could I have not known? I could feel it, Dani,"

So that was it? Was it all just one big coincidence Jack had solved the mystery? That night of all nights? One thing was obvious, we had a unique inexplicable connection that only seemed to be getting stronger. Was it fate? Did the universe have us set on a collision course?

"My dad was Victor's lab partner," I blurted, coming clean.

He rolled the rim of his empty glass with his thumb. "I know."

"And you don't want to kill me?" I asked, drawing in a long sip of my drink.

"Your father might have had a hand in the creation of the virus, but it isn't his fault what Victor has turned it into. And it certainly isn't your fault, either," he softly let out.

This went against everything Victor and the researchers had told me. Maybe Victor hadn't pegged Jack all that accurately after all. "You're sure you don't want me dead?"

"Far from it," he sighed, "although I'm sure you'll test my limits and I'll question that decision."

"How very charming."

Jack cracked a smile. After a few seconds, it faded, giving way to a softness.

"Are you parting ways once Ben is back to good health?" he asked. I knew he felt the tangle inside me. I wanted Ben to be back in good health. But I couldn't say that aloud. I couldn't let the universe hear and conspire against me.

"You don't want me to go," I said, partially a question, but I knew the answer.

"You know how I feel." A sternness washed away his gentle face, "And I can tell you want to hold your boot on my throat and watch me squirm." It was true. And part of it wasn't.

I didn't want to hurt Jack, I didn't want to watch him squirm in pain. But there was part of me that wanted to hear him awkwardly ask me to stay. To tell me I fit in, that I had found my place. But the truth was I had never had an anchor before, just a lighthouse. And I was a fraughtfully unfit sailor.

I was dying to get out of this conversation, to change the topic. Everything still felt so new, so different since I had been plunged into this world where I wasn't the only hybrid.

"I'm so sick of how everyone looks at me."

"I know," Jack sighed. I expected to feel pity run through him, but instead, I felt a warm tenderness. "Life has a different plan in store for you."

"You mean, Victor. Victor has a different plan for me. He knows there's a natural source of the virus. He'll come for me to get his answers, to make his little soldiers." I set my glass down a little too harshly, nearly breaking it.

"Once he figures out how to make hybrids like you," Jack admitted, "Then we'll really have our work cut out for us."

"Yeah, just wait until they're programmable like Victor intends."

"What?" Jack's eyes snapped up to look at me. Emily had told me so while I was held captive at Eyecon.

"That's the only way Victor can have his cake and eat it too. If you turn off the mind, you can control the beast. That's how he plans on taming it."

"Things are worse off than I originally thought," Jack admitted, "If he goes through with this, Victor will erase life as we know it."

"Whatever kind of new world order Victor has in mind, it will be cruel. He'll use his power to feed his greedy starving ego." I had already seen the frailties of Victor's ego, there was no length he wouldn't go to appease himself. Because he had a combination of the two most dangerous ailments, greed and self-righteousness.

"He'll start with us here in Reno and spread his hybrid soldiers like a fast-moving disease, implementing curfews and brutal laws. His hybrids will kill any challengers in the street. No trial. Just death for those who defect. He will be merciless, trust me, I've seen him at some of his worst." Jack's jaw was stone as a growl fell from his lips. One hand returned to thumbing over the scars on one wrist.

Jack's hand fell to his pocket, feeling around for his vibrating cell phone. Part of my heart sank as a hollow feeling overtook Jack. My attention focused on the call.

Is it Samuel?

No, Jack thought. His confusion intrigued me. *It's one of the officers on my team.*

I listened in on the conversation.

"Broady? What's going on?"

"Jack, you got some suits looking for you. When I said I'd cover for you, I meant like when you left a shift early or when you disappeared for a few hours at a time I'd take a couple of calls on your beat. Look, I don't want to get involved in whatever it is you're doing."

"Whoa, whoa, slow down. What do you mean suits?"

"You know what I mean. Feds. Two guys. Suits. Badges. Asking for you by name and badge number," Broady said, "I better not be getting wrapped up in this."

"No, no I promise you won't. Did you tell them anything?"

"I wasn't going to implicate myself, you kidding? No, I told 'em we occasionally respond to the same calls, but other than that, I told 'em I didn't really know you." The stress in Broady's voice was evident.

"Look, I owe you."

"Jack, I'm serious, I don't want to hear from you again. Consider this the favor you owe me." Broady hung up.

I stared at Jack as the realization set in. Eyecon was out looking for us. Actively looking for us. They weren't waiting around for our next move anymore. They were no longer playing defense. Jack had pulled the rug from under Victor and was holding his prized possession hostage. And Victor was out looking to get me back in his grasp.

Put your hood on, Jack told me. My mouth went dry. Pulling my hood up, I untucked my hair from behind my ears and pushed it further over my face than usual. *I don't know what's going on, but I know those guys weren't federal agents. We need to get out of here. Keep your face hidden.*

Nervously, I slid deeper into my sweatshirt and pulled the hood as low over my face as I could, almost over my eyes. As we walked away from our table, Jack reached up and pulled a sports cap off the wall which was intended as memorabilia. He adjusted the hat on his head, as he swung an arm around my shoulder, pulling me into him, attempting to make us look more casual, comfortable. The tingle of his touch was a bit comforting at the moment, it was familiar, expected. Something I wasn't used to having for the past few days.

Listen, if they're out looking for us, there's no telling what else they're up to, Jack told me, *Don't trust anyone.*

We were headed for the exit when I spotted two men. They wore nice suits that didn't match the run-down strip mall of the bar. One man's suit coat hung caught on a shiny piece of metal affixed to his hip. A badge. A pit in my stomach almost swallowed me whole.

Quickly turning on my heel as fast as I could, I tried to turn Jack around with me. I attempted to keep my body language as casual as possible. Jack knew what was happening before I could even get the message to him.

Jack, they're here. The thought came through to him shaky and in a panic, just as my voice would have.

Go! Jack placed his hand on my back pushing me in the opposite direction of the men. I sprinted towards the back of the bar hoping for an emergency exit. I didn't look back, but Jack did, and through his eyes, I saw the men tailing us.

"Stop!" a bartender yelled as he stepped out in front of us. I almost ran right into him. I ducked, knowing Jack was right on my heels. I already knew what Jack was going to do, I could feel it. Instead of stopping, Jack wound back his fist and punched the bartender right in the face. The bartender crumbled to the ground as we bounced over him. The fake agents pushed employees and patrons out of the way as they gave chase.

We busted out of the back doors of the bar into the alley and made a mad dash for the car. Jack fished the keys out of his pocket as we ran, the men were no more than fifty yards behind. Jack unlocked the car just as I reached for the handle on the passenger door. Once we were both inside, Jack started the engine as quickly as I could lock the doors. I caught sight of one of the men still running toward the van. The other pulled open the door of a black sedan.

In the glove box, Jack commanded. Without hesitation I pulled open the compartment, exposing a handgun. I stared at the firearm, then looked back at Jack. My mind was frozen, hesitant to touch it.

Grab it, Dani! Jack's mind screamed. The van flew down the street, screeching around corners. The gun was wrapped tightly in my hand. I could see the plan formulating in Jack's head. My eyes trained on the side mirrors, watching the Eyecon men trail us in their car.

If we can't lose them, we'll have to get rid of them, Jack thought as we slid around another corner blowing through a red light, only narrowly missing an innocent driver. The small black sedan showed no signs of slowing. Jack watched through my eyes while he kept his vision focused on the road.

My stomach bounced wildly as nervous energy built inside. My nerves and electrical circuits were running so high it was hard to control and contain the electricity racing through my body.

They're getting closer. Just as I thought it, Jack swerved so quickly I hit my head on the passenger window in his attempt to dodge cars through an intersection.

Shit, Shit, Shit, Jack was calculating the odds of things ending in our favor. It wasn't looking good. My hands itched with fire. They were so hot I could feel the power trying to peel through the ends of my fingers. It was taking every ounce of self-control I had to maintain my composure.

Jack, we have company. Barely audible were the distant sound of sirens. I could barely make out the patrol car in the side mirror weaving through traffic, catching up to us.

It has to be now before this gets too far out of hand, Jack thought. I watched the plan unfold in his mind as quickly as his hand shifted to the emergency brake. I rolled down my window. Jack simultaneously pulled the brake and turned the wheel. It was as if time slowed, like I had an infinite moment to take in the details, and I had two perspectives to view it from. As we circled, the black car screeched to a stop to avoid the collision. My view from the passenger window faced oncoming traffic as tires squealed. And I put the black car in the sights of the gun, staring.

I can't do it.

"Dani!" Jack yelled. My hand lay frozen on the gun, the metal hot in my palms as I froze with fear. For a split second, Jack considered pulling the gun from my hands.

Click, Click, Click. All I heard was the trigger pull as I closed my eyes, watching the gunfire from Jack's perspective. I was so scared my brain filtered out the loud booms of the discharging firearm as hot brass fell on my lap and the smell of gunpowder burnt my nose.

A cop car slid to a halt behind the whole mess. An officer jumped out of his vehicle, using his door as a shield, his weapon drawn.

Jack paused. And I caught the realization.

Broady.

It was Jack's coworker who he had spoken to merely minutes earlier. Broady lowered the barrel of his gun as he squinted over it to get a better look. Broady made the connection too.

Jack took advantage of the moment, flooring the gas. As soon as we were out of sight from the scene, Jack slowed to a normal speed. The easiest way to get spotted was to make a spectacle of yourself. Citizens would be calling in to report a reckless driver and the police would have a live update on our location.

"It was Broady," I said.

Jack bit his lip, his jaw was so tense I thought his teeth would crack under the pressure. I could feel the raw hollow aching hole inside him.

"If that wasn't Broady, we would've been dead," Jack lectured, "You hesitated."

"Well, it was."

"This isn't right," Jack mumbled.

The anger inside me rose, hot and lightning-fast. "Every second I spend with you, with the Rebels, every minute is a fucking risk. I need to get out of here. These people are out here looking for us, Jack! You brought *me*, Victor's prized possession, back to the compound. They're going to kill us. Has that not set in?" My words were hard, reflective of the feelings out of control inside me.

"Has that set in for *you* yet, Dani? I've been telling you this since day one. You froze. You hesitated to pull the trigger. You were going to *let* them kill you!" Jack was furious.

I wanted out and planned to run as soon as Ben was awake. I couldn't deal with the fact that every second, Victor was getting closer to us. And every person I associated with would share the target I wore. I had to get Ben, we had to get out and get as far away as possible. It had to be now. Before Victor got too close.

Chapter 26

Epicenter

Eyecon was upping their game. This was the first offensive move of many more to come. The first strike Jack had been warning about. I thought of Victor and what he would do to those men when they returned to Eyecon empty-handed— *If* they returned. Then I thought of what Victor would do to us had his men successfully captured Jack and me.

Getting away and concealing my identity was going to be a whole new ballpark. Eyecon was out in force. It was vital, now more than ever, to get as far from the situation as possible. Ben couldn't stay here. I would have to find a way to get him a new identity. Find a way to sneak off and get him some altered documents.

Jack drove in the most elaborate pattern on our way back. Avoiding anyone possibly tailing us. The tension lay thick as Jack replayed the scenario over and over in his head, scrutinizing every detail. He would never admit it out loud, but a small part of him wished we didn't have to shoot those men. But the most pressing thing on Jack's mind was Broady. The look on Broady's face when he had identified Jack. It made Jack sick to his stomach. Would Broady turn us in?

"How'd they even find us?"

"I think they're monitoring my credit card." Jack's grip tightened on the steering wheel. "We need to lock down the compound."

As we pulled around the corner to the industrial building, the garage doors rolled up. The van slowed to a stop in its parking spot when an eerie scene unraveled. Nate rushed out to meet us, breathless and red-faced. The pit in my stomach swallowed me whole. My brain activity went silent as Jack turned his phone over to reveal eight missed calls. Jack's thoughts were impeding on me. He was calculating what had happened. But, I didn't have the time to calculate. I ripped the van door open and ran towards Nate.

"Something's wrong with Ben, Sam can't get him back," Nate breathlessly spat out as I dashed past him. My feet felt like rubber, moving so fast beneath me. When I reached the room, Samuel was drawing a syringe. I didn't take stock of who was present because Ben was laying on his bed flopping uncontrollably. My heart twisted inside my chest.

"Sam, what's happening?!" I couldn't contain the fear seeping into my voice.

"A seizure, I'm giving him some medication that'll hopefully help."

Placing my hands on Ben's shoulders, I stood at the head of the bed, looking down onto his face. Fluids were leaking from his mouth. The monitor showed his heart pounding as quickly as a racehorse's hooves.

"Samuel?" I needed some fucking answers.

"I don't know," Samuel admitted. "It's not the Spectrum virus as we know it. They injected him with an extremely volatile mutation."

"What does that mean?" Samuel wouldn't look up from his work, intentionally ignoring me as he raced around recording vital signs and prepping a different set of medication.

"Get her out, Jack," Samuel commanded, sterner than I'd ever seen him.

"I'm not going anywhere!" Nate tried to pass me to Jack.

"Sam, he's crashing," Gus said, prompting Samuel to load another syringe with medication.

"I can help." I broke free of Nate's grip, running to Ben's side, grabbing his hand and wrapping it in mine.

"You can't," Samuel said bluntly, opening Ben's mouth, and pushing a tube down his throat as Ben's body brutally jostled. Ben wasn't breathing. My emotions were so uncontrolled I could no longer pick up on Ben's pulse. I couldn't differentiate between my wild heartbeat and what Ben's felt like.

"Dani, you have to let go," Jack pleaded, as I tightly squeezed Ben's hand.

I can't. I can't let go.

I know. Jack placed his hand over mine, gently prying my grasp from Ben's hand. Jack wrapped his arms around me as he pulled me backward, away from the unraveling scene, the unbecoming of Ben. I thrashed in Jack's grip, attempting to free myself. Jack's back pushed against the wall while we watched Sam try to stop the convulsions through various medications as Ben's body shook. And shook. And shook. A river of tears raced down my face. Ben's back arched in seizing convulsions, foam at his mouth. There was no air in my lungs. Ben's face was blue, his lips turned dark as the sea. My lighthouse had fallen from its perch to the rumple of the black ocean water. No. No. No. Stop. Please stop.

Jack turned me around in his arms to block my view. He held his hand against the back of my head, burying my face in his chest, muddling my screaming sobs.

I know, I know. It was all Jack could think, as my fist pounded against his chest. Over and over.

You said he would be fine.

Again. *I know, I know.* My legs gave out as I heard the never-ending repetitions of the convulsions beginning to slow. I imagined Ben's stiff body, crumpling into softness, his mind sailing away, sinking to the deep serenity of the ocean floor. Please, no.

Jack's shirt was drenched in all kinds of fluids leaking from my face. It hurt too much to inhale. There wasn't enough air in the room. I beat Jack on the chest with my tightly wound fist. We sat as an ugly tangled ball on the floor together. The amount of pain I felt was unknowable.

Samuel's words laced among the flatline of the heart monitoring machine. "I'm sorry."

Jack rocked me in his grasp. *I know, I know,* his brain repeated as I wailed louder than a banshee, my world crumbling. I was at the epicenter of a never-ending earthquake. Nothing but rubble left inside. Numb. Hollowness in my stomach flooded my entire body. Ringing in my ears overtook all of my senses, and everything was fading. My mind wouldn't track any noise or movement in the room.

In the stillness that death brought, I was spiraling in chaos.

The darkness opened its gaping mouth, swallowing me whole. One large silent, encapsulating bit. It was over. I was never going to be the same. I, as I knew myself, had come undone. For I was gone too. Lost to the tide.

Chapter 27

Souvenir

I don't know how long it had been, but inside only mere minutes had passed since Ben died. Jack had been dealing with all my aftershocks. They only appeared to come at night in my dreams, because the days were spent with pain that paralyzed my body. I had memorized the spackling pattern on the ceiling above my bed.

The dreams would bring surges of salty swell into my mouth as I thrashed through the waves. I was a hostage of the water, held at the will of the black sea. As I dove and paddled, Ben was never there. And I ended in desperation and anguish every time.

Jack slept on the floor next to me, to wake me when the dreams got bad, when he could hear me gasping for air, or screaming, or weeping. I'd caught sight of the bruises left on his chest, matching my purple fists. Jack looked like shit, but it was nothing compared to my condition. I don't know how many nights we'd been doing this.

I couldn't help but think the only reason Jack would stick around to wake me was that he couldn't bear the dreams when they leaked over into his brain.

Even though our minds were merged, I wasn't sure if Jack had mastered the ability to control his thoughts from invading my head— or if I had just mastered the ability to not give a fuck and just deny their existence. I didn't have the slightest idea of what was going on in the outside world, even outside the door of my room.

That was until Aaron barged in this afternoon, followed by Shauna yelling at him.

"What was it for, huh?" Aaron's words were sharply pointed at me. I could sense Jack had picked up on the situation and was headed over to intervene from some other location within the compound.

"Aaron, leave her alone. You don't understand." Shauna inserted herself between Aaron and my lifeless body as I lay on the bed.

"Ben gave his life to get you out of there, and for what? So you could lay here and pity yourself?" Aaron's face fell firm, his fist clenched. His other finger hastily pointed toward me. "If you loved him, you'd get off your ass and help us." What was he talking about? Help with what?

"Stop, Aaron," Shauna attempted to push Aaron out of the room. Jack finally made his entrance, breathless from the sprint he had made. Shauna flashed Jack an apologetic look, bowing out of her position so Jack could take control. Aaron, to no surprise, retained his pompous expression.

"Get out," Jack said.

"She deserves to know." Aaron shrugged his shoulders from Shauna's grip as he exited.

"She deserves to *mourn*," Jack firmly retorted.

Shauna turned and whispered to Jack before leaving behind Aaron, her face full of concern. "We both know this isn't healthy." Jack faced away from me, staring at the back of the door for a few seconds after closing it, rubbing his temples.

"What's Aaron talking about, Jack?" Maybe I wasn't as tuned in to Jack's thoughts because he was learning how to control them better. It was as if a fog surrounded his mind and the images in his head.

"Jack?" I repeated, my voice raspy. Jack turned from the door toward me, his face pale, almost sick.

"I didn't want to tell you because I wanted to give you the space you needed."

"Didn't want to tell me what?"

"Look, you don't have to get involved. You can say no and walk away from this all," Jack offered, "that's all you've ever wanted. You've given one of the largest sacrifices to this team."

"Ben gave the largest sacrifice to this team," I corrected him. "Walk away from what?"

"Victor's solved the puzzle," Jack's voice cracked. I shook my head back and forth. I was going into cardiac arrest due to the rising palpitations in my chest. "It's worse than any of us thought, Dani."

This couldn't be what I thought it was.

"A new hybrid has shown up," Jack admitted. "And Samuel doesn't know what he is."

"What?" I sat up straight in disbelief, stiff as a board. My legs hung over the edge of the bed. Jack stood. He ran his hands through his hair, tense jaw. Fleeting breaths gasped from my chest. Words were failing to form as my mind spun. I tried to put questions together, but they were all swimming through my mind and I couldn't make enough sense of them to get one out.

"Look, his infection level looks like yours, but it's worse. They inserted this computer— this chip into the base of his skull."

"Where is he? The new hybrid?"

"Dead," Jack admitted, "Sam's going to run an autopsy, full toxicology. Gus is working on the code from the chip."

"How'd you find him?"

Jack bit his lip and shook his head. I couldn't tell what was going on inside his mind. His feelings surrounding the situation were filled with dread, with hatred.

"Jack," I yelled, "where did you find him?"

"I didn't," Jack gazed at the floor, "he found me." Jack exhaled in frustration, "He, he—" words evaded him. He outstretched his hand. An invitation. Not that we needed to touch to share thoughts and memories, but that he wanted to.

I let my hand fall into Jack's. When our skin touched electricity danced across my fingers.

The snarling started, I could see it, a man facing toward him as Jack sat on the edge of the cliff overlooking the canyon. Jack had been there, lost in contemplation when he heard a scuffle in the dirt. And when he turned, it wasn't a man. Whatever was behind those eyes, it was no longer human. Its teeth gnashed as it snarled, running straight for Jack.

Sparks flew from its hands, reaching out in Jack's direction. Jack whirled to his feet, but it was too late. Victor's hybrid plunged Jack to the ground. They rolled across the dirt in an entanglement. The hybrid sent a pulse of electricity racing into Jack through their touch, nearly rendering him unconscious, it took everything Jack had to wrangle control of the electric high threatening to supersede him.

Jack wasn't much more than a human taser, a flawed hybrid. But this, this creature, it was Victor's best creation. And Jack stood no chance against it.

It lapped electric flames from its hands, taunting Jack. The hybrid smiled, sending another wave of electricity into him. Jack squirmed under his weight, trying to grasp at the metal tucked just under his waistband. Just as the creature pulled together a bundle of bright electricity in its palms, the gun had gone off.

A thud hit the dirt. Jack skittered backward, losing track of his gun in the process. The spray of blood had settled a red mist over Jack's clothes, and when he pulled his hands up to look at them, they were covered in red blots encrusted with dirt.

After he caught his breath, Jack crawled to inspect the body. He pulled the hybrid from the dirt, turning him over to reveal his face. In that moment, Jack saw that the wildness had faded from its eyes. Those eyes, he had seen those eyes before. *I had seen those eyes before, in the mirror. They looked like mine.*

Jack's heart nearly ripped in two as he pulled the teen boy into his lap. Tears fell from his face as he scanned the hollow lifeless cheekbones, the bullet hole left in his head. And Jack cried, gasping and torn as he filled with a pang of ugly mourning guilt.

I pulled my hand back from Jack before I could see any more, my chest consumed with a heaviness I thought not possible. I tried to not think of the incident with Darrel when I was younger.

Jack wrung one of his wrists as he shifted his weight. "He came with a message." I looked down.

"What did the message say?"

Jack shook his head as he clenched his fist. He had crumpled it after reading it, but I couldn't make out the words from his memory.

Jack reached into his pocket and retrieved a folded-up piece of tattered paper. He held it in his hand, debating sharing it with me. I pinched the end of the paper, readying to grab it from his grasp. His eyes met mine.

Jack exhaled through gritted teeth as he debated internally. I sat there, looking at him, speechless, still grasping the little paper bridge between us. A crevasse gaped inside me, trying to swallow me whole. Jack bit his lip, staring at me, reading the hollow ditches which deeply cut under my cheekbones. And I hated what he saw, what had become of me.

"You know, the hurt never stops, Dani. it never will. You just learn to grow around it, to become bigger than the pain inside, before it consumes you." I winced, not breaking eye contact with Jack. "You don't have to do this. We can hide you, get you out of here. Keep you safe," Jack pleaded. He scanned every part of my face before letting out an exhale accompanied by a frown. My heart sank. And after a long moment, he finally let go of the message:

'A souvenir from Lake Ophelia. I believe this means checkmate, Your Grace.'

I may have died alongside Ben, but who— or what— resurrected inside me was not the same. I was going to let the wild darkness in, and I was going to invite it to stay.

I was going to kill Victor Crowe.

Chapter 28

Anchor

All of this, every last bit had been because of Victor. Why my father had died, why I had become infected, why people were having their lives stolen, murdered, why Jack had been created, why Emily's team was being held captive, why Ben had died. All of it. And Victor wouldn't stop there.

Seething. All I could see was red. Victor had stolen everything I knew and crushed it. I wasn't going to let him get away with it, and I sure as hell wasn't going to let him go any further.

And now that Victor found the lake, I knew he had the answer to all his dreams. He had found the very thing that had given me my powers, the very powers he was so eager to emulate— to multiply and make his little dominions. Who knew how many hybrids Victor was turning out now.

No more. Victor could not play his game any longer. I had to save Emily's team. I had to come up with a way to get close to Victor and kill him. I had to stop him from implementing his rule because a life-wrecking disaster was certain. If this hybrid, this thing that attacked Jack was out there, and had clearly been sent by Victor, our time was up.

Victor had found the secret and was on the precipice of wrecking everything. Victor was going to overtake our city with his little creations, his stolen lives.

Jack turned to me. "I'd like Samuel to check you out. Since you were at Eyecon, it'd be a good idea to see if anything's wrong with you." I was already on edge, and Jack had just severed the last string holding the anger in.

"What's wrong?" I echoed in almost disbelief. I was trying to keep my voice down as I let the words slur from my mouth, knowing fully how well the hallway echoed every word.

"I fucking shoot lightning bolts out of my hands, I can control electronics and... and metals, I'm a lethal fucking weapon constantly on its last hinge. Ben died and who knows if I will ever be the same. Oh, and I forgot to mention we have entire conversations telepathically. Yeah, I couldn't imagine what could be wrong."

You know that's not what I meant.

"Want me to be your science project, Jack?" Anger and rage were building, "Are you jealous? Do you want to figure me out so you can be just like me? Want me to turn into Sam's little pet project? It's no different from Eyecon—from Victor. You want to figure out my powers too so you aren't so defenseless against Victor's soldiers? "

"Stop, ok. Just stop." Jack attempted to hold in his anger as he returned to pacing, keeping his back between us. "You don't know what you're talking about."

"Then what, Jack? What's the point? Why have all this concern? I'm not a little bird you can keep caged up. *I* am going after Victor."

"That's not what I said." Jack's anger ticked up a notch. *Besides, he didn't know you like I know you,* Jack thought.

The last time I had seen Jack's eyes so firm was on the beach. My brain replayed the images of Jack pinned on top of me.

He swallowed as he watched the memory of the event. Jack clutched his hands and let out a yell in frustration, pounding his knuckles into the wall. I almost took a step backward, but Jack looked at me and detected the hint of fear before I could react.

"Don't you get it, Dani?" Jack asked in desperation. "I'm concerned about you because I care about you." His mind was stuck on top of the canyon, on the moment we kissed before things had gotten royally messed up. "And for a split second, I thought you cared about me too." Bitter. So bitter.

"Don't worry," I bit out, "I don't. That piece of me, the part which cares for others, is gone." The electricity bounced inside as the anger raced around my body looking for a place to escape.

"Just going to pretend like we didn't exist, huh?" Jack scoffed, "Nice, Ophelia."

A dagger to the heart.

Jack had only known my real name because he had heard it in my dreams, heard it leak out of Victor's mouth as I replayed my memories. The pressure started seeping out of my hands, dancing like an electrical dust storm across my fingertips. Heat rose on my palms as if someone was holding them over a hot stove.

"Maybe what's wrong with me is you," I exhaled. "You being in my head all the time. I can't hide anything from you."

Jack was becoming aware of the threat I was suddenly turning into. The unhinged wild hybrid was on the verge of making an appearance.

At some point, I had pushed myself to my feet. Jack's heart was going to pound out of his chest. His hands raised as he scanned my face.

Dani, Jack's thoughts were slow, a soothing attempt. *You need to calm down.* But I didn't want to be calm, I didn't want to go quietly back into the cage I had known all too well. As if that part of me was gone, as if any lingering calmness had washed away with Ben.

Then I caught a glimpse of what Jack was seeing, catching enough of my attention to draw my eyes down to my clenched hands. My fists were filled with electric blue tendrils of light, a storm dancing across my skin.

I took a step back, not knowing how to control it. When I uncoiled my hands, bright blue flames lapped up from my palms.

"Jack?" I didn't know how to stop the flames. As my fear rose, the flames also began to rise out of control.

"It's ok, it's ok, you just need to breathe," Jack unconvincingly tried to coo. "Don't let it get the best of you." But I couldn't stop it, because anger mixed with fear was a deadly combination. And I couldn't talk myself down from the ledge. I wanted the feeling of release. I wanted to jump over the edge into its bliss.

Dani, listen to me. If you go over that edge, I don't think you're coming back.

Another shaky exhale left me. Jack was right, he could feel it too, the storm brewing inside. I had to get control. I had to stop my powers from taking over. Victor had warned me of this. Of the darkness. And I was knocking on its door. A rush of fear met with anger fell over me. I was falling into an irate state of uncontrollability. The emotions were a runaway truck speeding down a hill. I couldn't control it. What if this was the start of a rampage? What if I hurt Jack?

The storm on my fingertips grew, transforming from its spring shower into a category-five hurricane. I was so small, like a toy boat floating at the will of the sea during the most treacherous storm of the century. Where was my lighthouse? I needed my lighthouse. But he was gone. The prospect of a brighter future with Ben was no longer there. It had vanished. It had been *stolen* from me.

I tried, in a pathetic attempt, to sling my arms around, hoping to dampen the flames, but that didn't work. The flames grew. Things were going to get bad. Fast.

"Talk to me," I pleaded, my strands of blue shadowed on Jack's face.

"I'm here, I'm right here." He took a step closer to me. "And I will be here with you now, no matter how this ends."

Jack's arms wrapped around me, pulling my face into his chest. I didn't know what to do or how to stop this. Electricity was still bouncing across my fingers as I returned Jack's hug, placing my palms on his shoulder blades. He winced as my skin made contact with him, but when I went to pull away he grabbed me tighter, drawing me closer to his chest.

Jack was in the little toy boat with me, weathering the volatile storm together. He was soaking up some of the electricity, transferring from my body to be shared with him. Jack curled his toes as the energy flooded through him.

An anchor.

The storm was subsiding. Jack pulled back from the embrace. He slid his right hand behind my ear, parting my hair through his fingers as he wrapped them against the back of my head. His lips met the top of my forehead, dancing wildly with such a strong magnetic pull. Our heartbeats were synchronized. Our brains were completely plugged into each other. He peeled his lips from my forehead and returned to our hug, pulling me in and resting his head on top of mine. He smelled of sagebrush and cedar.

A recognizable feeling returned to me. A warm echo, a familiar impression. I could have sworn we had done this many times.

What are we going to do?

I don't know, Jack thought.

"You have to learn to control it, before it takes hold of you and we can't get you back," he whispered.

My voice was filled with nothing but rasp and sorrow, "Victor warned me."

"I know. His words linger over and over again in your dreams. So much I knew it had to be real." Again, I searched for the sense of pity I expected, but like before, there was nothing but a warm tenderness that filled Jack.

"I don't think I can kill him," I admitted.

"You can, I know you can. Just not yet." Jack's softness was so unexpected as if the curtain had finally and completely fallen. "And who said we can't use other lethal means?" Jack snidely asked. "Victor is so deep underground right now, we'd be lucky to find him."

"We can't sit around until he makes an appearance," I told Jack, "As he just passes down his pathetic orders through his army."

"We need to come up with a plan that'll stop him. Once we shut down his little project, it will coax him out of whatever hole he has crawled into to hide."

"Wouldn't it be nice to drown him in the lake?" I said.

"That's far too kind of a death for him. He doesn't get to do the kind of things he does and be able to die on a high. He doesn't get to go out like that, not after what he has done to you." The hole in my chest gave a giant ache at the reminder of Ben. Everything Victor had done to me was microscopic compared to what Ben's death was.

Jack left me to my own devices as I sat on my bed, drained of any energy and hungry for revenge— plotting all the ways I could kill Victor. But the reality was, I had to figure out how to get to him first, or rather get him to come out and play. And most importantly, beyond killing Victor, we had to shut down his delirious project and end his plans. We had to rescue the doctors and destroy every last trace of this stupid virus.

Gus entered the room hours later. He was holding a tray of food and his eyes were apologetic, as always. I thanked him.

"When did you, you know, become a hybrid?" I asked Gus

"About six months ago. I'm one of the newest Rebels."

"I'm sorry." Gus's eyes broke from mine. He glanced at the floor. I expected him to slip out the door, but instead, he opened his mouth.

"I was due to start interning at JPL after my college graduation this past spring. I didn't get to do either of those things, but at least I can help the Rebels in my own way."

"NASA would have been lucky to have you," I offered in solace.

Gus didn't linger, he knew I wanted to be alone. And I likely hit a soft spot asking him about his life before this whole mess had happened to him.

After Gus left, I didn't touch any of the food on my tray.

Instead, I listened to Jack's thoughts as he paced around the compound. He was failing to come up with a plan. The back service door he and Nate had slipped into days earlier surely wasn't going to work again. They had played their only card saving me.

Jack was trying to recall what the floor plan was. There was so much adrenaline in his system during his invasion he couldn't recall many details. He had been lost in rage, in fight mode.

I tried to remember all the details of the lab, all the spaces I had been in. Trying to help Jack.

Can you show me more? Jack asked. So I did. I shared with Jack every detail I could remember of the lab, the sleeping quarters, the lobby, the elevator up to Victor's lair. Sharing every memory of the floor plan with Jack was no easy task. I had to be forgetting some things. Making the conscious run-through of every space I had been in was a daunting task as I tried to remember every single element.

Start from the top, he said.

The top? "The top!" I shouted as I jumped from the bed. I could feel Jack's expression shift in response to me as if I were mad, perhaps I was. Jack was trying to follow my thoughts but they were formulating so fast.

I have an idea, but before we move forward I need a promise from you. I paced back and forth in my small room, trying to put the pieces together. Trying to hide it from Jack.

And what promise would that be? Jack asked, still deep somewhere else in the compound.

We need to get the doctors out safely.

They're a part of Victor's team, Jack responded, a hint of anger ruffled through his thoughts.

They're a victim of Victor just as much as you are.

Jack's dialogue went quiet as he debated in his head. *I'll get the team together. We need to start planning this. Tonight.*

Chapter 29

Postal

We met in Jack's makeshift office, our new war room. The last time we'd sat around this table, I volunteered in Ben's place to go into Eyecon. Chills shivered up my spine. Anxious expressions were exchanged between Shauna and Nate. Gus and Aaron sat across from them, while Jack and I countered each other at the head of the table.

"Does this mean we're finally going to do something?" Aaron asked. The room was quiet, save for Jack's tapping fingers.

Will it work? Jack thought. I was hesitant to let him in on what exactly I was thinking, I wanted the others to get all the information at the same time.

"We can't use the service door again, I'm sure Victor has taken care of that loophole. Or they're waiting for us to use it again like a trap," I said. Nate bit his lip, looking down as he remembered what he and Jack had done days earlier.

"Gus, are you able to access their system?" I questioned. Gus was hesitant to answer.

"Well, yeah, I can get past the firewall and see everything, but if I start to change anything Eyecon will be notified of the invasion," Gus admitted, "I can look, but I can't touch— It's impossible to make undetected changes."

Jack's posture stiffened, he was locked in a dead stare at me, trying to piece together my scattered thoughts.

"That's ok, we just need to be able to get in and get out before *they* can get to *us*," I said.

"What does that even mean?" Shauna snapped in a sassy tone.

Eyes from everyone shifted to Jack as he spoke with a stern and concerned tone. "Dani, do you think it'll work?" While everyone looked at Jack, he kept his focus on me. I could feel him looking around my mind, reading the plan as it formulated in my thoughts. Gus's eyes wandered to mine, and when we made eye contact I broke the silence.

"There's a glass atrium as the ceiling of the building."

"That's great, but in case you forgot, the lab is underground," Aaron pointed out.

"As soon as Gus alters their system to give us access to the basement floors, Eyecon will receive notification of the hack. But, if we can get down to Emily's team and the test subjects, destroy the lab and then get out quickly enough. We may be able to escape without interference," I offered.

"So you mean, you wanna do a drive-by?" Aaron taunted, "Yeah, let's just swing by and pick everyone up before Victor sics his dogs. Like that's gonna work." Aaron was always so snide and cocky, and this conversation was no exception to his personality, regardless of the importance.

"Whoa, wait. What do you mean by 'everyone'? You're not only talking about destroying the research and saving other hybrids but rescuing the scientists, too?" Shauna spat a huff of air, turning towards Jack for confirmation. "There's no way we're saving those fucking monsters." Her hands snapped up, raised with confusion and anger. "In case you forgot, they did this to us."

"They are victims too." I tried my best to stay cool. It was true.

But right on cue, Aaron rolled his eyes. "What's the point of saving these doctors if they can just go recreate Eyecon all over again?"

"They won't," I said.

A still very frustrated Shauna let her jaw snap open. "And how do you know that?"

"This isn't what they signed up for. Victor's held the safety of their families against them. They're good people. These doctors are just a product of their environment. You would do the same thing if you were in their position. We can offer them safety," I argued.

"I'd rather die," Shaunna's teeth were gridlocked as she and Aaron eyed each other in agreement.

"If we go in, we're saving the doctors. No more lives need to be lost due to Eyecon's dirty business," Jack said, silencing Shauna. Shauna glanced at Nate who gave her a reassuring look as he fell in line with Jack's commands. Jack gestured for me to continue explaining the plan.

"They *are* Eyecon," Aaron sneered. Jack pounded the table, silencing the riff-raff. Aaron exhaled, biting his tongue.

"Look, Eyecon is one of the leading security firms, we aren't going to go undetected. But if it's possible to just be faster, it might work— like a bank robbery. They have security and protections out the wazoo, but they still get robbed," I was trying to be as convincing as possible, trying to justify my thoughts. "Everyone on Victor's team is going to know we're there, everyone's going to know what we're doing. We are destroying Eyecon's lab." I glanced around. Everyone's faces were full of confusion, and hesitancy. "But if we can control how long it takes anyone at Eyecon to do something about it, does it matter if we've been detected?" I offered. I was trying to sell this idea. It was the only one I had. "Gus, are there glass-break alarms in the atrium ceiling?"

Gus bashfully looked up, "No, The glass-break alarms are only consistent on exterior windows from the ground up a few floors. The atrium doesn't have any glass-break alarms. Trust me, I've been pouring myself over their systems."

"So we have an entry point. Now we just need to get down the elevator which services the basement floors," I was eager. Trying to speak with confidence. Trying to win the team over with certainty things would work.

"There're motion sensors on the lobby floor," Gus said, dashing some of my confidence.

"And you need a key card to use the elevator that services the lower floors," Aaron pointed out.

"We have Gus," I said, "this is where the countdown begins." I nervously hoped I had this right, that my logic wasn't betraying me. "Jack, how many minutes on average does it take law-enforcement personnel to arrive on the scene of a break-in alarm?"

Jack hesitated to answer, wanting to curate his response to not intimidate the group. "It depends on multiple things, how many units are close by, if those officers are available, what kind of alarm code is sent to dispatch, and what other events are going on in the area."

"There is no way Victor's men have a better response time than the police. No way they're quicker if they aren't on-site," I confessed.

"I'm sure they have that place guarded 24/7," Shauna responded, attempting to discredit my plan thus far.

"Yeah, you're probably right. So we'll have to take care of a few guards who will be on duty," I said as I watched Nate shiver. He had been with Jack when they broke into Eyecon the last time. When they had killed some of Victor's men. "But Once Victor's offsite men get the notification their firewall has been breached we will be on a count-down to get out before the rest of them arrive. Jack, how long could this be?"

"Or the police." Aaron chimed in, stealing Jack's response time.

Jack eyed Aaron, then returned his attention to the question. "There is no way to tell. Maybe two minutes after receiving the call of a break-in police would usually arrive on the scene. I don't see how Victor's offsite men could be faster than the police."

"You want to 'go postal' in only two minutes?! Hah, what are you going to do with that?" Aaron laughed. I glared at him. Did he want to stop Eyecon or did he find demolishing our hope more enjoyable? Debatable.

"Let's take the cops out of the equation. What if the first thing Gus does after hacking into Eyecon's system is disable the alarm?" I asked

"No alarm, no cops. But Victor's men will still respond to the compromised firewall notification," Nate shrugged.

"If we can somehow slow down Victor's team and put enough obstacles in front of his men, maybe we can beat them to the punch?" I said. Nate's face told me he was considering this, but was skeptical. Jack seemed to be chewing it over too.

"You want to make distractions?" Nate asked. "I like it."

"We won't go undetected. But if we can try to hold them off long enough," I said.

Jack never broke his stare. "Where do we start?" A bit of relief set in. We were going to move forward with this.

"Why don't we target Eyecon during the festival? There's a Fourth of July celebration downtown in a few days. The streets are closed to traffic and will be filled with people for the music and fireworks events. This will put a slowdown on the arrival of Victor's team." Gus shyly spoke up. Jack smiled, approvingly patting Gus on the back.

"Why don't we get passes to the concert? I've got a friend," Shauna said.

Then Aaron asked, "Why do we need to go to the concert?"

"Not for us, you dipshit, the concert is on the south end of town. It's a VIP event, if we could somehow get as many of those passes to guards on Victor's team, and get them as far away from Eyecon as possible, it would slow them down," Shauna offered.

Aaron asked in a snarky manner, "You guys really think we can pull this off?"

Shauna rolled her eyes at Aaron. "Scared, Aaron?" She audaciously mocked.

Aaron glared a face at her before returning to look around the table for more suggestions. "No. I'm not scared. But none of this works without Gus."

Gus's face paled. Aaron was right— the plan hinged on Gus's abilities. And there was a lot of pressure on him to be able to figure this out.

"Gus, after disabling the alarm, how quickly can you get us access to the elevator, the lower floors, the lab, and the sleeping quarters of the scientists?" I asked, chewing over Gus's lengthy to-hack list.

"Uh... I mean, I can probably do it, but we won't know what we're dealing with until I can get into their system and start changing things. I don't know how long it will take," Gus admitted. Aaron leaned back in his chair rolling his eyes, proud he had yet again pointed out a risk.

"Look, this is the only way. If Gus needs time, we will find a way to buy him time," Jack sternly spoke, trying to crystalize the faith of our team. "Let's stop the bickering and come up with a solid plan, the only way this is going to work is if we all put our heads together to ensure there are no holes," Jack paused, inhaling a deep breath as Nate nodded in agreement. "If we go in knowing there's no plan B, we can perfectly execute this. This is likely our only shot because Eyecon is closing in on their plans. And we can't let Victor get boots on the ground, on the streets, on *our* streets."

We split up into groups, Gus and I had decided to work together to plan anything and everything to do with movement. We came up with a game plan for our strategy inside Eyecon. Each part needed to be dissected on a step-by-step basis to ensure Gus knew every piece of software code which needed to be hacked and edited.

We were also in charge of building our team's entrance and exit routes, which we poured hours over by bouncing everything off of Jack and his access to police records. We knew which roads were open, closed, or had roadblocks staffed with cops for the Independence Day events. All movements were going to be systematically planned and overseen by us.

Shauna was tasked with figuring out who all of the guards were. She would need to find someone to slyly get the concert passes to the guards who were on call during our raid.

Nate and Aaron were in charge of pulling all the gear together and training everyone on how to use it. Especially me, I had never rappelled down anything before.

Jack obviously couldn't settle in one group. He bounced between everyone, overseeing every minuscule detail. Although, this didn't seem to bother anyone. It was reassuring to know work was being triple-checked. The stakes were high if things went wrong, and no one wanted the responsibility to fall squarely on their shoulders. We were betting everything on this going right. As Jack said, there was no plan B— and if there was, we wouldn't have time to execute it.

Chapter 30

Magnet

Trying to keep my mind off the incident at the bar was grim. Squealing tires repeated in my head like an awful broken record. The hot metal of the gun was permanently imprinted into my palms. An empty pit at the bottom of my heart was consuming me whole, like a dark beast gorging on my conscience. The clicks of the trigger pull felt like a leaking faucet, never-ending. And worst of all, I could still smell the panic, feel the hair on the back of my neck stand as Nate's frantic voice delivered the news about Ben seizing. Or as Samuel's words proclaimed Ben as dead. A symphony— an ugly cacophony ceaselessly blaring in my mind. But that was better than the silence. When Ben died, and Jack held me as the weeping mess on the floor, the silence was the most suffocating experience I'd ever had.

"Try again." Jack rotated my hands in his as he inspected my palms. I was doing everything we thought we knew would trigger the flames to return to my palms the way they had earlier. I thought of things that made me mad, or angry, or scared.

"Maybe she needs more time to recharge or something. I don't know. I would think that kind of power would take a while to build up." Nate leaned against the dresser in my room.

"Last time it was like a dark angry wave crashing down on us," Jack admitted.

"Anger is a secondary emotion," Nate responded.

"What?" The frustration rising in my failed attempts to summon the flames.

"That's what they taught us in the army," Nate claimed, "Anger's what you see or feel on the surface, but it covers what's underneath." I pushed my fingers across my eyebrows, trying to rub away the stress.

I entertained Nate's idea. "So we have to figure out what triggers the anger?"

"Good luck with that," Jack laughed, "For many years, men have been trying to figure out how women work." His grin was wide and cocky as he joked with Nate. I jabbed my elbow into Jack's ribs. Prick. He winced as I let the taunting smirk crawl across my face. His hand fell to rub out the sting left from my strike. He deserved that one.

"I don't know, maybe it will just take time to learn," Nate offered.

"We don't have time," I exhaled. "As soon as we make our strike against Eyecon, Victor will rear his ugly head."

"Dani, it doesn't have to be you. We can find a way to take care of Victor," Jack said.

"He's mine." I slid the words of claim through my gridlocked teeth. "And I want to show him just what these eyes signify."

"What?" Nate was lost.

"Her eyes. They changed color after her infection." Jack cleared up Nate's confusion, then turned to me. "Look, when we get Victor, I know what you will do, and I don't want it to come to that," Jack admitted. He shifted his weight awkwardly as he ran a hand across the back of his neck. Nate moved to sit on the bedside.

"And what is that?" I questioned.

"Oh, there are multiple parts." Jack smiled, revealing a toothy grin. "You'll stoke Victor like a fire, and then you'll try and throw yourself over the edge attempting to douse him out." I wanted to pretend like it wasn't true, but that was exactly my plan.

"What does that even mean?" Nate asked, once again confused.

"She knows what it means." Jack held a momentary finger out toward me as he answered Nate's questions. "Have you not yet had the pleasure of fighting with Dani?" Oh, you prick.

"Jack," Nate grew cautious eyes in warning. "Have you lost your mind?"

"It appears to have wandered off long ago," I chimed in. "Jack's referring to my great skill of constantly being a lit fuse, and then blowing up." A trick I was considering at this very moment.

"You appear to do a fantastic job of honing in on the anger. I think that's why you're so good at getting under everyone's skin," Jack admitted.

"Oh, a compliment? So kind of you."

Jack's finger was still outstretched as if he hadn't finished his thought. "Dani, it's a miracle you didn't lose yourself to the darkness the last time you summoned the flames. You can't be in such a desperate ploy to kill Victor that you give yourself up, that you give into the darkness. I don't want you to lose yourself." Jack's hand fell, he bit his lip as he took a step closer to me.

"He killed Ben." I raised my head to meet Jack's gaze, his dark blue eyes. They reminded me of the evening sky. The moment you could see the stars after sunset, just before everything turned dark. "And if Victor has his way, he'll kill everyone else in his path."

"The way you talk, no one would know what a mess you are on the inside," Jack said, "as if you aren't afraid of anything."

"I'm not. Not anymore."

"I know." Jack's voice cracked as the words left his mouth. "Don't let him kill you too. If you lose to the darkness, Victor wins, even if he's dead." It was almost a whisper.

"Make me a promise?" I asked. But Jack was already aware of what my mind had thought up, of what I was about to ask him to do.

"Dani, No. Don't let it come to that. Don't you dare put me in that situation." Jack turned away from me as he plunged a hand through his thick, dark hair.

"If you won't, Nate will."

A baffled Nate stood as he tried to piece together what was going on. "Nate will what?" he asked. "Damn, it's like you guys are having conversations I can't hear." If only he knew how true his statement was.

"Shoot me," I confessed. Nate's eyes widened.

Dani, you can't make me do this. I couldn't do that to you.

"Jack, it wouldn't be me. You said it yourself, If I lose to the darkness, Victor wins. I wouldn't be me, I'd already be gone. Or worse..."

Silence lingered over the three of us as thoughts raced through Jack's head.

"I'll do it," Nate spoke up, "I promise."

"The hell you will," Jack challenged, stepping closer to Nate. "If it has to be done, *I'll* do it. And I'm the only one who gets to make that call."

"You don't get to make the call," I ordered. My voice was strong, it needed to be convincing. "Nate makes the call, but you can pull the trigger if you'd like." Jack winced, leaving his confrontation with Nate to stand in front of me. "Your judgment is too clouded, Jack. And with being merged, I will suck you down with me." Jack bit his lip and nodded once in agreement.

"Merged?" Nate asked. Shit, I'd said too much. Jack hung his head, grabbing for the bridge of his nose, annoyed too much had been revealed.

"Don't worry about it Nate," Jack said.

"You *are* having conversations I can't hear, aren't you? That's why you're so protective of her, isn't it, Jack?"

"I'm not..." Jack stopped himself. "Yes."

"Holy shit," Nate sighed in entertainment.

"Look, keep it to yourself, ok?" Jack warned. "Not even Shauna."

Nate gave a giddy smirk of acknowledgment.

"Are we done here?" I finally asked, trying to wiggle out of the entire situation that had come about. Jack nodded in agreement. Nate and Jack made to leave the room so I could clean up. But, I grabbed Nate's shoulder before he left, pulling him back. He turned and raised his eyebrows at me.

"I never said thank you." Nate didn't need to ask, he knew what I was talking about. Saving me at the beach, invading Eyecon with Jack, and most importantly, what he had just agreed to, shooting me if I lost myself to the darkness. Nate nodded with a gentle smile before pulling the door closed behind him.

Every time I was alone, my thoughts wandered back to Ben. The constant wall of grief continued to get harder and harder to hold off the longer I attempted to ignore it. Pushing down the thoughts was the only strategy I could attempt to pursue because when the sorrow broke through the veil, I was left in the clutches of overwhelming pain and grief.

The best I could do to keep my mind busy was to focus on ending it all. Stopping Victor, getting my revenge, rescuing Emily's team, avenging Ben, and ending the potential for a new human race of hybrid super soldiers that Victor could play king with. How hard could it be, right? God I was in over my head.

While we were working on plans to return to Eyecon, Gus had been acting differently around me. Even Aaron had a kinder-than-normal demeanor when he was around— a red flag he was feeling benevolent towards me. Maybe he knew we were all close to death, and the kindness was his making of amends.

I tried to stop thinking about Ben and focus on Jack's thoughts. Luckily, it seemed like he was too busy to do anything other than obsess over the plans. This made it easier for me to keep the anxiety and panic at bay. The constant need for Jack to create space and engross himself with the break-in plans was to my benefit. I could help work out the details. We used each other as a sounding board for ideas and troubleshooting.

I let Jack's obsession with the plan pull me in and grasp my attention the best I could. Jack attempted to refrain from listening to my thoughts. He was also desperately trying to avoid the carnival of emotions not only from me but from himself as well.

Jack was bathing in guilt. His thoughts were trying to persuade me he was responsible for what had happened with the shooting of Eyecon's agents. I never took the initiative to address the events with him, even though I didn't feel the same. It wasn't Jack's fault, but talking about it with him meant I had to acknowledge it was real. I had fired a weapon in the middle of the street, in broad daylight with plenty of innocent bystanders around. I thought I might have killed those men. It made me so sick.

But I wasn't the only one who had pulled a trigger recently. Jack was desperately trying to pretend the scuffle with that hybrid, that boy, never happened. That the small perfect circle in the center of his forehead didn't haunt Jack the way it did. I just wanted to tuck it all into the folds of my mind and pretend it never happened too.

A knock came at my door, it was Samuel. He entered and sat gently on the edge of my bed.

"You mind if I get a blood sample? Just want to make sure not only your hybrid parts are ok, but that your human parts are all in order too."

"Jack sent you, didn't he?" I asked, revealing the crook of my elbow. Samuel simply smiled and pushed the needle into my vein, drawing up a sample.

"You need to eat, tomorrow's the day." I gave him a soft smile. We both knew he was right.

"Call me if—"

"Anything weird shows on your sample," he smiled. "I will."

In the cafeteria, there was a certain kind of buzz. Not the electric kind I was used to, but one of excitement. The chatter between people was louder than normal, more constant. Some of the Rebels I didn't know had glanced over their shoulders at me in curiosity. Gross. But there was still a large cloud hanging over everyone. The possibility for things to go wrong loomed over us all.

I joined Gus and Aaron at a table after grabbing a tray of food that was poorly filled with the proper portions. Aaron's tray was eaten clean as he reached across, grabbing food from Gus's. Gus still had quite a bit of food on his plate, he'd been slow to eat anything.

Shauna and Nate joined us at the table.

"Ready for tomorrow?" Nate enthusiastically asked. My stomach churned and I pushed my tray away from me towards the center of the table.

"Can't handle the pressure?" Aaron scoffed, snagging some fries from my tray. Ok, maybe Aaron was still an asshole.

"More like, can't handle you." I snidely remarked, igniting Aaron's ego.

"You don't have to worry about me, I can handle my own." Nate gave Aaron an elbow to the ribs. Maybe that's why Aaron had been nicer to me lately— Nate had been guilting him into it. I grabbed my tray from the table and headed for the exit.

"Nice job, Aaron," Nate said sarcastically as I continued to walk.

I found Jack in the computer lab. It was empty, as everyone else was in the cafeteria. Jack sat at a table, staring at a blank computer screen, his eyes unseeing.

"Forget about Aaron, he tends to be a real dick when he's anxious." I didn't respond to Jack's advice. The tray rang out with an echo in the empty room as I slid it in front of Jack. He glanced down at the food, not thrilled about eating either. As I watched Jack, his jaw wiggled back and forth as he ran his hand over the top of his head.

"Why is he like that?" I finally asked, breaking the silence.

"Don't let the cockiness fool you. Aaron's pretty smart, had a full ride to Vanderbilt. He lost his scholarship because he disappeared on 'em," Jack admitted, "it all soured his attitude. I can't blame him."

I swallowed. Was I actually feeling sorry for Aaron? Maybe the mountain cat had a heart... somewhere deep, deep down.

"You ready for tomorrow?" Jack looked down as he rubbed his temples.

"Are you?" I asked, strategically dodging his question. I was not going to answer that.

"I've been waiting for this moment for quite a while. Just trying to make sure we didn't miss anything."

"What about you?" I asked. "How were you able to start all this? The Collective?"

Jack exhaled before answering. "My parents owned a farm. I sold everything when they died in a car accident," Jack said. "The land alone was worth a ton. It's been several years. I don't like to talk about it."

"I'm sorry—"

"It's ok."

"If you ever need to talk—"

"I know," he quickly said.

I pulled away from the table and turned to leave the room. "Well, get some sleep." I was going to need my sleep as well. But sleep did not come easy.

I found myself restlessly tossing and turning in bed. Tomorrow evening, we would be executing our plan. I would be returning to Eyecon to get my revenge, to rescue all those that Victor held captive in his dungeon. To burn Eyecon's lab down along with any trace of research from the scientists. Destroy every sample Eyecon had. To finish what my father couldn't. To finish what he had run from. And most importantly, it was the first strike in getting Victor to come out and play ball.

And then I would get my revenge on Victor for killing Ben.

Tires squealed, causing a jarring ringing in my ears. The van was spinning. I had one hand on the dashboard to steady myself.

Do it, Dani, now. Jack screamed at me. My hand was on fire. I couldn't hold it any longer. The gun fell from my grip and into my lap where it began to burn my skin.

What's wrong with you? Jack asked. I looked up at him, his eyes were piercing red, making me flinch. But I had to return my focus to the burning in my lap. When I looked down, the gun was gone. It had vanished. Jack's red eyes quickly regained my attention. They were now sitting behind the barrel of the gun.

Jack, what are you doing? His smile grew into a crooked menace, light catching on one of his canines. He wasn't Jack, he was Victor. I placed my hand on the pistol, trying to dislodge Victor's aim and grip, just as I touched the boiling metal of the gun: click.

I sucked in a deep breath of cold air as I sat up from bed. A shiver I couldn't shake crawled down my spine.

That's it, you're not going. Jack's thoughts barged in. He had been sleeping in his quarters for the past few nights, leaving me to myself in my room.

That's not fair, I have more of a reason than anyone to go after Victor.

Which means your judgment is more clouded than anyone else's, Jack argued, echoing words I had told him in a different situation. I couldn't believe Jack thought this dream would compromise me— compromise our mission. Everything was riding on our plan going off without a hitch. I was relying on this, to end Victor. To avenge Ben.

Let's not forget you were the one who begged me to help you, I pointed out.

You did. We have a plan now and it doesn't need to include you. You're safer here. That spiked my anger, bringing it to a boil. The electricity bounced around inside me, but I had to maintain control. Show him I could handle myself. How could he seriously propose I sit out?

You're a magnet for trouble.

A magnet? My ball of anger threatened to burst.

You were a train wreck in the woods, and the overdose, and Ben—

That's not fair, I bantered.

What about the Eyecon agent who nearly crashed into your van? Or let's not mention how you tried to kill yourself moments before being rescued, which inadvertently merged our fucking minds. And to top it all off Dani, Broady knows it was us. He knows we're in some deep fucking shit and how we shot at those men in the middle of the street. I've been too scared to even check the reports. And you know who they were all after? You, Dani. And we almost died because you hesitated to pull the trigger.

Jack's words were serrated, cutting ugly feelings as I processed them. He had given me a warning before to stay out of Eyecon, which ended disastrously.

You can stay here. It's not like you don't get to see a first-hand account of everything that happens. In case you don't remember, you get to live inside my damn head, you can guide me through anything that comes up, Jack said.

Sincerely, Jack, fuck you. I'm going. Ok, it wasn't the most sound of arguments. But my emotions were all over the place. I couldn't help it, I was fuming. My hands tightened into fists, balling up the bedsheets.

You can't control it, Dani. Jack's thoughts were firm. They almost convinced me it was best I hung back, but there was too much rage. It was Victor who had killed Ben, and I was going to take every shot at hurting Victor I could. I was not going to let Ben's death be the first blood to spill in Victor's impending battle for power. Undoubtedly, I was not going to sit this out.

You don't want me to get in your way, I calculated.

Can you stop and consider for one moment, maybe this isn't about me. Maybe this is actually about you. Jack inhaled a long deep breath. *Dani, we are dragging you like a lure in front of Victor if we put you back inside Eyecon. You'll be walking into the lion's den.* Jack said, trying to stay on track with his original argument.

And who cares, Jack? If we get the job done, and I go down while doing it, you have one less headache on your hands. That's the way you probably want it. You'll have me out of your head. And you won't have to pull the trigger yourself, I said.

The way I want it is for you to be safe. What don't you understand? Or are you still set on the fact that you believe I'm working for Victor? Jack was upset now. I could feel the hurt I had caused. I didn't respond. I tried to not think of anything, letting the words echo in my hollow mind, bouncing around as

I attempted to put up a mental wall. Looking for refuge. Looking for privacy.

I'm ok. I argued, trying to convince myself it was true. Having my mind merged with Jack's was hard. Especially when he was right, it was my fault we were merged.

Stop telling me you are ok, Jack said, *You're not ok.* His voice came through firmly. *Our minds didn't need to be merged for me to see the gaping hole you carry with you everywhere, the dark pit you so desperately try to cover up and pretend isn't there.* Jack's words hit me with a sharp sting.

Why do you even care? The thought lingered between us.

Jack was trying to not respond, it was like when I had just woken up to our minds being merged. When he was trying to hide the story of what Nate and he had done inside of Eyecon's lab. A movie strip, where things were out of order, holes all through every scene, every image. None of it made sense. It was as if Jack was putting up a veil, a fog in front of the damaged movie scenes. He was learning how to hide his thoughts from me. How long had he been doing that?

How did you do that? I asked.

It doesn't matter. Goodnight, Dani.

When I finally released the sheets from my grasp, they lay singed and black where I had bunched them in my hands.

Chapter 31

Tightrope

Tonight was it. The big plan.

My clothes were borrowed from Shauna, and naturally, I had selected all black.

Gus was posted up at his computer, ready to commence. A small group of Rebels surrounded him, setting up shop like NASA watching a space launch.

In the garage, Nate held Shauna's hand, and Aaron was naming off gear as Jack checked it off the list.

What are you doing here, Dani?

Ignoring Jack, I instead turned my attention to Shauna and Nate.

"Got everything in place?" I asked her, pretending I was checking over her work, even though I knew Jack had already obsessively checked and re-checked everything. Shauna smiled nervously.

"We're ready," Aaron announced.

"Load up," Jack said, nodding in the direction of the van. As everyone loaded up, Jack placed himself between me and the van. "Are you sure you can handle this?" His jaw stiffened and his eyebrow raised.

"Yes," I lied. Jack felt the hesitation within my thoughts, but he awkwardly shifted, letting me by. We scraped shoulders as I passed. "I don't need your permission to carry out my plan."

"*Our* plan," Jack bitterly corrected. I let it go as I climbed into the back of the van. Aaron was sitting shotgun.

Nate handed me an earpiece as Gus called roll to check out the comms system. I gave my verbal cue indicating I was online. The van ride was silent, save for the nervous breathing.

My stomach twisted into a terrible mess of bubbling anxiety. Electricity zapped around inside me like a dust storm filled with static. If I opened my mouth to say anything only two things could come out. Neither would be words. Puke or a stream of bright blue lightning bolts.

There was just one hitch. The Police had set up a perimeter around the Independence Day events. To get through to any of the streets we needed, we had to pass our first test.

The car came to a stop at the roadblock. This was Jack's part of the battle.

In the back of the van, Shauna, Nate, Aaron, and I pulled a piece of black fabric over the top of us while we listened to Jack's window roll down.

A police officer slightly leaned onto the car. "No uniform tonight, Jack?"

"Street clothes catch more criminals, Rick. You know that." Jack was laying the charm on thick, but it was natural. It was just the way Jack went about the world.

"Ah, explains why I haven't seen you around lately, I didn't know you were working a special unit."

Jack smiled, "have a safe night," he said, slowly letting off the brake.

As soon as we cleared the stop, Aaron ripped the fabric off the top of us and climbed up toward the front seat as I tried to straighten myself out.

The crowd thickened as we drove.

"Take a left," Gus directed, "You'll turn right on 23rd and then a quick left on 14th to avoid another stop."

Jack parked the van in an alley on the far side of a tall high-rise building just next to Eyecon. The building wasn't quite as tall as Eyecon, but it was set slightly closer than its other neighbors in the business district, hence why we chose it. And when Gus had checked their security system, he found a major flaw. It looked like this insurance company was more focused on pulling in more clients than they were focused on protecting those clients' information. Gus said their system hadn't been updated in months, making for an easy hack.

We all sat for a long moment, no one saying anything. Jack and Aaron got out first, checking the alley to make sure we had no unexpected witnesses. Aaron gave us the signal all was clear.

We each grabbed our black backpacks out of the van. Everyone was stocked with the same gear and we all wore solid black with our bags tossed over our shoulders. Nate and Jack both held rifles slung over a shoulder in addition to their bags. Shauna, Aaron, and I each had a handgun holstered on us somewhere. I elected to carry my firearm on my hip.

Jack approached the door labeled 'emergency exit only'. He glanced at Nate. Nate nodded.

"Alright Gus, let's get this started," Jack said.

Gus's fingers clicked as they furiously flew across his keyboard. "Alright, here we go. Three... two... one. She should be unlocked now."

Nate pried his fingers into the crack of the door, as there was no handle. The door was only ever meant to be an emergency fire exit, never intended for entry from the street.

"Scary how easy it is to get into their system. Shame they don't use services from just next door."

"Focus, Gus," Jack muttered.

I was trying to keep my focus. Jack's brain was dialed in on executing a perfect plan. While Jack reviewed each piece of the plan, I followed his thoughts, trying to stay calm instead of letting the fear get the best of me.

We climbed each flight of stairs. Aaron's breath became louder as we passed the tenth floor.

"I need to take a break," Aaron said just as we reached the fifteenth floor. Aaron leaned against a wall, letting his backpack slip to the floor at his feet.

"Are you kidding, right now?" Shauna questioned.

"Cardio isn't my thing," Aaron breathlessly admitted.

"We've noticed. Twelve more flights, then you'll have a few minutes to yourself while we get set up on the roof. Pull it together, Aaron." Jack grabbed Aaron's bag and slung it over his shoulder, carrying a double load of gear.

I grimaced at Aaron. I know right now wasn't the time, but oh, how it felt good. Aaron smirked at me, his lip giving a twitch.

"Let's go," Jack commanded. Aaron hesitantly began climbing stairs again. We reached the top of the stairwell, revealing a final door to the rooftop. Nate reached for the round knob, twisting it. The door didn't open.

"Gus? Can you open the door to the roof?" Nate spoke as he pressed his finger into his earpiece waiting for Gus's response.

"Fire code says roof access isn't to be locked. The door's alarm isn't even armed," Gus said.

Nate and Jack looked at each other. Nate tried shouldering the door as he twisted the handle. Again, the door didn't open.

"I've got it. Move out of the way," Aaron said, just barely catching his breath. Nate stepped to the side just as Aaron took a running leap toward the door, attempting to kick it. Aaron's foot made contact with the door, immediately springing him backward onto the ground.

Shauna placed her face in her hand. "Oh my god, this is embarrassing."

"Really, Aaron? That was your great idea?" Nate asked.

"Move," Jack commanded, pushing past Nate. Jack grasped the pistol from his waistband and aimed at the knob of the door. "Cover your ears."

Just as I placed my hands over my ears, the sound of the discharge reverberated through my body, the muzzle flash temporarily blinding my sight. Jack had shot through the knob, destroying the mechanical lock. As he twisted the knob, it fell apart in his hand. Jack stuck his finger in the hole, stripping away what was left of the knob mechanism. Nate pulled an embarrassed Aaron off the floor— I guess his ego could be bruised after all.

We stepped out onto the roof, my anxiety bubbled up through my stomach as if a thousand butterflies took flight inside me. Electricity floated around my body, all my nerves tickled with power.

You ok? Jack asked.

Never better. Ready to get this over with, I relayed back in a bold-faced lie. I let my eyes wander from our current rooftop up to Eyecon's rooftop. A three-floor difference. Jack and Nate pulled what looked like a grappling hook gun out of their bags.

"We only have two shots to make this work," Jack said "Why don't you try first, Nate?"

Nate nodded and fixed his sight on Eyecon's rooftop. He ran a hand through his midnight black hair, taking a deep breath as he steadied his aim. Nate discharged the grappling hook gun and the hook landed on Eyecon's roof. Jack and Nate exchanged a look in surprise.

"The moment of truth here, pull the rope and see if it catches," Jack said. Nate bit his lip and began pulling. The rope pulled taut.

Nate smiled. "Seems like we got a winner."

"Nice job," Jack said, seemingly pleased.

I pulled on the harness needed to make the journey across the gap. Shauna had already finished putting on her harness and was now helping Aaron with his. Then I did something stupid.

I peered over the edge of the roof and looked down. Holy shit. It was a long way down. I was going to crawl across that? Panic washed over me as I gasped in a deep breath of air. Jack's hands were instantly around me, pulling me back from the edge. The exchange of electricity almost put me over the edge— the emotional one. Everything felt out of control, making me ever so hypersensitive to electricity.

What were you thinking?

"I don't know, I wasn't,"

Are you sure you can do this? Jack asked. I stared at him, his emotions pinging all over the place. His eyes stared back at me, blue dusk, a thousand hidden stars just under the setting sun. His hands sat still around my waist as we exchanged our electric buzz. He knew. Jack knew how I felt, I was so ready to get this over with. To get back at Victor. But I was terrified I would slip up somehow and ruin the whole thing.

Jack brushed his finger across my cheekbone, then tucked a piece of my hair that had fallen from my ponytail behind my ear.

I know you can do this. You have no idea how lucky he was, Jack thought, *Even if it was just for a little while.* Ben. He was talking about Ben, being lucky. It caught me so off guard, I didn't know what to say. But Ben wasn't lucky. Ben was dead. Ben was dead because he had gotten tangled up with me. Before I could even think of a response, Jack had let go and turned away.

"Alright, I'll go first," Jack said, "Then Nate will help everyone get hooked in correctly. We go one at a time across the line."

You can do this, Dani. I gave Jack a thankful acknowledgment, appreciating the encouragement. Jack hooked his harness to the rope strung between the buildings.

The device Jack was attached to allowed him to pull himself across the line without sliding backward. The device locked after every bit of progress he made as he pulled himself forwards, preventing him from sliding down the line and back to the rooftop where he just started. It was going to be slow going across the rope, as it took quite a bit of strength to pull yourself across at such an angle.

Jack finally made it to Eyecon's roof after what seemed a century. Nate helped Aaron latch in next. Shauna and I patiently watched as Aaron pulled himself across the line onto the roof of Eyecon. He wasn't quite as fast as Jack.

"Dani?" Nate called my name, asking if I wanted to go next. My response must have been too slow, Shauna offered herself up instead. Nate hooked Shauna to the rope and kissed her. Shauna must not have crossed as quickly as Jack or Aaron, but it felt so very fast. Probably because I was next.

I stepped up to the edge of the rooftop, onto the half-wall that would keep any sane person from falling over. My hands wrapped tightly around the rope as Nate hooked my harness into the mechanism.

"Alright, you're all set, Dani. Take it slow." I gave Nate a thankful smile as I remained wordless, trying to keep the panic at bay. What have I gotten myself into?

Don't look down, Dani. Just don't look down. One hand over the other. Over and over again. I began pulling my body weight across the main line, suspended between the two buildings. A zipline. This was just like a backward zipline. Not so bad, right?

The windows of the Eyecon building reflected my image, almost a perfect mirror—— a mirage glowing with all of Reno and the mountains beyond. I couldn't believe I was here, doing this.

Ok. About halfway now. Fine. Everything was going to be fine.

My nerves were getting the best of me though, and my hands began to sweat.

Dani, calm down. Just breathe. Look, you're already halfway. Jack tried to soothe my nerves. But as I looked back at Nate on the lower roof, I made a mistake. I continued to look further down, until I saw the ground, noticing the tiny van so far below. My hands struggled to keep their grip on the rope as they profusely sweated. Before I knew what was happening, Jack's thoughts rose into a frantic wave. "Dani!"

No. No. No. My hands slipped from the main line, leaving me dangling by my harness. The angle of the rope made it nearly impossible to stay upright. My right hand fell to my hip as I tried to prevent my gun from falling out of its holster. I frantically swung my other arm around, trying to find the line that connected my holster to the main rope. But I couldn't find the connecting line before turning completely upside down and the contents in my backpack hit the top of my bag, jolting me and the entire line up and down. Not good. This. Was. Not. Good.

I was suspended upside down nearly three hundred feet in the air recoiling wildly, failing to gather myself. My free hand finally found the connection rope running from my harness to the main line. I grabbed ahold of it like my life depended on it. It quite possibly did.

Shauna gasped, covering her mouth.

Dammit, you shouldn't fucking be here! Dani, you have to pull yourself upright.

I'm trying! I don't know if I can. My bag and gun are holding me down. I admitted to Jack. *And it's a long fucking way down. My harness is starting to slip.* I was going to slip out. I was going to splatter across the pavement. If I was lucky, I would die on impact. Oh, god, I never seemed to be lucky. Blood rushed to my head, tunneling my vision.

Because I was nearly vertical, instead of a seated position, my harness was beginning to loosen and I was starting to slide out. As I dangled upside down, I quickly bent my knees and wrapped my legs around the connection rope to prevent myself from sliding any further out of my harness. I had my left hand glued to the connection rope while my right hand held my gun in its holster. Breathe. But it was becoming harder to breathe the longer I remained upside down.

I had to lose the bag. It was too heavy, and the way the weight was distributed prevented me from swinging myself right side up. To slip the bag off, I would have to remove my left hand from the connection rope and slide it through the backpack strap to free my left shoulder. I squeezed my thighs around the connection rope so tight, I thought my feet were going to fall asleep. All of my blood pooled in my head, making it harder to think. Breathe, just breathe.

Slowly, I let go of the connection rope, meaning I was only relying on my legs being wrapped around well enough to prevent me from sliding out of my harness and becoming a human pancake below. I slid my left arm through the backpack strap, freeing my left shoulder. This made it harder for me to keep my right hand on my gun. Ok, now we were getting somewhere.

I moved my left hand over to my holster, holding the gun in place while I slipped my remaining arm free of the last backpack strap.

No!

I catapulted upwards, losing my grip on my gun and its shitty holster. Instinctively, I grabbed the connection rope between my legs with both hands. The sudden weight change from ditching my bag sent me flinging like a fly on a jump rope.

My bag hit the ground below with a thud, followed by my gun just seconds later. I flinched. That could have been my body instead of my belongings.

Don't look down. You should be able to pull yourself up right now so that you don't have the extra weight keeping you upside down, Jack thought. *Deep breath, eyes closed.*

I focused on Jack's words as I held the connection rope between my legs. To swing myself right side up, I would need to unravel my legs from the rope. You can do this, Dani. Slowly, I unwrapped one leg, my fingers had a death grip on the connection rope. With one leg unwound, I found the weight distribution made it easier for me to maneuver. I needed to avoid having to only rely on my grip strength to prevent me from slipping the harness.

With one big deep breath, I unwound my second leg, using the momentum to help pull me upright. Oh, thank god. Relief washed over me as I finally faced the direction I needed to. I had to get to Eyecon's roof. I couldn't handle hanging out on this rope much longer. Reaching one hand up at a time, I grabbed a hold of the main line. Quickly, I frantically pulled myself closer and closer up to Eyecon's rooftop.

As I reached the edge of the rooftop, Jack extended his hand, grabbing mine. He yanked me up over the edge and into his arms. Jack's thoughts were a receding tidal wave, very much like mine. His arms braced me. The panic was subsiding and I was lucky to be alive.

Just as Nate came over the edge of the roof, I released myself from Jack. But he pulled me in one last time, his lips just above my ear.

"Like I said, you attract trouble like a fucking magnet," he whispered, then pressed a soft kiss against the side of my head. When he pulled back, his dusky blue eyes settled on mine and neither of us broke away until Nate chimed in.

"We have business to finish."

Jack reluctantly pulled away. I hesitantly refocused on Nate, on our mission.

Jack joined Nate as they converged on the atrium in the center of the roof as Shauna approached me, kneeling to fix my harness that had loosened on my frightening journey across the gap.

"Think you can handle this next part, princess?" Aaron whispered snidely as he passed.

"I'm fine, thanks." I flashed a foul gesture in his direction. Ass.

I pushed past Shauna toward the atrium, putting space between Aaron and myself before I strangled him. Attempting to recenter myself, I listened in on Jack's thoughts. Jack was already back to reviewing and rethinking every process and step of the plan. Aaron set anchors for each of us so we could rappel down into the lobby of the building. Nate tied my harness to the rope I would be rappelling with.

Here it was. This was the start of the plan I had thought up. From here on out, this entire idea had been conceived by me. I was terrified of what might happen if things went wrong. This was the start of what we were hoping was the end of Eyecon.

Chapter 32

Arrived

An elongated glass pyramid stood at the center of the building's roof. Shauna rose to dust herself off as Nate held her by the elbow. Nerves fired like sparklers inside me. I was terrified, but the excitement of pulling off such a feat thrilled me. Nate made the final adjustments to my harness as Jack finished establishing the anchors.

The entire Truckee Meadows valley was littered with blossoms of light as fireworks blew through the sky, cracking and exploding. Shadows of red and blue gleamed across us as we worked.

"Happy Independence Day," Aaron chided.

Shauna laughed and grinned to herself, "And it's only getting started." To the Rebels, this meant freedom from worry. Taking down Eyecon was the gift that ensured no others could fall victim to Victor's dirty plans. To me, it meant revenge.

Jack pulled a deep inhale as he pressed his finger to his ear.

"Are we ready, Gus?" The rest of us made awkward faces in anticipation of the events that would unfold.

"Here we go." Gus let out a shaky breath over the comms. "I'm in. Triggering motion sensor on the northwest side of floor eighteen now." The breaks between Gus's utterances were lightyears apart. This was a minor alarm, it didn't signify a perimeter break. Motion alarms could easily be triggered by a stack of papers falling from a desk simply due to the air conditioner kicking on. Motion alarms were unreliable, which meant they had to be verified by a guard before it begged a real response.

"Shauna's work paid off so far, one guard on the desk tonight," Gus said. Shauna's face didn't change. She was just as focused on what our next movements contained. "Guard is moving for the elevator. Here we go." Gus narrated what we couldn't see while we waited in the darkness for the cue. "He's on the elevator, doors are closing." Furious pecking of Gus's keys sounded through the comms. "Elevator stopped. Emergency call disabled," Gus called out. Jack let out a deep sigh of relief as he looked up at me. An unexpected chuckle escaped him.

"And you're sure there's no radio signal from the elevator?" Aaron asked, "This is our last chance."

"There's no one to radio, he's the only one on duty. As Gus said, I've done my research and my job," Shauna rebutted.

"Work quick." Jack shoved the top half of an ax through the glass. The fragments fell, ringing out with a final shatter as they crumbled on the lobby floor. It was like throwing a penny down a well and listening for the water. A long way down, like the pit in my stomach. Jack shattered the glass in front of the rest of us, giving us each space to climb through. Jack's thoughts were so focused on the mission, I could see why he was chosen by Victor to be a soldier— but that had not gone in Victor's favor.

Nate helped Shauna clear the glass from her pane. Aaron turned his attention to me as if to offer me a hand. I quickly broke eye contact.

You sure you don't need a hand? Jack barged in.

I can handle it. And I surely wasn't going to accept help from Aaron.

I kept firm as I quickly kicked out the glass from the rest of the frame, ensuring I wouldn't get gouged on the way through. Slowly, I lowered myself through the opening, giving more and more of my weight to the rope. The rope continued forever as if I was never going to have enough to make it to the lobby floor. We were racing against the clock, trying to beat a ticking time bomb. AKA Victor's men.

My sneakers swept shards of glass as I tried to place them and get my balance on the floor.

"Houston, we've got touchdown," Nate relayed over the comms as my fingers fiddled with the end of the rope, trying to free myself from its connection. We broke for the basement elevators.

"Dani, you've got clearance, I'm working on Jack now," Gus's voice rang in my ear. I reached my arm out to the access panel. It flashed green. The door gave a soft ding and rolled open. We all tumbled inside trying to move as quickly as possible. So far, so good. But I had told myself that before...

"Ok, Dani, Aaron, you are headed for the crew sleeping quarters with me. Shauna, Nate, you are destroying the lab," Jack commanded. Nate and Shauna each pulled a container of lighter fluid from their bags as we descended, a maniacal grin stitched on Shauna's face. The elevator doors reopened, meeting me with a flood of unexpected emotion. Nauseousness— expected— and confidence— unexpected.

"Jack, you should now have access too," Gus chimed in. We ran down the hallway where the lab doors stood. Jack swiped his hand over the access pad, letting Shauna and Nate inside. Just as quickly as the doors opened, Shauna began pouring lighter fluid. Jack, Aaron, and I continued down the hall toward the holding cells.

A fit of unexplainable anger was growing inside Jack. We came upon the first cell, Jack stood in the doorway while Aaron and I took position on either side of the door frame. I unlocked the door using the access panel. Jack pulled it open. Empty. What the hell? We repeated this another two times.

Where is everyone?

I don't know. Either way, we search every room, Jack. No one gets left behind.

Upon opening the fourth door, a shriek leaked out of the room. My heart flooded with relief, it was one of the researchers. She held up her hand, attempting to block the blinding light from the flashlight Jack held.

"Thank God, I was starting to get bored," Aaron mumbled.

"Dani?" She asked, "what's—"

"We have to go, grab some shoes. I need you to guide us to all the cells with your coworkers. Where's Emily and Lincoln?" I asked

"Lincoln's in fifteen, they keep Emily down in the last cell, twenty-one," She said.

Jack was already heading down the hall, eager to get business done as quickly as possible.

"I'll get Lincoln. Dani, I think it's best if you are the one to greet Emily." Jack glanced over his shoulder as he ran, remembering their last interaction where Jack had the barrel of a gun pushed in her face. We jogged down the row of cells. Fifteen, Lincoln's cell was right in the corner before the hall turned left. Jack and Aaron stopped to get Lincoln while I made my way to the end. Twenty-one. I swept my hand over the access panel. Green. Tugging the door open, Emily was in a crouched position, ready to fight.

"Emily?"

"Oh, god, it's you." Emily bounced off her heels with a sigh of relief. "I thought Victor was shutting things down. Taking us out. What— "

"Get your shoes, we have to go." This wasn't the time for catching up. What was I even going to say to her? I turned, leaving her room, planning to work my way back to Jack and Aaron as I opened the cell doors.

"Did you get the test subjects?" Emily followed so close behind that she nearly ran into me as I stopped dead.

"Not yet, how many are there?" My stomach was beginning to cannibalize.

"We got four in last week. There are only two here now, Victor took the first two." Emily's voice was sullen.

"One was gifted to us. Where are the last two?"

"Down a floor, I can show you." Emily slid on her shoes as she hobbled down the hall.

I'm going to get them, Jack. My chest seized as guilt washed over me. I couldn't help but think if we had implemented our plan earlier, maybe we could have saved all four test subjects. Maybe if I committed to stopping Victor sooner, I could have spared these innocent lives. But I was weak. I was so hell-bent on just running from my problems.

Go, I'll get the rest here. Jack was on board with the plan as he and Aaron rescued the remaining scientists. Emily and I ran past all her released coworkers who were flooding the hall. We reached the elevator again, this time, we took it down to its last stop. B2. When the door opened, it revealed a dark and narrow hallway with a solitary door at the end. Emily flashed her badge over the access panel. The light illuminated red.

"Shit, my access isn't working," Emily muttered.

"Here, let me." I extended my hand. The panel illuminated red again. Shit.

"Uh, Gus, we have a problem," I exhaled as I held my earpiece. "We are on Basement Level Two, I need access to the security panel."

"On it, this might take me a second though, there's another layer of security for this door," Gus said.

"How long?" Jack chimed in over the comms.

"Maybe sixty seconds max."

"Dani, we're going to start getting the doctors out of the service door. Meet us in the alley once you get the test subjects," Jack said.

"Copy," I recited over the comms. I relayed the plan to Emily as we waited for Gus's signal for access. My lip was tucked between my teeth as I paced back and forth in front of the door. Time. This was sucking up time, and that was the most important part of our plan's success. We had to get in and get out as quickly as possible. This hold-up was an unforeseen part of our excursion, but it needed to be done. We couldn't leave the test subjects here.

"I didn't think you would come back for us," Emily admitted. Would I have come back had Ben not died? How long would I have held out had Victor not sent us a thank-you gift? Maybe I never would have come. "Who was he? The guy Victor made us infect?" Emily asked. My stomach twisted. Ben. It was Ben. But before I could respond to Emily, Gus rang in my ear.

"Ok, Dani, try again."

I swiped my hand over the panel and it flashed green. Unlocked.

Pushing the door open, I let Emily take the lead to get the test subjects. We ran down a long sterile hallway with dim lights. Finally, at the end of the hallway, Emily notified me the last two rooms contained the test subjects. I waved my hand over the panel and the door slid open. A boy, maybe about sixteen, stared back at Emily and me, just as terrified. I wasn't ready to see that— a boy who was nearly my age when the virus had overswept me. A boy, nearly the same age as the one Jack had killed. I tried not to look at him,

"Hi Parker, we are getting you out of here," Emily said as she rushed over, ripping out different monitoring cords, trying to keep her voice calm. "This is my friend, Dani." I undid the straps which kept Parker tied down to the medical gurney. "She's here to help us, ok?" Emily kept talking in a calm voice, trying to keep Parker from freaking out.

The bags under Parker's eyes were practically black. He was frail and helpless. Sick. He looked sick. The pit in my stomach threatened to swallow me whole. He was only a boy, and look at what Victor had subjected him to. Emily helped Parker to his feet and slung his arm around her neck while she supported him by the waist.

"I know this isn't going to feel good, but we need to move fast, ok?" Emily pulled Parker onto his feet, his eyes meeting mine for the first time.

His eyes glazed over with wild darkness. Suddenly, he pushed off Emily, backing away into a crouch, ready to strike. Emily fell backward against some equipment. Why couldn't things ever just be easy?

"Shit," Emily whispered, "he's been activated." Just as Parker made his spring into action, Emily launched herself onto him. I flung myself in Parker's direction, attempting to grab hold of his flailing limbs. As soon as we made contact, Parker's body revolted in snarling convulsions. Electricity bounced back and forth through our touching connection as I pinned his shoulders down to the ground. This was not good. Not. Good. I straddled Parker's chest as Emily sat on top of his waist, our back's touching each other.

I held Parker down. His blood pulsated with anger. He wanted nothing more than to kill me. I almost recoiled against the recognition. But under the rage was a young boy, frightened. A boy. He was just a boy.

As Parker snapped his biting teeth toward me, his electric energy sputtered. He hadn't yet learned how to use his powers. Emily's hand reached up to a side table nearby, revealing a syringe which she quickly plunged into Parker's thigh. After a few moments, Parker subsided to the injection, his body fell limp. Emily and I both rolled off of Parker's body in relief.

"Help me turn him over," Emily commanded. Once Parker was on his side, Emily pulled the hair away from the base of his neck, exposing a deep gash sewn over with stitches. My stomach churned in disgust. She plunged a scalpel into the base of Parker's neck, hastily undoing the stitches. Blood pooled from the wound as she removed a small black capsule-like chip.

"Ready for round two?" Emily plunged another syringe into Parker, but this time he sat straight up, swinging his arms in fury. Emily called Parker's name as his swinging arms slowed. His hands pulled at his face as he began to recognize himself.

"I'm sorry, I know you just went through quite the ups and downs, but we need to get you on your feet and get you out of here." We each wrapped an arm under Parker. He groaned as we lifted him to stand, struggling to pull him out into the hallway.

"Dani, you need to grab Ruby while I get Parker squared away. She's in the next room over." I nodded and rushed over to the next room.

The door opened, revealing Ruby who was unconscious. I took a moment to inspect the back of her head but didn't find any indication she was chipped. Gently shaking her, I attempted to wake her. Ruby didn't open her eyes.

"Emily! She's passed out, what do we do?" Emily sat Parker down in the hallway and ran in to meet me. She was opening different cabinets, looking for something as I untied the leather straps fixing Ruby to her medical gurney. Time. This was sucking up so much time.

"Here, watch out." Emily drew back a syringe plunged into a vial. "This will do the trick." She pricked Ruby, injecting the liquid into her arm. Ruby sat straight up, gasping for air, appearing dazed and confused. "Hi Ruby, I know you aren't sure what's going on right now. This is my friend, Dani, and we are here to get you out of this awful place. Can you walk?" Ruby didn't say anything, she gave Emily a quick nod, and we left the room.

We returned to the hallway, where we met Parker who was doubled over and vomiting. Emily and I pulled Parker off the floor, practically dragging his feet as we all ran back to the elevator. We were almost out of here. Almost back to the others.

I swiped my hand over the control panel and it flashed red. I impatiently swiped my hand over it again. Still red. "Gus, we need you down here. We need access to the elevator from B2."

"Sorry, working on it, this might take a minute. It wasn't part of the plan."

"We don't have a minute," I anxiously yelled back. Emily stared at me with concern.

"Dani, I'm not getting a signal from that panel." Gus's nervous words immediately caught Jack's attention as he intervened.

"What do you mean, Gus?"

I placed my hand on the access panel, feeling the electric current. It was pulsing as if there was a malfunction.

My stomach had more than enough nervous energy ready to strike.

"Hold on." I balled the electricity up and pushed it through my arm. As it reached my fingertips, I sent it out in a pulse. I tried to read the signals much like how I did for ATMs, but something was wrong. The panel was malfunctioning. We were going to be trapped down here. A cage. Not another cage. No, I could not let that happen.

With a large push, I sent a pulse out of my fingertips, effectively frying the panel. The elevator door slid open. Emily sighed in relief as we pushed inside. We just had to get back to B1 and meet the others in the alley. As we stood in the elevator, I updated Jack on our movements.

"Jack, we're on the way back to B1." But as the elevator slid open, Jack was standing just behind the door. His face pale, but stern.

"Change of plans. We can't exit through the service door, it's been bricked over," Shit. We hadn't seen that coming. "We are going to have to go through the lobby. We'll have to go up in groups." Jack ushered some of the doctors into the elevator with us.

"I'll see you up there," Jack said, pushing me back into the elevator. I nodded as the doors slid closed.

As we rose towards the lobby, Gus made an announcement over the comms, "Guys," Gus exhaled, "We have incoming company."

"Where?" Jack asked, just as the elevator doors slid open again. I had arrived on the floor of the lobby, and so had Victor Crowe.

Chapter 33

Unhinged

Shit. Jack and I simultaneously thought.

As our group exited the elevator, I let another doctor take my place in helping Parker. Victor was sprinting across the lobby floor towards us. I instinctively stepped out in front of the doctors, shielding them. My hand fell to my empty holster and I silently began freaking out. Shit. I had lost my gun while shimmying across rooftops. No. No. No. Slowly, I raised both my hands.

The elevator doors opened again and Jack, followed by Shauna, Nate, Aaron, and the rest of the doctors stepped out, firearms raised.

Victor brandished a handgun, and it appeared I was directly in his sights.

"Don't," Victor warned, "or you can count on me ending her right here."

"You wouldn't," Jack growled.

"Willing to test that assumption?"

Jack quickly hesitantly placed his gun back in its holster as he digested Victor's words. The rest of the Rebels put their weapons down at Jack's lead— leaving them stuck with their hands up as they exited the elevator.

"Well, look who has returned." A sickening smile spread across Victor's face. He straightened his shirt and ran a hand through his black hair, fixing his appearance. I was going to be sick. Was this how it ended?

I took a step forward, closer to Victor, my hands still raised. He recentered his aim on my face. My throat was so very dry. Victor cackled, relishing the fact he caught us.

"What do you want, Victor? You want to rip these people away from their lives, from their families?" I asked.

"These people are not special. Look how selfish you all are!" Victor pointed with his gun. His eyes set deep into his face. "We are a disease on planet Earth! The human race cannot evolve quickly enough to beat the rising thermal and solar radiation levels we created. To save the many, we must sacrifice the few. So what's the price of saving the world, huh? What makes you people so special?" He grinned, waiting for an answer. "What would you give to make sure future generations have a life here on this earth?" Victor spat as he pushed his gun toward me. "Hybrids ensure the success of the human race, we have to become stronger if we are going to survive past the next ten years. Time is of the essence"

I stepped forward, toward Victor's ugly scowling face.

"And what kind of life would you give them? Stop lying to yourself. You aren't saving the world. You're trying to seize power. Create your elite army of hybrid soldiers to crush humanity. What you're doing is stripping people of who they are, shattering minds." I was calling Victor out. He quickly reminded me of the risky situation I was in, stepping closer, stretching the gun nearer to me. Cautioning me to be careful.

"How dare you," he warned, "You don't know what you are talking about." But I did, because I too felt the darkness that crept up in the back of my mind. The parts of the virus that wanted more than just electricity, the parts that wanted the power Victor had warned me about. I knew.

"You foolish girl, you have put everyone in jeopardy. You think you are so smart, so righteous. You may live long enough to realize the only way to win is with darkness. Because the world, people, they ruin everything. This is— this whole thing, this is for the good of everyone. They just don't know it yet."

"What about the gift you sent? Did that hybrid not know the chip in his head was for his own good?" Victor's gun was so close to my face, the heat radiated off of his hand. I leaned in closer, my forehead mere inches away from the barrel. "So go ahead, if you want to end this. Shoot me."

Victor frowned, lowering the gun. "Oh, Ophelia, so brave. But, didn't you know you have a weak spot?" Victor grinned, raising the gun again, pointing it straight at Jack. For a brief moment, Jack was struck by panic, followed by a wave of bravery.

"What do you want from me?" I quickly asked, trying to get Victor's attention from Jack.

"You know, I already found the raw source of the virus. But something isn't quite right, Ophelia. My... prototypes aren't like me, they aren't like *you*. I've felt your power. You have the potential to be undeniably great. I can show you the way. We can be great together," Victor said, "You are a natural leader... and with your powers, you can be boundless. You can take back the control that was so disdainfully ripped from you. You're a leader, Ophelia. People will need your guidance if we are to survive this."

Leader? Here we were, back to the same idea. Every single hybrid I had ever met couldn't help but tell me how powerful I was. I didn't understand. I didn't understand where everyone got this idea. This idea I could save them. This idea I had any inkling of understanding, that I knew what I was doing. I couldn't control myself, my powers— not in the way Victor had imagined it.

I was just Dani. And I couldn't even save Ben. I was shattered. Mangled. Twisted. All my fears were consumed into a single devastating unwakeable dream.

"No," I refused. The sound of the gun reverberated through my body. The deafening noise rang through my ears. I never even flinched. I was ready for it, ready to die if that's what it meant. At least surrendering to death was better than surrendering myself to darkness.

But, it was Jack who fell to the floor, blood pooling around him on the ground as he clutched his leg.

I didn't take my eyes off Victor who had returned to pressing the barrel of the gun against the center of my forehead, the fire-hot metal melting into my skin.

Jack's thoughts raced in excruciating pain. Every nerve ending in his body snarled in agony, popping with agonizing pressure. His knuckles whitened as he clutched them around his wound hoping for the torment to stop. Every part of Jack wanted Victor dead, and this just amplified it. Jack growled in rage as Emily quietly knelt to help him.

I needed to focus. I returned my attention to Victor as Jack's painful thoughts spread inside me.

"Stop," I demanded, refraining from letting the panic seep into my voice.

"You can't help but put yourself in front of those you care about, Ophelia," Victor said. "But who saved, *you*?" Then a chuckle. "No. No one. Too bad you didn't realize no one was ever willing to put themselves in front of you. Not even your father. A massive dose of the virus—— especially the raw source—— would've killed you. He was going to *let* it kill you. Your own father.

"He went off the absolute deep end, trying to secretly return to his precious raw source. Like a drug addict. He didn't care about you. No one cared about you. How do I know this? Because your father and I were microdosing one of the original samples of the virus together. For you not to die in the lake meant he was microdosing you too. He risked your life by giving you the virus. Your fate was always sealed, Ophelia. You were always going to be a hybrid. Doomed to the curse. We just didn't know you were going to be the strongest. And to be frank with you, I thought you had died alongside your father years ago. Overdosed on the raw source. Wiped from the face of the earth." Victor's smile grew so large his pointy canine teeth reflected light like the sick beast he was.

I was trying to make sense of Victor's words. Trying to decide if any of them held any weight. But Victor was so good at twisting the truth, at making me second guess reality.

"You're lying," I rebutted. But he wasn't lying. I attempted to stay calm as my brain tried to click all the puzzle pieces in place.

If Victor never had a sample of the raw source, the scientists could only ever use different iterations of the sample they had on hand— or what was left of it. That's how Victor had his powers. He had been infected with the original raw source. But the microdosing saved him from his binge on the remaining samples from the lab.

And the only reason *I* survived the lake was that my father had been microdosing *me*.

"When you went missing, who noticed? *Who* came looking for *you*? Oh, that's right... no one. You were just a kid. James was supposed to protect you, but instead, you were left out in the dark. *No one* cared. And when James disappeared, his betrayal shattered everything— you *and Eyecon*. We lost access to the raw source of the virus. But not anymore.

"And now, daughter of co-creator James Colburn, rising to control what nearly killed her? Taking that powerlessness and becoming powerful— to rise from the ashes. People will never doubt you again. *Show them...* show them all how they hurt you, what you've made of yourself, Ophelia. James may not have cared about you, but *I do*. I see you Ophelia, and I'll teach you. Imagine what we can conquer if we can just confront our own flimsy limitations, if we can transcend into a world where we don't operate under the burden of fear, if we can give in and harness the power we can unlock within us."

Victor was set on the fact that being James' daughter was going to be the soft spot he could use to call me home. As if rehashing the pain would convince me to abandon my humanity.

And maybe Victor was right. Maybe I should have been mad. Angry. But, had my father not been microdosing me, maybe I would have died upon first contact with the lake, ravaged by the infection. Chills raced up my spine. Who knew how high the kill rate of the raw virus was. Maybe the microdosing had saved my life. Maybe my father saved my life.

But there was no way I was stronger than Victor— especially now he had access to the lake which he so graciously named after me. And even if I was stronger, I didn't have the same kind of mastery over my powers. I had seen the control he possessed when he effortlessly threw Ben against the wall. Or when he smoothly lapped his electricity from his palms like flames.

Jack grasped his leg in pain, attempting to keep it under control. My thigh was burning where he had been shot. A hot iron jabbing through my leg and twisted about. All my neurons were firing at once with such a large input of information.

"How did you find the lake?" The question slid through my gritted teeth.

"Hansel and Gretel led me. You see, James had disappeared, and after you mentioned he died in a plane crash it got me thinking. If he had changed you into a hybrid, he wouldn't have fled without you. You both were in that crash, except you were the only one to survive it. Cross-reference the timeframe of James' disappearance with reports of a mysteriously found girl and suddenly... There. You. Were. Forgotten and found again in the Plumas National Forest.”

I think I actually growled as the exhale of my breath rumbled through my chest.

“I loved your little tree markers, by the way, it made the searching so much less cumbersome.” We had left the trail markers tied to the trees on our way in so we could find our way out. Never did we think to remove them. Never did I imagine they would have led to this.

“Three long months of direct massive exposure, Ophelia. And what a shame you don’t know how to control your powers,” Victor’s voice sang sickeningly sweet.

“So tell me your demands already.” I was sick of hearing Victor dance around. Sick of hearing his stupid words. His lies.

“You want to make me out to be your villain? Is that it? You have no idea what lurks around the corner.” The edge of Victor’s lip tucked up into a crooked grin. “That’s fine, if you need someone to hate, you can sink your sorrows into me. You can despise me. But be warned, you won't walk out the other side of this unscathed from the darkness. I can teach you how to use your power— how to be great.”

“You have nothing to offer me,” I bit out.

“Your father fell to the darkness, Ophelia.”

“My father *ran* from the darkness.”

He donned an all too polite smile. “Right, if that’s what you want to think. It’s only a matter of time until it swallows you too. What do you want to be, Ophelia?”

“Not like you.”

Victor’s eyes sharpened as he let out a snarl. “Let’s all go back downstairs.”

“No.” I stood firm. Victor fired another shot. This time into the ceiling. A panel of glass from the atrium above shattered, falling upon a few of the doctors. I didn’t dare move a muscle. Victor once again positioned the gun in the center of my forehead, this time with a frustrating force. He pressed it firmly against my skin.

I wondered if this was the part where I needed to make my amends and say my goodbyes. Victor could shoot me, and then the Rebels could take him out. It would all be over. I would be the sacrificial lamb for a cause greater than I could imagine. I would not grovel for my life.

"Back downstairs," Victor ordered, interrupting my thoughts of last wishes. This was something I refused to do. I was not backing down. I wasn't running away anymore. I stood firm. It was time to end this, all of this. And it all came back to Victor.

"I'm too valuable for you to kill," I confessed, "and I'm not going back, Victor. So, are you going to shoot me now?" I asked. He was realizing that killing me was his only option— the only win he would be able to garnish from this game.

Victor removed a single hand from his grasp on the gun, throwing a palm out toward me. Blue electricity lapped up, dancing in the dark. His light streamed across the gap, pooling into me. The energy flooded my system, overwhelming my neurons, firing so fast I couldn't comprehend what was happening. Victor had mastered how to use his powers, and how to concentrate them. And I had never built up any kind of tolerance to electricity. I was weak, paralyzed as I was overdosing on Victor's power.

My limbs gave way and my body fell against the cold hard marble floor, locked in Victor's electric grasp. I was a hostage to his power, caught in his deadlock. I couldn't move. I fought to stay conscious. White noise overtook my hearing as heat flushed through me. My vision blurred to darkness as the wave of power roiled through me. And then a familiar thing happened.

I was at the lake, wrapped in the warm euphoria. A dark blanket of night sky swaddled the stars above as I floated on the water's surface. And I was blissfully aware of how my mind was drifting further and further from my reach.

This was the end. I had been here before, but this time, I was alone and I found myself not wanting to return. Because the last time I had woken up from my escape, reality had crushed me under its relentless weight. The insufferable pain and hurt were unbearable. I had lost Ben, I was the reason his life had been stolen from him. My existence threatened everyone. So when the abyss called my name, I wanted to shut my eyes and let it take me, to suck me into the inescapable gravity of its black hole where I could remain free of all the things that hurt me. Where my existence could no longer hurt anyone else.

His warm voice swelled around me while I basked. "You see?" He asked. "Isn't it glorious?"

And when I looked over, Victor was floating next to me. His dark eyes glistened as they reflected the light off the water. He was nearly unrecognizable. His skin appeared soft, younger. His smile held a warm glow.

"I can give you what you've always wanted, Ophelia. A life without pain or hurt or suffering or fear. All you have to do is let go." His voice was so delicate as it floated over to me.

The energy of the water seeped into my bones, pushing the ecstasy higher with every passing second. Higher. Higher.

"Let go, Ophelia. I promise you, everything will be alright." I wanted nothing more than to give in to the comforting richness of the electricity. To the delirious indulgence. The lake was coaxing me in, welcoming me home to a place where I fit in, where I belonged. Home sounded like something I hadn't been privileged with in a long time. Home.

"Will you stay?" Victor asked, his wet black hair was almost silver as the starlight fell over him.

"Here you can find your true escape," He proposed. "Everyone is looking to feel something, but you? You're looking to not feel anything at all. You owe it to yourself, Ophelia, to let go, to give in. No more pain. No more suffering. I can give you the true power you are after. You can finally take control of your life. You just have to let go, let me in."

He was right. I wanted to let go, to give in. I wanted to be free of all the things that had shattered me into little broken bits. I wanted to be wrapped in the inconceivable feelings of the powerful lake. To bathe in the warm nothingness forever.

"You aren't really Victor, are you?" His black eyes stared at me, piercing my soul, their color almost a deep red.

A crooked smile swept his face. "No, I am not Victor."

But I wasn't scared. It was almost like greeting an old friend. I don't know if the electricity of the lake water was comforting me. Or if I was too naive to be afraid. Or maybe I had nothing more to lose.

Victor, or whatever Victor was, reached out and grabbed my hand. "Let me help you. I can teach you to be great." I did not move as I stared at his eyes, lifeless black pits.

"No," I whispered, shaking my head, weary of his offer.

"Then I'm afraid it's already too late," Victor said, throwing himself on top of me, pushing me under the water. The rush of warm liquid filled my mouth and my lungs. The power was intoxicating, stealing the final bits of my fluttering mind.

As I choked on my failing breaths, I thought of Ben and his endless love. The wisps of pink on his lips, how his thumb swiped my cheekbones when he tilted my chin to look at me.

Water flowed deeper into my lungs, a stinging cold swelling with powerful pressure.

I thought of Jack and the gentleness he kept hidden underneath. The vulnerable moments he'd let peak through. The undeniable connections that sparked to life, braiding us together.

A wildfire of pain spread through my body, burning my lungs, my throat.

I thought of my father and his never-ending will to protect me. Even through Victor's lies, even through my doubts, I knew the truth. I was loved.

The water was flooding my mind, drowning the last of my circuits.

I thought of the Rebels and the doctors and the lost friendships from the people who knew my secrets and weren't afraid.

A darkness was crawling, creeping through the maze of my mind, boiling in its angst to take over.

I thought of the people in my city and all of Victor's future victims.

I thought, and I cared, and I loved.

As much hate and pain as I carried inside me, I loved.

This was it. The last of me. The final bits of oxygen in my blood nearly evaporated as the power of the lake consumed me.

No.

No one would be able to stop Victor from hurting the ones I loved.

No.

Just as the power thrust me nearly over the edge, I opened the floodgates, letting it seep in even deeper, concentrating it. I pulled all the energy I could muster to the inside of my body where the all-consuming electricity awakened something deep.

I was not going to surrender myself to the darkness, ignore the hurt, run from the brokenness. A life without pain or suffering isn't a life. It's a shell, a human body devoid of compassion and empathy. It's dangerous. It's what had become of Victor. And I was not going to give up like this. I was not going to let whatever had overtaken Victor win. I was not going to take the easy way out of this.

It was never my choice to become a hybrid, to have this life. But these were the cards I had been dealt. And I'd be damned if I let the darkness win.

My eyes flickered open as I lay on the marble floor of the lobby, my body encapsulated by Victor's blue dancing tendrils of power as I fought for control.

I pushed my face up from the marble floor, looking at the shattered glass, the glossy sheen of the pristine white stone. And that's when I saw him. Emerald green eyes, as if they were floating in the depths of the water, under the silver moonlit lake. I stared, and he— *she* stared back. And at that moment, I understood. *Save yourself* had come from me.

He wasn't there. He was never there. There was no mystical warning. It was me. The whole time, it was me. No one was coming to save me from the lake, the grasp of its waters. The only person to save was myself.

As I stood, Victor grimaced in disbelief. He withdrew his electricity, realizing it no longer held me captive. A growl escaped him as I placed myself in front of his gun once again. Widening my stance, I smiled at him. He wasn't going to get what he wanted from me. It was my time to face the things I tried so very long to run from—— the darkness I pretended I didn't carry inside.

Victor threw his palm out again, overtaken by a wave of anger. Just as he thrust the power toward me, it was halted by my own stream of energy, holding it off. The light streamed in a gridlock, matched by the power flowing through one of my outstretched palms. Victor's eyes widened.

He sneered at me, dropping his stream of electricity. I did the same. I reached up, placing both hands on either side of the firearm, pressing it hard into my skin against my forehead.

"So you want to be a martyr?" he grinned, tightly grasping the gun, moving his finger hastily onto the trigger.

I could feel it, all the inner workings of the gun. The trigger tightening beneath his finger. He was going to pull it. The pin, ready to strike. I could feel the current as I pulled and directed it through my hand. Victor squeezed with all his might. But the trigger remained frozen. The power came seamlessly through me, giving me complete control over the weapon. His face froze at the realization.

I was going to end this.

I pulled the gun from Victor's hands, turning it back towards him. He backed, slowly retreating from me as his face sat within my sights. Pulling this trigger was something I wanted desperately, something I wanted for more than just me. Killing Victor was something I wanted for every single person who had ever had the misfortune of meeting Victor Crowe. Killing Victor was for humanity, for saving the world as we knew it. But most importantly, killing Victor was for Ben. My arm was outstretched, finger ready to fire.

Victor's hands were raised. Why was I hesitating? He was going to shoot me only moments ago. This man was an absolute monster. He had killed Ben, ripped him away from me. The fear surfacing in Victor's eyes was insurmountable.

I remembered Victor floating in the lake, the peacefulness over his face as he drifted near me. He was a version of his younger self, before the darkness had overtaken him. Before he had given himself up.

It's ok, Dani. Remember, you are not the monster you make yourself out to be, Jack pushed to me. *Victor is.*

The difference between Victor and me? I hated the way the mugger looked at me, how Anna's eyes raked my face, the fear lingering in the eye of the crow. But Victor? He thrived watching those squirm under his thumb.

But who I had seen at the lake wasn't Victor, it was the darkness wearing Victor's face. As I stared at his eyes, I was reminded of how he clutched my wrist in his office. Two dark lifeless pits mounted on his face. All consuming. Victor had lost himself to the virus, and he had never returned. It was by far too late to save him. He was already gone, having surrendered himself in greed for power, for refuge from all the things that make us human. He was weak, a coward. What was left of Victor had become a dangerous beast, and he deserved no mercy for the pain and suffering he had inflicted on others.

A flash of bright blue blinded my eyes as a stream of electricity pulsed the gun from my grasp, knocking it to the marble floor. Victor aimed again, directly at me.

Without hesitation, I outstretched my free hand, facing my palm straight for Victor's center mass. I had been waiting for this moment since I had met Victor, and the best way to get my revenge was to use the very powers he could only wish to wield against him. The energy siphoned from around my body, effortlessly pooling into my palm for my use.

I thrust the electricity into a bright blue stream as I centered it on Victor. He smiled as I heaved him against a marble column, pinning him so his feet floated off the floor. His grin widened the longer I held him there in my electric grasp. I knew this would happen. Victor had a tolerance for high amounts of energy. And I hated the gleam in his eyes as he fathomed how my powers had come to be. Hated how he soaked up my energy with that vicious little grin.

As I held Victor pinned against the wall, I could feel his heart race. I could feel the blood pumping through his body with its maximum oxidation. And it was my turn to crush him the way he had squandered the hopes, dreams, and plans for every hybrid he created, every life he came into contact with.

I could feel it, the vibration of electricity within his blood. And I had complete control.

My lips parted, and the words seeped out, "Checkmate, Your Grace."

I turned the push of power into a pull as I stripped the energy from Victor, pulling the electricity from his body. His face hollowed in a sudden panic as pain ripped through him. There was a hungry beast inside, overtaking what was left of Victor's mind. And it felt good to let the monster chomp on the bits of his lucid thoughts.

The remaining energy Victor had danced through his body. I had to stop it, crush it, get rid of it. Take it away from him. But, the electricity brimming into me from Victor was overwhelming, sending me so close to the edge. My body felt like it was going to crack open, and I was going to lose control of myself. The power was so intoxicating, I couldn't stop even if I wanted to. I was at the proverbial edge Jack knew I'd reach.

Everything. It was going to cost me everything to end him. It was the only way.

So I decided to toss myself over, out into the abyss. A place where I knew I wouldn't return from.

A place where I'd lay at the bottom of that dark lake and stare through its ripples, watching what nasty thing I'd become on the outside.

A place, if I was lucky, I'd forget whatever good bits about me I'd known. Then I couldn't cringe at what had become of me.

Power flickered through me, stretching into crevices of my body I'd never felt before as that dangerous energy reached into the free fall of the unknown. As I pulled the remaining bits of energy from Victor, sucking it through my hands, absorbing it, I was losing consciousness. A wild electric ball of concentrated energy sputtered in my stomach. The power was too much. The edges of my vision were beginning to blur.

Here it was. The void.

Everything shook as I stripped the power from Victor. All my neurons, my circuits, overloaded in a flooding rush of electricity. My hearing faded to nothing but the pounding of my heart, racing so fast it wouldn't be able to keep me alive much longer.

A scream left my throat as a giant blinding flash filled the room.

I became unhinged.

Light beamed from my outstretched palms, blasting into Victor. The last of Victor's thoughts were gone, ash in the wind. His heartbeat waned, dribbling off into nothingness. The stream that pinned Victor to the column withdrew. The thud of his body hitting the floor echoed across the marble lobby in unison with mine.

I thought I'd slip right through the marble floor into the depth of the dark waters of the lake. But the floor held as I gazed up at the shattered atrium above, staring at the blue and red firework-flecked sky.

Empty. I was so utterly empty. But there was one more thing that had to be done. I had to ensure Victor couldn't get up and walk away from this. That he hadn't made a deal with the devil for nine lives.

I crawled to Victor's lifeless body, dragging myself across the crushed glass bits scattered across the floor. Placing one of my palms on Victor's chest, I reached for the gun and waited, feeling for signs of life.

His heart was still. It was over. It was finally over.

Nate was right. Anger was a secondary emotion. I had always had control over the trivial parts of my powers, but maybe to harness its full potential I had to give way to the anger and rage and believe I could control the very thing I was ashamed of. To know that I would come close to darkness and find the strength to have courage. Maybe the thing about having courage... it wasn't about not being scared of suffering. Maybe having courage was about being afraid of the hurt, and looking it in the eye anyway. About plunging your hand into the depths and not being afraid of what surfaced.

Victor had been wrong in calling out my weak spot— putting myself in front of others. Because it appeared love gave me strength. It was what gave me control, like when I protected Anna, or Ben, or Jack and the rest of the researchers. It was the very thing that kept me from falling to the lake's darkness. Love gave me the ability to embody the monster inside, to not fall victim to its insidiousness. Love allowed me to hold the hand of darkness.

Smoke billowed out of the elevator shaft. Feelings I didn't understand began to wash over me, flooding me with emotions I couldn't comprehend. Lincoln approached me as my hand still held the gun. He placed one hand on top of the firearm, sliding the pistol from my hand into his own, grasping it as he wrapped his other arm around me, pulling me up off the floor to leave. Lincoln's eyes locked on me. "It's over, Love."

I pushed Lincoln's arm away and rushed back to Jack. Nate was already at Jack's side, helping him up as people rushed to leave. Sirens were building in the distance. I looked at Aaron, who was trying to shuffle people out of the building. Aaron's eyes went wide. He stared at me, mouth agape.

"Spread the word, those who don't have anywhere to go can come back to the Collective. We need the two remaining test subjects to come with us. They're only kids. Ruby and Parker," I ordered Aaron as we passed. I shuffled alongside Nate, trying to help him with Jack. "We'll see you at the van. Be quick," I said, "Hey, we need Emily and Lincoln too." Aaron gave me one swift nod and started looking for Ruby and Parker.

Jack's feet thudded against the concrete steps creating a trail of blood as Nate and I dragged him through the doors of Eyecon. Everything felt like chaos. I was trying to keep the terror at bay, but I could feel Jack starting to lose consciousness, our connection fading.

"Stay with us, Jack." The first time I ever made contact with Jack was in an alley, and it was beginning to feel as if it would be the place I lost him. Tears finally started rolling down my face. The confidence was no longer there, instead, it was being replaced by panic. The adrenaline was wearing off and shock was taking over.

"Jack, Please, you've gotta hold it together. We'll get you to Samuel, and he'll be able to help. Stay with me."

Jack's head lifelessly rolled around his shoulders as we dragged him. Sirens blared in the distance as smoke began rolling out of the Eyecon building. Shauna jumped in the van and reversed to meet us where we were. As she opened the back door, Nate and I pushed Jack into the van as best we could. Shauna flipped the van around, only stopping for Aaron who was assisting Ruby and Emily. They were trying to support Parker as they ran down the alley to meet us.

In the back of the van, Jack lay slumped across my lap. Nate removed his belt to use as a tourniquet on Jack's leg. The amount of blood leaking from Jack was astounding, and he had already lost so much. Placing my palm over Jack's heart, I tried to feel for his pulse. But I couldn't focus. I tried to push the hysteria aside. It wasn't going to help me. Blood everywhere.

I could feel his heart still beating. So much blood. Slowly, I started pushing some of my energy into Jack.

Shauna slammed on the brakes just as we were exiting the alley. Beams of red and blue lights glared in our eyes as a patrol vehicle came to a stop just yards in front of us. No. No. No.

The officer jumped out of his car with his gun drawn, yelling words to stop us. Shauna put the van in reverse, as she looked over her shoulder intending to floor it. But as I caught sight of the other side of the alley, another police car was making its entrance. The officer in front ran towards us, closing the gap.

Shauna's eyes met mine as she stopped the van in the realization we were trapped. The officer was now standing mere feet in front of the van peering into the windshield over the top of his weapon. Maybe this was it. Maybe this was where things truly ended.

"Out of the vehicle," the officer yelled. But no one moved as the officer circled to the driver's side. Just as the officer's chest rose to shout more commands, his voice softened.

"Jack?"

The officer's eyes met mine through the open window. "Broady."

Broady flinched, taking a few steps back as he met my gaze. We hesitated to move, expecting Broady to say something more, to give us a command, but he didn't. He stood frozen. Why? His face displayed confusion as he was trying to calculate what had happened. We didn't have time to calculate.

"Go," he grunted, lowering his gun. Shauna didn't spend another second guessing if it was the right choice. The van sailed to the end of the alley and Shauna made the tight squeeze between the patrol car in our break for freedom.

I had to shake the incident with Broady because I had to focus on Jack, on trying to help stabilize his situation. Red dampened nearly everything. Jack rolled his head from side to side. Or it could have been Shauna's crazy driving. She was honking at pedestrians to get out of the way as Gus provided directions for which streets to turn down. Emily checked over Ruby and Parker, ensuring they were stable.

Jack was coming to consciousness as he slowly opened his eyes. A foggy haze surrounded his thoughts. We both simultaneously flinched.

Jack thought my eyes were dark red. I saw it in his mind. I looked at myself through his eyes as he stared at me. Red? No. No. That couldn't be.

I looked over to Nate. His face was so pale it was almost translucent. We stared at each other, saying nothing. Was Nate seeing the same thing?

Does it hurt?

Does what hurt? I asked. Please don't be true.

Your eyes.

I swallowed loudly. Was this what Broady was reacting to when he stepped back?

You have to hold on, I told Jack, trying to change the subject, trying to convey what was most important right now.

I'll be fine, just lost a bit of blood. But it was a lot of blood. *At first, I thought I had lost you. I was so in tune with your thoughts I'd thought Victor had shot you instead of me.* The painful moment replayed in his mind, a wave of agony sweeping over him.

I held Jack's head in my lap, bracing his face with my red-stained hands. Blood smeared on his cheeks where our touch met.

When I fell to the floor, I still hadn't realized I'd been shot. I thought it was the pain you were going through. The pain of losing you. It was like when I held you in my arms when you had almost died. As if you'd been swept up by darkness. And then Victor struck you with his power, and... and I thought I had lost you forever.

I wasn't sure what to say. I was so focused on standing up to Victor, that I hadn't even flinched when the gun went off. I had never even looked back to check on Jack. Although, I knew what exactly had happened. I felt it. It was unnecessary to look. Unnecessary to put myself through that.

And then Victor nearly killed me with his power. The overdose had sent me face-to-face with the dark demon of the Spectrum virus. And if it would have gotten in, taken over... well things would have ended a lot differently.

But there was a moment inside me. It came after Victor was dead. After I finished off his last bit of energy. After I had stolen his final moments. Had I drawn up his darkness? And the words from the lake, just before not-Victor almost ended it all, echoed in my mind. *I'm afraid it's already too late.*

Chapter 34

Toxins

The brakes squealed as Shauna pulled the van into the compound. Nate and Aaron dragged Jack toward Samuel as he held the door open, hauling him into the lab, onto the very same table Samuel performed his research. Jack was still conscious, barely, as Samuel buzzed about the room grabbing the items he needed to tend to Jack's wound. Smears of red were already beginning to cover several surfaces in the shuffling.

Fire burned through Jack's thigh. Standing over him, I peered down at his face, watching him struggle with the pain, fighting to stay awake. I was using my energy to help him, but I was terrified about doing so. What if I could infect Jack with whatever this dark energy was? Would I turn his eyes red too?

Dani, as if he was calling from a long way off. I couldn't take my gaze off him. His eyes fluttered as he tried to focus on my face.

Don't do this, Jack. You're not allowed to do this. But I knew what was coming. And for a split second, I thought Jack almost chuckled between his gritted teeth.

I need to, before it's all too late and I never get the chance, he confessed.

You'll have the chance, Jack. Whatever it is. I'll make sure you have the chance. But there was so much red, so many smears of his blood lacing everything around us, crusted on the hand I used to cup his face.

Jack groaned as Samuel struggled to get an IV of pain medication together. Death was closing in on Jack, the same way it had started to close in on me when I tried to end myself. I could feel his thoughts slipping closer and closer to the edge. Was this how Victor won? By destroying everyone in my life?

Jack lay lifeless on the table. His lips parted, and a shallow rigid breath left him. His eyes gleamed, but no words escaped his mouth. Instead, tears glistened as he spoke through our connection. *I... I look at you and I've seen the universe.*

No. No. No. It's the lack of blood, lack of oxygen, I argued. But, one of Jack's hands tilted up, shaking as it reached out, reached for me.

Will you hold my hand? Jack asked. No one should die alone, without a hand to hold. My lips quivered as I tried to hold in the tears. I nodded, wrapping my hand in Jack's. No. Please, no.

A painful groan wracked through him. Then he was utterly still, as easy words found him.

I love you, Dani. Like the stars love the moon.

No. No. No. He couldn't do this. He couldn't say those things. He couldn't slip away. I couldn't do this again. I couldn't do this with Jack.

Placing a hand on one side of Jack's head, I tried to tune in with him as best I could. Oh my god. Was he even here? Was he already gone? His mind sat empty, an entirely empty human shell. I had to do something.

I drew my energy down through my arms into a small steady stream, slowly upping the ante. Jack was coming back online. But I too was running low on energy after the incident with Victor. I needed more electricity. My fuel was running out.

"Nate, I need a power source," I said. Nate's eyes scanned the room. He somehow knew exactly what I was after, what I was doing. Nate returned with a lamp, he smashed the lightbulb housed inside. Reaching down, I wrapped my hand around the socket. It felt so good, so powerful. But, the lamp was transmitting too much power. My focus on saving Jack was being compromised. I had to let go, but just like an addict, I was finding it difficult to part with the influx of euphoria. And after a night like this, I desperately wanted to not let go. I needed this. The electricity had never wrapped me in its addiction. I never faced the same temptations the other hybrids had, not in this way. Had Victor's energy tainted me?

Nate ripped the lamp from my grasp, realizing the battle ensuing inside.

"Like a phone charger or something with a lower amperage," I exhaled, trying to contain the rush of energy bounding inside so I could dispel it in a slow controlled manner to Jack. I wasn't capable of adapting to such a large power influx, not now.

Please, please hold on.

Nate grabbed a long phone charging cable, ripping the end off so its wiring was exposed. He outstretched his arm, cable in hand. Taking hold of the wires, the power was just right. Enough energy to keep me going, but not too much to send me over the edge.

My foot anxiously tapped as I monitored Jack. I could feel his presence, but it was as if he was laying on the periphery, sleeping. Jack was nothing but a thread floating in the wind, and I was grasping for him to hold on, to tether him here long enough.

"He's lost a lot of blood, he'll need a transfusion," Samuel said. Aaron rolled up his sleeve in preparation. Samuel ran an IV line from the crook of Aaron's arm into a holding bag then set up the next IV on Jack's free arm, preparing for the blood transfusion as Aaron's blood continued to drain.

Samuel wiped the sweat from his forehead as he tried to work as quickly as possible.

"Ok, ok, it's full," Aaron exhaled. Samuel ripped the holding bag of Aaron's blood from its place while Nate addressed removing the needle from Aaron's arm. Bright red filled the IV line running into Jack. A scream of agony ripped to life. Suddenly Jack was awake. Pain blared through our connection, open floodgates I could not control.

"Stop! Stop!" I yelled. No one in the room knew what was going on. Jack's arm lit on fire, hot poison rushing through his veins. "It's hurting him." Utterly broken words. I ripped the IV from Jack's arm. As soon as the blood line was out, Jack lost consciousness again.

"It's O negative, and it's hybrid," Aaron defensively said.

"Well, what do we do? He's lost too much blood," Nate stated the obvious situation we were all already aware of. Precious seconds were ticking away.

"I don't know." I was in a panic. "We need Emily, or Lincoln, or— or— someone who knows what they're doing." Nate took off out the door in search of Emily. She had made the van ride back to the compound with us but had melted off to assist Parker and Ruby.

"Dani, you and Jack have the closest infection level. He needs *your* blood," Samuel said, proposing we attempt to give Jack a transfusion of my blood.

My blood? Would I infect Jack? Time. We were running out of time.

"Dani," Aaron said, "What are you waiting for?" Samuel approached me with a needle in hand, ready to fill an empty bag full of my toxic waste. Was it worth it? If I subjected Jack to... to... whatever this new thing was?

"Dani," Samuel whispered. "He'll die if we don't try this." Tick. Tick. Tick.

Hesitantly, I pulled up my sleeve. I couldn't watch as Samuel made the prick in my arm. I didn't dare look as the toxins drained into their death pouch. Was this the final sucker punch that would do Jack in? Would I pass on an even stronger craving for electricity? Would I make the addiction impossible to avoid? Was this Victor's final parting gift? The passing of the torch?

Samuel began to set up Jack's new IV line to transfuse my blood to Jack. I kept my grip gentle, but firm on Jack's head. And as the blood trickled into Jack's arm, something peculiar happened. A sigh of relief washed over Jack. His heart rate was stabilizing and his breathing began to level. Samuel stared at me for a few seconds, making sure I hadn't picked up on any brain signals from Jack inclining us to stop. I gave Samuel a quick nod of approval.

Chapter 35

Eventide

I sat with Jack's hand in mine, listening to his dreams. Watching him replay all the events over and over again in his head. His mind lingered on my now dark red eyes. He was afraid of them, of what they meant. But he wasn't afraid of me, he was afraid *for* me.

Then his mind would kick off into a euphoric spree, remembering the way our lips touched with electricity. The way our brains, our souls, had danced back and forth seamlessly together on the clifftop, how his lips had felt like a river of warmth on mine.

Jack's thoughts and dreams pinged all over the place. But only one memory had truly caught me off guard. Jack had splashed a handful of water on me. We had been at the lake, swimming partially nude in the water. My eyes weren't red in this memory. Jack had commented how the electricity pulsed through them while we swam, how beautiful he thought their color was. *Even if it ended here, after just this little time. I would do this again and again, for lifetimes. To relive these short moments we had together. It will never be enough.*

A tear rolled down my cheek as emotion threatened to overtake me. I pulled my hand from Jack's trying to collect myself as I turned his words over in my mind. Jack had said something on the rooftop as he pulled me from my frantic glance over the edge. *You have no idea how lucky he was. Even if it was just for a little while.* I knew then he was talking about Ben, but I had never known the burning passionate affection Jack was holding onto. I had never seen the lifetimes he had imagined in his head. The seemingly insignificant moments that would mean nothing to a stranger, but kept Jack entranced. How he watched the hair fall over my collarbone or how I bit my tongue at his witty remarks. How he noticed the way I drew my breaths, and what the sound of each of them meant. Or the way my words would spill out differently when I was mocking him.

And the truth? I was pretending I hadn't noticed, but as Jack always said, I knew how he felt. And I had been so focused on pushing down everything, not letting a single feeling creep up to the surface where it could hurt me. I had been lying to myself. My life had come to a head, balancing on a delicate thread. And in order to see it through, I pushed everything in the periphery down. I had been focused on a single mission, and now that it was over, a flood so large was sweeping me away. Because I too had seen Jack.

I had watched him nervously thumb the scars on his wrists. Or how he flexed his shoulders back and pursed his lips when he was trying to hold in a laugh. I had noticed the numerous ways he held his stiff jaw lost in contemplative thought, and how it shifted when he settled on his decisions. And more so, I had seen his soft eyes, his gentleness under the bravado. Or how the skin under his eyes would wrinkle when he smiled—usually after some cocky joke.

But Ben was still there. I could still feel him, and the pieces of our stories, our moments. I was caught in the vast endlessness. In a space that didn't belong in this world anymore. But this was where I was now. And this was who I was now. I loved Ben so much, and I had been holding onto him by a thread far longer than I ever wanted to admit. Time doesn't heal if you refuse to move along with it. If you stay stuck in the past. And as much as I didn't want to, I needed to let him go.

Because I had never deserved Ben and the countless ways he cared for me. I had always fallen short of returning the love he deserved, the love he effortlessly graced me with. Ben had unselfishly served as my lighthouse, and I, for some unknown reason, was the center of his world. He had held me together, given everything for me. And even though Ben was gone, I had somehow found how to swim through the vast dark waters.

And maybe that's what eventide was for— letting go. For the goodbyes. For the night to come and sweep the everlasting moments all away in its quiet darkness. Because after the darkest hour comes the dawn. Washed anew for a fresh start.

Forever in my mind, Ben and I were laying on the white beach of Sand Harbor, soaking up the drifting rays of the Sierra sun. My head in his lap, his hand cresting my face as he read his books.

And I hoped he had found his 42, wherever he was. For he was once again nowhere and everywhere all at once. A part of me, forever. But free again. Free from me.

I loved Ben. But I couldn't love him in the way he deserved, the right way. I had hidden all of who I was. I had shied away from the moments, the connection, the vulnerability of sharing my raw, naked openness, my ugly truths.

And then I understood. 42 wasn't about looking for something, unveiling a great big answer. The complexities of life couldn't simply be boiled down. 42 was subtle, and personal, and self-fulfilling. 42 was about meaning and connection, and vulnerability. It was never about looking for purpose, it was about sharing it with each other. Because everything has purpose when you can share it with the ones you love.

I hung my head.

Ben never wanted us to find our 42, because I already *was* his 42.

It's just… I never let him be mine. All those moments that I let slip by me… all those moments will be lost in time, like tears in rain.

As I held Jack's hand, I couldn't help but think things were going to end the same way— Jack dying just as Ben had.

I sat for hours with Samuel and Jack in a small room. Everyone had melted off to give us privacy after Samuel had finished the surgery. For all I knew, the Rebels could be throwing the party of a century somewhere in the compound. But I doubted it. Jack was dearly loved by all the Rebels, and if they knew he was wrapped up in the infirmary, their grief wouldn't be lifted until he was well.

Victor had said the only reason I survived the lake was that I had been microdosed with the Spectrum virus. The same virus which ignited his cravings and overtook him. But I had not faced the same fate as Victor, I hadn't even had any strange symptoms while living with my father.

"Sam?" I whispered. Samuel's head rose to meet my gaze. "You once mentioned to me that I had been exposed to the virus before the lake." Samuel nodded his head, not understanding what I was asking him.

"If I had been exposed to the virus before the lake, why didn't I develop symptoms like Victor? Cravings?"

"I think your father saved your life," Samuel softly spoke, trying to not wake Jack. "Your blood didn't show signs of infection, remember? Your blood showed signs of resistance or immune response. Your father exposed you to the virus in the same manner a vaccine would work. He was trying to protect you." Some things were true. Victor and my father were microdosing the virus together. I suspected Victor had dosed too much, infecting himself, and when my father saw the effects, the darkness in Victor, he sought to protect me from ever becoming a hybrid. It likely started slowly as Victor consumed more and more of the virus. But once Victor had finally gone mad, evident that the experiment had failed, after my father had been made aware of Victor's plans, he would have fled. He would have taken me as far as he could to keep me safe. Little did he know the lake would swallow us on our escape, drawing him into its grasp.

"You're different. Created differently. Perhaps it's a double-edged sword. You're strong because of your losses. But, I think resiliency is what gives people true power."

Jack's hand finally stirred in my grip. Slowly his eyes squinted open as he uncomfortably groaned. I felt him become aware of his hand in mine, knowing I was there beside him.

Jack didn't say a word. His eyes were glued to me as he shook his head, focusing his line of sight, revealing the creeping glow of starlight through his dusky blues.

Not red.

I filled with relief. Samuel rose from his seat, walking over to make his inspection of Jack.

"How're you feeling?" Samuel asked.

Jack glanced down at his bandaged leg. "As if I got shot."

Samuel rolled his eyes and then excused himself from the room to give us privacy.

"Are you ok?" Jack asked me.

"Are *you* ok?"

"I thought your eyes might not have been red when I woke."

"Sorry for the disappointment."

"That's not what I meant," Jack corrected himself, "I meant I was hoping whatever it was, that you passed it to me instead. That I could take that burden from you." I pulled my gaze from

Jack, trying to casually look away. Trying to hide my expression, my red eyes.

"You know that's pointless, right? Looking away?"

"Don't make light of things. You were close to the end, Jack," I admitted, "I could feel it." His gaze fell from mine. This was something he didn't want to confess. "You told me after you'd saved me, after our minds had merged, you felt the black hole, the darkness that I already carried inside, battled with. You knew what it was because you hold the same weight. But you were just better at covering yours up than I was." A mask. He was quiet for a long moment, hesitating to speak.

"So you've seen me," Jack acknowledged. His face full of sorrow turned into a wide cocky grin. "You know, they aren't that bad, I could get used to red."

"It's not funny Jack," I renounced.

"Things will get better."

I think I laughed, but it wasn't in the humorous kind of way. It was in the gasping unbelievable kind of way. How could Jack say those words? Had anything ever gotten better?

"And what if this is all just senseless? What happens if I'm just chasing a fleeting version of myself that'll never exist. And for what? The only thing life has taught me is every time you take a step up, it's only to remind you of how much harder the fall is going to be. Because it's inevitable. We will all fall."

"Yes, we all fall. But you fail when you refuse to get back up, when you stand alone," Jack whispered, "and I will never let you stand alone." Could there have been truth in his words? Would I have found the power to overcome Victor had I stood alone, had I not put myself in front of Jack and the others? Had I not gotten back up to protect those I cared about?

"Jack..." I was trying to put my words together, "It's a long way down." I pulled my forearm across my face, begging the fluids to stay in. "Broken people can do horrible things. I'm capable of great destruction."

"Yes," Jack paused. "And broken people can do beautiful things," he whispered with his lips pressed against my forehead. "It's your choice."

I shook my head, running my hand across the back of my neck. How could he not get it? How could he not understand? Then Jack opened his mouth.

"I don't get how you don't see what I see...You get to look through my eyes and see everything I get to see every single day. How can these moments pass, and you not realize how fucking special you are." Jack's voice was rough, confrontational.

"I don't want to be special." The words were hoarse as they left my mouth, cracking with the threat of coming tears I so desperately tried to hold in. "I'm so sick of being different, of being so alone. Sick of how everyone looks at me."

"I didn't mean special because of your powers. Even if that was all gone, I would go to the ends of the earth for you." I shut my mouth then, to listen, to truly listen. "I mean strong, smart, cunning. I see a young woman who loves helplessly and selflessly. Who gives everything she's got to defend those she cares for. I see how you find the good even in the most broken of places. How you choose light over darkness day in and day out. It's natural, seamless for you. Not because you are some chosen one by the universe, or that you embody something you never asked for. You are special because you are you, and not a damn thing can take that away from you."

"That's not true," I whispered.

"You're hardwired differently, Dani. And I'm in love with it. I'm in love with you,"

"Stop," I breathlessly whispered. "You will become another thing I can't save. I couldn't save Ben, and I can't save you."

"Listen to me, I don't need saving. I need you. And I can't lose you, not again." Jack paused, biting his lip. His hands plunged through his dark hair as the skin under his eyes pulled taught. "He didn't know you like I do. Ben loved you before he knew you. Before he knew what you were or what you could do, before he *saw* you. And perhaps there's something special in that." Jack's voice was firm, unwavering. He paused, letting his hard eyes seep into mine. I traced my finger over the scars left on one of Jack's wrists.

"But I loved you before you knew yourself. Before you knew what you were or what you could do, I believed in you. I will always believe in you." The fire was blazing inside, lapping up through my throat. Tears were running down my face.

Jack and I were utterly connected and I could no longer deny it. Deny him. Jack was... he was the kind of person you'd been sharing secrets with since you were a kid. I had known him for lifetimes, I wanted to know him for lifetimes. *It will never be enough.*

"I see you, Dani. And you never have to stand alone again," he said. But the veracity of life meant that if something was important to me, it would be threatened. Taken away and broken into tiny irreparable pieces.

"I can't love you, Jack," I breathlessly choked out over my tears, "Because if I love you, I would have to leave you, I would have to let you go," I admitted as Jack's hand trembled, "But I'm too weak for that."

"Good, because I'm not going anywhere." Jack pushed his body over to one side of the bed, carving out a space. I pushed myself into the spot as Jack's arm fell over me, his mouth sitting just over my ear. He repeated a line he had said to me before. "And I will be here with you now, no matter how this ends."

And whatever this Spectrum virus was, it was clear we had some law-defying draw to each other, a magnetic pull that could not be broken. The poles of the earth, endlessly attracted to each other, their complementary other halves. There was no hiding from it, as it would persist wherever we existed. Forever.

But what was painstakingly obvious, I had been engrossed in the battle inside my head for so long, I think I had gone over into the abyss long ago, blurring the line between reality and the demons in my head. Forgetting to find the beauty in the world, in the moments, in how I shared them.

And then the darkness came, and it became me. And if I was the darkness, he was the comet in the night sky, striking and unexpected, lighting the way home.

I had left the ocean and taken to the stars.

And right then I knew the big bang in my life was in fact not the plane crash, it was colliding with Jack.

XLII

We sat on the bumper, the doors of the van hung wide. The canyon below us trickled with leftover waters from a recent rain. All of Reno was splayed before us, its unique lights bounding off the strip of downtown. The radio was turned up loud enough to drown out any thoughts threatening to take over the moment as the music wrapped us in its time.

Jack leaned over, handing me an object wrapped in brown paper.

"What's this?" But he didn't answer, instead, a grin cracked on Jack's face as he started to hum to the melody of the radio, missing the next few lines. His voice was a lovely smooth satin dancing through my ears, lifting my heart.

I knew this song. Jack smiled and raised his hand, pulling me from my seat on the bumper. He pressed his mouth against my ear, breathing his words gently. Electricity raced through me, dancing across the folds of my brain as he held me in his arms, swaying back and forth. A serenade.

"Strange you never knew." His words grew a smile on my face that I could not hide. I tilted my head back to catch his gaze.

"Open it," he whispered. The words barely parted from his lips as he sang along.

As I peeled back the paper, it revealed a book— Ben's favorite book. I tried to not let the tears well up in my eyes, but Jack already saw. He pulled me closer, sending the smell of sagebrush and cedar through me.

"When did you know?" I asked. Jack rolled his head across his shoulders, gazing over downtown, letting a smile slip onto his face.

"I think it's strange you never knew." He echoed again, ignoring my question. I smacked his chest and he let out a dry chuckle. He reached out, grabbing my wrist, and pulling it toward his mouth. His lips brushed the still-fresh black ink. *XLII.* Better known as 42. "I've loved you long before I've known you, before I'd met you." I rolled my eyes, thinking he was actually going to answer me seriously. Clearly, I had been mistaken.

"I'd loved you for all my time, and then I saw you, and I knew it was you in that second."

"Is that why you shot me with your taser?"

"Very funny," Jack chuckled. He bit his lip and pulled his eyes back to mine. "The moment we touched, that moment, I had known you forever. I had known you with all my being. You'd never need to open your mouth and I would have followed you into darkness."

"No matter how this ends?" I asked, repeating his own words to him. His lips found the top of my head, and he whispered, "It will never be enough."

And then his mouth found mine. And we were nowhere and everywhere, all at once.